PRAISE FOR T. I. LOWE

"A family's collapse under the weight of dysfunction and mental illness becomes a luminous testimony to the power of neighbors and the ability of a community's love and faith to shelter its most vulnerable residents. Readers will close the cover with a smile and a long, satisfied sigh."

LISA WINGATE
#1 *New York Times* bestselling author of *Before We Were Yours*
and *The Book of Lost Friends*

"With lyrical prose and vivid description, T. I. Lowe masterfully weaves the story of a teenage girl's quest to protect the ones she loves most in the wake of unthinkable tragedy. *Under the Magnolias* is a moving portrayal of the power of family—the one we're born into and the one we create—and the resilience of the human spirit. In this memorable and moving story, T. I. Lowe has hit her stride."

KRISTY WOODSON HARVEY
USA Today bestselling author of *Feels Like Falling*

"T. I. Lowe has done it again! I loved *Lulu's Café*, but I love *Under the Magnolias* even more. There is so much to admire about this book. T. I. writes with amazing grace and beautifully depicts the cost of keeping secrets when help might be available. This story is filled with rich, lovable characters, each rendered with profound compassion. Austin is an admirable young woman—flawed, but faithful to her family—and Vance Cumberland is another Michael Hosea, offering unconditional, lifelong love. *Under the Magnolias* is sure to delight and inspire."

FRANCINE RIVERS
New York Times bestselling author

"On a tobacco farm in 1980s South Carolina, we meet smart and spunky Austin as she struggles to keep the family farm together and raise her six siblings and mentally ill father. With a wide cast of fun, offbeat characters, a mix of heartbreak and humor, and a heaping handful of grit, *Under the Magnolias* will delight Lowe's legion of fans!"

"What a voice! If you're looking for your next Southern fiction fix, T. I. Lowe delivers. Readers of all ages will adore the spunky survivor Austin Foster, whose journey delivers both laughter and tears. Set smack-dab in the middle of South Carolina, this story will break your heart and put it back together again. A must-read."

"Plain-speaking and gut-wrenching, T. I. Lowe leaves no detail unturned to deliver a powerful story about a family's need for healing and their lifelong efforts to run from it. This is no 'will they or won't they' romance. Rather, it's a thorough exploration of the hidden depths of the heart."

"I loved *Under the Magnolias*! . . . Austin Foster is one of the most memorable characters I have ever read."

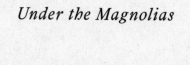

Under the Magnolias

UNDER THE MAGNOLIAS

T. I. LOWE

Tyndale House Publishers
Carol Stream, Illinois

Visit Tyndale online at tyndale.com.

Visit T. I. Lowe's website at tilowe.com.

TYNDALE and Tyndale's quill logo are registered trademarks of Tyndale House Ministries.

Under the Magnolias

Designed by Libby Dykstra

Edited by Kathryn S. Olson

Published in association with the literary agency of Browne & Miller Literary Associates, LLC, 52 Village Place, Hinsdale, IL 60521

Scripture quotations are taken from the *Holy Bible*, King James Version.

Under the Magnolias is a work of fiction. Where real people, events, establishments, organizations, or locales appear, they are used fictitiously. All other elements of the novel are drawn from the author's imagination.

For information about special discounts for bulk purchases, please contact Tyndale House Publishers at csresponse@tyndale.com, or call 1-855-277-9400.

ISBN 978-1-4964-5360-0 (HC)
ISBN 978-1-4964-5361-7 (SC)

Printed in the United States of America

27   26   25   24   23   22   21
7   6   5   4   3   2   1

To Teresa Moise

My dear friend, mentor, and running partner

Because of your unwavering confidence in me,

I felt confident enough to pour my soul into this story

PROLOGUE

1987

At eighty feet tall with a spread of forty feet, the southern magnolia tree was known to get out of hand in our part of South Carolina, which was nestled smack-dab in the middle of the heart-shaped state. The ornamental madam could get a wild leaf to lift her full skirt and take a squat in a yard if she wasn't made to mind. Owners had to be diligent with keeping the trees on a grooming routine or chance the entire yard becoming overrun by the Southern beauties.

The self-contained tree was a tidy guest though. Discarded limbs and leaves were kept hidden under her fluffy hem until the debris gradually returned to the very soil that gave it life.

Unlike most neighboring towns who were starting to plop

Bradford pear trees in the ground like they were the next great thing, our entire town was decorated with southern magnolias. Shoot, our trees had built-in storage, and Mother Nature wasn't the only one to take advantage of the unique hiding spots. High school students weren't as sly as they thought they were with hiding their cigarettes under the two fat twins flanking the bus lot so they could sneak a smoke between classes. The Truett Memorial Library didn't allow food or beverages past the door, so most folks used the limbs of a magnolia tree beside the building to hang grocery bags or set their cups just underneath to retrieve later on their way out. You just never knew what would be found under one of the trees. Diaries, love notes, a lost baseball . . .

The most notorious discovery had to be the skeletal remains of a runaway teen and the knife used to dismember her. As if that wasn't awful enough, her remains were found under a giant magnolia on the front lawn of the courthouse where the trial had been held and concluded years before, confirming later that an innocent man had been sent to prison.

But the folks of Magnolia didn't like to talk about that. No, they preferred to keep stuff like that hidden and shine up all the positives of the small town. Like the fact that our mayor had a direct connection to the Kennedy family—by way of a second cousin, once removed—making him and his family town royalty. And then there was the other family who were kin to the folks who made the Duke's Mayonnaise up the road in Greenville. Of course, they're considered town royalty, too. It *is* the best mayonnaise, so I get it.

The town was also big on bragging about its active church

community. With a church on every corner, it's no wonder there was always a lot to crow about. There was the First Baptist of Magnolia, the First Presbyterian, First Methodist . . . a lot of Firsts.

And just like the botched murder trial, Magnolia didn't like to talk about Dave Foster and his congregation out on Nolia Farms. Even though it wasn't the official name of my father's small country church, folks referred to it as the First Riffraff of Magnolia. Pa said they could call it whatever they wanted. People running their mouths was never something to bother him. No, he had much bigger issues than small-town gossip.

The one-room chapel could only hold thirty or so people. It was established back in the late 1800s by my great-grandfather, who was also a farmer with a passion to minister. Farm life didn't always allow much free time, so he built the chapel as a place of worship for any of the farm help and his family. My father was the third generation to pastor this church. Phoenix said it reminded him of the schoolhouse on *Little House on the Prairie* and was all about convincing Mama to teach us there instead of sending us to public school, but she wanted us to have time off the farm, so that never happened.

As the piano came to life, I sat a little straighter and scanned the small pews and felt certain the ragtag congregation near about represented any walk of life you could think of.

A fortune-teller accused of being a witch doctor. Check.

An ex-con with a glass eye. Check.

An atheist believer with a Polish accent. Check.

The town's undertaker whose sexual orientation was questionable. Check.

The town floozy with a penchant for neon-blue eye shadow. Check.

A poor farming family with way too many kids. Check.

A madman leading them. Check.

At the moment, said madman was going to town on the untuned piano like he was Jerry Lee Lewis. Shoulders shaking, long legs bouncing to the beat, singing an up-tempo version of "What a Friend We Have in Jesus," he had the rapt attention of the entire congregation.

Except me.

I was immune to his theatrics, so I turned my attention to the magnolia wreath hanging on the beam above the altar. Sunshine slipped through the filmy windowpanes and reflected off the waxy leaves. At least it made the worn plank floors and the chipped white paint look intentional, like the antique style was what we were going for. The wreath was one of Charlotte's creations. I would often catch my sister looking at the giant monstrosity with a big smile on her young face. I looked beside me and caught her doing so now, thinking nothing but happy thoughts, quite the opposite of my own. Instead of seeing the wreath as decor, I couldn't help viewing it as a monument to a bad memory. The bracket mending the beam was barely noticeable, but my eyes didn't have to glimpse the tarnished metal to know it was there, holding more than the weight of the broken beam.

The awareness of what was hiding in plain sight had my eyes snapping away and focusing on a head full of blond curls, trimmed to a respectable length and neatly styled. It made me want to dishevel the curls until they resembled the unruliness of better times we'd shared together. The mayor's son was the only one in this tiny sanctuary who was considered normal, but his being here amongst us misfits, sitting two pews up from me like he owned the place, made him the weirdest of us all.

Before I could look away, he glanced over his shoulder and caught me staring. Instead of offering me the typical dimpled, lopsided grin, Vance Archer Cumberland frowned. The ever-present sparkle in his grass-green eyes was absent.

I shook my head and glared a warning. *Not today.* He shook his head too, but with resignation. He was too handsome to look so sad and I wanted to live in a world where I was allowed to make him happy, yet his unhappiness was solely my fault. It didn't matter anymore. There was no point in wasting his or my time on what could never be.

I broke our gaze first when a flash of hot pink got caught in my peripheral vision. Charlotte had started swinging her legs at a rate that was sure to launch her slap off the pew if she kept it up. She was short still, but at age thirteen that would probably soon change. The inevitable growth spurt that accompanied puberty, if it was anything like my experience.

"Get still," I muttered out the side of my mouth and tapped my Birkenstock to her jelly shoe.

Charlotte huffed but did as she was told, stilling her legs. She picked up the end of her dark braid and began fiddling with it. My sister was my opposite. Prissy, loved dresses and silly shoes that were good for nothing but producing sweaty blisters. Today she'd paired the lacy plastic sandals with a floral sundress.

I'd carried the label of tomboy as far back as I could

remember, hated dresses, and chose shoe wear for practicality. Today's church attire was bell-bottom corduroys I'd lifted from Mama's side of the closet and a plain white V-neck T-shirt I'd lifted from Pa's side. It was as dressy as I was going to get. Charlotte liked to sass about me being stuck in the seventies, but she had no idea just how deeply I was stuck there and that I would do anything to go back.

You'd have thought with us being the only two girls out of the seven siblings that we would have had a tighter bond. Maybe if there had been less than the six years' age difference, or if I had been more agreeable . . .

Pixy bumped into my leg, grunted, and then plopped down on the worn pine floor at my feet. Her earthy scent mingled with the lemon oil I'd used yesterday to wipe down the pews. I moved over to give her more sprawling room, but that only made her scoot until she'd eliminated the space between us and was right back to nuzzling my foot. Pixy had issues. Namely her identity crisis. She thought she was a five-pound poodle. She wasn't. Pixy was actually a thirty-six-pound potbelly pig.

With the town viewing us as riffraff, it wasn't surprising to find animals dropped off near the front of our 850-acre farm. I'd found Pixy tied to the mailbox a few years back. Another time, we discovered a billy goat had wandered up to the house and was gnawing on the porch rail one morning. We named him Woody, for obvious reasons.

Animals weren't the only surprises people left for us. One time it was a stolen car left in the west field. Pa called the cops on that one. And he should have called about another surprise gift but chose to handle it in his own special Dave Foster way.

The guesthouse tucked in the western part of the farm was considered to have an open door to anyone needing a place to stay for a while. A Native American couple from the Lumbee Tribe found their way to Nolia Farms one spring. Some didn't care for that, namely grown men parading around like ghosts, and so a cross was erected in our yard and set afire. Pa, being Pa, rushed into the house, and we all prepared ourselves for him returning with the shotgun. Instead, he came outside with a bag of marshmallows and skewers fashioned from wire hangers.

As those fools in white robes and pointy hats watched on, we roasted marshmallows and sang "The Old Rugged Cross."

Their ringleader accused Pa of blasphemy, but Pa shut that down with a confidence Dave Foster wore better than his denim shirt. Mama said that shirt made her swoon, so there's that.

Pa jabbed a finger at the flaming cross. "No. You setting fire to this sacrificial symbol of freedom and love for *all* is the actual crime of blasphemy. Now how 'bout we set aside our differences. Y'all welcome to take those hoods off and enjoy a marshmallow with us."

Not having the desired effect of running off our guests, the Klan skulked off into the night and never bothered us again with their hate. I asked Pa why he didn't fight back or yell or something, thinking that's more like what they deserved instead of an invite for marshmallows. His answer has always stuck with me.

"Fighting hate with hate will only produce more hate."

"Whew-ee, is the Lord good!"

I snapped out of my thoughts and realized Pa had abandoned the piano and was now towering behind the small podium.

Shoulders as broad as the side of a barn, about six and a half feet tall, the man was a giant. The bushy black beard and matching thick hair helped to earn him his nickname: Paul Bunyan. I was his sidekick, always following him around. In my younger years it was so I could bask in the sunshine he seemed to carry, but now that I was older, it was to keep a closer eye on him for when the shadows seeped through.

Paul Bunyan, of course, was always seen with his big blue ox. So I didn't take offense to being saddled with the nickname Ox as my pa's constant companion. My five-foot-ten-inch frame was quite muscular and it was no secret that I was as strong-minded as an ox, even a fictional one.

A chorus of *amen*s and *praise be*s rang out as Pa dabbed at the tears streaking the tops of his cheeks. The only time he cried was when he was happy, but I wasn't judging him about it since my tears had abandoned me long ago in the good times or bad. I'd gone as far as hiding in the packhouse to pinch the fire out of my arm to the point of bruising just to see if I could find my tears, but nothing. They were gone. Like a lot of things in my life.

"The Spirit is calling for us to testify!" Pa's voice boomed around the small building. The windowpanes rattled from his enthusiasm as the small congregation agreed with their own shouts.

Phoenix groaned from the pew behind me where he sat with Boston and Raleigh. "We gonna be here *forever*."

I cut him a look over my shoulder and shushed him. He was just two years younger than me, and even though he liked to act big and bad, often running off at the mouth, my brother showed some respect by sealing his lips.

The sermon began in Genesis, leapt forward to Philippians, zigzagged through the Gospels, and rewound to Isaiah. An hour in, Pa was washed down in sweat with his denim shirt displaying the evidence of his vigor. And a chorus of growls were coming from the younger twins sitting to my left. At age six, I was impressed they were both still awake.

Knox tugged on my shirtsleeve. "Ox, I'm starving."

I looked down at him, his freckled nose wrinkled and his lips parted just enough to see the space missing a front tooth. He was identical to Nash with big blue eyes and a mop of dark-brown hair. Even their missing teeth were in identical spots. Having come prepared, I pulled a pack of Nabs out my back pocket, rousing Pixy from her nap long enough to snatch one before leaving the rest for the boys.

Without missing a beat, Pa went from preaching to singing and then returned to preaching. Don't get me wrong—he was magnificent and could capture anyone's attention when he had the right wits about him. But those times were getting fewer and further between.

How did we get here? Is there a route away from it?

Those questions haunted me more and more these days with things spinning out of control, and I wished we could just turn back the pages to a simpler, happier time.

Nights spent frolicking in the swimming hole just past a patch of woods at the back of the farm. The moon and stars the only light, making the entire experience even more mischievous.

Tobacco-worm grenade attacks, leaving us covered in neon-green goo and needing another swim.

Lazy Sunday afternoons on the front porch with each of us taking turns cranking the ice cream maker, churning out the best peach ice cream in the world.

One of Mama's laughing spells that wouldn't quench until the entire Foster house was infected. Laughing until fat tears rolled down our faces and we had deep aches in our bellies that only righted with some of that peach ice cream or a pack of the Hostess snack cakes that Mama always snuck in the buggy at the Piggly Wiggly.

Looking through the innocent lens of adolescence, those happier days were perfection. Sadly, they had an expiration date just like those snack cakes. Happiness staled and nothing was pleasing after that. But just like the expired cakes in a meager season, we had no other choice but to stomach whatever life tossed our way next.

Chapter 1

THE FORTUNE-TELLER

October 1980

Edith Foster was the poster child for hippie living. Her golden-brown eyes held a glassy appearance most of the time, but she was never high on anything other than life. Free-spirited, she didn't care that a new decade had arrived that was adamant about more being more. Bigger, brighter everything. Not Mama. Nope. She continued parting her long blonde hair down the middle, forgoing the thickly applied makeup and big bangs that were trending. She always tuned the radio to the easy listening songs from the sixties and seventies instead of the hip-hop and new wave sounds taking over the airways.

She and Pa said I was the spitting image of her, minus that dreamy expression and contented smile. On the cusp of teenage-hood, my only expressive setting seemed to be stuck on a guarded pout. I was full-on pouting at the moment as she spoke in that delicate voice laced with whimsy. She was propped up in her and Pa's bed, looking like a flower-child queen as she adjusted the daisy behind her ear that Charlotte had given her earlier.

"Austin, it's a beautiful rite of passage as a woman." Mama wrapped her hand around my wrist, trying to pull me into a conversation I wanted no part of. My gaze dropped to the mood ring on her index finger and I saw that the stone was blue. It was always blue. I recalled teasing her once that the thing was a joke and held no other color besides blue, so she insisted I put it on. I did and the color instantly turned as black as coal.

"Mama—"

"It's your body's natural process of preparing to—"

"Mama!" I tried pulling away from her, but there was no give to getting away from my spot on the edge of her bed.

"I'm serious. Any day now your flower—"

"Why do we gotta talk about something that ain't even happened yet?"

"To be prepared." She finally let go and resettled on the bed, nestling in a pile of fluffy blankets and pillows. It looked like the bed was swallowing her up, except for the giant ball that was her belly.

"Please, Mama. I'm so grossed out right now." My shoulders shuddered.

She giggled, finding way too much amusement in my discomfort. "I can't wait to see you with your own young'uns. You know that saying about your children being ten times worse than you were as a child."

An obnoxious snort slipped out as I scanned the dresser top. It held enough picture frames to cause an avalanche if someone stomped by it hard enough. "Well, I ain't having no young'uns, so there's nothing to worry about." I glanced at her just in time to see the smile slip slightly from her face.

"Why not?"

I waved toward the pictures, evidence for my conviction. "You done had enough for the both of us." I aimed a finger at her ginormous belly that held babies six and seven. "And you keep spittin' them out every time I turn around. Seriously, you and Pa need to apply that part about controlling your urges that you shared with me in the birds and bees talk. Time to slow down on some things, missy."

Her smile returned as she set into having one of her laughing spells. Holding her belly with both hands, she managed to say, "You keep getting me tickled like this and these two will be arriving early."

"Only two more weeks. They got to be about ready anyway."

"I'm ready to be out of this bed." She readjusted, lying more on her side, but the grimace that flashed on her face gave away the fact that she was miserable.

When the doctor had diagnosed Mama with preeclampsia— a word I'd never heard before—I'd ridden my bike into town and had Miss Jones at the library help me find a book about it. I ended up with a book about pregnancy that covered conception to birth to complications. Reading it from cover to cover, I learned things I wished I could unlearn. I also knew that calling that entire natural process *beautiful* was a crock of bull. Nothing floral about it. Mama could shine that mess up, sprinkling flowers and pretty words on it all day long, but I wasn't falling for it.

"You'll change your mind." She pulled her waist-length hair, the color of sand and sunshine, over her shoulder and began braiding it. The only times I'd ever seen her wearing it in any style other than down and free was when she was sewing tobacco or cooking. Seemed the last stages of pregnancy was the other exception. "I predict you'll have at least three children of your own one day."

"What? You a fortune-teller or something?" I rolled my eyes.

"No, sassy-pants. But I heard there's one at the fair. Perhaps you should pay her a visit. See what she says." Mama giggled, the real sassy-pants in the room.

I stood, sending out a creak from the brass bedframe, and pulled the piece of mail from my back pocket. "This came today."

Mama took it and opened what I already knew to be a map and began unfolding it. "It's Tennessee!"

I peeped over the edge of the giant rectangle she held with both arms spread wide. "Have you thought about backup names just in case you're wrong like last time?"

Mama had been sure the last set of twins would both be girls, so the towns of Charlotte and Elizabeth had been circled on the North Carolina map. Well, "Elizabeth" came out three minutes after Charlotte and had everyone gasping when it was quite obvious she was really a he. Poor baby boy went a week nameless until Mama decided on Raleigh. It's kinda funny, but we're forbidden to tease him about it. Mama said it could cause him identity issues if we did. He had big ears, and she didn't forbid that topic, so there's that.

Grunting, Mama reached to the side table and plucked a pen from its tiny front drawer. "These two are boys. I think they'll even turn out to be identical. There won't be any surprises with Nashville and Knoxville." I wasn't so sure. After all we got a mixed set last time when she predicted two girls.

She bit her lip while drawing careful circles around the city names, and I bit my tongue to keep from spewing a protest on those awful name choices.

Edith Foster was not only a hippie but also a homebody with a weird wanderlust that took her no farther than the library. She had a vast collection of maps and *National Geographic* magazines but had never stepped foot out of the state of South Carolina. And for some other weird notion, she decided to name each one of us after a city she took interest in.

Ruckus from downstairs echoed through the floorboards, reminding me I had other things to do besides chatting with Mama. But our one-on-one time was all but nonexistent and I was selfish, craving every second I could have her to myself.

Carrying twins back-to-back seemed to have taken a toll on her, but by golly, the woman loved being a mother. She adored us and was a natural at sensing what we needed. Boston needed frequent hugs and a listening ear. Phoenix needed a more stern approach, and she was quick not to baby him over his handicap nor would she let him by with his mouthy ways. I suppose she joked and teased with me more often than not, knowing I was too serious and needed loosening up. Charlotte and Raleigh were the soon-to-be-dethroned babies, a coveted place they'd had all to themselves for the past seven years, so they were spoiled rotten. I wondered how she planned on changing that, but I knew she'd figure it out. Shoot, she even babied Pa and he was a grown man.

I definitely did not inherit my mother's mothering instincts. That whole idea interested me about as much as getting a tooth pulled or talking about my period—both of which made me nauseous. I'd much rather be out plowing a field or sitting at the dining table with Pa, studying the *Farmers' Almanac*.

"I wish you were going with us," I mumbled, hearing heavy footsteps landing on the stairs.

Mama grinned over the edge of the map. "Me too. I bet those fair workers are from all over the country, if not the world." Her eyes went dreamy again. "Be sure to ask some of them where they are from." That was another one of her little quirks. At a chance encounter with someone new, her first question was always wanting to know where the person was from.

"Okay . . ." I brushed my hair out of my face and sighed. "You sure I need to tend to the twins tonight?"

"Yes. Your daddy needs some Boston time. That always cheers him up. Will you please do it for me?"

I wanted to ask what in the world did Pa have to be down about. It was Mama who deserved some fun time. But I kept that to myself, just like the weird name choices, and mumbled, "Yes, ma'am." The heavy steps turned into a fast-paced bumping sound, sending whoever was on the stairs bouncing down on his backside. "Ugh. I better go help Pa." Before I made a step away, Mama gathered my hand in hers.

"Sweetie, I know you don't like talking about certain things, but you still need to be prepared. I've stocked up on supplies. They're in the top of the linen closet."

I knew she was just looking out for me, so I chose to forgo my grumbling and be agreeable for a change. "Thank you." I kissed her cheek and made my way to the door, pausing there for a moment to give her one last tease. "You need to promise that these two babies are the last two!"

She rubbed her belly and giggled. "I'm making no such promise." She stuck her tongue out.

I stuck mine out too before dashing down the stairs to help herd the wild animals. Ages ranged from fourteen to seven. With one mentally challenged and another physically challenged, I had my hands full. Phoenix sat in the front of the truck with Pa and the twins, while Boss and I climbed in the back. It was a warm fall night and even though Boss liked to babble about nonsense, it was much more peaceful than sitting in the cab.

As Pa pulled into the fairgrounds, melodious music from the carousel filled the air as thickly sweet as the aroma of cotton candy and caramel apples. The wind carried over to us, along with squeals of delight from the roller coaster. Each plunge could be distinguished by the roar from the riders, wave after wave confirming that thing had one too many dips for my likings.

For all my grumbling with Mama earlier, I was excited to do something out of the routine of everyday farm life, which consisted of feeding the small flock of chickens and other critters before catching the school bus, a mundane school day, after-school chores, making sure the others did their homework and their own chores, helping with supper and then bath-time routines. With Mama on bed rest, I felt more like a warden than a preteen girl.

At the ticket booth, Pa divvied out tokens for rides and games along with three dollars apiece. "That should get ya a soda and at least two snacks. I'm gonna ride some rides with Boss, so if you run out of money, come find me or Ox. If you act like you got good sense, then I'll let you pick out a souvenir before we leave." He handed me another bundle of dollars. "Your ma said you wanted to take the twins on rides?"

Wanted was a strong word, but I nodded anyway. "Yes, sir." Even though fourteen-year-old Boston had the mind of probably a four-year-old, he was tall enough and adventurous enough to ride anything. I sure wished he was my fair companion for the evening.

"Peg, you good to go? You're welcome to hang out with us two." Pa hitched a thumb toward Boston.

"I'm good. I want to see about winning me a goldfish. It'll take concentration and y'all just be distracting." Phoenix turned and limped off toward the game section, the thick crowd immediately sweeping him away.

"Meet us right back here in two hours," Pa called, his deep voice skipping over the heads of people to reach a determined boy on a goldfish mission.

"Yes, sir!" Phoenix's voice somehow made its way to us even though he was out of sight.

Phoenix had more spirit and vinegar than anyone I'd ever met. He should have been born a redhead, but he was just as dark-headed as the rest of my siblings. They all favored Pa, with varying shades of brown hair and blue eyes. An unfortunate accident at age three when he'd tripped while chasing after the tractor left Phoenix minus a leg. His right leg had gotten caught in the discs before Pa realized he'd fallen. After months and months of surgeries and rehab, Phoenix returned with his leg gone from the knee down but having gained a cynical disposition even at such a young age. Now at age eleven, he mostly kept his smile to himself and was growing more and more argumentative about every little thing.

Boston was quick to let Phoenix know he looked like a pirate and renamed him Peg. No one, not even our newly ornery brother, ever disagreed with the Boss, as Pa had nicknamed him, after Boston's favorite singer, Bruce Springsteen. So the name Peg stuck better than the first prosthetics he had to wear. Thankfully, the doctors finally got that right with the help of the Shriners.

"We want to ride the carousel," Charlotte spoke up for both her and Raleigh as she always did.

I looked over at my little brother. He was nodding his head in agreement. "The carousel it is." Holding their hands, I moved through the crowd and started my night at the fair with most of the other tiny tots and mamas.

After riding the carousel twice, we took a moment to watch the bumper cars. Each time a car crashed into another, the impact sent the twins into a tizzy of gasps and giggles. Right in the middle of the action was the mayor's son, Vance Cumberland, steering his car into others as Malorie Fitzgerald sat beside him, clinging to his arm. Her father owned one of the only two law firms in Magnolia and was also kin to the Duke's Mayonnaise makers, so of course the town had Vance and Malorie betrothed before they could crawl. I didn't get it. A political family joining forces with a condiment empire? No. How about Duke's Mayo and the Merita bread folks? Add a tomato farmer in the mix. Now that would be a union made in heaven.

Even though Vance was a grade ahead of me, I knew more about him than any boy in my own grade, and it was Malorie's fault. She and I were in the same grade. With our last names beginning with the same letter, we were destined to always have lockers beside each other. Well, *doomed* was more like it, because I'd already had my fill of all things Vance Cumberland. It was Vance this and Vance that.

Vance just completed his Eagle Scout.

Vance was the best first baseman this county has ever seen.

Vance did volunteer work at the Y.

Vance, Vance, Vance . . . Yuck, yuck, yuck . . .

Malorie squealed and playfully popped Vance in the arm when he rammed two other cars head-on. I rolled my eyes and began leading the twins away from the perfect couple's obnoxiousness and toward the snack vendors.

Time passed quickly with me helping the twins on and off all the kiddie rides, buying more sweets and then popcorn to tamp down the sugar. We shared a grape slushy while I stealthily watched my classmates run around in freedom from one wild ride to the next. The ring-toss game became the highlight of my night, using the rest of our money to ring three of those crazy-tall soda bottles with the curvy necks.

By the end of the two hours, the twins were tired and whiny, my back hurt from lugging three oddly shaped soda bottles around, and Phoenix was missing. When he didn't turn up at

the ticket booth as instructed, Pa led us on a hunt that took us
to all of Phoenix's favorite places. When those were a bust, we
followed Pa around to the edge of the fairgrounds, where the
haunted house, the mirror maze, and other oddities were set up.
It was darker in that area too, except for one attraction.

A sparkly purple tent strung with a million twinkling lights
drew us to it like moths to a flame. Two flaps were rolled
back to reveal a round table dressed in black velvet with a
crystal ball perched in the center. The glow of it caught my
eye first, but then I noticed the two people occupying the
table. Plain ordinary Peg sat in a chair across from a dazzling
fortune-teller.

"Look, Pa." I pointed. "Peg's at the fortune-teller's tent."

"That boy," Pa muttered while leading the group over to the
table where Peg seemed to be in deep conversation with the
woman. "Peg, what in tarnation are you doing?" Pa tipped his
head at the fortune-teller, who was draped in glittery robes
and wearing a fantastic beaded head wrap I couldn't wait to
tell Mama about. "Sorry for any trouble my son has caused
you, ma'am. How much do I owe you?" He began to pull out
his wallet.

"A lot," Peg spoke up. "I want Foxy to be my souvenir. I ain't
even gonna be mad no more 'bout not winnin' a fish so long
as I get to have her."

All eyes turned to the stunning woman. Her dark face glowed
from the twinkling lights and her iridescent makeup, but her
expression remained neutral. The air shifted, taking the scent of
popcorn and earth with it, revealing a heady spice that swirled
around us. It was exotic and new compared to the plainness of

country living we were familiar with, so I knew it was a part of this woman as much as the silk material wrapping her head.

Pa apologized to her again before giving Peg a stern look. "Son, a souvenir is like those bottles Ox has or a stuffed animal or something. Not a human. And it's rude to even suggest that. You owe—" Pa read the sign leaning against the table—"Mrs. Deveraux an apology."

The fortune-teller waved a hand dismissively. "Phoenix has been perfectly fine. And please call me Foxy." Her voice was hypnotic with a different drawl than our Carolina twang. It was deep with a confident authority yet feminine enough to be alluring, and it made me wonder if it was part of her act. The twins seemed to be just as entranced as the rest of us and took several steps to get closer to her.

"Dave Foster." Pa extended his hand and she shook it.

"You sure are a purty Black woman," Boss commented, his grin spreading.

"Thank you, young man." Foxy's lips curled into a slight smile.

"Boss!" Pa nudged him on the shoulder. "Mrs. Foxy, he didn't mean no harm by that. Land's sake. You probably thinking I'm raising a bunch of heathens with no manners."

"No, I think you're raising truth speakers. I am Black. A woman. And my Jinx says I'm beautiful, too." Foxy discreetly tucked a stack of cards inside a wooden box when Boston reached for them. She handed him a beaded necklace and he instantly forgot about the cards. The rest of us were given necklaces as well. "Phoenix was trying to talk me into coming home with him. Said his mother can't even get out the bed and that Ox doesn't cook as good." There was a little bit of tease tingeing her tone, but her sparkling face remained neutral as her onyx eyes found me. She winked. "I told him I'm not a good cook either."

I expected Pa to scold Phoenix, gather us up, and move on. Instead, he grabbed a chair and struck up a conversation with the fortune-teller. "My wife is due soon with twins. We run a farm and Edie works enough for two grown men, but she's going to have her hands full with the babies. You wouldn't happen to be looking for a change from this, would ya?" Pa gestured toward the tent.

"Change is a part of life. I'm always looking for it." She tapped a long purple nail against her dark-red lips. "But my Jinx isn't one for change."

When Foxy shared with Pa that her husband worked the petting zoo and livestock exhibit, he left the young'uns with me and took off like a shot. I couldn't understand what kind of wild hair came across him to suddenly be looking for farm help. He was known for wild hairs, though, and it wasn't out of character for him to offer up the guesthouse out on the farm to folks.

Later, Pa returned with a frowning man. Average height but skinny as a rail, Jinx Deveraux was opposite of his flashy wife. He smoothed the thick mustache above his lips while Pa tried selling him on the idea of farm living.

"My granddaddy and my daddy done an' worked for the man. I ain't gonna let my queen live oppressed." Jinx bent and placed a kiss on Foxy's cheek, then went back to rejecting Pa's offer of food and board in exchange for helping out at the farm.

"But this can't have much freedom." Pa spread his arms

wide and we all took in the flashing lights and chaos of the fair. "Don't ya wanna plant some roots with your queen? You'd even have your own house and a piece of land to do it with. Us meeting is a divine appointment, my friend. Don't ya see that?"

They kept right on going round and round until the fair was shutting down for the night. After the Deverauxs agreed to think about it and Pa left them directions out to the farm, Pa bowed his head and prayed for God to lead Foxy and Jinx to us. When I lifted my eyes, I caught a glimpse of a smile tugging at Foxy's lips. It looked like she was in agreement but she didn't put any words to it. Only time would tell.

We began walking off, but I whirled around and asked, "Where are you from, Mrs. Foxy?"

"New Orleans," Foxy answered, and I knew Mama was going to love that answer.

I waved, almost losing one of those darn bottles, and turned to catch up with my family. It was a little chilly on the ride home, but I was too hyped up for it to bother me. Life was so routine that something as ordinary as meeting someone new was extraordinary to not only me but the rest of the Foster clan. We were all chatty, Boss and I leaning through the open back glass of the truck to talk about it with the others, all the way to the farm.

As soon as Pa pulled up to the house, I cradled the awkward bottles to my chest and jogged straight up to tell Mama about Foxy and her rad costume. Each hurried step made the bottles clang together, ringing out a warning of my imminent arrival. I collected all the details to share with her, hoping not to forget anything. I knew how easy it was for a moment to get tangled up, some parts shifting while other parts faded like sneakers left in the sun too long, until a memory was only a muddled reflection of the truth.

I barreled through the door to share one memory only to collect another one I would spend years distorting, reshaping, and wanting to forget. My arms went limp, glass shattered, liquid soaked my feet, and my throat burned from the scream ripping through me.

One blue baby on the bed, strangling on a whimper.

The other baby weakly crying where he was nestled in my mother's lifeless arms.

The daisy wilted and tangled in her sweaty hair.

A stream of crimson leading away from my mother's still body.

The Tennessee map on the floor, dotted with blood.

I instantly collected the details only to remember things we should have thought about before leaving for the fair.

We never should have left her completely alone. Upstairs, with the only phone in the house way down in the kitchen. I should have done something besides sassing and sticking my tongue out at her for our last memory together . . .

"Peg! Peg, get help!" I screamed, trying to unstick my feet to get to the blue baby.

"Bless your heart."

"Sweetheart, we praying for y'all."

"The First Methodist is bringing supper in a bit."

"Let us know if y'all need anything, dear."

Each awkward half hug accompanied some line of condolence as people filed past me, yet I sat on the back pew,
stiffer than the wood bench, giving no reply or hug in return.
I couldn't. Finding Mama dead had stolen my voice, my heart,
my hope, my—

"Honey, don't you want to join your family?" Morty Lawson
whispered in his soft voice. He was directing the funeral, trying to keep it on track, I supposed. Pa had led my siblings out
behind the casket and pallbearers moments before without
even realizing he was missing me. It had been four days since
Mama's passing and he had been sleepwalking ever since. We
all were, to various degrees.

I shook my head and kept my eyes down, staring at his
shiny penny loafers. The prissy man wrapped his arms around
me, pressing my face against the coolness of his silk shirt. I
wanted to experience the luxurious fabric with my palms, but
I kept my hands fisted in my lap.

Morty patted my shoulder before letting go and disappearing out with the others. A few more folks tried engag-
ing me into a mournful moment, but I wanted to share my grief
with no one but Mama, so I kept my head down and let my long
hair drape as a shield around my face.

The hushed chatter began to fade outside when a throat
cleared in front of me. Through a small crack in my hair curtain, I could see he was facing me, one knee resting on the
pew as he sort of leaned toward me. I lowered my head more,
hoping he'd get the hint.

He cleared his throat again. "I'm Vance Cumberland."

I swallowed before muttering, "Okay." The one word felt prickly leaving my throat.

When I offered nothing else, he spoke again. "And you're Austin?"

Even though he was asking me to confirm, I only repeated a scratchy "Okay."

Behind me, a stern hand squeezed my shoulder. Nothing else followed, not even placating words, before the person stomped off. And then a familiar sound reached me from outside the door. One I'd begun to expect over the last several years.

Vance gasped. "That old lady just spit on the steps of the church."

"Yes." I confirmed what I already knew.

"Yes? But why?"

Sighing, I kept my head down but tucked the hair curtain behind my ears. "That's Miss Wise. It's okay."

I'm sure he wanted to ask more about Miss Wise and her odd behavior, but I was thankful when he didn't. I had no energy or desire to explain that woman, especially when I didn't understand her myself.

The chapel finished emptying, leaving just the two of us. The quiet was sweeter than the cakes and pies lining the counters and any other free space found back at the house. The past three nights had been spent tending to the newborns with my other siblings camping out in my room to find some semblance of comfort, which had me running on very little sleep. Seemed there was always someone crying who needed me to hold them. Or someone thirsty and needing me to get them a glass of water. Or someone hungry and needing me to get them a plate of food.

As soon as Morty drove away from the house that night with Mama in the back of his funeral home van, Pa had checked out. And he'd yet to return. With no grandparents, I was on my own. Pa's parents had passed away within months of each other when I was in kindergarten and Mama never knew hers because she was raised in a group home.

Some friend of Mama's had come in from Nebraska to pay her respects and had volunteered to watch the newborns during the funeral, so my plan was to sit here alone for as long as I could get away with it. Vance made no move to leave, so my alone-time window was closing rapidly.

"Listen, Austin . . ." His warm hand pressed my knee briefly before retreating to the other side of the pew. "I . . . I never want to know how you feel right now."

I had expected another regurgitated line of condolence, so his blunt words had my eyes snapping up to meet his. Green as a grassy meadow on a summer day, they weren't looking *at* me but *inside* me, taking on a portion of the pain I was struggling to carry on my own.

"Vance, Son, we need to head out." His mother spoke from behind me, breaking the moment and sending my head to lower once more.

"Yes, ma'am." The pew creaked as Vance stood. He walked away.

It would be the last time we would exchange words for many years. It was only a handful of words, but they comforted me when it seemed nothing else would.

I learned some hard truths during that terrible fall. One truth was that a person could be dead even with a pulse. The stench seeping from my parents' bedroom was proof. I'd let it go on for a week after the funeral, but today there was no other choice but to put a stop to it.

Steeling myself after getting everyone off to school, I shoved open the door and nearly threw up. The room looked and smelled like a crime scene. Pungent body odor; picture frames toppled like dominoes, a few scattered and broken on the floor; clothing strung and strewed; a limp body on the bed.

I hurried over to the window and yanked it open to let in some fresh air and hopefully push out some of the staleness. My stomach twisted when I caught sight of the bloody bedding crumpled in the corner. Turning my back to it, I faced the bed and the unmoving giant. He still wore the suit from the funeral. Shoes untied yet they remained on his feet. One arm slung over his face.

"How have you been able to stand wearing these all this time?" I pulled his shoes off and the new stench that action released sent me into a bout of gagging. I tossed them across the room before realizing the noise could wake the babies down the hall. Cringing, I perked an ear and held my breath. Thankfully, the house remained silent.

"Pa, you gotta get up." My request was met with no response, so I shook his leg. Finally he moved a little. "Please, Pa. I really need you to get up. The babies are low on formula and diapers."

No response.

No matter how much I pleaded with him, he remained unresponsive, and eventually I got good and mad. I marched to the bathroom and collected a glass of water. Returning, I emptied it over his greasy head. He barely blinked in acknowledgment. Didn't even turn his head to dodge the water. I'd have rather he'd jumped up and got ahold of me for that.

As I swallowed my tears, another hard truth became clear. Mama wasn't there to protect us from Pa's dark seasons anymore. A hard question followed that hard truth: Would I be able to step into her role and protect my siblings from them?

Whatever was going on with Pa went beyond normal grief, but I was too young to understand what exactly it was. With Mama's shield no longer in place, I fully experienced the shadows that fell from Pa's presence for the first time. It was a murky place, dim with very little understanding.

But Mama had never let him hide this long, so I knew I couldn't walk away and allow him to continue rotting in this room.

With the time ticking down to the newborns' next feeding, I began to panic. Fear crawled up my neck and tightened my shoulders as I treated my father in a way I'd never done before. My pa wasn't a mean man, but I didn't know the hollow man unmoving on the bed. There was no choice but to push and face whatever repercussions arose.

I talked hard, whisper-yelling, "You need to stop acting like a baby!" When that didn't work, I tried talking even meaner. "You should be ashamed of yourself. Mama would be so disappointed in you for doing this to us young'uns." Tears burned my eyes, but I refused to release them. "So suck it up and get your sorry tail out of this bed."

Pushing and pulling and shoving at his deadweight, I was finally able to coerce him up and into the bathroom. "And you stink. Like really, really bad. Like that time Boss got sprayed by the skunk and then thought the mud in the pigpen would mask it . . ." I grunted while depositing him onto the closed toilet lid. His big ole form slouched in such a defeated manner that pity tapped my anger on the arm, but I held tight to the fury in order to get through this moment. Pity would do nothing but shove me inside his shadows, and that wouldn't do either one of us any good. "Yeah. No. You stink worse. So you better use the whole bar of Irish Spring." I jabbed a finger toward the shower after I set the water to warm and stomped out. I wanted to slam the door for good measure but remembered the babies in time to squelch the notion.

While he washed, I stripped the sour sheets off the bed and collected the stiff bloody ones from the corner. After setting the sour ones to washing and tossing the stained set, I gathered clean clothes for Pa and placed them just inside the bathroom door and waited for him to dress. I stood there and gave him instructions on brushing his teeth as if he'd never done these small tasks once in his life. When I had to open the tube of toothpaste and squeeze some onto his toothbrush for him, I began to wonder.

By the time I had Pa settled at the dining table and was force-feeding him grits, exhaustion hit me hard, but the soft cries coming from my room let me know there was no time to be exhausted. Staring into my father's hollow, bloodshot eyes that held no acknowledgment of his newborn sons' cries, another hard truth twisted my insides.

I had become a mother before I'd even become a woman.

Mama's talk that night before she died came to mind, and I knew for certain she was no fortune-teller. She'd predicted I would have three children, but there was no way that was ever going to happen. I already had seven to take care of, and one of them was a grown man.

Chapter 2

THE WITCH DOCTOR

April 1981

An unassuming spoon covered in mayo was no big deal until it slipped and clanged to the floor. White dots galore all over the kitchen cabinets, the floor mat in front of the sink, my bare feet. I grabbed the dishcloth and bent down to wipe up the mess while Peg continued adding bologna to the sandwiches we were assembling for lunch. I wasn't much on cooking, and so Saturdays, I stuck to cereal and sandwiches. Tomorrow I would give it more effort and add something like Beanee Weenees or canned stew to the meal rotation.

"Oooh! We gonna have company!" Peg announced as he took a step away from the mess I'd just made.

"No. The ole wives' tale says it has to be a spoon you're cooking with that falls. I'm not cooking."

"That's about as close to cooking as you get," Charlotte sassed from the other side of the kitchen.

I looked over my shoulder to glare at her, but Knox being smothered by his blanket caught my attention. I pointed to the blue swing that we'd designated for him. "Get that blanket off the baby's face. And crank Nash's swing again." Nash was kicking his tiny legs in the green swing beside his twin. The only way the others could tell which was which was that I kept Nash in green and Knox in blue. Due to spending so much time with them, I could tell them apart by subtle differences in their six-month-old features. Knox's nose was a little wider at the tip and Nash outweighed his brother by a quarter pound, making his face a bit fuller.

Charlotte did as I asked without giving me any lip. We'd all learned quickly that we were a team and teams couldn't perform well without unity. The baby twins were the most well-behaved babies in the history of babies. Perhaps they understood from the get-go that it was in their best interest in order to have better odds at surviving. We were pretty much on our own.

Fortunately, I only missed a few weeks of school until the day care at the First Baptist agreed to take the twins, even though they didn't have spots available. They also looked the other way when my thirteen-year-old self pulled up in Pa's truck to drop the babies off and pick them up.

Looking back on the juggling act I pulled off, it's amazing I didn't drop the ball on something. Thankfully, the school made an exception in my case and set up a short-term homebound program for me. It was also helpful that book smarts always came easy to me, even though nothing else did.

Pa had finally snapped out of the darkness after Christmas, only to begin obsessively planning for the next tobacco season. The past month, he'd all but slept in the greenhouse, germinating seeds and then tending to the sprouts like they were fragile children needing their father's care and comfort. Never mind the fact that he was neglecting the seven actual children he had, who were relying on each other to weather losing not only their mother but also, apparently, their father.

At least he was still breathing, and that meant there was hope he would return to living at some point.

I leaned against the counter and took a few deep breaths while rubbing my forehead. Nothing felt good, from my head to my stomach, yet I kept sucking it up and moving on to task after task. There was simply no other choice.

"What company?" Boss asked, late to the party even though he was sitting on the floor beside Charlotte talking gibberish to the babies.

"No company," I mumbled, returning to my task of topping the bologna with cheese and second slices of bread. I glanced out the window toward the greenhouse, wondering if I should bother bringing Pa a sandwich.

"Ha!" Peg shouted close to my ear as he pointed out the window at a boxy van pulling up. "Told ya!" He turned and began limping toward the back door.

Pa came from the greenhouse, beating Peg to the unfamiliar vehicle, and was opening the passenger door in a blink. His face pulled into a spastic grin, reminding me of Jack Nicholson's face when his character fell off his rocker and went totally mad in *The Shining*.

I saw the shimmery head wrap before the woman's face as she stood from the van. Instead of being mostly hidden in layers of robes like last time, her revealing outfit of hip-hugging jeans and a blouse tied above her belly button hid nothing. A pair of giant white-framed sunglasses concealed her sharp cheekbones and onyx eyes, but there was no mistaking who it was. Foxy Deveraux was the kind of intriguing woman you couldn't help but gawk at, and at the moment Peg was clinging to her bare waist like she was manna from heaven.

Swallowing hard, I gripped the edge of the sink to suppress the overwhelming desire to rush out there and cling to her too. To say the last six months had been difficult was like saying an infestation of red bugs was mildly irritating.

Outside, everyone's smile disappeared as Peg animatedly told what I knew had to be the nightmare of losing Mama. Foxy's blue-tipped nails covered her frown as her head shook. Jinx rounded the side of the van and clasped Pa's shoulder. More condolences, I was sure. Wanting no part in it, I gathered the sandwiches and started divvying them out to the young'uns sitting cross-legged on the floor in front of the baby swings as if they were the twins' guardians.

"Who's here, Ox?" Charlotte asked, eyeing Raleigh in a way that told me it was a question he wanted answered. He'd not spoken much since last October. Couldn't blame him. I didn't too much care for sharing words either anymore.

"I'm hoping it's a remedy."

"Like a doctor?" Charlotte questioned before taking a bite of her sandwich.

"Like a healer."

Not caring for my answer, Boss finished the last bite of his sandwich, hopped up from the floor, and joined me in peeking out the window. "Foxy!" Bits of food flew from his mouth as he shouted enthusiastically. He nearly made me topple over with his hasty retreat out the back door.

I gathered everyone else to go join the welcome wagon.

Pa introduced each of us by our actual names but barely got the babies' names past his lips. Foxy was nice enough but when I tried handing Knox to her, she took a step backward and patted him on his bald head instead. Like how someone ain't a dog person but can appreciate the cuteness of a puppy from a polite distance.

Her standoffish behavior was a bummer, because I was hoping the healing she could bring to the farm would be that of a motherly kind, being's that I was the worst at it. She and Jinx were two adults, nonetheless, so at least we weren't stuck with just one broken adult any longer.

Over the next hour or so, I corralled the young'uns inside so the adults could have an adult conversation. After I got the babies down for a nap, Pa asked that Boss and I go with the Deverauxs to the guesthouse to help them move in.

"Ain't this place groovy," Foxy said in a dry tone, although she somehow sounded sincere.

I glanced at the two-bedroom cabin, sky blue with yellow shutters and trim. "My mama painted it. The place is small but clean, and it holds a lot of Mama's heart." I had no idea where that defensive attitude came from, but I sure did feel it in my stinging eyes and warm cheeks.

Foxy took a deep breath and scanned the exterior with

a tilted head. "I thought we was about to move into a shack. It's a lovely surprise is what I meant, Austin, and I promise to honor your mother by taking good care of it." She slid the giant sunglasses off and tucked them inside her suede shoulder bag with long fringe hanging from the bottom. She turned her attention away from the house and studied my face as Boss and Jinx walked by lugging a big trunk. Once they were inside, she leaned closer to me. "Is this your first cycle or have you had your monthly before now?"

Face instantly heating, I gawked at her. "First time. Did you read it in my aura? You really are a fortune-teller."

Foxy sniffed, maybe her way of laughing. "No. I acted as one for the fair, but I don't need to be able to read minds or the future to know." She reached a long, cool fingertip toward me and gently tapped my chin. "Acne, and your emotions are running a little high. And . . . you have this look on your face like you're constipated. Sweetheart, that's a dead giveaway."

Good grief. This woman was just as candid as Mama used to be. Oh, the ache in my chest that thought produced.

I followed her onto the porch and stood in the recesses of the shade. A slight breeze rustled by and sent the wind chime to singing a delicate melody. "Well, that's nowhere near as magical as you reading my aura . . ."

"Yeah, and that's the reality of reality. Do you need anything?"

"A potion to make it go away would be nice." I couldn't believe I was having this conversation with a perfect stranger, but she was a woman and there was no way I was talking to Pa about it. "Mama . . . she stocked up on stuff I'd need, but . . .

my, uh . . . my stomach hurts and I feel really tired . . . Should I take Pepto or aspirin?"

"You need Midol. I have some." Foxy rummaged around in the giant bag, retrieving a plastic medicine bottle and handing it to me. "Take one and repeat as directed." She twisted the bottle like a dial and pointed to the directions on the back. She raised her voice slightly, speaking over her shoulder. "Jinx, baby, will you bring in my medicine trunk next?"

"Yes, my queen." He pushed the screen door open and headed to their van with Boss following, the door smacking shut behind them. They came from around the side of the van with another trunk, but this one was double in size. "Where you want it?" Jinx grunted as he and Boss both appeared to be struggling to carry the bulky thing.

Foxy eyed me. "How many bedrooms did your daddy say?"

"Two. But the back porch has been closed in, so that's like an extra den or something." I shrugged.

Foxy led the way inside, her platform sandals tapping against the linoleum floor until reaching the back room. With one glimpse of the closed-in space, she claimed it as hers. The guys placed the trunk in the corner and headed out to continue unloading the van. It was slightly musty in the house from being closed up for the better part of a year, but as soon as she opened the lid of the trunk and rested it on the clapboard wall, the room took on a spicy scent that reminded me of the aroma from her fortune-teller tent last fall.

She knelt beside it and began sifting through tiny glass jars and metal tins. "This is what you need." She handed me four mesh pouches filled with yellow dried leaves.

I held the pouches to my nose and sniffed. "It smells like flowers."

"Because it is. It's evening primrose tea. Steep it just like a cup of hot tea and sip it before bed." She pulled out a glass bottle of clear liquid. "And this is witch hazel oil. Dab it on your pimples to help clear them up. Don't go mashing them."

I studied the bottle in one hand and the tea pouches in the other. "Are you a, uh . . . witch doctor?"

Foxy let out three quick sniffs, her lips turned up, amusement squinting her onyx eyes. "You make me out to be so much more interesting than I am." She took the bottle of oil and showed me how to apply it to my face. She seemed no more motherly than me, but there was care and attention in her actions. It was the first time in six months that someone had taken care of me to any degree. I'd forgotten how wonderful that felt, and it almost had me finding my tears.

I told the young'uns earlier that I hoped a remedy had arrived in that van. Sitting on the floor beside Foxy's trunk of potions, I was pretty sure I'd been right.

"How do you know how to make this stuff and what it's used for?" I held the pouches a little higher before lowering them to my lap.

"Back home in New Orleans, my grandmother was big into natural remedies. She grew her own herbs and plants. I was probably about your age when she began teaching me her craft. Some swore she was a witch doctor." Another laugh-sniff. "But there's no hocus-pocus about it."

Foxy could brush it off all she wanted, but I was downright impressed and quite curious about all the trinkets and bundles of herbs she filled that little room with—even more so after using the witch hazel that made my pimples magically disappear.

Too bad by the time summer came around, the folks of Magnolia had formed a strong, less impressed opinion about Foxy and her herbs.

———————

Jinx Deveraux was not a social man. He kept to himself mostly, only seeming to want to converse with his queen. Who could blame him there? Everyone wanted to spend time with the fascinating woman, even the ones gossiping about her around town.

Jinx's skin was several shades darker than Foxy's pecan tan, but his eyes were butterscotch. Even though they were light and inviting in color, there was no openness to Jinx. Except for when it came to my brother Peg. Why he took to Peg of all people is baffling. Ain't like there weren't plenty of us who were more pleasant to be around to choose from. It was probably because Peg gave him no choice, always hanging out at Foxy's, as we had started calling the guesthouse after they moved in. Some unspoken truth was conveyed that the couple were not guests but permanent residents and everyone was fine by that.

For as much as Jinx liked to protest about working for "the man," he had no issue with working hard. From sunup to sundown, he could be found somewhere on the farm, either tending to a field or setting up a piece of farm equipment to work on a field.

And for as much as Foxy liked to protest that it weren't her place when it came to Pa and his odd behavior or when it came to us young'uns, she sure made it her place to implement changes to the farm. Within the first month of them living there, she'd claimed an acre across from the chapel to turn into a garden. Herbs, flowers, vegetables, and fruit were planted meticulously. She nurtured and cared for that garden in a way I wished was directed toward me and my siblings. But it *weren't her place*.

By the summer, a farm stand had been set up by the road and we were in business. On top of the tables was bountiful produce and underneath was lined with elixirs and such. She had quite a large clientele for what was under the table, even though those same folks wouldn't so much as look her way when they crossed paths in town.

The first harvest to come from Nolia Produce was the fattest, sweetest strawberries I'd ever tasted. Seemed Clive Thomas thought the same thing from the cardboard trays of berries lining his truck bed.

"You gonna make a lot of jam or something, Mr. Thomas?" I asked the heavily freckled man as I placed another cardboard tray beside a fifty-pound bag of sugar.

Clive cackled, baring his buckteeth. "Somethin' like that." He pulled a wallet from the front pocket of his overalls. "How much I owe ya, gal?"

"Foxy, how much does Mr. Thomas owe for the strawberries?" I hollered, which brought her out from inside the small room of the farm stand in her standard farm outfit of high-waisted jeans, off-the-shoulder shirt, and a printed head wrap. She began counting the trays but Clive spoke up before she got started good.

"You that witch doctor, ain't ya? I thought these was Foster berries. Not—"

"Nice berries?" Peg interrupted as he limped over, standing between Clive and Foxy like his tiny self could protect her. Even though he was third oldest in a line of seven, it looked like he would end up being the runt of the Foster litter.

"I ain't wantin' these nasty berries. Get 'em outta my truck." Clive's face turned redder than the berries.

"But, sir, they ain't nasty. Why you say that for?" Peg asked, tilting his head as if he were confused. He might have only been eleven, but he didn't think like a kid. His mind had always been years ahead of his age.

"That colored witch done been messin' with 'em." Clive wrinkled his bulbous nose like the air was foul.

With an inflection of faux innocence only a child could get away with, Peg pointed to Clive's face. "But, sir, you colored too. With all them spots you at least half-brown. You know what you remind me of? When two kinds of dogs mix and the puppies come out all different colors. My pa calls 'em mutts. Are you a mutt, sir?"

Clive's fat, freckly hands balled into fists as he sneered at Peg. "Why you little smart-a—"

"All right now. You watch your language around these innocent ears," Foxy spoke up in her cool monotone.

"Ain't nothing innocent about that young'un." Clive hurled one of the trays to the ground, berries scattered and splattered at our feet. He yelped and held up a bleeding finger that must have gotten sliced on the sharp edge of the cardboard.

Peg hurried over to inspect the minor cut and gasped.

"Look, Foxy, he bleeds the same color as you and me. Maybe Clive ain't a mutt after all. Just a jack—"

Before Peg could finish muttering evidence on how un-innocent he really was, he was plucked off the ground and tossed over Pa's broad shoulder. "Mr. Thomas, I'm awfully sorry for my son's rudeness. That's no way to treat another human being."

Chin jutted out, full of indignation, Clive bellowed, "You dang right! Shame on him. And shame on you for raising him no better than that."

"Yes, sir. Shame on me indeed. And shame on you for mis-treating that lovely lady." Pa tipped his head toward Foxy, who was retreating inside the little room.

Foxy hightailing it from any form of confrontation would be something we'd all get used to over time. The woman did it better than anyone I'd ever met.

"Her's a nice person," Boss added from his perch on the tailgate of our truck, but no one acknowledged him.

Pa leaned closer to the fuming man and lowered his voice to say, "And shame on your parents for not raising you no better than that. Now I think the best thing you can do is load up and go get to work on that batch of wine you gonna bootleg."

Clive looked at the berries and then at his wallet.

"Foxy and Jinx are a part of our family and we don't take too kindly to anyone mistreating them, so we don't want your money or your business here ever again. Take the berries and get."

Clive spit and sputtered on his pride, but he ended up taking the beautiful free berries he had no real right to and kicking up a dust storm on the way out of the farm. Once he was out of sight, Pa whirled on his booted heels and started off toward the house with Peg still dangling across his shoulder playing possum. My brother's scrawny arms fell limp, and I half expected his tongue to droop out the side of his slack mouth but it didn't.

"Ox, round the young'uns up and meet me inside the barn. Now!" Pa kept beating a path up the dirt drive, on a mission that I hoped would lead to Peg's first ever butt whupping. He'd been asking for it, in my opinion.

I directed the older twins and Boss to get in the back of the truck while I scooped up the babies from the playpen underneath the shady elm tree and loaded them in the floorboard. They were pretty good at sitting up by themselves as long as I took the drive slow, and I was in no rush, not wanting to catch up with Pa. No worries there since it seemed he sprouted wings and was at the barn well before we arrived. I handed Knox to a confused Boss and placed Nash on my hip. Even though Boss's mind was slow, he took orders considerably well. Best part was he never questioned me. Just did as he was told—opposite of Peg. Man, life would have been so much smoother if we'd figured out how to take a page out of Boss's simple book.

We quietly crept toward the dark barn, Raleigh and Charlotte filing in behind us. We stepped inside the packhouse that no longer held the sweet appeal of cured tobacco but the musty aroma of years gone by. The loft was mostly used for storage and the first floor as a graveyard for broken things. A bicycle missing a front tire. The rusted two-seater tobacco

setter that had been replaced with a shiny red four-seater. If
I looked hard enough, surely my hopes and dreams could be
found buried in one of the corners.

The front and back doors were slid open, giving the sunshine permission to filter through enough to allow a fair view
of whatever consequence Peg was about to receive for his
misbehavior. The uncertainty of what Pa would do had the
sweat trickling down my back. I moved Nash to my other hip
and pulled the collar of my T-shirt away from my damp skin.

Pa placed Peg on his feet and began unbuckling his belt
and unsnapping the buttons of his shirt at the same time. Fact,
Pa had never been able to follow through with a whipping of
any sort. He'd get as far as tearing a switch off or undoing his
belt buckle, but never—not once—did the thin wood or thick
leather meet any of our skin. Mama was just as soft, and it's a
wonder we all didn't run around acting like a bunch of wild
heathens. What our parents lacked in corporal punishment
was always made up in chore punishment, though, so maybe
that's why we all didn't end up ruined.

We stood in a somber line as the belt swished from the last
loop of Pa's britches, all eyes watching Peg squirm. He knew
and we knew that he deserved a few lashes from that belt. But
we also knew Pa wouldn't see the punishment through.

Knowing all that certainly didn't prepare me for what Pa
would do.

"I'm no better father than this?" Pa's wild eyes were trained
on Peg as he shrugged off his denim shirt and let it fall to the
ground. It was the most emotion I'd seen him openly display
since Mama's passing. A flash of Pa lying in that bloodied

bed, screaming for Mama not to leave him, slammed into my thoughts, almost making me drop the baby. Holding Nash tighter, I blinked the image away as best I could.

Pa doubled the belt, gripping it with both hands to form an O and then snapping it into a loud thin line. Seven bodies flinched, including the two babies.

"I'm s-s-sorry, P-Pa," Peg stuttered between whimpers.

"You acting like you don't know any better than to be disrespectful." Pa's arm coiled back, preparing to deliver a blow as Peg's eyes rounded with fear. Leather biting into skin echoed through the barn. Peg yelped and took a big step backwards, falling on his backside as Pa retracted the belt from where it wrapped around his own giant shoulder. His back was toward the line of us as he stood over Peg, so the angry welt rising against his skin was on vivid display.

Pa just struck himself? I could hardly believe what my eyes had so clearly just witnessed.

Both babies wailed, reacting to Peg's sobs and the thick tension shoving against our better judgment. It was stifling, but none of us dared to leave for fear that belt would find us next. We just stood in shock and terror as Pa flicked his wrist at lightning speed to send the belt rapidly snaking around his own waist.

Whack!

Another red line bloomed across his back.

Whack!

With each lashing Pa condemned himself as a parent, as a man, as a Christian.

Whack!

The sour stench of sweat and urine filtered around the dank space. I looked down the line of Foster kids and caught the dark spot blooming on the front of Raleigh's pants.

Whack!

"I've failed at being a father. God have mercy! I've failed!" Pa's words screeched through his clenched teeth as his chest heaved violently. The Bible reference about weeping and gnashing of teeth came to mind. Was Pa living in his own hell? Were we?

Each time a new red line streaked across his skin, we all winced as if we could feel the pain. In a way, I suppose we did. I'd never felt the brutal deliverance of a belt against my skin, but the effect couldn't have been more traumatic than witnessing my father whipping himself until blood trickled down his back. From the sobs and trembling bodies, my siblings felt the impact just as viciously as I did. As Peg did. As Pa did.

Pa eventually collapsed to the ground on all fours, panting and moaning. His large frame shook as he pointed the belt toward the door. I didn't have to think past a second on obeying him. I made my way outside, ushering a procession of stunned and frightened children away from the thick despair of his shadows.

Where did the sun go?

Will it ever shine again?

Can it at least peek through the storm clouds every now and then?

Those questions haunted me as I settled the babies down for a nap as quickly as possible so I could go tend to the others. With shaky hands, I helped Raleigh out of his soiled clothes and into the shower, neither one of us saying a word. He was so very tenderhearted, but I had no idea what to do for that, so my focus was always on his physical needs. Like getting him cleaned up from peeing himself. I set his clothes to washing, not realizing yet how often that would become an added chore in the following years.

Charlotte was the next one to be checked on. She sat on her bed, brushing her doll's hair, always finding another task to do to separate herself from whatever episode had just occurred. I figured it was a blessing that she could pretend something didn't happen, but we would both learn later in life that pretending something away was no better than constantly dwelling on it. Both produced impactful wounds that tended to fester in other parts of living.

I slid a Twinkie out of my pocket and left it on her nightstand, my way of giving her a piece of Mama's comfort. Raleigh would find one on top of his clean set of clothes when he finished washing.

Leaving Charlotte in her denial, I went on a hunt for Boss, finding him doing a poor job of hiding inside his tiny closet. One thing about us Fosters, we tended to grow on the big side, but Boss hadn't realized his formidable size yet.

My own body had shot up so much recently that I was left with no option but to take clothes from Mama's side of her and Pa's closet. After one of my closet raids, I ran into Pa in the hallway. A stricken expression hung heavily on his face while taking in one of Mama's outfits I was wearing.

"You . . . you look just like your ma." It was the first time he'd mentioned her to me while actually making eye contact, and it would be the last. It would also be the last time my father

looked directly at me. From then on, it was only fleeting glances, as if looking at me any longer than that would result in him turning to stone.

I took another Twinkie out of my other pocket and placed it onto Boss's lap, wedging in beside him, and we remained quiet for a spell. Silence was another way we dealt with things poorly out on the farm.

Lastly, I peeped in on Peg. He was huddled on the floor beside his bed, staring at his hands with a deep frown on his dirty tear-streaked face.

Standing by the door, I told him, "You taking up for Foxy was the right thing to do, but the way you went about it sure did stink."

"Just leave me alone," he ordered, turning away from my view.

"Phoenix, you cannot fight hate with hate. It only produces more hate." I delivered a quote from Pa and decided not to give my brother a Twinkie for fear it would be rewarding bad behavior. "Stay up here and think about that for a while. Then come on downstairs and help me with supper." I left without waiting for a reply, knowing he'd make his way to the kitchen eventually.

After a meal of beans and franks with sliced cucumbers and tomatoes on the side, I got everyone washed up and in bed early that night. I'm ashamed to admit I didn't go nowhere near that barn to check on Pa until then, sensing it was going to be a similar situation to when Mama died and he holed up in their room. I had no desire to face anything like that again, yet there was no way around it.

Working side by side with Foxy was like second nature—in the garden, in the kitchen, in her little room mixing herbal remedies. But I never imagined we would work side by side in the packhouse, patching Pa back together.

He was sprawled out, facedown, on an old quilt we managed to get him on before he passed out, snoring heavily from the elixir Foxy had whipped up. About 90 percent of it was made from 100-proof moonshine. With him no longer writhing in pain, we knelt on the edge of the quilt and went to work on dressing the angry slashes crisscrossing his back.

"I don't understand today," I whispered, holding the small pot of salve for Foxy.

She dipped her fingers in and then applied it to a welt on Pa's hip. "What part?"

"All of it . . ." I wanted to voice my concerns about Pa losing it, but as always, the subject of Dave Foster remained trapped inside me. That feeling of needing to vomit and knowing I'd feel better after the purge hit me. Swallowing it down, I broached the other part of the day that bothered me. "Why do people act like Clive Thomas? The civil rights laws done and declared that we are all equal."

Foxy let out a humorless snort and shook her head but offered no other response to my question.

I pulled the salve out of reach so she had no choice but to focus on me. "Why are people not understanding the law? It's clear as day."

Sighing, Foxy took the pot from my hand but kept her eyes

on me. "Honey child, you can change the law all day long, but you can't change people's opinions. That fool today was probably raised to believe I ain't nowhere near his equal."

"That's just pure stupid."

Foxy sat on her butt with arms crossed, looking lost in her thoughts for a spell.

I sat back too and listened to the symphony of crickets and such just outside until she cleared her throat.

"What if a new law came out tomorrow that said you could no longer worship God? Would you suddenly stop believing in him just because the law told you to?"

Huffing, I swiped my thumb against the leg of my shorts to remove a smudge of salve. "It's not the same. Believing in God is a great thing. Racism and hate is a bad thing."

"I know. Just trying to help you make sense about not being able to suddenly change someone's beliefs if that's all they've ever known."

"God should have just made us all white or black or . . . purple. Sure would be easier if we all looked the same."

"There's nothing wrong with being different. The problem is people who don't accept that." Foxy screwed the lid onto the jar, eyes flicking to Pa as he went to roll to his side. Flinching in his sleep, he resettled and stayed on his belly.

"You got anything that Pa could take to maybe fix whatever is broken on his inside?" I whispered once he returned to snoring.

"That . . . It ain't my place." Foxy quickly whispered her excuse as she stood and pointed to the figure lingering by the door. "My Jinx is gonna stay in here with Dave for the night. Go on to bed now." With that she knocked the dust off the seat of her pants and started out of the barn.

"No. It's *my place* to tend to him. Thanks just the same, Jinx." My tone was sharp with enough irritation to have Foxy glancing over her shoulder but not slowing her stride.

This would be my first attempt at building a barrier between us Fosters and everyone else. The barrier was rickety at first when I'd become overwhelmed to the point of feebly reaching out for help, but with each rebuild it eventually became ironclad.

Chapter 3

AN ATHEIST BELIEVER

November 1982

Tobacco seasons had a trusted pattern—prep, plant, harvest, repeat. There was comfort in this pattern. One that was dependable. As I watched the cringeworthy show of Pa preaching while standing on top of the front pew, there was no denying another dependable pattern. One in which no comfort could be found. The highs reminded me of brilliantly sunny days jacked up on speed. So bright and glaring, it was too overwhelming to take in directly. Then the pattern would shift into a treacherous dormancy where everything became shrouded in gloom and dread.

For the most part, we'd had normal, somewhat-comfortable days for more than a year, ever since Foxy and Jinx moved in.

It would have been easy to think Pa was finally settling down, but I was never quite able to convince myself of that possible outcome. As sure as the tobacco seasons rolled around, here we were rolling around to another one of Pa's jacked-up spells. And it was one of the unchangeable truths of our family that the darkness would inevitably follow.

A loud groan from the pew caught my attention as Pa danced three steps from one end to the other. Surely he could hear the poor wood yelling at him to get his giant self down. His face shone in high color, his smile blinding as he spoke animatedly. Pa hopped off the pew and reached to give the town's ex-con, Tripp Murphy, a high five.

Tripp laughed but returned the high five with enthusiasm. If I'd done what the town's ex-con did on his very first visit to this church, I'd probably go along with whatever Dave Foster came up with, too. Last month Pa got the wild hair to go pick Tripp up before service, not even giving no mind that the feller was two sheets in the wind.

Pa had practically dragged him inside and propped the drunk man up on the front pew. During Pa's sermon, Tripp staggered to the altar. He opened his mouth and we all seemed to hold our breath, expecting him to confess his sins right then and there. Instead, his body spasmed and then an explosion of sour booze shot out of him. Tripp stumbled to the small part of the altar he hadn't desecrated, curled up in a ball, and started snoring.

Pa had scratched the side of his beard, thick eyebrows drawn close together, and studied Tripp sleeping peacefully. Pa's lip had twitched as he lifted his blue eyes and scanned the small congregation. "I reckon we just performed our first exorcism."

I guess he was right because Tripp had shown up on Sundays ever since, sober and attentive. Pa said Jesus only wanted us to come as we were, so he would always be inviting all, no matter their circumstances.

Covered in an array of colorful tattoos with a silver hoop in one ear, Tripp Murphy caught people's attention, but it was his glass eye that I had the hardest time looking away from. I'd find myself following its roaming track instead of his steady eye when he talked to me about his landscaping job for the city, cleaning up under the magnolia trees in town.

The city must have felt bad for sending him to prison for the murder of the teen whose remains had been discovered right in front of the courthouse, hidden under one of those magnolias. In the very same prison where Tripp was serving time, an inmate bragged to another about getting away with the teen's murder, going into detail about hiding her body under the tree at the courthouse as a joke. Some sick joke, if you ask me. I think Tripp felt the same way. He was dedicated to his job and making sure nothing ever went undiscovered again under one of those voluptuous trees.

Considering the town had never accepted Tripp, even after he was found innocent and had wrongfully served over three years behind bars, the poor guy needed acceptance. He found it amongst the First Riffraff of Magnolia.

This morning Pa was dancing up and down the aisle, and I'd have thought he was the drunk if I didn't know better. No one seemed to pick up on how ridiculous he was, quoting

Scripture one minute and then singing George Harrison's "My Sweet Lord" the next. And it was a great song and so most everyone joined in, including grouchy ole Peg. It seemed Pa was in a Beatles kinda mood, because the next song was "Here Comes the Sun," and I couldn't help but hope my darnedest that he was relaying the message that this dark season of ups and downs was coming to an end.

The closing prayer finally showed up but in a lengthy rambling. As Pa took a breath and launched into the second part of the prayer, an impatient huff came from a few pews in front of me, followed by heavy feet hitting the wood floor.

I peeked open an eye and watched Helena Wisniewska head toward my pew, wearing her usual funeral attire—black wool skirt and jacket—no matter if it was hotter than hades. I sweat just looking at her. Tall and thin, her figure reminiscent of a winter tree stripped down to its spindly branches. Slightly stooped, her posture suggested the inability to hold her six-foot frame upright any longer. Gunmetal hair in a severe bun and dull gray eyes. A hooked nose hovering over thin lips in a permanent grimace. Miss Wise was one woman we all took considerable lengths to stay clear of. She moved to Magnolia from somewhere up North, but her thickly accented words hinted that her roots hadn't been formed in American soil. No one even knew how to properly pronounce her last name, which was why it was shortened to Wise. She clucked her tongue the first time Pa called her that, but she never corrected anyone for it.

My *amen* was whispered a good five minutes ago, so I felt no shame in turning my attention to Miss Wise. Human behavior intrigued me to the point of staring, and if something was interesting enough, I'd have Miss Jones at the library help me find books about whatever caught my attention. She always gave me funny looks, like when I asked her to help me find a book about witch doctors and herbal remedies since Foxy was stingy with sharing much about herself, but Miss Jones never refused to help me satisfy my curiosity about something.

As Miss Wise reached the threshold of the church, she leaned over with her lips puckered, but she froze, eyes fixed on the sky. A few motionless beats later, she began trembling like a withered branch in the midst of a winter storm. Her lips parted and let loose a bloodcurdling scream. Pa's melodious nonsense cut off and all heads popped up.

Rushing outside to see what had her freaking out, we found billows of thick smoke just past a thin line of trees in the direction of the west tobacco barn. The wind shifted and the acrid odor of smoke entwined with the sweet aroma of curing tobacco, creating a new scent I'd wish I'd never been introduced to. Breaking out in a sprint, a long line of us hurried to the burning barn.

Jinx and Tripp got busy trying to douse the flames while Pa worked on cutting the gas from the barn's furnace. I focused on moving anything within the flames' reach out of the way. The more the men struggled to snuff the fire, the more it fought back. Through a fallen wall, we helplessly witnessed the beautifully sewn tobacco we worked months and months to produce incinerate within a blink. A hissing sound started rising above the cacophony of shouting and crackling.

"Run!" Tripp shouted, scooping up the two-year-old twins

like Pac-Man collecting dots while trying to outrun the ghosts. I did the same, making Boss help me carry Peg while pretty much shoving the older twins to keep them in front of us.

We'd barely made it to the line of trees when the boom shook the ground and sent a thick shower of ash to rain down on us. There was no gathering the barn or its contents back together ever again, so the soot-covered group of us plopped on the ground and attempted to collect ourselves instead.

Eventually Foxy took action, checking each one over for injuries and then directing Tripp and Pa to follow her so that she could dress their minor burns. The rest of us returned to the chapel to gather what was left behind, having no clue we'd left a distraught Miss Wise until finding her on her knees in the side yard. Her entire body and mouth vibrated in silent sobs, as if someone had hit her mute button. It was disturbing yet so eerily captivating that I couldn't look away.

Similar to approaching a rabid animal, we crept closer, arms extending and then retracting, indecisive on whether to reach out to her or keep at a safe distance. Suddenly the tremors paused and her dull gray eyes widened in horror as Miss Wise began slapping at her hair until it started unraveling from the bun.

"Get it off me!" Miss Wise screeched, batting the ashes off her suit jacket while completely spazzing out.

At a loss as to what to do, I ordered Peg to take the others home and asked Charlotte to help me load Miss Wise into her Cadillac. Charlotte took a step away from the car to close the door, but Miss Wise practically yanked her inside.

"Don't leave me, Irene! Please!"

"But I'm Char—"

"No. We can't let them separate us . . ." Miss Wise's entire body trembled in an unfathomable fear.

Charlotte's worried eyes connected with mine, neither one of us having a clue who Irene was, but the pain in that woman's deep, raspy voice had me nodding my head for my sister to get in the back seat. I hurried around to the driver's side and drove Miss Wise home.

Home was a gloomy wooden structure that faded into a weathered gray, looking as dreary as its owner.

"Sure could use a coat of paint," Charlotte muttered as we pulled up. At the age of nine, my sister already seemed to have found her calling for decorating and such, always sprucing something up or rearranging furniture.

"And some of Foxy's flowers," I added, eyeing the barren yard and empty flower boxes under the two front windows that didn't even have shutters dressing them up. I put the car in park and cut the engine, angling slightly to the stooped figure in the passenger seat. Her tangled hair barely held on to the lopsided bun. "Miss Wise, we got you home."

She lifted her head and slowly blinked. After a few more blinks, the trancelike state cleared away. "Huh?" Her unfocused eyes cut to me.

She went from a trance to a state of confusion, so I didn't know if we should walk her inside or go to the hospital. "Uh . . . Charlotte and I . . . we drove you home from church. Are you not feeling well? You need to go to the emergency room?"

Miss Wise exaggerated a blink, then scrubbed her hands down her face. "No, no. I'm fine," she said from behind her hands and then dropped them to peer out the windshield, appearing uncertain as to what to do next. Her and me both.

I looked at Charlotte in the rearview mirror. She whirled a finger beside her ear and mouthed, *Crazy.* I shook my head, took a deep breath, and opened my door. "Let's get you inside, okay?"

"Oh . . . Okay."

I hurried around to Miss Wise's side of the car and opened the door. She unfolded her long, narrow body from the car with Charlotte climbing out behind her. Her stride was so feeble that my sister and I instinctively flanked her all the way to the door. Once she unlocked the door, we retreated down the three porch steps.

"Do come in," Miss Wise said.

I don't know if we were more stunned to be invited in or by what her opening that door revealed. After wiping my eyes and scrutinizing the dreary exterior, I stepped into an episode of *The Twilight Zone.* The show was weird to say the least, but Foxy liked to watch it while I helped her sort through dried herbs. At the moment, the real-life episode went from a grainy black-and-white to full-on Technicolor. Everything inside was bathed in pinks and whites and trimmed with gold finishes. Crystal figurines and porcelain knickknacks, lacy doilies and fluffy throw pillows . . .

"Whoa, it's like a life-size dollhouse." Charlotte shuffled around the living room, mouth gaping, eyes wide in wonder. I followed behind her doing the same.

"I . . . I need to freshen up . . ." Miss Wise walked down a hallway. A door shut and then we heard the muffled sound of a running faucet.

"I guess we need to start the walk home," I whispered to Charlotte. My growling stomach reminded me we still had to figure out Sunday dinner after the three-mile journey.

Ignoring me, Charlotte pulled in a deep inhale. "It smells like a rose garden in here." She lifted her nose and breathed in again the way the old bloodhound that took up at the farm this past summer did every time something in the air caught his attention.

I sniffed my collar and winced. "We smell like a smokehouse." I shoved my soot-smudged hands deep into the pockets of my corduroys. "Don't touch anything."

Charlotte held her hands out and twirled slowly. "I didn't get dirty."

"You never get dirty," I grouched. My little sister was the queen of getting out of farmwork or anything that put her directly in contact with dirt. At least she didn't mind keeping the laundry done and watching after the younger twins. Heaven knows, both were full-time jobs.

"Don't fuss at me. I made sure the twins stayed out the way for y'all." She placed her hands on her hips and rolled her eyes. In a floral chiffon dress and with her brown hair in pigtails, Charlotte looked like the doll that went with this dollhouse.

Refusing to argue with her in the middle of a stranger's home, I beckoned her to follow me. "Let's go."

Before we could slip out the door, Miss Wise walked back into the room. Another dimension of this *Twilight Zone* episode unfolded with the new version of this woman. For the first time ever, I saw her in a short-sleeved blouse and a pair of lounge pants. Her feet were bare, showing off sparkling toenails in bubble-gum pink. Blinking away from her feet, I looked up and noticed her dark-gray hair had been freshly gathered in a long braid that hung over her right shoulder.

"Would you young ladies care for something to drink?" Miss Wise asked, voice heavy with an accent but much smoother than the normally garbled delivery that certainly never included pleasantries or offerings. It was so peculiar how the spindly branches of this woman had magically sprouted a few blooms within the walls of the dollhouse.

"Yes, please," Charlotte answered before I could find any words.

Miss Wise gestured for us to follow her to the kitchen. It was an immaculate space dressed in all white with touches of pink and chrome.

Charlotte tapped her knuckles against the glossy white countertop with subtle gray veining through it. A faint ping echoed through the quaint room. "Wow. This ain't Formica. What kind is it, Miss Wise?"

Miss Wise pulled three sets of dainty teacups and saucers from a cabinet, her eyes moving to where Charlotte stood ogling the counter. "White marble."

I regarded the pink rose pattern on the cups, not wanting to be rude but certainly not wanting coffee or hot tea after fighting that fire. I decided that after taking a few sips we would bolt but changed my mind when she opened her fridge and pulled out two glass bottles of Cheerwine soda. Besides milk and tea we kept a pitcher of Tang in our fridge, but never soda. That was only for special occasions.

Miss Wise popped the tops with a bottle opener with such

ease like she'd done that very thing a million times. When she opened the cabinet below the sink and tossed the two caps inside a nearly full bucket, I supposed she had. After pouring the three cups of soda and placing them on a lace-topped round table with a fresh bouquet of flowers in the center, she glanced my way and took in my darkened hands and dingy shirt. "Perhaps you'd like to clean up a bit?"

Face heating, I nodded, beelining to the bathroom she pointed out. I turned the glass doorknob, using only my fingertips, and entered the prettiest bathroom I'd ever laid eyes on. A claw-foot tub was the centerpiece of the room. Beside it was a bench lined with elegant bottles of bath salts, bubble bath, and other fancy canisters.

I washed up in the pedestal sink, using the pink liquid soap that reminded me of springtime in Foxy's flower garden, scrubbing up to my elbows and also my face. Completely opposite of the harsh Irish Spring we used at home, the soap smelled so perfume-fresh and felt so silky that I wanted to bathe my entire body in it.

"Dang it," I grumbled under my breath at the grimy mess left in the sink. It took another squirt of soap and some elbow grease to clean it away. Satisfied with that, I hurried to the kitchen, where Miss Wise and my sister were sipping soda from fine china.

"Join us," Miss Wise said quietly.

I moved to the chair where the third teacup of soda had been placed. Choosing to stand, I picked up the delicate cup that felt fragile in my hand. It only took three sips to drain it dry. The cherry-flavored cola was refreshing but left me wanting more.

Sensing as much, Miss Wise took another bottle from the fridge and refilled our fancy cups.

"Thank y—" My words stalled when I caught a glimpse of a blurry row of numbers in bluish-green ink lining her left forearm.

Miss Wise quickly moved her left arm behind her back, making it clear the odd tattoo wasn't up for discussion. As soon as I took the last sip of my second cup, she cleared her throat and I knew what was coming before she spoke.

"It was kind of you two young ladies to come visit me. Please see yourself out." With that, she disappeared down the hallway again.

I tugged on Charlotte's arm. "Hurry up. Let's get out of here before she morphs into another version."

We cut through a few yards before hitting the road. It didn't take long before the houses disappeared and we were surrounded by trees.

"That lady is so strange," Charlotte observed about a mile into our walk home, as she teetered on the white line on the road like a tightrope. "Did you see that faded tattoo on her arm? She don't look like the tattoo kinda person."

"Yeah. And I was rude staring at it. It was my fault she wanted us gone." I pulled my long hair off my neck to allow the breeze to cool me some.

"She sure did have a pretty house though. I wish it was ours."

"Yeah."

A horn beeped, startling the both of us, as a Jeep slowed almost to a stop. "Lookee here. I didn't think y'all were allowed off the farm," Levi Sullivan taunted from the driver's seat. He was the ringleader of the cool kids. Well, that's what they thought of themselves, but reality was they were a bunch of spoiled brats.

The other guys laughed, but the only one who drew my attention was the only one not bothering to participate in the heckling. Eyes closed, a pair of headphones nestled amongst his wild blond curls, head nodding to the beat of whatever song he was listening to on his fancy Walkman, Vance Cumberland appeared to have no care in the world. I wondered what a world without care felt like.

"Keep walking," I told Charlotte, ignoring the guys altogether and guiding her onto the shoulder of the road.

"Y'all want a lift home?" Levi asked, sounding more teasing than sincere. He and Cody Elvis, who was sitting behind him, were practically hanging out the windows. The Jeep swerved closer and he extended his arm and flicked the ends of my hair. "You hear me, Texas?"

"No thanks." I waved him off and sped my stride, wishing another car would appear in the opposite direction to force him back to his side of the road.

Someone made a dumb comment about being surprised we were wearing shoes, laughter ringing out after it, but we kept our lips tightly shut.

"You sure? 'Cause I won't mind letting you sit on my lap, *Texas*." Cody cackled, slapping the side of the Jeep.

The other two guys catcalled, making a lot of noise, but my ears concentrated on the silence coming from Vance in the back seat. I chanced a peek and saw that he was still in his own music world, totally oblivious to any of us.

"We're good." I used my body as a shield, moving Charlotte

even farther off the road until we were tiptoeing on the edge of the ditch.

"Suit yourself." Levi dropped the Jeep into another gear and revved the motor.

I kept my eyes trained on the uneven terrain on the side of the road, determined not to give the jerks even the tiniest amount of attention as the Jeep rolled past with the tires crunching the asphalt.

Charlotte clucked her tongue. "That Vance boy just looked out the rear window at you." She lifted her hand, but I batted it down.

"Charlotte, you don't give people like them your attention." I held my breath, worried the Jeep was going to come back, but it vanished around a bend in the road.

She yanked away and huffed. "But he was waving."

I gave her the side-eye. "Sounds like he was looking at you then."

She scrunched her nose. "Why couldn't they give us a ride? My feet are hurting and we ain't even close to home yet."

"It's those dumb jelly shoes for ya. They ain't fittin' to wear."

"And your Moses sandals are any better?" She flicked a wrist toward my dingy brown Birkenstocks.

"*Obviously.* Moses did have to lead that bunch in the desert for forty years." I rolled my eyes and we both laughed. "But seriously, you never, *ever* ride with strangers. It's dangerous."

Charlotte hitched a thumb over her shoulder. "But we just drove a stranger home. Same thing."

"We've been going to church with Miss Wise for years. She's not a stranger."

"We don't know anything about her. She kinda is a stranger."

"You know what I mean." I halted and gripped her shoulder, making her stop too. "Promise me you'll never accept a ride from boys like them or strangers."

"Strangers I agree, but there was nothing wrong with those boys. Especially the mayor's son." She giggled. "He sure is nice to look at."

There was no denying my sister was right about that, but I played it off with a snort. "Girl, you got better things to be noticing besides dumb boys. Remember that crowd we live with? Well, the ones in that Jeep are just like 'em. Besides, you're only nine. Way too young to be looking at boys." I veered us around a flattened squirrel.

"Yeah, and you're fifteen. Ain't it time for you to start looking at them?" Her sassing was accompanied by a snicker.

I'd made an art form out of *looking* at Vance Cumberland on the sly, watching him at lunch and in the hallways. I kept to the edges and corners of high school life, participating in nothing more than classes, so it was easy enough to go unnoticed. Every minute at school was used to get in as much homework as possible, considering there was never much time for me to get it done at home.

And Vance was always surrounded by his friends and followers, everyone vying for his attention, too much in demand to notice a nobody looking at him. Having a secret crush on the most unattainable guy at school was the only teenage act I indulged in. That unattainable part made it seem safe enough since nothing could ever come from it.

Clearing my mind of Vance and refocusing on the road,

I mumbled, "I don't have time for such mess as that." We walked in silence and focused on swatting at a pesky horsefly to prevent it from landing a pinching bite. After listening to Charlotte's shoes tapping against the asphalt and mine keeping a rhythmic flapping for a spell, I gave in and asked, "You sure he was looking at me?"

Charlotte nodded her head and giggled, making me crack a smile. It had been one warped day, so to give in and simply act like silly girls for just a moment felt pretty good, no matter how short-lived.

On my way to pick up Nash and Knox from day care Monday afternoon, I decided Miss Wise would become my new puzzle to study and perhaps solve, so I stopped by to check on her.

I climbed the three creaky steps and knocked on her door. After several moments with no answer, I knocked again and hollered, "Miss Wise, it's Austin Foster."

"Come in!" she hollered back.

With the idea of just poking my head in and offering a quick hello and goodbye, I opened the door and instantly changed my mind. If heaven has a scent, I would want it to be the exact aroma that greeted me. Warm, robust chocolate.

Leaving my dirty coat and shoes on the porch, I followed my nose to the kitchen and found the willowy woman hunched over the counter. "Whatcha doing, Miss Wise?" I watched her smear melted chocolate on the marble top with what looked like a spackling trowel, making a fine mess that I would not have minded cleaning up with a spoon or straw.

She worked silently for a few more minutes, smoothing and smearing the glossy brown liquid. "I'm tempering the chocolate."

"Oh . . ." I moved closer but was careful to stay out of her way. "Was it misbehaving?"

She looked up, mouth pressed in a thin line, seeming to not care for my lame joke, or maybe she didn't catch it in the first place. "It will if I don't get the temperature correct."

"Oh," I repeated but didn't have a clue what she was talking about.

Miss Wise reached into a covered dish and came out with a little chocolate bar with a few flakes of salt dusting the top. "Here. Take this and break it in half." She held it out, giving me a clear view of the five faded numbers lining her arm. I managed to keep my lips sealed and held my palm up, only to have her quickly retract the offering. "Wash your hands first."

Feeling a bit like a schoolgirl being scolded by the teacher, I stepped to the sink and scrubbed my hands twice and was prepared to do it a third time if it meant sampling a piece of that chocolate. Thankfully, she granted me the candy and I broke it in half as directed.

"Did you hear that crisp snap?"

"Yes, ma'am." I held a tiny piece in each hand, waiting for permission to eat it.

"Perfect. Taste it. You'll see."

I placed a piece on my tongue and let it melt. She was absolutely right. It was perfect and by far the best piece of chocolate I'd ever eaten. Humming, I slipped the other piece in my mouth and savored the salty-sweet combination.

"You like?"

I shook my head. "I love."

That must have been the magic answer because she handed me another treat, but this one was round like a Reese's cup and filled with peanuts and nougat.

"It tastes like a Baby Ruth candy bar, but way much better." I licked my fingertips, longing for another piece. "How do you know how to make such fancy chocolates?"

"It's my trade." Miss Wise swirled the chocolate again and then scooped some into a mold with at least a dozen square forms. Once they were filled, she upturned the mold and banged it against the counter, splattering chocolate goodness everywhere.

She spoke softly while working, about studying under a top chocolatier in France and then becoming one herself. She'd spent most of her career at a gourmet candy shop in New York City and still provided private orders every now and then as a favor to the owner.

"How do you manage not eating all your work?" I snuck another round treat and was tickled when she poured us each a fancy cup of Cheerwine.

Time was ticking away on the gold wall-mounted clock, reminding me the day care was going to close in less than thirty minutes, but there was no way I was going to waste a drop of that soda or the conversation about the art of chocolate.

Shoulders relaxed, I took a sip of my soda and then made the mistake of opening my mouth and ruining everything. "Miss Wise, what's that number tattoo stand for?"

Her spine straightened and stiffened into a six-feet-tall

wall. "It is time for you to go." She grabbed my arm and ushered me out, yanking the cup out of my hand before shoving me outside.

The door slammed behind me, muffling her words in a language I'd never heard. Stunned, my gaze traveled the weathered porch that gave no clue to the extravagance just inside. It also gave no clue to the odd woman who was hiding behind it and her reaction to my simple question either.

I spun around and knocked, even though there was no chance of her opening up, literally or figuratively. "Miss Wise! I don't know what I did, but I promise I didn't mean it!" When a few minutes passed in absolute silence, save for a dog barking next door, I cut my losses and headed out. If she wouldn't tell me about her tattoo, I knew a place that could probably provide some answers, so I made a quick stop by the library.

Miss Jones lifted her gaze when I walked up to the desk. "Austin, what can I help you with today?"

"Umm . . . anything on chocolatiers?" I asked, starting with something easy. From the breath the librarian exhaled and her eyebrows relaxing, it was a good choice.

Moments later, she handed me a culinary book about pastry and confectionary careers. "Anything else?"

I glanced around, confirming we were alone, and leaned over the desk, nearly knocking over a pencil holder. I righted it and straightened a stack of bookmarks I'd disturbed before whispering, "Do you have anything about tattoos?"

Miss Jones's eyebrows shot up and then pinched together, her normal look for when dealing with me.

"I saw someone with a row of numbers on their arm." I ran

my hand over my forearm, indicating the location. "They were faded real bad. Greenish blue."

The librarian's eyes hardened with some sort of understanding and then softened. "I think I know what you're talking about. It's . . . well . . . it's an awful thing."

The word *awful* drew too many pictures. Was Miss Wise a member of a corrupt gang? Was it her prison number? I had no clue. But it was no longer a *want*, but a *need* to know. "Do you have a book about the awful thing?" I checked the time on the clock behind her desk. "I'm kinda in a hurry."

Miss Jones rushed around and I ended up leaving with three more books to go along with the chocolate book. One that I skipped reading once I cracked open *Night* by Elie Wiesel later that night.

When the sun rose the next morning, it reflected a much different world. Miss Wise was no longer the weird lady spitting on our church steps. She was Helena Wisniewska, a survivor of the darkest evil I had ever read about.

I wasn't a fan of fiction, always preferring facts, but after reading all three books about the Holocaust, I really wished with every bone in my body that this horrific time in history was a horrible work of fiction. Devastated by my findings yet needing to know more, I returned to the library a few days later. The microfilm reader in the archive room provided more visual facts than what I had bargained for: images of living skeletons, corpses stacked like building blocks, dark smoke billowing from crematoriums . . .

Miss Wise's freaking out about the ashes from the barn fire finally made sense. But at the same time, it made no sense whatsoever. How could this gruesome genocide have happened to millions of innocent people?

The need to right things with Miss Wise consumed me, but she made it impossible by not answering the door. I spent the week leaving her notes of apology, potted plants from our greenhouse that I knew would bloom pink, satchels of dried lavender and fresh mint for her chocolates. They would disappear from the porch before the next day, so at least I knew she was still alive behind the locked door and silence.

When Sunday arrived and she did not, I felt personally responsible.

In the kitchen after the church service, I loaded plate after plate with tater tot casserole and green beans while the young'uns whined about me being too slow.

"Hurry up, Ox. I'm starving," Peg complained.

"You don't have the first clue about starving." I looked over at the dinner table, six sets of expectant eyes on me, but all I could see were images from the library where protruding ribs of men could be counted and the hollow cheeks and dark eye sockets of young children testified of their torture. I swallowed the queasiness as Pa came in and helped me divvy out the plates.

"You know where Miss Wise was today?" I asked Pa as I set plates in front of Raleigh and Boss.

"No. I'll have to check on her." Pa took his seat at the head of the table and said grace.

Everyone immediately dove into their food. It was one

of the few dishes I'd gotten fairly good at making and they'd declared it a favorite, but the sight of the overflowing plate made my mouth taste sour. Poking at a tot with my fork, I mumbled, "I tried checking on her every day this week on my way to pick up the twins, but she wouldn't answer."

Pa took a swig of iced tea and then wiped his mouth. "That's odd."

Peg snorted. "Everything about that ole bat is odd. I think she's an atheist. Why she even come to church if all she's gonna do is hock a loogie on the steps?"

"Eww! We're eating," Charlotte snapped at him.

"Watch your mouth, Phoenix." Pa plucked the fork out of Peg's hand before the bite made it to his frank mouth and pointed it at him. "You best not disrespect Miss Wise like that ever again. She comes to church for the same reason any of us do. Looking for God. I don't care if Satan himself shows up looking, by golly he's welcome to find God there, too." He handed my red-faced brother the fork and went back to eating.

"What's atheist?" Boss asked.

"Someone who doesn't believe in God," Charlotte answered. "Ain't that sad?"

"Atheists are believers," Pa retorted firmly. "They just too bullheaded to admit it."

Everyone was too in their own heads to pay me or my lack of appetite any attention that day and for several more days after. Nothing looked or tasted appealing, so I stuck with coffee to keep me upright and a saltine cracker or two when stomach cramps got the best of me.

By Saturday morning, my behind was dragging slower than

Peg's gimp leg when he was trying to miss the school bus on purpose. He'd succeed at least once a month, but Pa let him get by with it or simply did not notice.

Our morning started before daybreak, unloading the two south barns and preparing the tobacco to go to market. Oddly enough, the smell of cigarette smoke repulsed me. It was nothing like the spicy-sweet aroma of cured tobacco. What happened to it in the factories, I hadn't a clue, but it sure did tick me off that the product we worked so hard to produce ended up ruined.

Once that was finished, we gathered around the charred remains of the west barn as Pa gave instructions on cleanup. My head was hazier than the ribbons of fog lingering around us by then, so I leaned against the side of the truck while waiting for my orders.

"Ox, you hear me?"

I blinked out of the daze and tried focusing on Pa. "Sorry, what was that?"

Pa tipped the bill of his hat up and gave me a careful inspection. "You feelin' all right?"

"I guess." I used the collar of my shirt to wipe my sweaty upper lip.

"I said for you to grab a wheelbarrow and start collecting anything metal." Pa pointed to a coil of wire springing from a pile of ashes.

"Yes, sir." I donned a pair of work gloves and got to it.

The others tore down what the fire hadn't demolished while I rummaged through the ashes with a garden rake. Tools, bolts, hinges, and such were scattered throughout the debris, making my task a constant exercise of bending and squatting.

Two loads in, the wheelbarrow began to tilt. Or maybe it was the earth . . .

A heavy weight pressed against me as I opened my eyes and squinted up at the overhead sun.

"What in tarnation?" Pa stood over me. Jinx and Boss were across from him. All three staring down at me.

"How'd I end up on the ground?" Something poked me in the back, so I reached underneath me and came back with a stick. Tossing it to the side, I took a deep breath and struggled to sit up.

"You passed out. What's going on with ya?" Pa's large hands grasped under my arms and set my reclined body upright. "Just sit there. Boss, get Ox a cup of water."

"Yes, sir." My brother's heavy footsteps pounded the ground over to the tailgate, where I'd set up the water cooler earlier. Moments later, he returned and thrust the paper cup into my hand a little too forcefully and splashed some of it on my arm. "Sorry, Ox."

"It's okay. Thanks." I chugged the water and received another while the others murmured about what to do with me.

Pa clapped his gloved hands together once. "I'm taking Ox up to the house. Y'all get back to work."

I expected my father to walk me to the truck, but no, the big lumberjack carried me as if I were a child and I let him with no protest. I settled in the seat, rested my head against the window, and let my eyes drift shut until the driver's door slamming sent them popping open.

Pa cranked the engine and reached for the radio, turning it

down until "Don't Stop Believin'" faded to the background. He reversed out to the drive and then headed in the direction of the house. "Ox . . . you wanna tell me why you ain't been eating? Don't think I haven't noticed." He glanced my way, a thick eyebrow arching up before he focused on the road.

"I haven't had an appetite."

His eyes cut over to me again. "Is this . . . Is this a . . . uh . . . body issue? 'Cause you're skinnier than a rail. And I gotta say you looked a lot better a week ago when your clothes weren't all saggy." His grip tightened on the steering wheel as a look of guilt twisted his face. "If us calling you Ox done this, tell me now and I'll put a stop to it. But it ain't ever had anything to do with what you look like. You my sidekick is all that means."

"I know that, Pa."

"Is it some fool at school then? Tell me their name and I'll go first thing Monday morning and handle it." The fire blazing in my father's deep-blue eyes left no doubt he would handle it.

I lifted both hands, shooing his assumption. "No. Nothing like that."

Pa parked the truck somewhere in between the shade and sunshine, giving me a glimpse of the Dave Foster from my past for the first time in a very long time:

The old soul who sat on the porch with his young'uns surrounding him while whittling a stick and singing a Creedence Clearwater Revival tune.

The father who patiently helped Phoenix overcome his fear of tractors once he was released to come home from rehab, taking him for slow rides around the farm on the smaller John Deere at first and then the bigger ones.

The sensitive man who noticed Boston's slow development before the doctors and teachers and then made sure my brother received the best care and education opportunities.

The romantic who used to lead Mama in a slow dance around the living room while Mama's Percy Sledge record played. Serenading her when their song, "When a Man Loves a Woman," would come on. And boy, could Pa sing. Boss and I would hide at the top of the stairs and listen to him. Both of us giggling every time Pa made Mama giggle.

All those memories collected, forming a major contradiction to the Dave Foster I'd been living with in the last two years.

"Does . . . ?" His lips trembled and the life began fading from his eyes again. "Does this have to do with you missin' your ma?"

My throat tightened. "I miss her every day, but this has to do with Miss Wise." I took a deep breath and spilled it, explaining everything about the lady, the biography books, and the research at the library, and how my appetite had vanished somewhere in the midst of discovering the disturbing history of the Holocaust.

Once it was all spilt, we sat in the truck staring straight ahead at the newly plowed field between the house and the packhouse. A flock of crows were rummaging the rows for anything that might have been unearthed.

Pa took a deep breath and blew it out as he shook his head. "If only the world was filled with bighearted Austin Fosters, it sure would be a much better place to live in."

I snuffled, not having enough energy to snort. "Not sure many would agree with you." I felt pretty insignificant in the whole scheme of life.

"Hogwash. People would have to be blind and deaf not to notice." Pa reached out and placed his giant hand on my shoulder. The weight of his concern offered such a comfort, the way my quilt did on chilly nights. "But, sweetheart, you gotta get back to eating."

"Okay." My cheek met his hand briefly before I reached for the door handle. "Right now, I just want to go lie down awhile, if that's okay." I pointed my other hand toward the packhouse. I'd converted the loft into a hideout during one of my bouts of restless nights.

Pa rubbed the side of his beard. "You able to climb up there?"

"That water I drank helped clear my head. I can manage." I gave him a forced smile, yet it wobbled as bad as his did, and exited the truck.

"I'll check on you in a bit."

"Yes, sir." I closed the door and made my way inside the packhouse, up to the loft, and onto the sleeping bag I'd stashed up there. The world dimmed and faded before I even heard the truck drive off.

The creaking of the ladder that led up to the loft and the grunting of someone climbing it pulled me from a deep sleep. I rubbed the sleep from my eyes and focused on the top rung to see who was coming up. Another creak and grunt later, dark-gray hair came into view and then the narrow eyes that matched it.

Sitting up, I croaked, "Miss Wise?"

She didn't answer, just kept climbing until maneuvering into the loft with a canvas bag over her shoulder. Pretty impressive for such a tall older lady. I was about to say as much, but she called me stupid first, effectively halting the compliment from leaving my lips.

"Beg your pardon?"

"You heard me." Hunched over, Miss Wise shuffled toward me while scanning the area. She pulled a stool from the corner and placed it by the sleeping bag before plopping down on it. The bulky canvas bag rested in her lap with her long arms wrapped around it.

A stare off ensued as dust motes filtered around the tension between us and the late-afternoon sun slanting through the windows. I had six siblings to keep in line, so stare offs were my specialty. Several moments passed, indicating Miss Wise was too.

Her eyes remained fastened to mine as she finally spoke. "I just finished speaking with your father." She unwound her left arm from the bag and held it out so that the numbers were on display. "I assume you know what this is now, yes?"

"Yes, ma'am."

Miss Wise tsked, placing her arm back around the bag. The contents inside rattled together. "Transported in cattle cars and tagged with identification numbers, we were treated worse than animals off to the slaughter. At least the animals were fed properly before being killed."

Stooped on the tiny stool, Miss Wise told me her story. A teenage girl taken from her home in Poland to work at Auschwitz with her younger sister, Irene, who died of typhus only weeks before the camp was liberated. She was never reunited with her parents or other siblings, learning years later that they all perished at the hands of the Nazis.

"First they stole our jobs. Then our homes. Our possessions. Our families. Our humanity. They didn't stop until stealing everything. Even my soul."

I pulled my knees to my chest and wrapped my arms around them, thinking about what she'd shared for a long time before I spoke. "So you don't believe in God? Why go to church then?"

Miss Wise sucked her teeth. "I believe in God."

"But you go spittin' on the church steps every Sunday."

"Because I am mad at him."

"Oh . . ." I didn't know what to say to that, even though I understood to some degree. After losing Mama, it would be a lie to say I hadn't been mad at God too. I apologized later and the Bible says he forgives if asked, so there's that. "Aren't you tired of holding on to that anger for so long?"

She sniffed, lips tugged down into a fine grimace. "I know no other way."

My stomach let out a rumble, sounding as if a monster was working on clawing its way out of me. I pressed my palm against the pain and slowly drew in a breath.

"You stupid girl."

My head popped up. "Huh?"

"You live in a land of plenty. Yet you make yourself sick for no good reason." She rummaged in the bag. "No grieving, no cursing, no crying, no fasting . . . nothing can amend what happened in that awful time and place. I will not put up with you starving when there is no need. You eat." She pulled out a foil-covered plate and thrust it into my hands. "Now."

My hand shook as I peeled off the foil, feeble and apprehensive that I wouldn't be able to stomach the contents until seeing what was on the plate. "You brought me candy?"

"No. Petit fours."

"Petty what?"

"Squares of sponge cake layered with strawberry jam. Covered in dark chocolate."

"Oh. Thank you." My mouth watered for the first time since leaving her house almost two weeks ago. I plucked one of the fancy confections off the plate and took a tentative bite. As expected, the treat melted into an array of flavors. Vanilla. Strawberry. Dark chocolate. I didn't stop until half the plate was clean and probably wouldn't have stopped then if she hadn't offered me an icy glass bottle of Cheerwine.

I took a deep pull from the bottle, drinking it too fast. A burp escaped with such force it tickled my nose and burned my chest. My hand flew up to cover my mouth. "Excuse me."

Ignoring my rudeness, the prim woman crossed her legs and flicked a wrist toward the wall. "What is all this?"

Miss Wise had shared so much with me that it was only right for me to do the same. I washed another tiny cake bite down with a sip of cola while studying the collage I'd made, using polyurethane to seal it. "They were my mother's maps. She always loved the idea of traveling someday." I placed the plate on the floor and scooted over to the wall, using the tip of my finger to trace the circle around my name. "She named us after cities she wanted to visit." I scanned the other maps until spotting each sibling's name. Smiling at the crossed-out circle around Elizabeth on the North Carolina map.

"Edith was a fine woman. She would be proud of you." Miss Wise offered the compliment along with another plate from her bag. This one had an array of dainty finger sandwiches with the crusts cut off and everything.

Her kindness made my eyes sting and my chest ache, but I swallowed that down with the cucumber sandwich and followed it with an egg salad sandwich. While I worked through cleaning another plate, Miss Wise told me the next part of her story, a happier part. One that took her on a journey to France and then to the States, where she indulged in her love for food by making a career in the culinary world, vowing she would never go a day hungry again.

Trucks had pulled up outside sometime in there, so she packed her canvas bag and stood. "Now, no more of this foolishness. Eat." She wagged a slim finger at me and began climbing down the ladder.

"Miss Wise," I called. She reappeared, peeping between two rungs at me. "I know I'm just a *stupid girl* and don't know much." I paused when she scoffed and rolled her eyes at my snide remark. "But I do believe God gets blamed for a lot of stuff that he shouldn't. . . . And I also believe forgiveness and getting over being mad is a gift for ourselves, not for the ones who wronged us."

Silence and a meaningful look passed between us before she left me in the loft. I leaned over the side railing and watched her retreating form below.

"Miss Wise," I called again, but this time she continued

walking away. "You deserve to be happy. Not angry. I'm gonna be praying for you!"

She lifted her arm in a haughty wave and replied over her shoulder, "You do that." And I be dog if she didn't smile at me before exiting the barn.

That, in itself, was an answered prayer.

Chapter 4

LIFE AIN'T FAIR,
BUT SUCH IS LIFE

January 1983

"It ain't fair." Peg's face scrunched tighter than a shriveled-up prune as he seeded the flats with more force than necessary.

"What are you griping about now?" I grabbed the flat and shoved topsoil over the top like smoothing icing on a cake. Well, it's the closest to icing anything I'd ever come to doing. Nails black and hands stained, no one would want me touching a cake anyhow. "At least it's warm in here and we have stools to sit on instead of having to stand." Pa had given us the seed-sprouting duty this year while he worked on rebuilding the tobacco barn.

"Us stuck working all the time while Boss gets to play. Ain't fair." Peg gathered some of the teeny-tiny seeds from the paper bag and began on another flat. Even though he was making us both miserable, he'd worked steady through all the whining.

"Hopefully Jinx will sell Pa on the idea of sowing seeds instead of like this." I held up the flat that I'd just filled half-way with soil and plopped it in front of Peg. "That practice bed seems promising. It looks like a mini greenhouse."

"Boss knows how to do this. Don't take a genius to shove stupid seeds into dirt. He should be here." Peg grumbled a few sentiments under his breath, pushing the flat in front of me on the long wood table.

"I'm just glad Pa let him participate in the special needs program. Shoot, take your leg off and whine in front of him and I'm sure he'd let you participate too." I poked that sore spot, because Peg might have been the biggest complainer I'd ever met, but he never used his disability to get out of something or into something.

Before he could lay into me for even suggesting it—and the sharp look he gave me sure did indicate he was about to—the deep purr of an engine prowling up our driveway interrupted him. Peg slipped off his stool and hobbled to the greenhouse door.

"It's the mayor's son." Peg let out a harsh snort. "I'm surprised Rich Boy would let dirt touch his fancy wheels. Why's he always in the middle of charity junk for?"

"Looks good for his family, I reckon." I wiped my hands on the front of my coat and joined Peg by the door.

"So Vance just takes Boss to the movies or the batting cage and that looks good for his family." Peg snorted again as we watched the shiny sports car creep closer. If it went any slower, it would be standing still. "Tough life, right?"

"Yep," I answered, agreeing wholeheartedly. Crossing my arms and turning my back to the chilly January wind, I bumped my shoulder against Peg's to get his attention. "But watch your mouth when they get up here. No need in ruining this fun for Boss."

The shiny black car finally came to a stop. It looked like it belonged out on Nolia Farms as much as a sparkling diamond ring belonged in the midst of cow manure. Peg walked over to the car with a good bit of care, almost dragging the prosthetic leg. His limp had grown more pronounced lately since hitting a slight growth spurt, so it was time to make an appointment for another fitting. I added that to my to-do list.

Boss climbed out of the passenger seat and almost plowed Peg over. "Peg! I hit the ball real far this time!"

He looked like a giant compared to Peg. Something else that concerned me. The Fosters were all tall and well-built, except Peg. He was short and frail, tending to pick up colds and bugs easily. It made me wonder if his accident had also stunted his growth somehow.

I heard the driver's door open but kept my eyes on my two brothers. "Boss, I thought Pa was picking you up."

"He never showed." Boss shrugged.

Even as I told myself not to look, my eyes betrayed me. Blond curls came into view before the rest of Vance Cumberland emerged from his side of the car. Green eyes connected with mine and then he slowly blinked as if he'd never seen me before now.

Lips curling into a lopsided grin, producing deep dimples in both cheeks, Vance strutted around the car and joined us. "Boss, you didn't tell me you were growing beautiful girls out here on the farm." He winked at me. "Think I need to pluck this one for myself." Arms stretched, he lunged in my direction.

I dodged his advance and turned around in time to kick him square in the butt. Peg cackled behind me, but I crossed my arms and kept my focus on the flirt who was rubbing his backside. The guy certainly had the weirdest idea of condolences or greetings. Only two times he'd spoken to me, and both times were far from predictable. It was hard not to find that appealing.

"Did you really just kick me?" Vance's eyes narrowed but a smirk formed on his lips.

"Yeah. And you try something fool like that again, and I can guarantee the next kick won't be in the butt."

"I was just playing around. Lighten up, will ya." Vance tsked.

"This here is one fine car ya got, man," Peg commented with way too much admiration in his voice for it to actually be genuine.

I slid my eyes over to where he was running a dirt-coated hand along the black hood that shone in such a gleam it looked like a mirror.

Vance winced, evidently catching on to the nasty smudges Peg was leaving all over the car. "Thanks, man."

"Peg, go get to work," I ordered, and even though he grouched about it all the way back to the greenhouse, he did as he was told. That was Peg's mode of operation—obedient in the most disagreeable way possible. Life hadn't been easy on him, so he'd stubbornly determined to not be easy about anything. Period.

"Vance, we have a swimming pool," Boss blurted, face lit with enthusiasm.

Vance's lips drew downward as he nodded his head with an air of being rather impressed. "Wow, Boston. Ain't y'all fancy."

Boss shook his head. "No. We're farmers. You wanna go see it?" He was about to head that way, turning and waving for Vance to follow, but I grabbed his elbow to stop him.

"It ain't a pool. It's an oversize pond. And, Boss, we have chores to do. Change into some work clothes and go help Peg in the greenhouse. . . . Thank Vance for this afternoon."

"Thanks, Vance, for this afternoon." Boss grinned so big his eyes closed.

Vance waved him off. "No problem. The movie theater has an early showing of *E. T.* tomorrow. That cool with you?"

It was surprising that Vance would choose to spend a Friday evening with my brother rather than his group of friends or a girl for that matter. Malorie Fitzgerald came to mind and her incessant chattering about Vance even though he paid her very little attention at school, not even sitting with her at lunch. For the last month, he'd actually been sitting with Boss while his friends gave him questioning looks. I wondered if hanging out with my brother was his choice or the doings of his parents, who liked to keep the Cumberland family on the front page of the paper to show off their do-gooding.

Boss, close to two hundred pounds and over six feet tall, clapped his hands and jumped up and down. "Yes! Yes! That's real cool!"

Vance smiled, producing dimples. "Cool."

Boss finally hurried inside after a little more encouragement from me. As soon as the door slammed shut, it was opening again.

Charlotte stuck her head out the door, eyeing the flashy car and then Vance while hollering at me, "Ox, it's time to get the twins from day care!"

"I'm about to leave!" I hollered back, checking my coat pocket for the keys. "Look, Vance, Pa gets busy and can be absentminded. I appreciate you bringing Boss home. From now on, just let me know where y'all will be and I'll see to him getting picked up."

"It was no trouble driving him home." Casually tucking his hands into the front pockets of his jeans, Vance lowered his head slightly and looked at me through a thick fringe of lashes, intensifying the green of his irises. "I can tomorrow, too."

Knowing nothing good could come from ogling the guy, I started toward the truck. "Just let me know from now on, please, instead of my father. I'll pick him up."

Vance seemed reluctant but finally took the hint and headed toward his car. "Okay. The movie should be over by eight. See ya then." Eyes squinted, he gave the farmhouse and then me a slow perusal before closing his door.

Shaking off the flustered feeling that gave me, I loaded up and swung by the new barn on the way out. I put the truck in park and leaned toward the windshield to get a better look at the structure. It was at least twice as big as the old barn with a deeper overhang that would make days of filling it with tobacco much easier.

Pa's truck wasn't there, but I beeped the horn anyway. A moment later, Jinx came around the corner from the far side of the barn with a tool belt barely hanging on to his skinny waist.

I cranked the window down and angled out to holler, "Have you seen Pa?"

Jinx dusted his hands off and retrieved a crumpled pouch of Levi Garrett from his back pocket. As he walked closer, he loaded a good-size chaw of the tobacco into his mouth, working it until his hollow cheek poked out like a chipmunk. "He left about an hour ago. Needed to grab some supplies from the hardware store and then pick up Boss."

"Okay. The barn sure is looking nice."

Jinx puckered his lips and sent a long brown stream of spit to the ground. "It's gettin' there."

Knowing that was all the conversation he'd care to share, I reeled the window up and reversed into the driveway and drove off.

Jinx and Foxy were a major blessing to the farm, both working persistently to make it a more bountiful place. Aside from attending service on Sunday morning, they kept to themselves. And even though Peg spent a few hours after supper each night up there where I suspected he was watching old westerns with Jinx, I got the sense that the Devereauxs didn't want to get too close to any of us. It didn't stop Peg and it sure didn't stop my late-night visits to help Foxy with her herbal remedies. Last night's visit was spent making tea bags from a mix of ingredients for a mix of ailments. Mint, ginger, and licorice root for indigestion. Chamomile, valerian root, and passionflower for insomnia. Echinacea, hibiscus, and lemon peel for colds and coughs.

The thin ribbons of lemon peel had such a delicious aroma that it conjured memories of Mama's lemonade. As we worked, I kept sniffing the container holding the peel, longing for my mother to the point I almost broke down. Before I left, Foxy gave me a mesh pouch filled with lemon peel without saying a word about my odd behavior. I tucked the pouch inside my pillowcase and met up with Mama on the front porch in a dream where we were giggling between sips of her lemonade.

I could almost smell it now as I drove a loop around town in hopes of spotting Pa's truck. Unsuccessful, and annoyed that there wasn't enough time left to pop in and check on Miss Wise as was my new routine, I picked up the twins and returned to the farm. With no sign of Pa and knowing there was nothing I could do about it, we got busy with supper and night routines.

"Where's Pa?" Boss asked as I passed his room after checking on the twins.

I backtracked a few steps, contemplating what to say to avoid upsetting him. All eyes lingered on our father's empty chair at supper, but no one voiced any concern since that had become a regular occurrence. Him not coming home by bedtime was not.

"He's probably down at the barn," I whispered, keeping it simple.

"Okay." Boss grabbed me in a constricting hug, my feet lifting from the ground, and then released me. "Good night, Ox."

"Good night." I waved him off to get in bed and then headed downstairs to lock up.

It was unnerving to be left alone with six kids depending on me to take care of them so late at night. To ward off feeling vulnerable, I re-dressed in a pair of clean jeans and a sweatshirt instead of pajamas. Time in the daylight hours flew by with so much to get done, but in the dead of night, time seemed to be in no hurry to go anywhere when sleep was evasive.

Three in the morning, I was lying in bed wide-awake when the rumble of a truck traveled up the driveway. Relief and apprehension warred with each other, glad Pa finally showed up but weary as to which version of him was down there unloading something onto the front porch.

I climbed out of bed and peeped out the window. Below, Pa's shadowy figure slid a cooler out the bed of the truck, the sound of it scraping making it through my closed window. He lugged it to the porch before going back for another. A total of five in all.

Steeling myself, I tiptoed downstairs and out the front door to see what on earth he was doing. A briny smell hit me as soon as I stepped onto the porch. "Pa?"

He reached inside the cab and gathered a brown paper bag. "Yeah?"

"What's going on?" I crossed my arms to keep from shivering.

Pa closed the truck door and started my way. "They were saying at the hardware store that shrimp season was still open and so I thought I'd go grab us a mess from McClellanville."

That coastal town was three hours away, and a mess of shrimp was more like five pounds, not five coolers. I lifted the lids, each one brimming with seafood.

I was madder than a wet hen about him just taking off like

that without telling a soul but tried tamping it down by taking a few deep breaths. "What happened to you picking up Boss?"

His head snapped up from the bag he was rummaging in. "Ah, shoot. I knew I was forgetting something." He wheeled around and started down the steps.

"Where are you going?"

"To get Boss," Pa replied in a tone that should have been followed by a *duh*, and it made me want to scream at the top of my lungs.

"Wait! Vance Cumberland already brought him home."

Another one-eighty sent Pa back toward the porch, moving too fast to keep up with. "Oh, good. I'm starving. How about getting that big wash pan so we can shell some shrimp. I got everything we need. Cornmeal and oil." He opened the door and flipped the living room light on. "Where's everybody at?"

"In *bed*. It's three in the morning." I reached past him and switched it off. There was plenty enough light from the one I left on in the kitchen.

Pa looked over his shoulder at me with a look of confusion on his face. "Really?" he asked and I confirmed with a head nod. "Humph. Time must have gotten away from me somehow." He continued on to the kitchen with no consideration to those sleeping, tossing the grocery bag on the counter, slamming cabinet doors, sending pans clanging while pulling out the wash pan. The whole house would be awake if he kept that up, and no one else needed to be witness to his current state.

Thinking fast, I suggested, "Why don't we take this stuff to the packhouse? That way the house don't get all stinky."

"That's a good idea. We got some shelling to do. Come on."

Scooping the supplies into his brawny arms, he made his way to the front door, his work boots hitting the floor loudly.

With no other choice, I followed, tiptoeing as if that could cancel out all his noise.

By the time the sun started rising, I'd shelled shrimp until my fingers ached with tiny nicks making them sting. The only break was when Pa had a batch fried up and insisted I help him eat it. We feasted past being full and I was on the cusp of being sick and barely able to keep my eyes open. Not Pa. He cycled from cooking to eating to belting out songs to carrying on about different ways we could prepare the shrimp.

Once the sky shed its dusky-gray coat and warmed into yellows, I mentioned it was time to get everyone up and ready for school.

Pa's eyes widened. "Go put on a pot of grits so we can surprise the crowd with fried shrimp and grits."

Oh, my siblings were surprised all right when they were greeted by a smelly crazed man, showing off a ridiculous amount of shrimp that he expected them to eat for breakfast no less.

I managed to grab a shower to wash the stink off while they finished eating, and then we all fled out of the house and away from the crazy to go to school.

Eyes gritty and stomach sour from too much grease and my father's alarming behavior, I drifted through the day and could hardly recall picking the twins up from day care and getting us home safely, just thankful I had. I was even too foggy to recall much about my brief visit to Miss Wise.

After handing the little ones off to Charlotte and Raleigh,

I beat a path to the packhouse to assess the damage, expecting most of the shrimp to probably be spoiled since Pa hadn't
iced the coolers and the day had been unseasonably warm.
The ripe smell of seafood was strong, but after inspecting the
coolers and finding them empty and washed out, I realized the
smell was coming from a barrel with an army of flies buzzing
around it. I swatted the air and peered inside, marveling at the
amount of shrimp hulls and trying to figure if it was humanly
possible for Pa to have shelled all that shrimp by himself.

Leaving the shells to deal with later, I hurried inside and
checked the fridge. A large bowl of clean shrimp with plastic
wrap over it sat on the top shelf. Opening the top freezer next,
I found it overflowing with shrimp, but it still wasn't enough
to account for five coolers. I headed to the laundry room and
opened the chest freezer, which held a massive amount of
shrimp. I stood there staring down at the contents as the icy
air seeped out, not having a clue what to do with that much
shrimp—or with Pa. This was clearly not normal behavior.

"Oh, good. You're home!" Pa spoke from behind me.

I jumped, dropping the heavy lid. It slammed with a loud
thud as I turned my back to the freezer to face him.

"I'm going to put in a few hours at the barn before dark." Pa
tapped his knuckles on the doorframe and was gone in a blink.

I hurried through the house to catch up with him, wondering where all that exuberant energy was coming from. "You get
some sleep today?"

Pa paused by the door and let out a jaunty chuckle. "You
think that shrimp cleaned itself? I ain't had time for sleep." He
waved a hand dismissively as if sleep were trivial and there

was absolutely nothing wrong with having enough shrimp to start our own seafood market.

The door slapped shut behind him, leaving me with the lion's share of responsibilities as always. Chores needed to be divided and conquered, supper to be figured out that would no way be including shrimp, and then I would need to go get Boss afterwards, but fatigue nailed me to my spot until I remembered the batch of double chocolate chip cookies from Miss Wise that I'd left in the truck. I found just enough gumption to go fetch them and call the young'uns to the porch, not caring if it spoiled their supper or not.

Before I could take the first bite of my cookie, we all turned toward the sound of a vehicle.

"Here comes fancy pants," Peg garbled between bites, pointing his cookie at the black car slowly coming up the drive.

There was still a good two hours before I was to meet Vance at the theater to pick up Boss.

Cookie clutched in my hand, I sprinted off the porch as Boss opened the passenger door. "Something wrong?"

"The movie projector broke down," Vance answered as he climbed out of the driver's seat. He closed the door as if he might stay awhile.

"But we went over to Vance's and played Atari!" Boss nearly squealed. I heard Peg huff in jealousy. "Cookies?" Boss asked, eyes rounding as he licked his lips.

"Yeah. They're on the porch." I barely got out of the way as he shot past me. "Great day, Boss! They ain't going anywhere!" My own cookie waved in the air as though it were making some point it didn't care to share with me.

Vance grabbed my wrist, brought the cookie to his mouth, and took a monster bite, leaving just a pitiful morsel between my fingers. "Mmm . . ."

We didn't know each other well enough for playful cookie thieving, that's for dang sure, so I yanked my arm free and pinned him with a stern stare while he stood there smacking. "Just because you're the mayor's son don't give you the right to take whatever your spoiled little heart desires!"

Perhaps I laid into him harsher than necessary, but I was irritated and his handsome face made for an easy target. The lack of sleep and the tiny stinging nicks covering my hands from having to clean a gazillion shrimp at an ungodly hour in the morning were to blame. Not to mention, I really wanted that darn cookie!

Vance raised his palms and licked his lips. "Why don't you lighten up a little. Sheesh."

"Why don't you grow up *a lot*!" I tossed the tiny chunk of cookie, nailing him in the forehead with it. He didn't even flinch.

"I've been told I'm plenty grown. How about I take you behind that magnolia tree over there? One kiss should prove it," Vance declared while wiping his forehead with the palm of his hand, leaving a tiny smear of chocolate I wasn't about to point out.

"You just think you're *so* cute. Go on back to town, where I'm sure you'll find plenty of girls falling over themselves to be teased by you." I jabbed a finger toward his stupid sports car.

"Why can't you just be nice to me?" Vance snapped.

"Because it puts me in a bad mood!" My arms flung up before slamming against my thighs.

He shook his head, a smile playing at his lips. "You sure are pretty, even in a bad mood."

"Why are you still here flirting with me after I done and told you to get?"

"Heck if I know." Vance ran his fingers through the wild curls covering his head. "Would it hurt you to flirt back, though?" He straightened, apparently remembering we weren't alone. He glanced in the direction of the peanut gallery watching our exchange from the porch.

"You musta got dropped on ya head as a baby," Peg supplied as that scoundrel plucked the last cookie from the container.

"Phoenix Foster! That's mine!" I charged the porch and snatched the cookie from him even though he'd already taken a bite out of it. Maybe that made me look just as childish as I'd accused Vance of being, but it didn't stop me from wedging the entire cookie in my mouth at once to prevent any more thieving.

Once everyone finished laughing at my expense, I handed out chore orders and they scattered. Boss and Peg on animal-feeding duty, which included a bunch of chickens, six pigs, two dogs, and a few cats. Raleigh and Charlotte on twin duty, which included keeping them out of mischief.

I collected the empty container off the porch steps and was about to head inside to work on supper, but Vance grabbed my wrist, gentle this time, and waited for me to meet his gaze. When I did, it jolted something inside me.

Heaven knows, I was only fifteen, but my heart knew what my heart knew. It began to race as heat rose along my neck. Mama got in a few *love* talks before she passed away, telling me about the warning signs of attraction and how it would make me feel sick to my stomach, dizzy, and flustered when it struck. I figured she was just messing with me, because there was seriously no appeal to being attracted to someone if it involved symptoms similar to a stomach virus.

Standing there with Vance's total attention on just me, each one of those warning signs was present. Honestly, I'd crushed on him from a distance for years, just like every other girl at Magnolia High, but this was different and nothing about it felt safe.

"You okay?" Vance asked softly. "You look beat."

I shrugged a shoulder and lied, "Just a bad night's sleep."

"Anything I can do to help?" His thumb drew continuous circles on my wrist, making it hard for me to breathe.

The moment grew too serious and we were too young for such and I was too tired to avoid making a fool of myself if we didn't move away from it soon. I broke the stare and sassed, "Another cookie would help. Too bad you stole mine."

Vance tilted his head and laughed. "You were holding it up to my mouth. I didn't want to be rude by not accepting it."

That made me laugh in spite of myself, because I probably was, without realizing it. "I did no such thing!"

We bantered back and forth a little longer, neither one of us making much effort to end the visit or his hold on my wrist, but responsibilities were still waiting on me, so at my insistence he finally left.

The following week, Vance showed up again with cookies and that lopsided smile he wore so well.

I eyed the Tupperware container he'd cracked open to

show off the goods while watering plants in the greenhouse. "Where'd you steal those?"

"No more cookie thieving for me. I've changed my ways." Vance swiped a cookie, took a bite, then held it out for me to do the same, but I hesitated. "Our cook made them for me. Peanut butter chocolate chip." He tipped his head, beckoning me to take a bite.

I accepted the treat but struggled with accepting just how different our worlds were. *A cook?* Bet he had a maid too. "That's almost as good as Miss Wise's cookies. Thank you." I opened my mouth and he delivered another bite.

He finished off the cookie and licked his fingers. "Why don't you take a break and enjoy another cookie? Maybe spend a few minutes being nice to me?"

"Too much to get done to be taking a break." I turned to water another section. "And why would I want to waste time being nice to you?"

"Hmm . . . I think you're flirting with me." His accusation had me whirling around and accidently watering his sneakers. He danced out the way, laughing.

"Ox! Pa won't answer me! I'm about to—" Peg came to a halt just inside the door. "What y'all doing in here?"

I held the hose up and glared hard at him. "What's it look like?"

Vance popped another cookie in his mouth nonchalantly, taking his time chewing and then swallowing. "Were you trying to call your dad?"

"What?" Peg's eyes snapped up from the container to ping-pong from Vance to me. "Oh. Uh, no. He's in his room."

"I think he has a headache. What do ya need?" I said slowly, enunciating each word to add an unspoken warning for my brother to watch his mouth.

Peg's eyes narrowed at me. He hated the pretending game we'd perfected playing when it came to our father. "Nothing... I'll take them cookies inside for you." He snatched the container out of Vance's hand and hobbled off.

I let him get away with it too, considering the eggshells we'd been constantly walking on since Pa crashed from his frenzied shrimp fest. It was a reminder how bad of an idea it was to be encouraging Vance Cumberland in any way, other than sending him packing.

"Thanks for the cookies. I'll bring the container to you when I get Boss tomorrow. Y'all going bowling, right?"

"Yes," he answered hesitantly.

"Okay. I'll be there to pick him up." I rolled the hose onto the rack and led him out of the greenhouse. "Bye!"

Vance sighed, giving me a look that expressed he wanted to say a thing or two, but left me in peace.

I expected he would tire of my brush-offs and distracted conversations, but the trips out to the farm continued. Sadly, the visits were basically repeats of a little banter with me shooing Vance away before he got close enough to see what was really going on.

One afternoon, things went sideways when Pa had a meltdown and started tearing the kitchen apart. Emptying everything out of the fridge and cabinets onto the floor, only to get distracted halfway through sorting it all. His rabid attention fastened on taking the cabinet doors off because he thought they were hanging crooked. Fearing the house would be completely destroyed, I forgot about Boss. Fortunately, Vance brought him home after I was a no-show.

I met Vance and Boss in the yard and started rambling off my apologies before he could get out of his car. "Sorry! I got busy helping the kids with their homework."

"No problem. I already told you I don't mind." Vance went to close his car door, but I grabbed the top, earning me a curious look.

"I have a lot to get done," I explained and then glanced over to Boss. "Homework?"

"Yep."

"Go get to it. I'll be there in a minute to help you." I waved him off and he ambled into the house. It was a cool winter day, but my forehead was damp with sweat.

"Your dad around?" Vance eyed Pa's diesel truck.

I dabbed the sweat away with the back of my hand and stared at the truck to hide the truth. "He's sick in bed." It was sort of the truth.

"He's sick a lot," Vance commented with a hesitance in his voice. "He . . . he doesn't have . . . cancer, does he?" He cringed in a manner of pity.

Cancer was like a curse word that no one dared say, fearing the word itself could conjure the disease.

"No." I gave my head a firm shake. "Nothing life-threatening," I declared, although the words tasted of uncertainty as they passed my lips.

Raleigh walked up behind me and tugged on my shirtsleeve. Once I leaned down, he whispered in my ear, "I can't get the feed bin open." Poor guy was still shaken by what was happening in the kitchen.

I met his watery blue gaze. "I'll be there in a sec to help you, okay?"

My timid little brother nodded, stole a quick glance at Vance, and hurried inside the packhouse. I turned to Vance as the front door of the house opened.

"You got an hour before twin pickup!" Charlotte yelled from the porch before revolving back inside like a cuckoo clock. She was good at keeping me on schedule if nothing else.

I sighed while staring at the front door closing. "Look, I need to get to it. Chores, cooking supper, and my English paper won't get themselves done." Before I could move, Vance wrapped his hand around my wrist. It was a soft grasp as always. Never forceful, conveying a choice that I could accept him or pull away at any time.

"You take care of this place, but who takes care of you?" The corners of his eyes tightened with nothing but concern reflecting in them.

Focus around Nolia Farms was either on Pa or my siblings, never on me, so Vance directing concern toward me was more of a gift than he realized. And that right there made me realize just how much I liked him, probably much more than I should.

"I'm a big girl. I can take care of myself," I answered with a false confidence, brushing off his hold on my wrist as well as his worry.

"It's not fair how hard you have to work all the time." Vance sounded genuinely peeved by that. He scanned his surroundings, as if looking for what he was missing.

Before he could figure it out, I gave his firm bicep a nervous squeeze, then another, and then a pat. "Yeah, well, life ain't fair. Goodbye." I followed the awkward arm touch with a spastic wave and started toward the packhouse.

I'd learned the lesson of life not being fair a long time ago, but once Vance had started coming around, the truth of it was getting harder to accept.

Chapter 5

THE DEAD
SHOULDN'T DRIVE

February 1983

Fifth-period study hall was my time to sit without the world bearing down on me. That one hour allowed me to just *be*, with no expectations or responsibilities past being a normal teenage girl who could choose to get her homework done or shirk it altogether. Of course, homework always took precedence over goofing off, but the idea that I *could* was comforting. Because of this extra time, I was able to double down and actually get ahead in my classes. Hands down, it was my favorite period of the day.

To be honest, that also had something to do with a certain senior who had the same study hall as me. Vance could be depended on to show up to class with his easy, dimpled smile and a pack of Razzles. He was good at sharing with whoever stretched a hand toward him, but I was the one who got all the purple ones. He knew somehow that they were my favorite.

To say I was ticked was putting it mildly as I found myself sitting in the ER waiting room with a police officer instead of sharing Razzles and flirty remarks with Vance during study hall.

"Your father is lucky those kids cut school."

If that wasn't the most peculiar statement, then I didn't know what was, but I simply nodded my head at the officer.

"I'm sure you're in shock. That's understandable." Officer Hicks patted my shoulder. "But your father is just bruised and scraped up a little. He's gonna be fine."

It almost slipped past my tongue to ask if he'd promise that to be a fact, but my lips stayed in a tight line to keep from saying something I'd regret.

"Undoubtedly, the brakes must have gone out. The tires didn't leave any skid marks." Hicks shook his head, as baffled by what had transpired as I was that he didn't see what was obvious. "That road don't even get used anymore since the county closed the bridge for repairs. You reckon Dave forgot?"

Nope. And the brakes were just fine, too, until he drove the truck into the pond. I wasn't sure if I was madder about losing my study hall time or that truck. We needed it, but I was fairly certain it had drowned like I'm fairly certain Pa was trying to pull off.

I finally unhinged my jaw and asked, "So can I take him home?"

Officer Hicks gave me a questioning look but pretended,

like most every other adult I knew, that I didn't just snap at him. "Umm . . . let me see if they're done stitching up his forehead."

His shoes squeaked against the tile floor as he hurried away from me and my nasty attitude.

There was just no shaking it either, but I chose only to nod at the nurse as she gave me care instructions and say nothing at all to my bruised-up father. I stomped out of the hospital ahead of Pa, not caring if he was following me to the diesel truck or not. Thankfully, Jinx and Foxy had dropped it off while I was inside fetching the broken man who was now dragging his feet behind me. It had a flatbed, so that would make it tricky to haul all the young'uns around, but that would be something to stew about after I'd had my fill of stewing over the stupid stunt he'd just pulled.

The ride home was silent, except for the rumbling *chuga-chuga-chug* of the engine. Pa gave no excuses or apologies and that was fine by me, because I wasn't in the accepting mood. He limped into his room and there he remained until the smell began meeting me in the hall a week or so later. It was time to hard-love him out of the bed again, when all I really wanted to do was hit him hard.

A few somber weeks passed by before Pa managed to shove off the shadows and return to full-on sunshine. We couldn't make heads or tails of it. Dave Foster and his moods were exhausting. We began tiptoeing around the house as we had become shadows ourselves, scared to death that if we stepped on a creaky board, it would set him off. We were like a bunch of paranoid delinquents, constantly looking over our shoulders or peeping into a room before entering it. Sometimes I think we forgot how to even breathe in our father's presence. Anticipating, watching, and waiting. It was an unpredictable quest for survival.

We were gathered on the porch after school, doing homework and debating on whether Pa had just gone to town or gone off a deep end somewhere, when a horn started blaring way down the road. Listening for a few seconds, I could have sworn someone was blowing the horn to the beat of a song.

In a mighty dust storm, a limo shot down our driveway like a silver bullet. As it neared, the long car fishtailed, performing a couple donut spins before coming to a stop near the porch. Once the dust settled, the driver's door opened and Pa climbed out. His hair was past due a haircut and was dancing about in the wind. If he didn't get it cut soon, it was going to take a Bush Hog to get the job done.

"Ah, shoot. Pa done an' stole the funeral home's limo," Peg said out the side of his mouth, and I was pretty nervous about my brother being right in his assumption.

"Whew-ee! What y'all think?" Pa asked, waving an arm toward the dusty car. The engine ticked loudly, sounding spent from being driven hard and performing stunts it wasn't designed to do.

"About what?" Peg asked, drawing the two-word question into a thick line of skepticism.

"About our new car. It's a Fleetwood!" Pa grinned and continued waving at the car.

"No way," Peg grumbled.

"We going to a funeral, Pa?" Boss mumbled without receiving an answer.

"But that's the Lawsons' funeral limo." I stated the obvious. "For dead folks' families to ride in."

"It ain't no more. Morty just got a new one, so I bought this one off him for a steal. Come check it out." Pa beckoned us to move but we remained glued to the porch.

I swatted a fly away and crossed my arms. "That's just one step away from riding around in a hearse."

Pa pushed the wild locks of dark hair off his forehead and glanced at the car, looking proud. "Nonsense. Morty called it a family car. That's what we are . . . a family."

My eyes slid over to where Nash and Knox were driving Matchbox cars along the steps. I wondered if Pa was including them in his statement. It burnt my hide that he never paid them a lick of attention. Those poor babies' first words should have been *mama* or *daddy*, not *Ox*. I was pretty sure they thought I was a combination of mama and daddy. I thought I was failing at both.

"I ain't riding in that thing. I'll walk if I have to," Peg sassed, slamming his math book shut.

"We need something that'll fit all y'all. It was either the limo or the short school bus the county is selling." Pa's hands landed on his hips, daring us to talk back.

Oh, the options of transportation . . . Both came with stigmas attached to the vehicle titles.

We gave Peg the final say-so and he all but cussed us for even implying he needed the handicap bus. The one-legged hothead jabbed a finger toward the funeral limo, making his choice, before hobbling inside the house. We were none too happy and understood his frustration.

Unfortunately, Boss didn't have enough wits about him to drive, so the old Lawson Funeral Home limo, which we renamed the Silver Bullet, became my first vehicle. So much could have been said about me being the designated chauffeur of a barely breathing family, but I didn't. Only because Peg beat me to it most days.

Tuesdays after school, rain or shine—and I'm referring to Pa's moods—I chauffeured the Foster kids to the Truett Memorial Library, where we'd stay until closing. The two-story brick building had originally been a bakery until the founder, Robert J. Truett, decided at age fifty-five to hang up his apron and in doing so, he discovered a new love to take up his time. You see, Truett didn't actually learn to read until after his retirement. So inspired, he began moving the ovens and pastry racks out and refilling every nook and cranny with books, spending a substantial amount of his savings to do so. It hadn't served as a bakery in nearly a century, but the aroma of yeast and smoky molasses permeated each and every book housed in the building. You couldn't help but get a hankering for something sweet and doughy upon cracking one open.

The enchanting library was our place of solace, and we knew it like the backs of our hands. We were more familiar with the card catalog than some of the library assistants. Boss spent his visits putting away returned books without being asked and no one had ever tried stopping him. Peg's main gig at the library was to sit behind the long desk that used to be the bakery's checkout counter and scold patrons about overdue fines and hush chatty visitors. He was a natural. Charlotte took it upon herself to arrange books in the glass display cases that were originally pastry cases. Raleigh always served as her assistant.

With the younger twins at day care and the others settled into their own library routines, I was free to do as I pleased. If my homework was complete, I usually hid in the reference section or the archive room with White Lily flour bags and Dixie Crystals sugar sacks papering the walls, but today I had errands to run, so after settling everyone in, I told Peg to keep an eye on them.

"Why can't I go with you?" Peg whined, following me to the door.

"I gotta go make a payment at the funeral home," I answered, knowing that would stop him in his tracks.

"Morty's so weird." Peg wrinkled his nose.

"Oh? And you're so normal?" I patted my pocket, making sure the check was still where I'd put it.

"What kinda fool parents who own a funeral home name their kid Morty?" Peg sucked his teeth. "Sick."

"You really want to go there about weird names, Phoenix Arizona Foster?" I lifted my brow.

Peg plowed ahead, on a mission to be disagreeable. "Why didn't you just give it to him on Sunday?"

"I don't feel right about paying bills on the Sabbath, and I ain't sure how Morty would feel about it either."

After Pa made the deal with Morty about making monthly

payments on the limo, he talked him into coming to church. Morty hadn't missed a Sunday since. The flamboyant young man fit right in with the rest of us riffraff.

Peg snorted. "You always making everything nice and easy on everybody. Especially Pa. He should remember to pay the dang bills himself."

I glanced around to see if anyone was close enough to hear him mouthing off. Luckily, no one was. "Watch your tongue." I pinched his arm and didn't acknowledge his yelp, just turned and walked out the door.

That mouth was going to catch up with Phoenix Foster one day, if I couldn't figure out a way to tame it. He would be turning fifteen before the year was up, so it was probably best just to chalk up my attempt at child-rearing him as a big fat F and move on to doing a better job with the four younger ones.

Brushing off my frustrations and doubts, I focused on crossing the street. Surely I could at least pull that off with success. When I arrived, Morty was unloading a gurney from the funeral van with a black body bag resting on top.

"Hi, Morty. You got a minute?" I wanted to send the check over to him like a paper airplane and take off, but Pa had raised me better than that, so I reluctantly took a step closer.

"Sure, honey. Come on in." Morty motioned for me to follow him and the dead body to the side entrance.

I pointed to the front door. "I need to settle the car bill with you. I'll just go wait up front."

"No time for that today. My schedule is full tilt boogie. I have to finish setting up for a viewing and then I need to start work on Mr. Winkle here." He daintily tapped the body bag.

There was no choice but to follow behind Morty and the squeaking wheels of the gurney. Once we were through the doors, the surprising revelation of us walking down a ramp and into a dark basement had my shoulders bunching. The harsh odor of chemicals, mixed with a heavy floral scent, amped up my internal freaking out by several notches.

Morty flipped a switch, causing the overhead light to flicker a few times before staying on. The light might have eliminated the dark, but what it illuminated had my throat going dry and my stomach dipping. On a metal table lay one of the school lunch ladies dressed in a lavender pantsuit with no hairnet in sight. I'd only ever seen Mrs. Fannie wearing a white uniform with a plastic apron, so it was hard to decide which was odder: her being dressed in something besides the cafeteria uniform or her being laid out dead.

"Don't worry, honey. Mrs. Fannie no longer yaps like a Chihuahua. She's perfectly pleasant company nowadays." Morty situated the gurney to the dead lunch lady's left and then turned his attention to her. He clucked his tongue and straightened a gaudy gold broach on her lapel. Once he seemed satisfied with its placement, Morty began fluffing her orangey-red bouffant even though it already looked perfectly fluffed. Comfortable as could be, he handled her with such ease and care.

Everyone knew Morty had taken over the family busi-ness after his father suffered a stroke on the heels of Morty's brother dying in a boating accident, but I wasn't sure if it was a choice a colorful man in his twenties would have willingly made. In a silk paisley shirt, pressed trousers, and shiny penny loafers with no socks, with his highlighted hair feathered back, he certainly didn't look like a mortician.

Pa would scold me for being judgy, so I cleared that thought from my mind and moved on to categorizing all the weird stuff lining the small space. Hair spray, a curling iron, a bottle of industrial-strength glue, a hacksaw, a drill . . .

Rubbing the chills from my arms, I asked, "You don't get creeped out being around the dead all the time?"

Morty's soft blue eyes locked with mine. He winked one of them. "Honey, the living creep me out. Not the dead." He picked up a cosmetic brush and touched it to Mrs. Fannie's pink cheek. "The living can be cruel, judgmental, quick to complain, and slow to please. The dead never yell or cuss you out. Or call you ugly names." There was such a sadness to his gentle voice.

Even more uncomfortable now, I pulled the check from my pocket and offered it to him, but he was too immersed in inspecting the dead lunch lady's face to notice.

"Morty—"

"My brother and I used to sneak down here and practice applying makeup on each other." Morty snickered as he straightened the row of makeup containers.

I shook my head and took a step back.

"It's all about contouring and blending. We eventually got it down pat . . ." His voice grew distracted and then he glanced at me out of the corner of his eye, making me halt my retreat. "I would have never guessed I'd actually have to apply the makeup to Donald postmortem. He was only twenty-two . . ."

As Morty told me about the boating accident that took his

brother's life, the black bag behind him caught my eye and I could have sworn it shifted. After a few heartbeats of not daring to blink, I chided myself for letting my nerves get the best of me.

"I'll just put this check on your desk," I said, my voice so hoarse I should have followed up with a *ribbit*.

"Don't rush off," Morty insisted, breaking through the rising ringing in my ears.

I blinked, blinked again, but could not look away from the body bag. My eyes must have been playing tricks on me, because it sure did look like that bag shifted again. I squinted to try focusing on it better, and then a bloodcurdling scream rushed out of me as the bag jackknifed.

"What the . . . ?" Morty spun around at the same time a raspy voice began a muffled protest. He quickly unzipped the bag to reveal a wild-eyed, gaunt man with wisps of white hair sticking in every direction. "Mr. Hal! Goodness' sakes. You're supposed to be dead!"

My butt landed hard on the cold cement floor. Scared stupid, I didn't bother getting up as I watched Morty help the zombie sit up.

Mr. Hal scratched his whiskery cheek, paying no mind to the crinkling sound of the body bag still wrapped around his legs. He glanced around the dim room filled with hoses, bottles of clear liquid, and stainless steel tools. "If I'm dead, then does this mean I'm in hell? 'Cause I ain't never imagined heaven looking like the funeral home. Is that . . . ?" He squinted. "Is that Fannie Agnew? Ah, heck. I am in hell."

Morty picked up the paperwork from the gurney and

skimmed over it. "This says your wife found you nonrespon-sive on the bathroom floor. The coroner pronounced you dead and then called me to pick you up." He dropped the paperwork and pressed two fingers against Mr. Hal's neck, tilting his head in concentration. "Humph. You're very much alive now, sir, so no heaven or hell for you today. Great news, right?" His voice grew quite high, but he somehow remained calm, considering the circumstances.

Mr. Hal rubbed his eyes. "I must have gotten my night and day pills confused."

Morty tsked, waving a hand in the air. "You about made me pee my pants." He finished removing the body bag and helped Mr. Hal climb off the gurney and into a chair. After getting the old man a cup of water, Morty crouched in front of me. "Oh, poor Austin. Mr. Hal done gave you a fright too, didn't he, darlin'?"

I could only nod my head as Morty helped me off the floor and into a chair of my own beside the desk. My eyes remained trained on the newly alive man while keeping the dead lunch lady in my peripheral vision in case she decided to wake up too.

Morty stood by his desk and picked up the phone to make a call. "Ted, this is Morty Lawson. We, uh, have a little issue over here at the funeral home. . . ." He glanced over his shoul-der at Mr. Hal and then me before turning to face the desk, his fingers anxiously twisting the coiled phone cord while he quietly spoke. After concluding the call with the coroner, he made another. "Mrs. Winkle, this is Morty Lawson. Honey, I've got some great news for you. A miracle, if you will. Are you

sitting down?" He peeked again at Mr. Hal. "Good, good. So . . .
um . . . there's no need to make funeral arrangements. You see,
um . . . your husband was accidentally declared dead, but he's
very much alive." Morty paused a moment and then let out a
nervous laugh. "No, ma'am. It's the honest-to-goodness truth.
The coroner is coming over to see for himself. After that you're
free to come get your husband. Ain't that grand?"

I could hear a high-pitched voice breaking through the
phone but couldn't make out what she was saying.

Morty glanced over at Mr. Hal again, who was staring into
his cup, looking as stupefied as I felt. "I know I picked him
up, ma'am. That's my job, but it's not my job to return a body.
Living or dead." Morty hushed when the high-pitched squab-
bling started up again. "I understand. . . . I'll make an exception
just this once. . . . Okay . . . I'll bring him home shortly." Morty
hung up the phone and took a deep breath before leaning in
my direction and whispering, "I told you—the dead are much
more agreeable than the living. His wife won't come get him
because it will interfere with watching her soap operas."

Oh, I mouthed when nothing more brilliant came to mind.

Morty bent down in front of Mr. Hal and removed a paper
tag from his big toe. "Just be glad you came to before I started
the embalming process." He released a nervous giggle.

Having had enough of the funeral home to last a lifetime, I
snuck out and booked it back to the library to find Miss Jones.
As soon as I stopped in front of her desk, she gave me her usual
look that was a combination of amusement and apprehension.

"What can I help you with this time, Austin?"

"Umm . . ." I fidgeted although I knew she'd help. Shoot, I'd already had her look up an array of odd subjects, why not one more? "Embalming?" I hitched a shoulder, trying to brush off the weirdness with no success.

Her eyebrows pinched, lips screwed into a pucker, but she went on a quest to find what my curiosity was seeking. I didn't think this request was much worse than male puberty last month. I was pretty embarrassed by that one but more concerned as to why my brothers were smelling like corn chips and soured onion dip. Answers were needed, pronto. Good thing she found a book about the subject, because other concerns came about shortly.

The subject I really wanted to ask her to find material about was always on the tip of my tongue. But I held back, knowing if I asked for books about grief and mood behaviors, it would tip her off to what we were hiding out on the farm. I'd plunder the shelves every so often to see about finding something myself, but there wasn't much on the subject. It was probably hiding in plain sight, like a lot of things.

After Peg stamped the due date in the backs of my two books and offered his declaration about me being weirder than Morty Lawson, I gathered the crew up to head out so Miss Jones could lock the doors. As soon as we rounded the corner, a familiar face was there waiting as he had started doing most every Tuesday in the past few weeks. And like most every Tuesday, my heart took off in a happy dance. A brown bag in hand, Vance scanned the parking lot before meeting us by the limo.

"Hey, Vance." Boss welcomed first as always.

"Hey, there." Vance was surrounded at once, each kid eager

to accept his ever-present treat. With packs of M&M'S in hand, they piled into the limo.

Not a one of them ever called shotgun, always wanting to ride in the back and pretend to be famous folks being chauffeured around. Except Peg. He just didn't want to be seen riding around in the funeral home limo, so he hid in the back. Fine by me. I liked having the radio to myself and pretending I was alone.

I knew not to linger with chores and supper preparation waiting to be done at the farm, but I dragged a little when climbing into the driver's seat. I cranked the car and pressed the button to send the window down. The Silver Bullet did have its perks, like automatic windows and seats, so there was that. I glanced at the dashboard clock to make sure I still had a little bit of time before the day care closed.

Vance looked both ways before leaning into my open window, a mischievous grin tilting his lips as he passed me a pack of Razzles. The handsome devil smelled like he'd already eaten an entire pack. He stuck his blue tongue out to confirm my suspicions.

"Why's Ox get Razzles instead of M&M'S like the rest of us?" Peg complained with an edge of sourness.

Vance looked at him over my shoulder. "The chauffeur deserves something special for having to put up with you." He was good at dishing out whatever attitude Peg liked to serve him.

One stubborn curl loved to wiggle free from the others and rest against his forehead. I'd stared at it for years but something struck me today to finally tuck it back into place. It was soft and slightly damp from the humidity. His eyes lit up and that boyish grin stretched to full capacity.

"You just couldn't stand it any longer, could ya?" Vance's dimples made a show.

I rolled my eyes, playing it off. "That curl aggravates me."

"Use that as an excuse all you want. I don't mind you touching me. And if my messy hair is the ticket to more of that happening, then I'll be tossing my comb."

This guy flirted casual as you please and we had an audience, so I changed the subject.

"You'll never believe what happened at the funeral home..." While bags being torn open and then smacking cut off the chatter in the back, I gave Vance the short version of Mr. Hal Winkle being resurrected from the dead.

"You made that up." Vance scoffed but his dimples made a show, letting me know he got a kick out of my tale.

"I ain't that creative. Trust me." I sighed, getting caught up in the depths of his vivid-green eyes. "I really need to go pick up the twins from day care and get home."

"Yeah, I need to get home too." Vance gave my lips a lingering look before tapping the top of the limo and walking away.

Staring into the side-view mirror, I watched him stroll down the sidewalk with his hands nonchalantly in his pockets. It annoyed me how he seemed to not have a care in this world. And I was even more annoyed that I didn't want him to leave.

The pinging sound of candy meeting metal tore my eyes away from Vance's receding form and had me twisting in my seat to see what was going on. "What was that? Did someone spill their candy?" I wasn't crazy about the set of wheels I'd been stuck with, but I took care of them just the same.

Boss pointed at the ashtray on the door as Raleigh plucked an M&M out and popped it in his mouth.

"We got a candy dish in our car," Raleigh garbled out, a stream of green leaking from the corner of his overfilled mouth. He wiped his mouth with the back of his hand.

"Eww . . ." Charlotte made a face. "That's gross."

"You know it's never been used. It's fine. He's fine." I dismissed it, even though it grossed me out too. I'd learned early on to pick my battles and also that boys were just gross and there was nothing we could do about that. My little brother choosing a clean ashtray for a candy dish certainly wasn't the worst thing to happen.

No, witnessing a dead man come back to life while another dead person was laid out beside him was worse by far.

But even worse than that was Vance making sure he wasn't seen in town conversing with me. Yeah, that stung.

Chapter 6

TOBACCO SICKNESS IS BAD, BUT LOVESICKNESS IS EVEN WORSE

May 1983

That spring, Vance Cumberland made himself right at home on Nolia Farms. Quite an odd occurrence to have town royalty parading around dirt and plants. Even odder, it seemed like he'd been there from the start, along with the tobacco barns and chickens. The guy wore fun and carefree so fittingly that he somehow drew Raleigh out of his shell and calmed Peg's moodiness. Sure, Vance disrupted our routines and chores, but he was such a good sport about slopping the pigs and collecting eggs from the henhouse that we decided to put up with him.

From comments whispered loud enough for me to hear in line at the grocery store and questions asked at day care pickup, it was pretty clear that Vance was using the guise of befriending Boss as his reason for spending so much time out on the farm. My hands were too full with tending to the kids and dealing with Pa's moods to really care one way or the other.

Or that was what I repeatedly told myself until Malorie Fitzgerald started carrying on and on about going to prom with Vance.

"I already have my dress. It's fuchsia, tea-length, with lots of ruffles. Vance will love it. He likes me in pink." She pulled a history book out of her locker, closed the door, and leaned against it, swooning like a fool.

Why that prissy girl thought I'd want to know all that made no sense. In stained jeans and a plain black T-shirt with my long hair in my face, I looked nothing close to Malorie's teased brown hair, pale face painted with makeup, pin-striped Jordache jeans, and bright-orange top.

"My mom is on the prom committee and so I got to choose the theme. It's going to be a paradise theme after *The Blue Lagoon*. Vance could totally be Christopher Atkins's twin, don't you think?"

I had no idea who that guy was, but I nodded my head like I did. Malorie was already rattling on about helping make tissue-paper flowers the exact same pink as her dress, so I zoned out and focused on the *Just Say No* poster on the wall behind her. I know the First Lady Nancy Reagan's campaign was to say no to drugs, but I sure wished I could *just say no* to other things. Like playing nice to this girl when I'd rather whack her with my history book for going on and on about Vance as if she were making a point to claim him in front of me.

"Are you going to the prom?" Malorie asked.

I looked away from the poster and gazed at nothing in particular inside my locker. "No. It's not my thing." Wanting to get away from her, I fumbled with wiggling a notebook free from underneath the clutter in my locker, nearly causing an avalanche.

"Here, let me help." Malorie reached around me to shove the tower of papers and books back in while I yanked the notebook out. Her perfectly polished nails in some peachy color landed next to my bare nails with nothing but yellowy stains from setting tobacco every evening for the last week.

Embarrassed by the striking contrast, I quickly withdrew my hand and mumbled, "Thanks."

"You're welcome," Malorie said brightly as ever. "Oh, I have a swatch of the fabric in my purse I want to show you."

After producing the tiny strip of shiny dark-pink fabric and practically shoving it in my face, Malorie jabber-jawed about wearing her hair in a twist and having to get her shoes dyed to match the dress while I struggled to keep the hurt and jealousy from showing on my face. I leaned inside my locker, angling my back toward her, as heat lit my cheeks and stung my eyes.

Thankfully, she drifted down the hall, nagging someone else about her awesome news.

When Vance showed up at the farm later that afternoon in all his happy, handsome glory, I sufficiently ignored him. The plan was easy enough to pull off until he cornered me in the feed room in the packhouse. A bucket of chicken feed and my pride prevented him from getting too close to me.

's up your craw?" He formed his question as a joke,
like he always did when he thought he was being cute.

rt was, he *was* cute, coming straight from the ballfield in
actice uniform. His hair curled around the edges of his
kwards ball cap. Completely cute, making it hard to stay
d at him.

It was a question I couldn't answer without giving away the
fact that I was jealous, and that in itself might have been ridiculous because he'd not made any verbal commitment to me. I
believed in actions speaking louder than words. Obviously I'd
misinterpreted his actions. But what else could have been the
meaning of him holding my hand when we sat in the porch
swing, or the weekly batch of cookies he gave me to right his
cookie-thieving wrongs, or the way he placed his palm to my
cheek when no one was looking?

"Talk to me, Austin. What's the matter?" He tilted his head,
the smile slowly fading. "Did I do something wrong?"

I clutched the bucket closer and shook my head. My jaw
refused to unhinge until he reached to touch my cheek. I
flinched out of reach and blurted, "I don't think your prom
date would think too highly of this."

His relaxed expression tightened. He yanked his hat off and
ran a hand over his messy curls before slamming it down on
his head.

"That's all my mother's doing. She had the date scheduled
before Christmas."

"Then you don't have any business coming around here dal-
lying with me when you already have a girlfriend."

"Malorie isn't my girlfriend."

"Does Malorie know that?" My eyebrows shot up. "Does your family?"

Vance scrubbed a hand down his face. "It's complicated."

I snorted. "Wow. What a big word to cower behind." I used the bucket to shove him to the side and stomped away. "Go hang out with Boss like everyone thinks you're out here doing anyway and leave me the heck alone!"

"Austin! Don't be like this!"

His pleas didn't slow me down, and it was easy to put a wall up between us when a couple of weeks went by with no farm visits. It stung how quickly he gave up, but it was for the best.

Vance's privileged world continued trucking along while I remained anchored to the farm and my anger. I was even mad at myself for keeping track of him with the help of the local paper.

It was unsurprising, albeit upsetting, to find a photo of him with Malorie, decked out in prom attire with the addition of crowns and sashes, on the front page. Of course they would be crowned prom king and queen. The only credit I gave him was for the fact that he also escorted Boss to the prom, even ensuring that it wasn't turned into a headline to make his family look good.

Thankfully, Pa managed to pull himself out of his shadows long enough to take Boss to rent a tux from the department store in town. My brother was elated, standing between the couple in most of the pictures Pa took when he dropped Boss off at the mayor's mansion. Malorie, not so much, if the tight smile that didn't reach her eyes was any indicator. Oh, I felt her pain, skipping my junior prom to babysit a herd of rambunctious young'uns while the guy I couldn't stop daydreaming about was giving his attention to someone else.

A week later, I attended the graduation ceremony to watch Boss receive an honorary diploma, which basically noted my brother put in the required years. Vance gave the valedictorian speech with his eyes pinned to me the entire time as he spoke about future goals and taking chances, and that made me spittin' mad. My life was complicated enough as it was; there was no room for whatever game he wanted to play. I made sure our paths didn't cross afterwards, hightailing it as soon as we were dismissed.

Avoidance became easier as life got busy with tobacco season for me and a shared family vacation with the Fitzgeralds for Vance. Even though an odd ache developed in the center of my chest, I shook the dust off my shoes and moved on.

By late June, hades had decided to visit Magnolia and settle its blistering heat on us so thickly that the simple task of walking out to the mailbox would require a trip to the altar of the deep freeze afterwards.

I wonder if it's empty enough I could wedge my entire body inside.

Those thoughts abated at the sight waiting for me at the end of the drive. While the sun scalded my neck, I stopped by the mailbox and contemplated what to do with the little surprise tied to the post. Round as it was tall, with a cookies-and-cream color pattern, it squealed at me to decide already. Before I could, the familiar rumbling of a car engine came from a ways down the road. Sure, it could have been someone besides him, but not with my luck.

"Shoot!" I grumbled. The pig agreed with another squeal as I fumbled to untie the knots in the rope so we could get out of Dodge. My heart leapt when the car approached and slowed, making it clear there was no getting away from having to speak.

The sound of a window smoothly whirring down and then, "Whatcha got there?"

Without looking away from the rope, I gestured toward the pig and then went back to unraveling a stubborn knot. Whoever left the stumpy little creature sure didn't want it getting loose. A pink bow dressed its neck, indicating that perhaps it was female and a pet and should certainly not be tied to a random mailbox.

The glossy black car crept past me and parked by the chapel. Moments later, a long shadow fell on the other side of the mailbox. The scent of his cologne grew stronger as his tanned arms circled around me and replaced my shaky hands to take over freeing the rope. I gave in and stole another inhale of his scent. The crisp freshness of it was so much more appealing than the sharp, spicy scent of Pa's Old Spice. It was another thing about Vance Cumberland I wished I didn't like so much.

"You got a secret admirer leaving you a potbelly pig?" Vance teased. His heated chuckle brushed the side of my neck, sending a tingle along my shoulders.

I ducked under his arm to put a little distance between us and readjusted my ponytail that had gotten knocked askew in the process. "So now that your date duty is fulfilled for your adoring public, you can come talk to riffraff again?"

Vance finished undoing the last knot and turned to meet my glare head-on. "You told me to leave you alone, so don't go blaming me."

I yanked the rope out of his hand, scoffing with enough indignation to kick up a dust storm. "You are to blame for being a dang coward. Prancing around with Fancy Girl in public while pretending Miss Nobody doesn't exist." I tapped my damp chest just above the tank top clinging to my skin. The thin top and short cutoffs suddenly made me feel exposed and vulnerable. Even though it was sweltering in that moment, I longed for a long coat with a hood.

Vance took a step toward me and actually growled. "Austin." My name formed into a reprimand leaving his frowning lips. "There is no pretending you don't exist. You're all I think about. I've missed you."

A truck zoomed by, beeping the horn. Vance threw his hand up and waved but did a poor job containing a grimace. "Can't we go up to the house and have a talk?"

"I ain't gonna get caught in the middle of this farce, so the best thing you can do is go on back to your mansion and Malorie." I tried making a hasty getaway up the drive but the blame pig ruined my effort by digging her hoofed heels in and refusing to cooperate.

"At least let me give you a lift."

"Nah. We're good." I tugged on the rope, but the squirmy little thing wouldn't budge.

He motioned down the dirt drive. The house was so far down the lane it wasn't even visible from the road. "That's a long way to make this little darlin' walk." Ignoring my protests, he gathered the pig in his arms and walked over to his car, fumbling to open the passenger door while keeping a grip on the squirming animal, and motioned for me to get in.

With a whole lot of reluctance, I did. He placed the pig on my lap and closed the door. I scanned the interior. Leather seats, lots of buttons and knobs, and clean as a whistle. It reminded me of the car show Pa took us to in the spring where all those fancy cars were on display. No doubt about it, this car was attractive. And the scent? Yeah, even better. My limo held a persistent smell of carnations no matter how much my smelly gang rode around in it with the windows down. And the diesel truck stank as a diesel truck should, exhaust fumes and sweat. Not this sports car. Nope. I was surrounded by the alluring scent of Vance's cologne and new leather, marred only by a hint of pig. My eyes landed on a dark bottle wedged inside a cup holder. I plucked it up and read the label. Halston. A quick sniff confirmed it was Vance Cumberland in a bottle.

The driver's door opened and I nearly bobbled the cologne but it somehow landed in the cup holder. Rather loudly. But Vance was decent enough to overlook my snooping. Instead, he settled in the bucket seat and cranked the beast of a motor. It roared to life, and as he grasped the gearshift between us and deftly shifted the car into first, my eyes latched on to the strain of muscle in his forearm. I was disgusted with myself for being so attracted to him, but not enough to stop staring.

"What's with that farm sign?" Vance asked.

I blinked out of my daze. "Sign?"

Vance sent a sidelong glance my way, connecting those

emerald peeps with mine before looking forward. "The one by the road. It's pretty gnarly on one side."

I twisted to look behind us at the weathered white sign with *nolia Farms est. 1875* written in faded-blue paint. Fixing it up was actually on Charlotte's project list for the summer. "Oh. That's Pa making a statement to your precious town." I resettled the pig on my lap and ran my palm along her back. She was surprisingly soft. "That sign used to say *Magnolia Farms*. But folks didn't care for how Pa ran the farm after he took over from his father. He let people who were down on their luck stay in the guesthouse and had all kinds showing up for Sunday services in the little chapel. The town said he had no business doing such and the farm wasn't fittin' to carry the name Magnolia, so Pa took a saw to it and hacked off the first three letters. He refastened what was left to the post, renaming the farm Nolia."

"For real?" Vance gave me a quick look.

I nodded. "It even made the front page of the paper. My mother showed it to me. It was a picture of Pa standing by the severed sign with a quote underneath. He said, 'There's nothing wrong with being different. What's wrong is when people refuse to accept it.'"

"Makes sense."

"Yep." I tore my eyes away from watching him, from admiring the gray polo shirt and how the sleeves hugged his bicep and the faded jeans taut on his thighs. Good grief, I was a hot mess of hormones. Focusing back on the driveway, I realized we weren't even halfway there yet. "I could have walked faster."

Vance chuckled. "Nothing wrong with taking your time, Austin." He let go of the gearshift and gave my knee a gentle caress before moving to pet the pig, and I declare if the fat little thing didn't mew like a cat. "And I like spending time with you."

I took a calming breath and blew it out. "Vance, what do you want? School is over and whatever friendship charity you had going on with Boss doesn't have to continue, so you have no excuse being out here anymore."

"That's why you thought I was hanging out with Boss?" He cut me a look filled with hurt.

"That's what it looked like. The town's golden child hanging out with the special-needs boy."

"I'm offended by that. I genuinely like hanging out with Boss. And the rest of your family, for that matter." Vance huffed, a deep frown marring his handsome face. "Plus, I'm a grown man. I don't need an excuse." His grip tightened on the steering wheel, turning his knuckles white. "I go wherever I want."

"You trying to convince me or yourself?" My sharp remark caused his full lips to produce a pout, but I plowed on. "Grown man? Pff. You too soft to be a man."

He stopped the car and placed a palm to my cheek. "Soft in only the right places." He grinned until I shoved his hand off. Frowning, he let off the brake and turned the radio up until we could hear an unfamiliar song over the roar of the engine.

By the time Vance parked in front of the house, the porch was lined with expectant faces.

"Where's Charlotte?"

My sister was the only Foster kid not present, and it was impressive how he noticed it right away.

"She's at Miss Wise's, where she's been most every day this summer."

Charlotte had taken my spot as Miss Wise's taste tester. It didn't sit too well with me, but at least one of us was getting a break from Nolia.

"I thought you were checking the mail?" Peg hollered as soon as I wiggled free from the car.

Before I could answer, the crowd surrounded me to check out the pig. "I found her tied to the mailbox. Forgot to check it."

Boss pulled the squirmy thing from my arms and plopped in the grass so that the twins could reach it. My hope was that Vance would roll out a little quicker than he arrived, but I was used to not getting what I wanted. He got out of the car with a brown bag and divvied out several Pixy Stix candies to each kid before grabbing my hand and leading me to the porch.

I unraveled my hand and motioned for him to take a seat. "I'll be right back." Parched, I headed straight into the kitchen, filled a glass with tap water, and took a big gulp.

"What happened to the cabinet doors?" Vance asked from behind me.

Choking on the water, I spun around. "You startled me!"

He wrapped his arms around me and pulled me into his chest, patting my back while chuckling.

It seemed more like a ploy to touch me than to help clear my airway, so I moved out of his arms. "We're doing some remodeling," I said, excusing it as truth since the word *remodel* pretty much meant to alter. It was another thing I'd picked up when it came to protecting Pa—justifying my lies with half-truths and omissions.

Vance studied the exposed dishes, pots and pans, and dried goods. "Can't believe I've never been invited inside this house."

I wanted to point out that he wasn't invited this time either but bit my tongue and placed the glass in the sink. "Let's go sit in the swing." I laced our hands together and pulled him along with me, hoping to hurry him out of the house.

Vance set the swing to motion before angling toward me. "Will you give me a chance to explain?"

I kept my eyes on the identical boys, smiling at them smiling at the pig, their little mouths already stained red from the candy powder. "Explain what?"

"What's expected of me from my family."

"It's none of my business." I tried to let go of his hand, but Vance's grip tightened.

"Austin, I think it is." He sighed as his shoulders slumped. "My family and Malorie's have been close friends for all our lives. There's always been expectations about us, but I've made it clear to my parents that's not happening. The thing is, it's an election year, so my father asked that I not ruffle any town feathers. That includes the Fitzgeralds."

"Then why are you out here with me?" I asked slowly, feeling like a record player stuck on repeat.

"Because this is where I want to be." Vance squeezed my hand, tilting his head to capture my gaze.

Unwilling to meet his eyes, I looked toward the kids sitting in the yard and grimaced. "Nash, don't feed that pig a Pixy Stix!"

The little stinker kept pouring the powder into the pig's mouth while giving me an innocent shrug. "But her likes it!"

"You're really good at taking care of your brothers and sister," Vance commented.

"There's no other choice but to take as best care of them as I can." I focused on Nash and Knox. "They're my world."

"You have to understand that's how I feel about my parents and the sense of duty I have toward them."

We rocked in silence for a while, listening to the creaking of the swing and the giggles from the yard. What Vance said started sinking in. Truthfully, I did get where he was coming from about his father's election and his duties. Although we lived in two completely different worlds, family came first. Protecting my siblings and my father from himself was top priority, so what I wanted rarely mattered.

Vance nudged my arm. "You understand, right?"

"Yeah, but it still doesn't warm me to the idea of being treated like your little secret," I admitted.

"My parents know I like you, so it's really not a secret. And it's none of the public's business who I hang out with anyway."

"Except for when you're hanging out with the town's princess with a camera at the ready?" I retorted, tugging my hand free and crossing my arms.

"The Fitzgeralds are not only big campaign supporters but also investors in my dad's financial firm. On top of that, Malorie's mother is on the city council." Vance sighed heavily, stopping the swing to rest his elbows on top of his knees. "I told Dad I would be polite to Malorie, but no more dates, and not to expect me at any more family gatherings this summer. But, Austin, that's all I can do at the moment."

I pitied him, knowing how it felt to have the weight of your family's world bearing down on your shoulders. I settled my hand on his tense back, moving it upward until combing my fingers through the curls at the nape of his neck. "So your parents know you like me?"

Vance nodded, his body relaxing under my touch. "Yeah. They've known for a while now."

That sent a thrill through me until I cringed, recalling my own father didn't know about whatever sort of friendship I had going on with the mayor's son. As a sultry breeze filtered through the porch, I decided to give Vance another chance, if for only the summer.

"As long as I'm the only one you're holding hands with, then I guess we can hang out." I dropped my hand when he sat up to show off a giant grin and those darn dimples.

I bit my lip to contain my smile and shook my head, knowing we were both being selfish with wanting to hold on to a friendship that had already proven to be of the fickle variety.

"You're the only one. Promise." Vance leaned toward me and placed a kiss on my cheek.

A shiver skated along my body. Pushing out of the swing to get away from the bizarre reaction to his lips touching me, I bounded down the steps and joined the boys.

"Let's play hide-and-seek!" Boss suggested and everyone else agreed.

One great thing about living on a farm is the endless places to hide. "Just be careful to not step on a snake," I warned as everyone dispersed in different directions, except for Peg, who took the pig to the porch swing.

On round three, I ended up wedged between the branches

of the magnolia tree in the side yard with Vance crowding me in. The perfume of the tree and the crisp allure of his cologne surrounded me, almost taking my breath away.

"Go find your own hiding place." I shoved him, but my touch seemed to be magnetic and drew him closer. "I think you need a lesson on personal space."

Vance's eyes roamed over me. Between his heated look and the heat index of hades, I was close to melting. "And maybe you need a lesson on letting someone in." The words fell from his lips in a low drawl, too solid in conviction to be a flimsy flirt.

I stepped over a branch to put some sort of barrier between us and was surprised he stayed put, though he reached across and took my hand. Not knowing what he was up to, I prepared to throat punch him, but then the scoundrel did the sweetest thing. He laced his fingers with mine and gave them a reassuring squeeze. It felt like the message in his gesture was letting me know that even though I wasn't ready to let him in, he'd be there regardless.

Or maybe that was wishful thinking on my part.

While Vance and I stood nestled in the skirt of the tree holding hands, Raleigh ran right by without spotting us.

Once the coast was clear, Vance rested his chin on the branch between us and whispered, "Have you ever been kissed?"

My cheeks heated as I shook my head.

Vance let out a low whistle. "Sweet sixteen and never been kissed . . ." He leaned close again, but I shoved him out of the way.

"The same day you turn up after ignoring me for a coon's

age, you're actually gonna try a stunt like this?" I pointed at his lips.

"I can't help it. I've wanted to kiss you ever since that day you kicked me in the butt." He gave my hand another gentle squeeze and looked up from the thick fringe of eyelashes. "Will you at least promise to let me be your first?"

"Not today!" I yanked free and pushed the limb out of my way, ready to make a run for it, but Vance caught my wrist.

"Another day. When I've earned your trust?"

"Gotcha!" Raleigh hollered, grabbing my other wrist and saving me from having to commit one way or the other about that kiss.

I let go of the limb after letting Raleigh pull me out of the hiding place, sending it to smack Vance in the chest. Understanding why he had to play nice with Malorie and how he ignored me in public was one thing, but I certainly wasn't going to be a pushover for him to toy with either.

Most of the summer would go by with him asking for that kiss and me denying. I didn't trust our friendship to last past the season.

The morning of the first cropping arrived along with Vance Cumberland. He came strutting into the kitchen, wearing cut-off jeans that looked like he'd hacked them off on the way over here with rusty scissors. A pink polo shirt with the collar flipped up, a Magnolia High baseball hat, and stark-white Adidas with no socks completed his getup.

"What on earth are you wearing?" I asked over my shoulder,

dumping the leftover pot of rice into a heated cast-iron skillet. Sizzling and popping indicated I had it too hot, so I adjusted the burner setting.

Vance scanned his outfit and shrugged. "Boss said to wear old stuff that I didn't care if it got ruined."

I grabbed the butter and two cartons of eggs from the fridge. "How are you going to ruin it?"

"I'm *croppin' baccer* today." He grinned, all proud of himself for looking like a fool and sounding like a farm hick.

"Why?" I snickered, grabbing a spatula and stirring the rice with it.

Vance joined me by the stove and caressed my cheek with his warm palm. "Because I need to toughen these soft hands and start being more of a man like you told me to do."

I paused the stirring and gave him a sidelong glance. "Don't do that for me." A half step moved me out of his reach. He got the message and dropped his hand, but that didn't remove the dimple creasing his cheek.

"Too late. This is all about you, Austin Texas Foster." Vance crossed his arms and inspected the kitchen. "Y'all haven't finished the cabinet doors yet?"

"Umm . . . no. Pa got sidetracked with tobacco season," I offered as an excuse, when the truth of the matter was the doors had disappeared into thin air. I'd looked high and low for the darn things, prepared to rehang them myself, but Pa couldn't recall where he put them. "I kinda like the open look. Makes it easy to find what you need."

"I suppose."

Needing to move his focus to something besides our

jacked-up kitchen, I pointed the spatula toward the cabinet holding the dry goods. "How about grabbing the can of Nestle's Quik out of there?" While he plundered for the can, I retrieved the new gallon of milk from the fridge and poured one glass.

"Here ya go." Vance set the yellow can beside the glass of milk while I pulled the funnel out of the utensil drawer. "What are you doing?"

I placed the funnel into the mouth of the milk jug, popped the lid on the chocolate powder, and commenced to pouring it into the milk. "Making it by the jug is easier with my crowd." I certainly didn't have the time or the patience to be measuring one glass out at the time.

A flume of sweet powder rose above the funnel as I tapped the can to release more. Vance took a deep inhale and sputtered a cough. I'd learned that lesson long ago and leaned away from the chocolaty cloud. Sure, it smelled delicious, but the tickle in the back of the throat wasn't worth it. Once the can was empty, I removed the funnel and screwed the cap back onto the jug and handed it over to Vance. "How about giving that a good shake for me?"

"You didn't leave any for that glass on the counter," Vance pointed out, already holding the jug with both hands and shaking it over his head.

The vision of the lid giving way nearly made me giggle like a silly girl. Tamping it down, I turned to the stove and gave the rice a good mix. "Boss isn't a fan of chocolate in his milk. The plain glass is for him."

The swishing of the jug abated as Vance's eyes cut to me and then to the skillet. "Are y'all having rice for breakfast?"

"Eggs and rice, yes." I began cracking eggs, two at a time, dotting the top of the steaming rice.

"Like Chinese fried rice?"

"I don't know nothing about Chinese rice, but this is just something we've always made with leftover rice. The crowd likes it." I finished adding the eggs, salting and peppering the tops before taking the spatula and folding them into the rice.

Vance tossed the shells into my compost bucket and then placed the empty cartons by the door where we kept a stack of them. "It sure smells good."

"You're welcome to eat with us. You'll need the fuel if you're serious about working today."

"I am serious."

And he most certainly was. After he scarfed down his portion of eggs and rice and asked when I planned on making them again, Vance soldiered out to the field with the rest of the cropping crew while Peg and I set up the stringer.

"Only an idiot would be that excited about cropping baccer. You reckon purty boy is going to make it through the morning?" Peg asked, concentrating on loading a spool of twine into the machine.

"Your guess is as good as mine." I rolled the cart of tobacco sticks over to the conveyer belt. I scanned the bountiful fields surrounding the barn. The distinct peppery scent of tobacco welcomed me to the first gathering of the season. The mustiness underneath the barn overhang and the lingering fumes of the tractor added to the familiar cologne of our summers. I inhaled deeply to capture it all, wincing slightly when finding the note of Mama's honeysuckle lotion missing. I let a brief moment of mourning her pass and refocused on the ramblings of my brother.

Peg let out a haughty laugh. "He's going to get sick as a dog."

"Probably. I tried talking him into changing into a long pair of Pa's pants and shirt, but he said it was too hot." We had all gotten tobacco sickness once or twice when the heat won out over our better judgment to cover up to cut down on so much tobacco exposure.

An hour later, the first tractor puttered up with a trailer full of beautiful fat tobacco leaves glistening in the early morning sunshine. Boss and Vance rode on the back end, all smiles. They hopped off so Pa could back the trailer behind us and the conveyer belt, close enough to put the tobacco within arm's reach. As we got started loading a single layer of leaves, topping it with a stick and then another layer of leaves, Vance stood on the other side of the conveyer, filling me in on how easy the morning was going.

"It wasn't hard at all." He grinned ear to ear.

"Yeah . . ." I straightened a crooked row, slinging another handful of leaves on top. "Let's talk again later after, say . . . ten more loads."

Vance's grin dropped. "That many?"

"More than that," I warned, twisting around to grab more leaves.

He pulled his hat off and dried his face with the hem of his already-stained shirt. "If there's that much left to do, then what am I doing up here?"

"I'm giving you an out, boy. I suggest you take it," Pa

answered before I could. He finished unhitching the trailer from the tractor and began climbing onto the seat.

Vance sidled up to the tractor in three long strides. "But, sir, I told you I was here to help today."

"And you did. Now ya free to go spend the day with Miss Malorie Fitzgerald. Heard you two were an item." Pa arched one thick eyebrow as he looked over at me.

I quickly glanced away, not wanting him to read the hurt his comment pushed on me.

"No, sir. We're just friends, is all." Vance laughed it off.

"Ain't what folks around town are sayin'." Pa put the tractor in gear; the puttering sound grew louder.

Vance jerked a shoulder up, his lips flattening. I waited for him to rebuke Pa more, but he didn't. Just hopped into the empty trailer Pa was hitching to the tractor. They headed back to the fields and I didn't see another glimpse of Vance until four trailer loads later.

This time, he wasn't sitting on the edge with his legs swinging, smiling away. Nope. This time he was laid out on top of the tobacco, as green as the leaves surrounding him. The pink polo shirt was gone and his exposed chest was speckled with black tobacco gum and something slimy. Vomit, if I had to guess.

Pa parked the tractor and hopped off the side. He unloaded Vance and propped him up against the side of the barn.

"Ox, take this boy down to the swimming hole to see about getting some of the tobacco juice off him." Pa pointed a finger at Vance's hunched body as it convulsed from the dry heaves.

"Me? He's Boss's friend. He should take him." I turned to the conveyor, preparing another row of leaves.

"With the way he couldn't shut up about you today, I believe you're his friend too."

I don't know why Pa was in an antagonizing mood, but I wasn't up for it. "Boss should."

"Boss might accidentally let him drown. Best you go. The quicker you can get him washed off, the better. He's already upchucked everything he had in his gut. Get to it fore he gets any sicker." Pa shouldered me out of the way and took my spot, going to work and leaving me no choice but to obey.

To be on the safe side, I helped Vance into the bed of the truck and drove to the front of the farm to see Foxy. I climbed out, peeped over the side, and told him to stay put. He answered with a groan and wheeze.

"Hey, Foxy. We got a problem."

Foxy looked up from the basket of zucchini she was sorting. "What kinda problem?" She adjusted her tie-dyed head wrap and eyed me with a pinched expression. This woman got jumpier than a cat in a room full of rocking chairs if things ever got out of sorts.

I hitched a thumb toward the truck. "It's Vance. First time in a baccer field. He's sicker than sick. I'm about to take him out to the pond to see about washing some of the juice and gum off, but I was wondering if you got anything that can help."

Her shoulders relaxed. "Let me see."

Foxy plundered through her medicinal supplies, handed me a mason jar of one of her steeped teas, a salt scrub, and a jug of water. "This tea should help with the nausea. Have him sip it, and keep offering some water, too, to rehydrate. Use the salt scrub to help wash him off." She broke a few leaves of mint off from the plant growing beside the farm stand. "When he's in better shape, have him chew on some of this."

"Thanks, Foxy." I put everything on the seat while she leaned over the side of the truck and took in Vance's whimpering body.

She hummed a disapproval. "You didn't think to tell him to wear more clothes? All that skin exposed—"

"Of course I did, but the fool didn't listen. Said it was too hot," I retorted as Vance's groan turned into another dry heave.

Foxy patted his bare shoulder. "I hope you feel better, cutie. Do what Austin says, okay?"

He mumbled something before dry heaving again. Man, his stomach muscles were getting a wicked workout. Foxy and I glanced at each other and then back to the contracting peaks and valleys of his abdomen, tilting our heads to get a better look.

"Is it wrong to enjoy the view with him in such misery?" Foxy whispered out the side of her mouth without looking away from Vance.

"So wrong," I agreed with little conviction. Shaking my head and blinking out of the daze, I climbed into the truck and drove to the back of the farm, where fields gave way to acres of trees and the giant pond with a dock jutting out to nearly the middle.

A hidden oasis, this quiet place was a refuge of peacefulness. A treasure trove of happier memories greeted me every time I would venture out here alone late at night. The pond and the packhouse were the two places I'd begun to haunt during late hours of restlessness. It was a restlessness that always awakened as soon as I had everyone settled down for the night. I blamed it on the infant years of the younger twins, when my body adapted to receiving little rest and being on alert even in sleep in case one of them cried out with a need.

I pulled the truck in the shade beside the shallow part of the pond and prepared to take care of someone else's need. "Scoot to the end of the bed and I'll help you out," I directed and patiently watched him roll, moan, wiggle, and dry heave until making it out of the truck bed.

"I can hardly walk. No way I'm up for swimming," Vance rasped as he leaned heavily on me while I struggled to maneuver him to the edge of the pond.

"It's only about two feet deep right here, so all you have to do is sit." With one arm supporting him around the waist, I unsnapped his butchered jean cutoffs.

"I'm definitely not up for that." How he managed a tease in this shape was beyond me.

"You got underwear on, right?"

"Yeah."

I unzipped the pants and pushed them down to his bare feet, not even taking the time to ask what happened to those bright-white Adidas. And certainly not looking anywhere near his midsection. "Your pants are soaked through with tobacco juice. That's what's making you sick. Step out of them." I held on to his wobbly body as he did so with a few staggered steps.

After propping him up in the water, I returned to the truck and grabbed the salt scrub and tea from the cab. With some coercing he took several sips while I sat behind him and scrubbed his body with the salt and eucalyptus mixture. Thankfully, it washed away the pungent odors of sweat, tobacco, and puke clinging to his stooped body, leaving behind a minty aroma.

"I wish I felt better," Vance slurred as I massaged the salt into his firm shoulders and back, "so I could enjoy your hands all over me."

"Behave, or I'll make you do it yourself," I warned, focusing on keeping my hands steady. Boy, was it testing my resolve to keep Vance at arm's length and to behave myself. To say his body was nice was an understatement. Even in this puny state, his lean, athletic build was admirable.

His head bobbled around, taking in the sight before us. "The water is so clear you can see all the way to the bottom."

"The pond was cut out of rock is why. About a hundred or so acres back here are nothing but rock."

Pa had made a pretty penny off the rock that was dug out for the pond, and the contractor begged and pleaded with Pa to let him quarry the rest of it, but he refused. Between a small inheritance from his father and the rock money, I never had to worry too much about finances, at least. There was enough to worry about without that.

I pointed a ways off to the right. "You see the red wagon on the bottom over there?"

"Yeah."

"It's forty-some feet deep in that one spot. Pa had them dig until they hit a natural spring, so it could feed our swimming hole."

"How'd the wagon get down there?"

"Boss and Peg got the wild notion that the wagon would float like a boat. Took about a minute to realize their mistake.

It sank too fast to rescue. They confessed to Pa what they did, wanting to know if there was any way he could fish it out." I cupped a palmful of water and rinsed Vance's chest before scrubbing some more salt against a stubborn spot of gum near his side, making him flinch. "Ticklish?"

Vance grunted when I hit the same spot again. "Yeah. So your dad couldn't get the wagon out?"

I'd forgotten all about the story and had gotten caught up in cleaning his torso. Face heating, I relocated the wagon underneath the glittery clear water. "He said he could, with a backhoe, but he left it there as a lesson." I offered him the jar of tea when his body spasmed into another heave.

After only managing one small sip, he handed it to me and asked, "What was the lesson?"

I was impressed he could keep focus in the midst of this sick state, considering my difficulty focusing in my state of perfect health. His mostly naked body was to blame. Blinking away from it once again, I fastened my eyes on the wagon. "When something is created for a certain purpose, don't go playing God, thinking it's needed for another."

"Humph." Vance ran a hand along my calf. "You can take your jeans off too. Don't want you to get sick . . ." Perhaps he wasn't as good at focusing as I thought.

I popped his upper arm and was going to leave him to float away, but before I could, Vance reclined until he was resting in my arms. I widened my legs to accommodate him, using my body as a chair of support. The back of his head rested against my chest, and I feared he could feel the wild beat of my heart and the quickening of my breath.

Watching him for a moment, I raked my hand through his damp curls to move them out of his eyes, combing through much longer than necessary. Of course Vance didn't mind a bit. I finally made myself stop touching him, but not before tracing the bronze line of freckles along the bridge of his nose with my fingertip. The tiny specks were only a few shades darker than his skin. I'd never found freckles appealing before seeing them worn by this guy. With him reclined in front of me, the view was much more intimate and everything about him was alluring.

Vance took a stuttered breath, his body tensing, putting my mind back on the reason we were out at the pond.

I picked up the jar from the grass behind us and held it to his mouth. "Here. Drink some more." After getting a few more sips of tea into him and it staying down, I placed the jar on the ground and started to work on his speckled forearms, where most of the gum had been collected.

"How do you stand working with this mess?" Vance tried helping me wash his arm, but his fingers were like limp noodles, so he plopped his hand into the water and snuggled closer to me.

"It's what my pa's family has done for a living as far back as I know." I lowered his arm into the cool, clear water, tamping down the urge to scold him for not listening about how to dress properly. He'd learned that lesson the hard way, and it was doubtful he would ever forget it.

Once his body was free of the gum and I'd talked him into chewing on a mint leaf to help combat the funk of his breath, I planted my hands behind me on the rocky bottom of the pond and raised my face to the sun. Vance leaned back until his head rested against my chest. We both closed our eyes and got still for a minute. The distant puttering of tractors was a reminder that we weren't as secluded as the surrounding shelter of trees made it appear, but it was still easy to imagine we were alone in the middle of a country oasis.

Hiccuping, Vance opened his eyes and revealed a glassy green gaze. "If I wasn't burping egg and mint, I'd kiss you."

I cracked up, even though I was certain he was being completely serious. "Well, I appreciate you restraining yourself."

"I will for now," he warned, quietly but firmly.

"Let's get you in the shade before you get sunburned on top of being sick." It took some finessing to get him to agree to move, but we settled against a tree trunk, and there we remained until Foxy came looking for us. We trekked to the house, where Foxy made Vance drink another glass of water and offered him a slice of bread. When it stayed down, she concluded that he was fit to drive home. It was tempting to send him home nearly naked, but I gave in and found him something of Pa's to wear.

The following Saturday, Vance showed up in a totally different getup to crop tobacco—a bright-yellow rainsuit and matching rubber gloves. Pa commented that if nothing else, Vance at least provided entertainment for the rest of us.

By the end of the summer, the sports car had been replaced with a pickup truck and the sneakers for work boots. Calluses formed on his palms, but they still felt pretty nice when caressing my cheeks. Vance had only changed in appearance. Knowing he did that for me had left me dealing with a mix of elation and guilt, because the voice in the back of my mind kept reminding me he could do a lot better than the likes of me.

If only Foxy could mix up an elixir to cure lovesickness as easily as she did for Vance's tobacco sickness that day, I'd guzzle it by the gallon. But there were no herbs or potions, and the longer I fought against it, the harder I fell in love with that carefree boy. He was sunshine in rain. A cool breeze on a humid day. A constellation of stars wiggling past a cloudy night.

My reality was nothing like that, and so it was inevitable for my stormy life to ruin his. But at only sixteen, I did what most teens would do. I selfishly ignored it until it was too late.

Chapter 7

DUSTING OFF MEMORIES
WHILE MAKING
NEW ONES

January 1984

Fashion in the Foster house was defined by having everyone dressed in the right sizes, with no inappropriate body parts on display. Color, cut, and style meant very little to me. All in all, I kept my siblings decently outfitted, which was no easy task with the growth spurts that were arriving in frequent intervals lately. Trips to the department store seemed to always be on my to-do list.

At least my clothing needs could mostly be met by rummaging around in Mama's drawers and her side of the closet. Pa hadn't done away with anything of hers but didn't seem to mind that some of her things had walked off. Each of us children had, at some point in the last three years, snuck in and swiped a memory.

Boss kept Mama's robe tucked underneath his pillow. Raleigh had a mostly empty bottle of her honeysuckle lotion sitting on top of his dresser. I'd caught a glimpse of him sniffing it a time or two on shadowy Pa days, with his patchwork baby blanket clutched to his chest. It was the same blanket made by Mama that we older children had been swaddled in until Raleigh claimed it and wouldn't let it move past his infant season. We all grieved for Mama and dealt with Pa's madness in private ways, so I'd always backed away from his bedroom door without saying a word. I had placed several framed pictures of Mama around the younger twins' room, so they would at least know what she looked like. I knew Peg had swiped something, but I'd yet to discover what it was, and he wouldn't let it be known unless he wanted to, anyway.

Earlier today, I'd ventured into the small selection of dresses in my parents' closet for the first time, and I was still uncertain that it was a good idea as I fastened the last of the tiny pearl buttons lining the front of the ankle-length dress. The bodice was fitted and the skirt flared, giving the illusion that my boyish frame held a few feminine curves. I smoothed a palm over the silky material and angled sideways to inspect myself in the antique cheval mirror in the corner of Charlotte's room. The mirror was her item of choice that had belonged to Mama and I thought it was fitting for my prissy sister to have it.

"It's very festive," Charlotte commented.

I gave the red dress with tiny white polka dots one last look before turning to find six sets of gawking eyes trained on me. Giving myself another once-over in the mirror, I found nothing out of place. The dress was buttoned properly and the hem wasn't hung up in the back of my panties. The bobby pins were still holding the braided bun softly in place at the nape of my neck. The light dusting of blush and one swipe of mascara was the only makeup I allowed Charlotte to put on me, so there was no clown resemblance.

I turned to the wide-eyed bunch and held my arms out. "What?"

"You look like a real lady," Raleigh answered, awe and wonder in his voice.

Nash tugged on the skirt to get my attention. "You real purty."

A natural blush joined the cosmetic one on my cheeks. "Thank you." I knelt down and kissed his forehead. Knox wandered over for a kiss too and then the next thing I knew, each of my silly siblings lined up and I gladly gave out kisses. Affection wasn't my strong suit, but the more Vance held my hand and pulled me in for hugs, the more I understood just how much my siblings were in need of it. I still hadn't granted Vance that kiss he kept teasing about, but I was glad he kept coming around all summer and fall, even once he got busy with the big class load he was taking at the community college. I still figured it couldn't last, but I decided to just enjoy it while it did.

Feeling light and carefree, I gave in to the silly notion to twirl, sending the dress skirt to flare like an open umbrella and making the little twins giggle. I curtsied like a *real* lady before shoving my feet in my sandals.

Charlotte clucked her tongue. "You can't wear Birkenstocks with a nice dress like that."

Peg crossed his arms in disapproval. "Especially when you're having dinner with the mayor."

The others threw in their two cents.

I held my palms up to hush them. "It's either these—" I kicked the Birkenstocks off and stepped into a pair of mile-high platform wedges, black suede with a thick cork base, that sent me towering over them—"or these things that make me look like a giant." I mimicked Frankenstein, stomping around in the monstrosities with my arms flapping in front of me. The twins squealed while darting out of my path.

"Mama didn't have anything else dressier?" Charlotte asked.

I wiggled out of the platforms, stepping way down to meet the floor. "I thought she had a pair of black heels but I can't find them."

Charlotte picked up one of the wedges and examined it. "I wonder if these float?" she asked, reading my mind about their resemblance to boats.

I snickered. "Probably as good as that red wagon." My comment had Peg grumbling behind me.

She dropped the shoe and it landed with a loud thud. "Can you borrow a pair from Foxy?"

"My foot is two sizes bigger than hers, so no." I lifted a shoulder and sighed before returning to the Birkenstocks.

"No!" Charlotte protested.

We went back and forth, annoying Peg to the point that he stomped out of the room. It was a wonder he'd stuck around that long.

I had one sandal on and was playing tug-of-war with Charlotte for the other when Peg reappeared. He thrust a dusty pair of black leather heels my way. I let go of the Birkenstock and accepted them, sending my sister flailing backwards until Boss caught her.

"Whatcha got those for, Peg? You can't wear 'em with only one good foot," Boss pointed out.

Peg's face turned pink, but it didn't appear to be from what Boss mentioned. After giving the shoes a meaningful look, he lowered his head until the mess of brown hair flopped into his eyes. "I remember the day Pa brought them home to Mama. She stopped washing dishes, sat right on the kitchen floor, and put them on. Then Pa danced her around the living room." Peg offered a sad smile, pinning his watery gaze on the shoes once again. "It was a happy day."

I swallowed the knot of sentiments building in my throat. "I remember. It was a very happy day. Thank you for letting me borrow the shoes. I'll return them as soon as I get home tonight."

Peg took one from my grasp and used his shirttail to wipe away the dust. He handed it back and did the same with the other shoe. Sniffing, he shook his head. "Keep them. . . . Just promise me you'll make a happy memory while wearing them tonight. I . . ." He stopped, batted a tear away, and coughed. "I think Mama would really like if you did that."

I placed the shoes gently on the floor and wrapped my arms around him, holding on tight. The others joined in, creating a big circle of shared embraces and sniffles. We remained that way until a flatulent noise broke us apart.

"Eww . . . ," Charlotte screeched. "You boys are so gross!"

"I couldn't help it. Y'all squeezed too hard!" Raleigh whined, sending a sputtering of laughter to follow the crowd out of my sister's room.

By the time we made it downstairs, Foxy and Jinx were at the door. I motioned them in and turned to gather Mama's white shawl and the bag holding gifts for Vance's parents.

"Foxy, you sure you don't mind watching the twins?"

"I don't mind a bit since Peg and Raleigh will be the ones actually watching them," Foxy answered in her dry tone and the wink that always followed it. "Boss and Jinx will help too." She and Jinx were taking the boys—and the Silver Bullet—to their house for the evening. Vance would drop me off there and I'd bring them all home later. Charlotte had been invited to spend the night at Miss Wise's house. Even though everyone was squared away for the evening, I was still hesitant.

"I should be home by eleven," I reassured Foxy while shrugging the shawl over my shoulders.

Foxy helped straighten the shawl. "If you're home before midnight, I'll be mighty disappointed in you."

I whirled around. "Midnight?"

"Yes. Make the most of your New Year's Day. It won't hurt you to act your age for once."

Each of the boys filed past me, giving my cheek a kiss before heading out to load up in the limo. Jinx was their designated chauffeur for the night.

"I thought I did act my age," I said absently, leaning out the door to peer down the driveway. Headlights crawling my way sent a smile to my lips. "Charlotte, Vance will be here soon!" I yelled toward the stairs.

Foxy scoffed. "No. You act like a forty-year-old mama."

"Yeah, well, I feel like one most days." I opened the bag to make sure I had everything.

"What all do you have in there?" Foxy leaned over to peek inside.

I held up a long rectangular box, beautifully wrapped in gold and silver. "These are peanut butter–filled bonbons that I helped Miss Wise eat, I mean make . . ." I replaced it inside and tapped the tops of two jars with a red plaid circle of fabric and green ribbon dressing each lid. "A jar of the strawberry preserves and a jar of the blackberry preserves you and I made."

"Very nice. You must really want to impress them." Foxy glanced out the window at the growing headlights. "Where's your father?"

"He . . ." I paused when Charlotte started down the stairs. "He had some errands to run." I told her the bold-faced lie, knowing Foxy wouldn't believe it. Today was Sunday, and Pa never ran errands on Sundays. Last week he announced there wouldn't be a service today due to the holiday, but it was just an excuse in my opinion. He'd been finding reasons to cancel services quite a bit lately.

Before Mama died, New Year's Day was always the day Pa set aside to spend with her, mostly snuggled on the couch, saying he wanted to be doing just that for the rest of the year. Since her death, he'd continued spending New Year's Day with her, but instead of snuggling, he hunched over her grave. I'd gone out to the cemetery earlier to encourage him to head back to the farm, but with a heavy fog overtaking him there was no getting through to him. Selfish as it was, I didn't want to cancel my plans with Vance or ruin Charlotte's plans. Miss Wise's house had become a safe haven for my sister.

Foxy eyed me, her purple-glossed lips in a firm line. She knew something was up and was already putting up her defenses to stay away from it.

"Okay, then. So the rules for my night are . . ." I held a finger up for each. "Don't act my age, break curfew, and what else?" I asked, wanting to lighten things up.

The firm line curled into a grin. "Oh, honey. Dressed like that, I expect you to let that good-looking fella steal a few kisses." Foxy winked again, and all was well, except for the flutters seizing my belly at her suggestion.

The pickup truck finally came to a stop in front of the house. I wouldn't admit it to Vance, but I wished he'd kept the fancy car. He stepped out and closed the door. Looking up to where Foxy and I were standing on the porch, he slapped a palm to his chest and staggered into the side of the truck.

"Mercy!" He braced a hand against the hood and pulled in an exaggerated breath. "Austin Foster, you tryin' to kill me?"

Foxy snickered at the handsome goofball. "If you don't make out with him tonight, you're grounded," she whispered near my ear before moving down the steps. "Vance, sugar, show my girl a good time tonight, will ya?"

"I'll do my best." He tipped his head toward her and backtracked to the truck. He reached inside the cab, then beelined to the Silver Bullet, idly waiting for Foxy to get in. He handed Jinx a brown bag, and voices of excitement rang out from the limo.

As the limo drove toward Foxy's place, Vance turned toward

me and straightened his shoulders as if he were preparing for battle. In a white dress shirt and gray slacks, he looked more ready for a cocktail party or board meeting.

"Austin, Austin, Austin . . . you look so, so lovely tonight." As a raspy groan rumbled up from his throat, Vance placed his palm to my cheek. "Making me fall hard, babe."

I popped his chest with very little force and said with no conviction, "Knock it off."

Charlotte hurried between us. "Stop mooning over each other and take me to Miss Wise's already."

Vance took her bag and guided Charlotte to the passenger side of the truck. "Yes, ma'am, but with your sister all dolled up, I can't help mooning over her."

Vance and that blunt tongue of his . . .

Charlotte stopped by the door, waiting for me to get in first, and gave me a once-over. "Vance, if you didn't moon over her tonight, I'd think something was seriously wrong with you."

I rolled my eyes at her before climbing inside the cab. It was no hardship sitting in the middle on the ride over to Miss Wise's house. Close enough to Vance to enjoy the subtle scent of his cologne and the warmth of his hand as it held mine.

"So, Miss Charlotte, we're taking you to the church-spitting lady?" Vance made a left at the end of our driveway, heading toward town.

Charlotte scoffed. "Miss Wise doesn't do that anymore."

"Yeah?" Vance kept his eyes on the road and squeezed my hand. The stinker had to have already known that, considering he'd become a regular at Sunday services after the election. He'd even joined us for dinner afterwards on Pa's good days.

I squeezed his hand in return. "Yes. She's made peace with some stuff and says she's not going to hold it against God anymore."

"She's a Holy Cost survivor," Charlotte piped in.

"Holocaust," I corrected.

"Really?" Vance asked in a serious tone.

"She doesn't broadcast it, but yes."

"I just wrote a ten-page paper on that for my world history class. Man, that research tore me up." Vance sighed. "I really wish I'd known that. You think she'd speak with me sometime?" He glanced quickly at me before turning in to her driveway.

"I'll ask, but it's doubtful. It took her a long time to open up to me."

"She doesn't shake as bad as she used to when we talk about it," Charlotte supplied. "I think it's done her good to talk."

"Then I'll ask her when I come to pick you up tomorrow." I gave Charlotte a side hug as she opened the door.

"Have fun tonight, Austin." She placed a quick kiss on my cheek and darted out the truck.

Vance hopped out, collected her bag for her, and walked her to the door, where Miss Wise was already peeping out. She lifted her hand and waved in my direction. I waved back and settled into Charlotte's spot by the door, smiling to myself. It had been a long, bittersweet journey to find friendship with that woman, but the journey had been worth it.

After spending a few moments chatting, Vance returned to the truck. He gave me a measured look before reaching over and looping an arm around my hip. One swift tug returned me to my original spot in the middle of the bench seat, closely tucked beside him. The thrill of his affection had me near about giggling like a foolish girl.

This is what acting my age feels like, and I like it.

"So . . . tell me about this lake house?" I asked as Vance reversed out of the driveway.

"It's on Lake Murray. We do so many public events during the holidays that Mom declared New Year's Day the official Cumberland Thanksgiving/Christmas redo. This is our private celebration. No cameras, no guests, no servants. Just the three of us."

"I'm crashing your private family holiday?" All those sappy feelings froze midflight and fell flat in my stomach. Before I could slide over to the passenger window, Vance stopped me by holding my hand.

"Don't even start this mess, Austin. It was my parents' idea to invite you. They want a chance to get to know you privately and thought you'd be more comfortable meeting them for the first time away from the public." He lifted our entwined hands and placed a kiss on the back of mine, giving me a brief glance before resetting his focus on the road. "You are very important to me and that automatically makes you important to them, so you can go ahead and put away the defenses."

I swallowed and took a deep breath, holding it a few beats before releasing it. This guy was from a different world than me, yet we shared a key similarity of having to grow up before our time. Him, due to family tradition and expectation. Me, from family tragedy and no other choice. Sure, he hid behind those irresistible dimples and wild blond curls, but Vance Cumberland was a man. And I was a woman, albeit a young one, who was about to officially meet his extremely important, slightly famous family.

Putting the title of mayor to the side, there was still an impressive history of an accomplished family dynasty. On a library visit or two, I'd done my research on the Cumberlands' background. Old money, ties to the Kennedys, and a financial firm that Vance's father had started over twenty years ago. Edward had his brother take over the reins temporarily so he could dabble in town politics. Shoot, even Vance's mother had a legacy all on her own. The former Miss South Carolina came from a political family and was active in charitable causes for women and children. Definitely a power couple.

I tried not to dwell on it, but there was no way not to recognize the fact that Vance was the sole heir to all of it. It made me more aware of my inadequacies and question why on earth he was wasting his time with a nobody such as myself.

Again, I tried brushing the worries off for at least one night and settled against Vance's side. When he took a few detours to show me some spectacular Christmas light displays, the worries were all but forgotten. His childlike reaction to seeing lights and decor was contagious, and his warmth and cologne helped erase the anxiety.

But by the time he pulled into his parents' circle drive, the truths about my inadequacies slammed into me full force once again. How naive I was to think we were going to arrive at a small cabin on the water. Nope. The gate we had to enter to even get to the property should have been an indicator to what was ahead, but nothing had prepared me for the redbrick, white-columned monstrosity. Thousands of white Christmas lights highlighted the three-story waterfront mansion.

"Are you kidding me?"

"It's old, but we like it." Vance shrugged, as serious as could be, and put the truck in park.

The structure before us could be considered an antique, refined and well-kept. But not *old*. No, *old* was my family's farmhouse, where even the small boxed rooms couldn't prevent the cool winter air from seeping through the seams, where more floorboards creaked than not and windows stuck and door hinges groaned. Chipped paint, sagging porch . . . I could go on and on.

Shutting the engine off, Vance opened the driver's door and exited before offering me his hand to exit from his side as well. "You're forgetting the gift bag," he reminded once my feet were on the ground, the heels of my shoes clinking against the stone pavers.

I eyed the bag and considered the meager gifts inside, knowing nothing I could offer would reach anywhere near the standards I'd been thrown into. Vance didn't allow me the chance to figure out an excuse to leave it. He simply reached past me and plucked it from the floorboard.

"There you are. It's about time," Mrs. Cumberland called from the brick staircase leading to the double front doors. All of it was dressed with real garland and burgundy velvet bows.

"I had to show Austin the Christmas lights," Vance told her as he began leading me up the steps at a fast pace. *Click, click,*

click, my shoes continued in a rapid beat, matching the pounding of my heart.

"Ooh! Did you take her down Duke Road?"

"Yes, ma'am."

My mouth remained on mute, even when she stepped forward and wrapped her arms around me. For a petite lady, Mrs. Cumberland packed a punch and had me stumbling a bit before catching my balance.

"Austin, it's so nice to finally meet you." She patted my back and leaned away. Eyes the same color as her son's took me in. "Vance has told us so much about you." Then she moved in for another embrace.

Clearing my throat, I said, "It's nice to meet you too, Mrs. Cumberland." Even though I towered over her, the lady was intimidating.

"Please call me Maggie, sweetheart." She offered another pat and finally released me to gesture toward Vance's father, who'd appeared on the porch at some point during our embrace. He was dressed similar to Vance, but with a suit jacket and red tie. "And this is Ed. Call him *Ed*."

Chuckling, Ed extended his hand and offered a polite handshake. "Nice to meet you, young lady."

I returned the handshake with a firm grasp, hoping he didn't notice the calluses or uneven fingernails, before letting go. "You too, sir."

Introductions finished, we finally moved inside the mansion, entering a foyer bigger than my living room and kitchen combined. Shiny wood floors with no creaks and intricately detailed wallpaper that looked more like tapestry than paper.

Even a fancy coat closet off to the left of the door where Vance hung my shawl. We only had an overloaded coat hook on the wall at home.

The crinkled gift bag dangling from Vance's fingers looked as out of place as I did, but I was an invited guest and would extend my humble gift along with the Southern manners Mama had instilled in me.

I took the gift bag from Vance and handed it to Maggie. "Happy holidays."

"Oh, you shouldn't have." Maggie smiled warmly, and I expected her to drop it on the round table centered in the middle of the foyer and continue on. She did place it on the table but only so she could plunder inside the bag with more ease.

"Those are homemade preserves," I explained when she pulled the jars out and inspected them.

"Austin, dear, this is so thoughtful and will be perfect with the biscuits I've made." She retrieved the box of candies next.

"Vance told me that you both are big fans of peanut butter." I began nervously rambling, filling them in on making the chocolates with Miss Wise and her being a classically trained chocolatier.

We stood around the round table with a fancy floral centerpiece as Maggie handed out the chocolates. Her enthusiasm and sincere appreciation for my "thoughtful gifts," as she described them, had my shoulders beginning to relax.

"I could eat the entire box, but perhaps we should have dinner first," Ed commented. He led us to the dining room with a table long enough to seat my entire family with chairs to spare. The surface was dressed in a white lace tablecloth, white-and-gold china with matching platters and serving bowls brimming with a holiday feast. Prime rib roast, mashed potatoes, gravy, whole green beans, and more than I could take in.

Ed led us in prayer and then worked on carving the roast, fork-tender by the looks of the knife slicing through it like butter.

The food was delicious and the ease with which Vance continuously touched me was even more delicious. Throughout the meal, his hand would rest on my knee or on the back of my chair, with his fingers pressed along my neck. He would reach over and squeeze my hand while sharing something about me with his parents. His comfort with showing affection in front of his parents seemed to make our relationship more genuine, as if we were more than just a pretense.

"What are your plans after graduation this spring?" Ed's formal tone made his question sound more on the lines of a job interview than dinner conversation.

"Oh. I won't be graduating in the spring." I took a nervous bite and focused on the gold rimming my water glass.

"Why not?" Vance spoke up.

I chanced a brief glance his way and found a look of curiosity holding tightly to his features. "I, uh, I had enough credits and so the school allowed me to finish before Christmas."

"So you've already graduated?" Vance didn't seem to believe me.

"Yes," I answered slowly, meeting his narrowed eyes with a glare. "I can show you my diploma when you take me home."

Maggie cut in. "Well, that's a rather impressive achievement, Austin."

I blinked away from Vance's stern stare and looked at his mother across the table. "Thank you, ma'am."

"What college have you chosen to attend?" Ed inquired before taking a sip from his glass.

"I won't be attending college." I spoke to my plate.

"Why not?" Vance repeated.

Defensive and a little irritated, I sat up straighter. "I have family duties just as you do. Mine are to help run the farm and to take care of my siblings." I fixed my attention on his father. "We're implementing some big changes at Nolia Farms this season."

That was the beginning line to a long-winded spiel about decreasing our tobacco crops to begin producing more soybeans, which was a rising movement in agriculture due to all of the health risks surrounding tobacco use. I then carried on about crop rotation and ways we were cutting down on pesticides. His parents were generous enough to act enthralled, but Vance didn't even try hiding his disinterest. He seemed offended for some reason.

"Sustainability and being more kind to the land is in the forefront," I concluded and had to refrain from smacking myself on the forehead for suddenly sounding like a salesman.

"Soybeans are a smart route. Corn and cotton are replacing a lot of tobacco fields also," Ed added.

I nodded in agreement, thinking about the tizzy Jinx got worked into when Pa had mentioned cotton. He said it would be offensive to his ancestors if he did, but Pa checked the label of Jinx's shirt that declared it 100 percent cotton. Then Pa pointed out how Jinx could honor his ancestors by working side by side with him, showing the world how they were equals. Jinx didn't much buy it, so we were sticking with soybeans for the season.

Vance sighed several times during my discussion with Ed but said nothing. Then it was my turn to stew after complimenting the Cumberlands' lake house.

"It's always been Vance's favorite home, which makes it perfect that he'll be moving in before the spring semester begins." Maggie doled out this tidbit along with an extra helping of potatoes.

Appetite gone, I poked my fork into the potatoes before setting it down. "Moving?"

"For school," Maggie answered for her son. "He'll stay here instead of in the dorms at USC."

"I'm transferring there," Vance clarified, but it still didn't make any sense to me.

"Transferring?"

"My Vance gave up a semester to stay near home for Ed's election. He certainly knows about family duty as you mentioned." Maggie smiled warmly at me and took a dainty bite.

"It makes sense to live here. It's only about thirty minutes from Magnolia one way and about the same distance to Columbia the other." Vance brushed his hand against mine but I moved it to grab my glass of water.

"What's wrong with the community college you're attending now?" I directed the question in almost a whisper to Vance, but his father beat him to the answer.

"USC is a Cumberland family tradition. It also has the top business program in the state." Ed's chest seemed to puff up with pride. "Vance will be best prepared to take over Cumberland Finance."

I smiled, or I tried to, anyway. Truthfully, I had no room to be let down by his opportunity in Columbia any more than he did about me not attending school at all.

Dinner concluded not much later after those bombs were dropped. Dessert was served in a large yet cozy den with wall-to-wall windows that showcased the moon glancing off the subtle ripples on the lake. Thankfully, no one noticed or at least drew attention to the fact that I didn't touch my slice of pecan pie.

"We're meeting the Hortons next door for nightcaps, Vance. Would you and Austin like to join us?"

"No thank you. I'll need to take her home in a little while. I thought she and I could hang out here until then." Vance stood from the leather couch we were sharing in front of the crackling fireplace and offered his hand to help me to my feet.

"Austin, sweetheart, we'll have to do this again soon." Maggie gave me a hug and Ed offered another handshake.

"Thank you for the lovely meal." My voice sounded wooden to my own ears, but again his parents appeared to be oblivious to it. I'm sure it's some sort of political social trait not to draw attention to odd behavior.

As soon as we were alone, I moved away from Vance and stood by the long windows. His reflection joined mine, followed by the heat of his body against my back. He wrapped his confident arms around my waist and pulled me close to his chest as his chin settled on my shoulder. With similar heights, we fit perfectly. Too perfectly in fact, considering we were so different.

"I'm ready to go home." I took a side step but he eliminated the space just as quickly, returning me to the protection of his warmth. I hated how much I loved being right there in it.

Vance gently squeezed my hip. "Why?"

My throat felt too thick to answer, so I fixed my gaze on the rippling water past the window and remained silent.

"You're mad. Why?"

My eyes became itchy. Swallowing that nonsense down, I whispered, "Why didn't you tell me about transferring to Columbia?"

"I planned on telling you, but you've had . . . a lot going on. And it's not a big deal. It's not like I'm moving hours away. Just minutes, really."

Spending so much time out at the farm the past few months, Vance had caught the tail end of a couple of Pa's episodes. Maybe having some distance wouldn't be such a bad thing. At least it would be easier to keep Pa's issues tucked out of sight. I'd have to keep telling myself that until the ache in my throat and chest alleviated.

His heavy huff pushed past my shoulder and fogged the window. "You're one to talk. Did you have any plans on telling me you quit school?"

I tried pushing him off, but he wasn't having it. "I didn't quit. I graduated early."

"What about college?"

"I already told you college isn't a part of my plan. I have the farm to help run and children to take care of." My eyes began to sting again, so I sniffed real hard to tamp it down.

We grew quiet. The only sounds echoing in the den were the popping and hissing of the fire and my silly sniffles. I'd not properly cried since Mama died and was annoyed that I was this close to bawling over a boy, no less.

"They say what you do on New Year's Day, you do the rest of the year." His words tickled the side of my neck as he nuzzled closer. "Austin, I don't want us arguing the rest of the year."

Even though our differences and the impossibility of us overcoming them weighed heavily in my thoughts, Foxy's orders from earlier talked over it. For once, I wanted to act my age just as she had suggested, even if that meant a lot of pretending. I wanted to pretend my only issue past that moment in Vance's arms was getting caught by his parents.

I slowly turned around and met his crestfallen eyes. "Then I want to spend the rest of the year kissing you."

Vance's head inclined back but quickly returned forward with a hungry smile curving his full lips. "Do you now?"

I shrugged and downplayed the frenzy of excitement wreaking havoc inside me. "Yeah. Sure. Might as well get it over with."

His low rumble of laughter echoed around us. Dimples on display and those glorious green eyes squinting with mischief. Danged if he wasn't the most handsome guy ever. "You've certainly made me wait long enough for something that you want to just *get it over with.*"

I smoothed the crisp collar of his shirt and warned, *"Vance."*

"Just so we're clear, I guarantee you won't ever get over me kissing you." He placed a finger against my lips to hold in my retort. "And I won't ever be getting over it either." Vance slid his finger away from my lips, feathering along my cheek before coming to a halt to cup the back of my neck, just under the loose bun. He used this hold to gently tilt and angle my head as he leaned toward me. Warm breath met my lips. "There's just no getting over you, Austin Foster."

My entire body trembled when the heat of his breath was replaced by the cool of his lips. It was just a delicate press to the corner of my mouth. Then he repeated the action against the center of my lips. I'd pressed this exact same kiss to my siblings' cheeks or foreheads, but never did it leave me dizzy. I returned the gentle press, but when Vance changed the angle and deepened the kiss, the only thing I could do was follow his lead.

This! This was dessert. The most indulgent dessert I'd ever tasted. And as he leaned away to end the kiss, I insisted on a second helping. If I was going to act my age for just one night, I was adamant about enjoying my fill of Vance Cumberland's lips. And boy, was he in a giving mood.

After a gluttonous amount of kissing, we agreed it was best to stop while we were ahead. The ride home was mainly silent. I sat beside Vance, holding his hand, relishing the newly experienced tingle on my lips that sort of reminded me of chapped lips but in a pleasant way.

"If you keep licking your lips like that, I'm gonna have to

pull the truck over." Vance brought our entwined hands to his mouth and placed a kiss on the back of mine.

I giggled like a lovesick fool. "We're on my driveway. You're gonna pull over in the field?"

He smiled against my skin, placing another kiss before dropping our hands to rest on my lap. "I will if I have to."

Snickering, I sassed, "Don't even think you're rounding the bases with me, Vance Cumberland. First base is as far as this is going."

Vance's charming grin dropped, his handsome face growing sincere in the glowing lights from the dashboard. "I'm not looking at stealing second or third or playing any sort of game with you, Miss Austin. And the only home I'm interested in is making one with you someday. I want a future with you. Don't you get that by now?"

Face in flames, I liked the sound of that way too much. I bit my lip to tame the grin, but nothing could contain it during the bumpy ride down the old farm road.

A song came on the radio, catching my attention. "Ooh, will you turn it up?"

"You like this song?" Vance did as I asked, smiling as he glanced over at me.

I stopped humming along. "Yes. I think it's called 'Heaven' by Bryan Adams."

Vance put the truck in park and hopped out. He rounded the front of the truck, his form flashing in the beams of the headlights. My door opened and then he was helping me get out.

I giggled. "What are you doing?"

"Dancing with my lady." Vance wrapped my arms around

his neck and then placed his hands on my hips, swaying us to the slow melody.

We danced quietly, listening to the angsty lyrics about love lighting the way and being all that we needed.

"I think this should be our song."

I lifted my head and our gazes connected, much the way I felt our hearts had. Natural, as if it were meant to happen all along. "I think you're right."

Vance's head tilted back as he chuckled. "Finally she admits I'm right about something." He angled forward and gave me a soft kiss as the song concluded. Too bad there was no way to set the radio on repeat.

Before we let go, "Girls Just Want to Have Fun" came on, sending Vance into a silly hip-swinging dance with his hands lifted in the air. He pranced around me in the dark as I could do nothing but stand there and laugh.

"I love your laugh, Austin Foster!" Vance nearly sang his words, so carefree and sweetly boyish. "I wish you would do it more often!" He danced over and gave me a popping kiss, making me laugh more.

Truly, it felt good to just laugh and be silly. Life hadn't afforded me many lighthearted moments, so I indulged in it until the song came to an end.

It was over too soon and we left the dance party and returned to the truck.

As soon as he had parked in front of Foxy's house, Vance angled toward me and sighed. It was as if the gesture pushed away the giddiness to bring the seriousness front and center. "We'll be just fine with me living a little farther down the road,

Austin. Heck, now that I'll have my own place, we'll finally be able to spend time alone together. We're always surrounded by lots of people, so doesn't that sound appealing?"

I fiddled with the fringe on my shawl. "You might figure out you don't like me all that much if it's just the two of us."

"I think we already proved tonight that I like you even more when it's just the two of us." He waggled his eyebrows, and just like that, the heaviness dissipated.

I elbowed his side and started scooting to the passenger side, but that only spurred a goofy wrestling match between us that ended up with another serving of sweet kisses.

Lost in the feel of Vance's soft lips moving over mine, the tapping on the window scared the tar out of me. Planting a palm to his face, I shoved him away and turned to see Foxy staring at me. The full moon glanced off her smirk and seemed to illuminate the lavender head wrap tied perfectly around her head. I opened the door and moved to climb out, but she stopped me.

"Everyone is asleep. Jinx will bring them home first thing in the morning." Foxy made a shooing motion and leaned around me to eye Vance. "My girl is allowed to kiss you, but you better not even think about going anywhere near her virtue."

"I'm a perfect gentleman, Miss Foxy. Austin's virtue is safe with me." Vance winked, so full of himself. "I promise." He tipped his head overconfidently. *The arrogant doofus.*

Foxy regarded him coolly. "You break that promise and I may have to learn some of that voodoo this town accuses me of knowing and cast something on your cute behind."

After a few rounds of teasing with Foxy and then a firm

promise to behave, Vance took me home. Even walking me to the front door for one more kiss.

With my fingers pressed to my smiling lips, I stood on the porch and watched the truck disappear down the drive before heading inside. The faint crooning of "Have You Ever Seen the Rain" drifted toward me as soon as I closed the door. Holding my breath, I stood still to see if any other sounds would register. Nothing but the chorus, so I released the lungful of air on a heavy sigh and moved to the living room to see what form of Pa awaited.

He sat slumped on the couch, head leaned back, eyes closed. At first I thought he was asleep, but then his lips began to barely move as he sang along quietly. I took a step back, hoping to slink off to bed undetected just as his eyes opened to half-mast, halting my getaway.

"Hey." Pa's rusty voice made me jump. He lifted his head and took in my outfit. Lips tugging in a heavy grimace and brow puckered severely, it was evident the sight of me hurt him.

I pulled the sagging shawl up my shoulders and wrapped it tightly around my torso to shield him from the pain of seeing me wearing Mama's dress. "Hey."

"Finally decided to come home, huh?" He rubbed the heels of his hands against the dark smudges underneath bloodshot eyes. He'd spent the last week in continuous motion, not even slowing down enough for sleep. Like a jolly machine raring to go and declaring things needed to get done. At first it was to repair a few floorboards after taking out the Christmas tree and noticing a water ring. Then it escalated until half of the flooring was ripped out.

My eyes strayed across the room to the hole in the floor and the pile of planks by it, knowing I'd have to figure out how to get the floor relaid before the planks wandered off to never be seen again like the kitchen cabinet doors. I was beginning to worry that Pa's ultimate goal might be to slowly tear down the entire house, both literally and figuratively.

"Yeah. I'm home." I glanced at the clock, relieved to see it was two minutes past midnight, which meant it was no longer New Year's Day. It gave me a flimsy hope that I wouldn't be standing in front of the brokenness of my father for the rest of the year.

Pa reached over to the turntable beside the couch and replaced the needle on the record to start the song over. He'd done it so many times, he hit the spot between songs with precision. His movements were so slow it was as if his muscles and bones were half-frozen, so I knew he was crashing and taking my flimsy hope down with him.

"It's late, so . . ." I retracted a step.

Pa unfolded his brawny form from the couch and held out a hand. "Just one dance first."

Recalling a happier time when Pa taught me and Charlotte how to dance one afternoon right in the middle of a tobacco field, I accepted his invitation and the tension eased from my shoulders. We'd not danced since Mama's passing, but the gesture was so familiar we fell right into step like second nature.

After making a turn around the room, Pa dipped me playfully and brought sweet memories to the surface of when our family was whole. When Pa was whole.

"Charlotte would be so jealous if she knew we were dancing

without her," I said on a giggle, evoking another happier moment where my sister and I wriggled between our parents one night to steal a dance with Pa. He had a way back then of making each of us feel like we were the most important girl in the world.

Pa's chest rumbled with a chuckle but it didn't reach his somber face. "What Charlotte and Austin don't know won't hurt them."

"Pa?" I slowed the already-slow dance. "*I'm* Austin."

He blinked sluggishly, narrowed his eyes, and sighed with acute disappointment. "Of course you are." His bottom lip trembled as he stared past me.

We made another slow turn before Pa reached over and restarted the somber song. Between that and Pa confusing me with Mama, I was close to splintering into pieces just like the pile of flooring.

"You ever hear of bloodletting?" Pa asked out of nowhere, snapping me from my inner turmoil.

I looked up and found his expression serious. "Umm . . . no, sir. You?"

He nodded. "The guys at the hardware store were talking about it the other day. One of 'em saw some documentary about it. Said in the olden days, doctors would withdraw blood from sick patients because their health was off-balanced or something . . . Bloodletting righted it."

I didn't know what I was supposed to say to that, so I said nothing. Just continued letting Pa lead me in this awkward dance as my body tautened with anxiety tighter than an overstretched rubber band. One that was ready to snap at any moment.

The glassiness of Pa's eyes intensified. "I'd imagine it would be quite a relief to purge out impurities with just a simple cut ... and feel right." His voice trailed off for a few beats. "Don't ya think?"

What I thought was Pa needed to stop his visits to the hardware store. I made a mental note to add hardware store supply runs to my to-do list even though that list was already to the point of making me buckle under the load of it. It's why I rushed to finish school. It was either that or just drop out, because something had to give.

Clearing my throat, I finally commented, "I don't think bloodletting is in practice nowadays."

"Maybe. Still think it would be worth checking into."

"Maybe it would be better to go talk to a doctor about you not feeling balanced," I suggested.

Pa deflated, shoulders sagging from a weight I would never completely understand. It appeared my realistic advice robbed him of some delusional hope he seemed to have found in a morbid, outdated practice. He let go of me, and with a sluggish flick of his hand, the needle screeched across the vinyl. Saying nothing else, he lumbered past me and drifted up the stairs to his room, where I knew he would remain for another dark spell.

Panic burned my chest as I switched off the record player and made my way toward the kitchen to put a Band-Aid on the gushing problem within the walls of this farmhouse.

Constantly glancing over my shoulder, I pilfered each and every knife from the drawers and dish strainer. Clutching them with shaking hands, I scanned the space for a safe hiding spot.

With no cabinet doors, the options were very limited. A giant roasting pan sitting on top of the fridge seemed as good an option as any, since we rarely used it.

I placed the bundle of knives on the counter as quietly as possible and pulled the pan down. Taking off the lid, I loaded the inside with the knives, cringing when one pinged off the side. Pausing stock-still, my eyes shot toward the doorway. When it remained empty after several staggered breaths, I finished my mission by replacing the top and shoving the pan back into place. Thinking better of it, I rummaged around until deciding on a few chipped coffee cups to line in front of the pan.

Out of sight, out of mind.

What a ridiculous notion, but one I took comfort in, none-theless.

After double-checking for any stray "bloodletting" tools, I took the stairs two at the time and locked myself in my room. I fumbled with the buttons on the dress, nearly coming unglued when the numbness and trembling in my fingers made it close to impossible to unfasten them.

Somehow I managed to change into a sweatshirt and jeans. In a blink, I found myself in the packhouse loft, staring at the maps glued to the wall like they would magically reveal the right direction I needed to take in this difficult life. When nothing but wasted time revealed I was too lost to be found, my body crumpled in a heap on the floor.

My thoughts began pinging all over the place. The odd mix of elation from my first kiss with Vance skipped around the confusing conversation with Pa. The sparkling water of the lake morphed into the sad pile of splintered flooring. The breathtaking, glittering Christmas lights Vance had shared with me, and the dull void of Pa's gaze when he realized I wasn't Mama. Everything I'd tried my darnedest to manage on my own suddenly intensified to the point of piercing through the barrier I'd built around myself.

Wrapping my arms around my knees, I gave in and allowed the pain to seep past my eyes, escaping down the contours of my cheeks and descending past the tip of my chin. The submission released a river of fear and uncertainty as my body rocked back and forth. It was violent and raw, like a wild animal being freed from the confines of its cage for the first time, and the only thing I could do was just sit in the violence of it until it chose to release me.

When it finally did, my shirt was drenched. I stared down at the mess, wondering if this was sort of like bloodletting. Was it possible to purge the soul of impurities through tears? Finally my eyes dried, and I knew they would remain that way for another long spell. And nothing about the deep-seated anger taking over my soul felt pure.

Chapter 8

SNAKE CHARMING

March 1984

Warm temperatures and newly developed blooms of all sorts proudly declared spring was in the air, the vivid sunshine and cloudless sky reiterating it. But the only thing in the air at Nolia Farms was attitude, of the nasty variety. Each one of us was carrying it around like the burden it was—shoulders slumped, feet dragging, heavy frowns. Talk about a sour bunch.

Me, especially, and my attitude was close to spilling out all over the place as I scrubbed water troughs that Peg's ornery behind was supposed to be cleaning. I'd just had it out with him after he mouthed off about chores for the umpteenth time. When I finished ripping him a new one, I expected my brother to do what was right and get to work. Instead, he'd slung a bag of chicken feed to the ground, spilling it all over the place, and said, "To heck with it all!" before storming off as fast as his gimp leg would let him. Seemed we were all at the end of our patience.

So Peg was sulking somewhere out of sight, Boss was lying down on the couch with an earache, Charlotte had snuck off to Miss Wise's, and I didn't even want to think about Pa and the useless state he was in at the moment. That only left Raleigh and the three-year-old twins to help get things done, which basically meant I was on my own since his hands were full with keeping an eye on the little ones.

On my own . . . always on my own, and I was getting right sick of it.

On that night back in January, something broke inside me and a bitterness had poured out of the wound. Vance happily packing up and moving did nothing but make that bitterness spread like an irritating rash. Shoot, I couldn't even stand myself most days lately. His school workload was hefty. When he managed to come home, it was for a family function that I didn't have time to attend. Our visits had become a hit-or-miss deal, and when he did show up, it was always accompanied with treats for the kids and lots of sweet-talking and sugared-up excuses for me. Something else I was right sick of.

Grumbling under my breath, I pushed Vance—and missing him—out of my thoughts for the moment so I could focus on washing the gunk off the goats' trough. The smell was just as sour as my attitude, reminding me of how long Peg had ignored this particular chore.

Peg came hobbling over again, and so I waited for him to

start the next round, but instead his face looked more per-
plexed than furious.

"What now?"

"You seen the new chicken coop?"

"Yeah." I dropped the scrub brush and grabbed the hose. I
doused the trough, sending a stream of green goop and suds
to puddle at my feet.

"No. I mean have you got a real good look at it?"

I picked up the scrub brush and held both it and the hose a
little higher. It was all I could do to not knock him upside the
head with the brush. "I ain't got time to inspect a lame chicken
coop since I'm stuck doing your chores!"

Peg yanked the brush out of my hand and sent it to the
ground. "You need to see this." He started toward the coop and
shouted over his shoulder, "For real, Ox!"

Resigned to go see what else mess awaited, I dropped the
hose and wiped my damp hands on the sides of my jeans before
following him. We came to a stop in front of the new structure
Pa had just completed last week on one of his whims. He'd
expanded on the old one and even added a second story to it.

"What?" I huffed.

"Notice anything about the wood he used?" Peg jabbed a
finger at it as if the coop was offensive.

Crossing my arms, I focused on the mismatched wood
slates. Squinting and angling closer, my eyes roved over it until
settling on a set of small holes in one of the slates and an outline showing where a hinge used to be. My breath hitched. "I'll
be danged." I was dumbfounded that the wood grain, which
matched the kitchen, hadn't caught my attention before now.

"The mystery of the kitchen cabinet doors is solved," Peg said with disdain instead of relief or amusement. For us, there certainly wasn't anything amusing about it.

It had been quite frustrating, though, not knowing where in the heck Pa had put those doors. Those things had went missing for more than a year, and I'd even lost sleep over it.

"Awesome detective skills, Peg." I leveled him with a stern glare and pointed toward the unfinished water troughs. "Now do you think you can make yourself *useful* and go do your chores?"

He muttered an oath, but I was too annoyed with Pa to worry about it. Instead I focused on the little nuisance who had just joined us and was now underfoot as I grabbed the slop bucket and stomped off to the pigpen.

"*These* are your people, Miss Priss. You should at least give them a chance." I opened the gate to the pigpen and motioned for Pixy to follow me, but the spoiled thing scooted in reverse instead. I crouched down and angled the slop bucket toward her, but she stuck her nose up at it. "This is Charlotte's fault," I mumbled, and she let out a snort of agreement.

Pixy Pig preferred canned dog food, bananas, Pixy Stix, and most any other type of candy. Her newest favorite was Miss Wise's cherry-filled bonbons that Charlotte liked to slip her while painting her hooves with nail polish.

I pointed to the rooting pigs, oinking away on the other side of the fence. "At least go speak to them."

Pixy snubbed her snout at the farm pigs like they were beneath her and pranced her neon-pink hoofed self toward the back porch, where her pillow bed was set up.

Shaking my head, I had just turned to wade into the pen when Raleigh started hollering from somewhere up front. Dropping the bucket, I rushed around the house and slowed as I caught sight of Pa on the front porch.

Catatonic, he sat motionless in the rocking chair, staring off into the distance of nothing. His formidable body was there, but his mind had checked out once again.

"Hurry, Ox!" Raleigh yelled.

"No problem," I sassed at my father with enough venom that should have had him off that porch to get ahold of me. "I'll take care of it like everything else around here! You just keep sitting there doing nothing to help out."

He didn't even blink.

"Ox!" Raleigh yelled again, waving both hands in the air while jumping up and down.

Huffing, I stormed in the direction of the equipment barn. As soon as I reached him, he grabbed my hand and led me to where several tractors were lined up below the overhang, pointing to the first tractor, which was parked cockeyed.

"What's wrong?" I asked, already peering over the side of it to see for myself. At first I thought I was looking at a coil of rope, but the rope hissed and sent the hairs on the back of my neck to stand on end.

From the diamond-shaped head and the clay-and-dirt banding, I was pretty sure it was a copperhead. Its forked tongue flickered out, pointing toward the sound of a whimper. Knox stood pressed against the barn wall, only a few feet away.

I'd warned the kids so many times about playing around the farm equipment, about the possibility of getting on a snake. It was not unusual to find them curled up in corners of the barns or underneath feed sacks. I'd made sure to instill a fearful respect for snakes, repeating a good bit about them being poisonous and how much they could hurt you. Sure, not all snakes are poisonous, but I didn't tell the kids that. I didn't want to chance them messing with any type of snake, period.

"Oh, Knox . . ." Fat tears rolled down his cheeks as his little body shook so severely that his brown hair had movement. "I'm gonna get you out, buddy. Don't move."

"What's all the fuss?" Peg complained, coming up behind us.

"Stay back," I warned as Raleigh whispered, "Snake." With my mind reeling, I hurried over to the tool rack, selected a flat-head shovel, and retraced my steps. "Peg, go tell Pa."

"Fat lot of good that's gonna do," Peg grumbled but hurried off anyway.

I eased over to the tractor, only to realize my arm span wouldn't allow me enough reach to behead the dang thing. Pa would be able to reach it, no problem. I glanced over my shoulder to where Peg was screaming in his face. There was no sign of Pa snapping out of his stupor any time soon.

Turning back to Knox, the idea of snatching him up by the straps of his overalls crossed my mind but fizzled as fast as it formed, considering that would give the aggressive snake a moving target to strike. Raleigh began crying behind me while Knox's whimpers grew louder in response.

"Shh . . . It's going to be okay. Just stay still."

The snake hissed again and started uncoiling its thick body in Knox's direction, jolting me into action. Wielding the shovel like a trident, I scaled the top of the tractor and blindly stabbed it into the ground with all my force. In a blink, I had Knox by the armpits. "Catch him, Raleigh!" I yelled just before hurling Knox over the tractor.

Clenching my teeth to prevent the litany of screams and ugly talk from spewing out of my mouth, I uprooted the shovel, gripped it with both hands to plunge it through the slithering creature near my foot. Leaving the shovel stuck in the earth with a piece of convulsing coil on each side of it, I clambered to the other side of the tractor.

Raleigh had Knox in his arms, actually comforting the little guy. "He's okay," he told me assuredly.

The air in my lungs stuttered out. "Good. Good." I placed a wobbly kiss against Knox's temple and started limping toward the limo. "Load everyone up in the car, Peg."

"Why?" Peg called, hurrying to catch up with me.

"Because I need to go to the ER," I said through gritted teeth as a flame started consuming my leg. "I can't do that and keep an eye on the young'uns."

Peg choked. "It bit you?"

I whirled around and leveled him with a stern glare, hoping it conveyed that we needed to keep the kids calm. "I need you to drive." Spots formed in my line of sight, either from the venom or the adrenaline overdose, and each step turned into agony.

"I can't drive!" Peg ushered the twins and Raleigh into the limo.

Pressing the back of my hand over my mouth as a wave of nausea rolled through me, I struggled to swallow. Once it passed, I told him, "Just use your left foot like you do on the golf cart."

Peg didn't argue. Instead, he helped me into my seat and closed the door. Running in some skipping manner, he rounded the front of the car and got behind the wheel in a flash.

The rear door behind him opened. "We going somewhere?" Boss asked while rubbing his groggy eyes.

"Just to town," I answered but the words barely held a sound. A cold sweat broke out on every inch of my body as everything started spinning. My eyes slammed shut as a tremor seized me.

"In or out, Boss? Hurry it up!" Peg yelled. The car jostled and then the door shut as Boss mumbled something about Raleigh sliding over. Then the engine revved and sent the car in motion.

The panic must have tripped a switch on Peg's tongue, because the boy alternated between praying and cursing all the way to the hospital. I was appreciative of his prayers but was in too much pain to get ahold of him for the poor language, not to mention the whiplash we all probably sustained each time he hit the brakes.

"My neck is gonna snap in two if you don't quit," Boss complained.

"I can't help it! My foot keeps gettin' tangled!" Peg grouched.

They bickered for who knows how long, but my ears were ringing too loudly to catch most of the exchange. One minute I was staring at the bleary road, the next a stark hallway while being pushed in a wheelchair. Another blink I was in an exam room with a doctor poking at my leg as the world closed in on me. The next tattered image was of a hospital room with an empty bed beside mine.

"Head count," I vaguely remembered mumbling.

"Six," Peg answered by my side. "I picked up Charlotte."

The habit of only sleeping four hours at the most in one stretch and the constant workload had started taking a toll on me as of late. A weariness pressed just as firmly on my body as the bitterness had done to my attitude. Reassured that everyone was okay for the moment, I gave in to the exhaustion and drifted off . . .

Daydreaming about being alone with Vance, his intense green eyes adoring me and his warm lips kissing me, was what got me through most days and many lonely hours at night when sleep wouldn't find me. The daydream was always set on a sunny beach or the lake. It had certainly never been set in a hospital room with Vance staring at my leg in sheer disgust.

"Looks like someone took a crowbar to your leg, babe." Vance shook his head, face scrunched as if he were the one in unbearable pain.

"You better not let Pa hear you call me babe or you'll be the one with crowbar issues."

"It's not going to fall off, is it?" Vance's focus remained centered on my bloated purple leg.

The blasted thing throbbed with a fevered beat in tune with my pulse. I was about to the point of wishing it would fall off. I slung the cover over the revolting sight and barely contained a wince. The lightweight fabric was as unbearable as if it were an elephant sitting on my leg.

Vance folded the cover away with much more gentleness than I'd used. Embarrassment flashed hot on the rest of my normal skin, remembering I was only wearing an open-back hospital gown and underwear. Glancing at the white-tiled ceiling and flipping through my memory, I cringed when it finally hit me that I'd pulled on a pair of Wonder Woman panties that morning. The product of a quick sweep through the department store where I was only looking for size five bikini cut and paying no mind to pattern or color. Needless to say, the crowd had made plenty of jabs about them at my expense and now there I was stuck in a hospital bed wearing them and knowing someone undoubtedly had caught sight of them during my snakebite frenzy.

When Vance reached to reposition the cover again, I batted his hand away and tucked the sides under my thighs to help conceal my silly underwear choice. "What are you doing?"

"The blanket is making it hurt worse."

"So?"

He leaned forward to level me with a stern look, sending his blond curls to flop into his eyes. "So I don't want you in any more pain than you have to be."

The blistering pain was beyond anything I'd ever endured, so there was no patience or strength to tamp down my nasty attitude. Vance's sweetness and concern did very little to soften it. My mouth blurted, "Why are you here?"

His brow furrowed, a mix of irritation and hurt. "You're in the hospital because you've been bitten by a *poisonous* snake."

I crossed my arms and stared down at my maimed leg. "You should leave."

"Careful now, Austin. Your mean side is showing."

I tucked the blanket tighter under my thigh. "But someone might see you with the riffraff."

Vance moved closer until his nose touched mine, arms braced on either side of my hips. "I've had enough of you calling yourself that. No more, Austin. My girlfriend, who is dynamite, is hurt in the hospital. I will be nowhere else but by her side." His drawl pulled each word until they were filled heavily with meaning.

Before I could get good and choked up over his declaration, murmurings interrupted the moment and reminded me we weren't alone.

"Austin is a girlfriend!" Nash gasped.

We both looked over at the row of spectators sitting on the other bed. The little twins looked confused, but the others were fighting grins. Well, not Peg. No, he looked ready to punch something.

I didn't want to address the girlfriend comment, so I glanced at Vance and asked him, "How'd you even know I was here? And what about your classes?"

"You. Were. Bit. By. A. Poisonous. Snake." Vance enunciated each word carefully, his eyes rounded for emphasis. "Classes are the last thing on my mind." He tipped his head to the line of whispering spectators. "Peg called me. I gave him my number before I moved in case you were too stubborn to call if you needed me."

I worked on gathering a retort but a knock on the door interrupted me.

A nurse came in with the doctor for the hourly check. They both froze, looking between Vance and me.

The doctor cleared his throat. "Mr. Cumberland." He extended his hand toward Vance. "It's a surprise seeing you here, young man."

Vance shook his hand, the action resembling his father while on mayor duty around town. "Good to see you too, sir." His tone polite and posture straight, there was no denying Vance's proper upbringing as town royalty. He let go of the doctor's hand and reached over to hold mine. The gesture made it clear as to why he was in my hospital room and surprised me more than the doctor or nurse.

The nurse smiled at our entwined hands while the doctor examined my repulsive leg. He made another line with a marker to track the purple swelling rising up my leg, and then he checked my vitals and made a few notes in my chart.

"You're still having shortness of breath, so I'm going to keep you overnight for observation." The doctor glanced at the other bed. "We need to call your father to come pick up your siblings."

"He's sick." I tried sitting up but settled on slumping against the pillow. The snake might have bitten my calf but every blame thing hurt. "I can keep an eye on myself at home. Just . . . maybe another nap before I go."

"It's in your best interest to stay overnight," the doctor argued as anxiety began rising in my chest.

"I can take them home," Vance offered.

"No!" I coughed. "Thank you though, but Pa . . . he has a nasty virus . . . coming out both ends . . . so I don't want to expose you." My eyes clamped shut so I wouldn't have to face the guilt of lying to him. "Can we just keep trying Foxy's number? They should be back to the house in another hour or so."

"As long as no one comes in needing the other bed, that should be fine," the doctor answered.

My eyes remained closed until the door clicked shut at their departure. I peeked over at my siblings and then at Vance. His eyes were trained on the younger twins, who were beginning to whine.

Vance placed a firm kiss on my forehead. "I'll be right back." He turned to the others. "Boss, will you come with me?"

Boss scooted off the end of the bed and followed Vance out.

They returned a while later with arms filled with cans of cola and candy bars. Soon after, a hospital staff member came in wheeling a portable TV stand. By the time it was plugged in and tuned to *The Price Is Right*, the whining had abated. The next hour or so sailed by with the kids munching away on junk food and shouting their price guesstimates at Bob Barker as if the host could actually hear them while I dozed off and on in what felt like some sort of flu-like haze.

It had been a long time since my siblings and I had a break from the farm, making Nolia feel more like a prison and not a homestead. I sure did hate that I had to suffer a snakebite, but my suffering was worth it to give them an afternoon of normalcy away from the farm and the hopeless situation with Pa that was beginning to take a severe toll on all of us.

Foxy and Jinx arrived much later than I'd promised the doctor, but the hospital staff all looked the other way. Probably due to the presence of Vance Cumberland.

"You have any potion that'll fix this?" I asked Foxy while she inspected my right leg that was double in size as my left.

"No potion, no." With a straight face, she added, "But I could chop off your leg. I'm sure Phoenix would share one of his prosthetics."

Jinx began corralling the kids by the door, but Knox

wiggled loose and came over to my bed, looking like the day had finally caught up with him. His big blue eyes swam in tears. "Ox, I'm real sorry." His eyes skittered to my rotten leg as his lips puckered. Fat tears plopped down his dirty cheeks, making me realize the unkempt state he and the others were in and also making me feel even more like a failure.

I swallowed down the guilt and pain as best as I could and reached over to comb my fingers through his knotted hair. The brown tresses were sticky from the combination of sweat, dirt, and whatever candy he'd enjoyed while watching TV. I needed the little guy closer and Vance seemed to sense this as he lifted Knox over the bed rail and tucked him against my left side, bringing me and my brother eye to eye.

"I know you are, buddy. We just need to be more careful where we play from now on, okay?"

Knox nodded his head, still looking sick with worry. I pulled him close and placed a kiss on top of his head, taking a deep inhale to capture the sugary-sweet scent and earthiness of boy mingling together.

Someone moved close to the bed, sniffling. I glanced over my shoulder and found an older version of Knox.

"It's my fault. I was supposed to be watching the twins . . ." Raleigh's voice broke and tears streaked his weary face.

I took his hand in mine. "Then it's my fault too, because I'm the one who promised Mama I'd take care of all y'all." As soon as I said it, my guilt and shame at failing her bit harder than that snake. We were all spiraling, barely surviving. I eyed the others behind Raleigh. They looked ready to break too. "Will y'all forgive me?"

Foxy cleared her throat, sending my eyes her way. Of course she was starting to fidget and it made me want to scream for her to just leave but I needed her too much at the moment. And boy, did I hate admitting that even to myself.

"Foxy, there's money in the car's glove box. Peg has the keys. Will you and Jinx take the kids to Duffy Dogs for burgers and fries and then let them spend the night with y'all?" I turned to drop another kiss on top of Knox's head, not wanting to meet anyone's eyes while lying. "Pa's got a virus. Best to stay away from the house."

Jinx spoke up. "Sounds like a plan. I just got a VCR, so we can stop by the video store and rent a few movies." He waved for the crowd to head out.

"Can we get *Raiders of the Lost Ark*?" Peg asked as they shuffled toward the door.

"If it's there," Jinx answered.

Excited at his offerings, everyone was quick to give me hugs and kisses and then it was just me and Vance.

Vance eased onto the bed beside me, careful to not jostle my leg. He settled me against his chest and kissed the top of my head, much in the same manner as I did Knox earlier. I hoped it had comforted my little brother as much as it did me.

"Shouldn't you be heading back to Lake Murray?" I asked even though I was snuggling closer to him.

"I'll go straight to school from here in the morning."

I tsked. "That'll make for a rough day."

"I don't have a class until ten and so what if I have a rough day. It still won't compare to the level of rough you're going through. Man, Austin, I hate you got hurt, babe."

Even in pain, I managed to find humor in his convoluted statement. "You just called me a man, by my name, and *babe* in the same sentence. Not nearly as eloquent as you were earlier with the doctor while in Mr. Mayor's Son mode."

He dropped another kiss on my head. "It's your fault. You hurting has my eloquence shot."

The door opened without a warning knock. We glanced away from each other and eyed the startled nurse as she took in me being held by said Mr. Mayor's Son.

She released a subtle cough and busied herself with studying the chart. "It's time for more pain meds. Do you need help visiting the bathroom first?" she asked, much to my relief and embarrassment.

"Umm . . . yes, please." And that was an ordeal I wanted to wipe clean from my memory. There was no dignity with having to flop and scoot out of the bed and then hobble-wobble to the bathroom with my backside hanging out. No one said anything, thankfully, just helped me in and out of bed.

By the time I returned to the bed, I was washed in sweat and my cheeks streaked with tears.

"Sweetie, how about trying to eat something?" Lettie suggested. We were on first-name basis and nicknames after the bathroom visit.

Swallowing a sob, I could only shake my head.

Lettie patted my hand that was fisted in the sheet. "I can give you something for the nausea too, and maybe later you'll feel up to eating something. How's that sound?"

I nodded, still unable to talk. With the earlier pain meds worn off and my siblings gone, there was no holding it together, so I fell apart. Sobbing and moaning until the medicine kicked in.

"Vance, you're welcome to the other bed since no other patients checked in." It was surprising that she never said a word about Vance laid up in my bed, but maybe it shouldn't have been, considering he was town royalty.

Once I calmed down and managed drinking about half a bottle of ginger ale with the medicine, Lettie left us alone to watch TV, which was something I'd never done at home. Weird how something so dire as a snakebite came with privileges.

"The town is going to know all about you being here with me," I warned him as a lightness grew through my limbs.

"Good. I want everyone to know I'm here with my girlfriend." Vance lifted my palm, kissed it, then flattened it against his chest. The rising and falling of his breaths and the steady beat of his heart were as soothing as the kiss.

I snickered. "Nash was too cute about the girlfriend declaration."

"Yeah, but not near as cute as your Wonder Woman panties."

"Ugh. You didn't have to admit to seeing them." I attempted to pull my hand off his chest, but Vance's large palm trapped it there. "Save me some sliver of dignity."

"I respect your choice of underwear." His expression was the very definition of innocent just as his lips curved on one side to reveal the tease.

"Keep it up and I'll make you leave," I warned, but my voice slurred slightly, so it killed the sternness I was going for.

We settled down and turned our attention to the TV set up

at the foot of the bed. Halfway through an episode of *The Fall Guy*, I started nodding off.

Vance brushed my hair away from my face, waking me a little. "I like how you handled Knox."

"What do you mean?" Grogginess from the pain meds settled a lethargic weight over me, but thankfully the pain was dulling too.

"You were straight up with him instead of brushing the mistake away and corrected him without being all mean about it." Vance traced my fingers with the tip of his index finger. "You're going to be a great mother one day, Austin."

Slipping under the blanket of unconsciousness, I think I muttered, "No . . . I don't want children."

And I think his reply was something along the lines of him having to change my mind about that.

Two weeks later, I hobbled into the library. Before I could voice my request, Miss Jones handed me a stack of books with titles that all included the word *snake*. It was actually comforting to know this woman truly got me.

Chapter 9

NOT EVERY ITCH
NEEDS SCRATCHING

August 1984

Summer shifted into a slow conclusion with several things coming at me way too fast. The twins were starting pre-kindergarten. And Vance would soon return all of his attention to college. Then it would be just me on a daily basis with Pa, since Tripp got Boss a job shadowing him in the city.

Tripp Murphy had turned out to be a genuinely decent guy who, like most folks, had made some poor choices. Choices that were his response to being wrongfully accused of committing murder. If I lost years of my life sitting in jail for something I didn't do, I would probably lash out worse than a few drunken bar brawls.

I once heard Pa say that Tripp had an unlucky knack for

being in the wrong place at the wrong time. Tripp had never met the teenage runaway he'd been accused of murdering, but he had been at the place where she was last seen. Witnesses at the bar said Tripp left only minutes after her, and so that was twisted into him following her. He was alone that night and had no alibi to discredit the claims, which easily made him the scapegoat for the crime.

Tripp not only lost years, but also his fiancée. She chose the public's opinion instead of standing by Tripp's declaration of being innocent. To add insult to injury, while he was in prison, she ran off with the friend who was supposed to be Tripp's best man. Magnolia spread that news quicker than when he was acquitted.

Once he put the alcohol down with Pa's help and got a job with the city, Tripp started performing yearly tree sweeps. He thoroughly checked each magnolia tree in town, using a rake, to make sure no secret would ever go uncovered again.

"Where'd you go, babe?" Vance trailed a fingertip along my sweaty neck.

I blinked and refocused on the handsome sweaty guy sitting beside me. "I was trying to teleport us to Antarctica, but it's not working."

Nearing midnight, the late hour hadn't calmed the temperatures that were still hovering in the high eighties with the humidity at nearly 100 percent. The heat was palpable, making the skin weep in misery. There was no seeing the threat, but one certainly could feel it pressing down on all sides.

"You'd think up here would be cooler." Vance nudged the opening of the loft's upper window with his toes. We were both wearing shorts and T-shirts, but he suddenly fisted the back of his soaked shirt and whipped it over his head, revealing a glistening chest.

"Ugh. That is so not fair!" I pinched the collar of my shirt and fanned myself, but it did very little to alleviate my discomfort or tirade about to reach a boil.

Vance used his shirt to mop over his head and chest. "What's unfair?"

"Guys have it so much easier than girls." I stabbed a finger through the muggy air and started ticking off my grievances. "You can take your shirt off in public. You don't have to shave your legs or armpits. Just your face—and that's only if you feel like it. And the whole peeing-while-standing bit. Err. So not fair. All you gotta do is pull out your hose and take a leak whenever nature calls."

Vance's chuckle cut me off. "My *hose*?"

"Yeah." I shrugged. "When I have to talk to Nash and Knox about . . . stuff, I refer to . . . well, I call it a hose."

"Why not use the technical term?"

"Change the subject," I demanded, face scalding.

Vance bit his lip, but it did nothing to hide that smug grin or those darn appealing dimples. "I think the current subject is fairly interesting. I see your point about the unfairness, and I'm perfectly okay with you taking your shirt off too." He reached for the hem of my shirt.

I popped his hand, but that only egged him on. Chuckling, he leaned in for a kiss, but I palmed his face and shoved him away. Vance retaliated by tickling my sides, only making the heat escalate past tolerable.

"It's too hot for this mess," I growled and then squealed. We probably sounded like a herd of elephants. Good thing we were alone. And good thing I knew how to deliver the most effective horse bite, considering I'd had plenty of practice with my rascally brothers. I clamped just above his knee, digging my fingers in, sufficiently putting a stop to his tickling attack.

Vance yelped, rivaling any farm dog by far, and rolled away from me. "That's gonna leave a bruise!"

"That's what you get!" Out of breath and patience, I hurried to my feet and headed for the ladder before he recovered. "We need to cool off."

"Where are you going?" Vance grumbled.

"To the pond."

"Night swim?" His voice lifted with anticipation.

I rolled my eyes. "No. We're just going to go stand by it and think ourselves cooler."

"All right, smart aleck." Vance followed me outside.

"Take Boss's bike." I pointed at the tallest bicycle and then climbed on mine.

We raced the mile-long stretch to the back of the property, jumping off the bikes before they even came to a stop, and continued the race on foot down the dock, cannonballing off the end and into the icy-cold water. I think I heard our skin sizzle at contact, and we both released a moaning sigh when we reemerged. Under a clear sky hanging heavily with stars and a crescent moon, we swam the heat away until growing tired before moving to the shallow spot under the dock, out of sight. It was almost completely dark, so only the outline of Vance's face could be made out as he wrapped me in his arms.

I'd expected his lips on mine while we clung to each other. Instead, Vance whispered wistfully about dreams and goals. He admitted to having a trust that would be freed to him upon graduating college. It was enough that he'd never have to work a day in his life, yet he was adamant about family loyalty and working to honor it. He spoke about making the lake house his permanent home since it was closer to the firm he would eventually take over when his father and uncle decided he was ready. He talked long and passionately about his future.

I wasn't so passionate about the outlook of mine, so I remained quiet and just listened. It wasn't a hardship. His voice had become deeper in tone and more refined in the last year.

A lifetime passed with us in our little bubble before we made it back to the packhouse. Instead of heading home like he should, Vance pulled me to the sleeping bag and wrapped his arms around me.

"Vance, this ain't a good idea." I snuggled closer and placed a kiss on the side of his neck. The scent of summer clung to him. A mix of earth, heat, and water.

"Just let me hold you a little longer; then I'll head out . . ." He let out a contented sigh. "Promise."

My eyes grew heavier with each breath. "Seriously . . . you need to go home . . ."

"I will . . . soon . . ."

I woke up surrounded by warmth. Nothing unusual considering most mornings I'd find a kid or two had ended up in my bed. But what was unusual was arms that were holding me in a comforting embrace instead of needing one from me.

Opening my eyes slowly, I took in the wall of maps before

me and then the strong arm around my waist as the night before came tumbling back. I wiggled to get from under his arm, but it tightened to hold me against his body.

"Vance."

Nothing.

"Vance." I wiggled some more, this time evoking a gravelly groan. "Vance."

"Yeah, babe," he mumbled, his voice a sleepy rasp.

I pushed against his forearm as he nuzzled closer. "We fell asleep. You gotta get out of here before Pa catches you."

"Just hush for a minute . . . please."

I shivered when his lips skated down my neck. "Why?"

"I want to practice some more." He cocooned me, slinging a leg over mine.

It was heavenly and extinguished the alarm rising rapidly in my chest. "Practice what?"

"One day . . ." Vance trailed off and remained quiet just long enough for me to wonder whether he'd dozed off again. "One day I'll get to wake up every day with you in my arms."

"Says who?"

"God, if he's willing to answer my prayers," Vance answered, his husky tone thick with sincerity.

"Ain't none of your prayers gonna be answered if Pa catches us up here like this. He has a shotgun, ya know." I rolled to a sitting position and rubbed my eyes. "I need to get some breakfast put together for the crowd soon."

Vance rubbed his flat bare stomach, which had remained as defined as it was back in his high school ball-playing days. "I could eat. What are you making?"

I tossed him his shirt and watched him pull it on, covering all that tanned, toned skin. "What part of you needing to leave so Pa doesn't introduce you to his shotgun do you not understand?"

"You're a terrible girlfriend. Just going to send me away starving and neglected." He pouted out his bottom lip and scooted closer, wrapping me in his arms. "Kiss me and I'll forgive you." He cupped my cheek and brought our lips together, continuing until we were both quite hungry for something besides food. The day was already offering another hefty dose of heat, and this guy only made it worse.

Lips tingling and stretched in a wide grin, I climbed down the ladder. I reached the bottom, turned, and faced terror head-on, sending the grin to fall to the floor as my body froze.

Propped in a chair by the door, Pa sat with his massive arms crossed and a severe scowl on his face. Eyes locked on mine, an eyebrow arched as if to ask, *Whatcha gotta say for yourself?*

Vance bumped into my back and laughed an apology, yet to realize the impending danger. His arms wrapped around my waist to steady us. His body suddenly went rigid. We both morphed into living statues holding our breaths.

"'Bout time y'all came down from there."

"Pa!" A nervous giggle hiccuped out, unfreezing me. "You scared the tater out of me." Another stilted giggle. "I didn't realize you were in here."

He sat forward, sending the front two chair legs slamming to the ground. A cat dashed out the door and I sure wished I could have done the same. "Yeah. You didn't notice me last night either when you two snuck back in here after your swim."

Oh, boy. We were sitting ducks. Only thing to do was step out of Vance's arms and brace for impact.

"S-sorry, sir," Vance stuttered, something I'd never heard him do, and took a step ahead of me. A gallant act that wouldn't be earning him any favor with my father. Surely we were past that. "We . . . I . . . didn't mean to fall asleep."

Pa huffed a rumbly chuckle even though his glower held strong. "It happens."

Vance laughed in response.

Pa waved his hand, shooing Vance's stupidity. "Especially if you sneak out somewhere at ungodly hours to fool around till close to dawn. Falling asleep is understandable."

Vance quit laughing. At least he was a quick learner.

"I was your age once, son. Had me a purty little thing I couldn't get enough time with. Me and Edith liked to sneak away together too." He pawed the side of his bushy beard, his stormy-blue eyes tightening with mentioning my mother. "Difference was we were husband and wife. So until your intentions are to marry my daughter, it's best you forgo any more plans of galivanting around my farm in the middle of the night without my permission."

Vance's shoulders deflated in front of me as he cleared his throat. "Yes, sir. I'm real sorry for disrespecting you, Mr. Foster."

"Apology accepted." Pa leaned his elbows on top of his knees. The man was sitting as we stood before him, yet he still managed to crush us with his intimidation. "You owe one to my daughter, too, for talking her into staying up there with you. It sure ain't respecting her when she told you good and well it weren't a good idea."

Ah, dang. He not only knew we were up there in the loft, but Pa had heard everything we'd said too. My face went up in flames while my heart galloped all the way up to my throat.

Vance turned to me, his face high in color. "Austin, I was selfish. Wanting to spend as much time with you as possible . . . I'm sorry."

I wanted to kiss him and let him know it was okay and that he was the sweetest thing, but with Pa just a few feet away watching us like a surly hawk, I only nodded my head.

Pa stood slowly and stretched his arms over his head while releasing a weary yawn. It spoke of the enormity of his exhaustion, which only served to deepen my guilt for robbing him of any piece of sleep he could have found during the night.

Lately, life had been okay, but it wasn't all right. No label seemed to fit just precisely to what was wrong. Like an itch you couldn't quite pinpoint. It nagged yet eluded. Pa had been present, leading church every Sunday for the last few months. Sure, the surface looked normal, but just underneath I caught subtle glimpses of some unseen force snuffing out my father's brilliance.

"Austin, we got a long day. Field work and chores. Then you're taking the kids to town for haircuts." In a rare agreeable mood, I nodded again. "Now get on inside and start breakfast. I'll walk Vance up to the front barn, where he *parks*."

The emphasis on the word *parks* made it clear he knew all about the other nights that we thought we were hiding Vance's visits. It was also clear that Pa was more present and aware than his typical comatose demeanor let on.

I hightailed it out of the packhouse without sparing Vance

so much as a glance and beat a path straight to the kitchen. I rummaged the pantry to find something to help right my wrong by any measure. A new box of Bisquick mix and the sticky bottle of Cane Patch syrup would be a good start since the foolproof biscuits and syrup were Pa's favorite.

The front door opened as I slid the biscuits in the oven. "Pa, I got biscuits going. And the coffee is ready," I called over my shoulder, hoping to butter him up, but the only answer I received was his heavy footfalls up the stairs.

By the time the crowd was settled at the table and digging into the hot biscuits, Pa still hadn't joined us for breakfast. "Y'all save some for Pa. I'm gonna go check on him."

"How many we gotta save him?" Boss asked, eyeing the mountain of biscuits on the platter like there wasn't enough.

"Save him five," I said, going with a higher number, knowing they would leave exactly how many I ordered.

Upstairs, Pa's room was empty and the bathroom door open, eliminating the only two places up here he would be. I eased down the hall and checked each room until finding him perched on the edge of Raleigh's bed. Through the small open crack of the door, I watched Pa pull in deep inhales from Mama's bottle of lotion. It was a scene I'd witnessed many times over the years, but with my brother instead of Pa. Just as I'd always done for Raleigh, I backed away from the door and allowed Pa his moment to remember, to mourn, privately.

Taking charge downstairs, I put Raleigh and the younger twins on farm animal feeding duty. He'd been reluctant to have responsibility of Nash and Knox after the snake incident, but I figured it was best to just put him back on that horse to get over it. Even though it took quite a bit of time, he was comfortable with watching the boys once again.

"The rest of y'all are to help me in the fields." I pointed a finger at Charlotte as soon as she started to protest. "You're driving the tractor, so don't even start with your whining."

She pouted out her bottom lip, but that was that.

After a quick lunch of bologna sandwiches and freshly sliced watermelon, we loaded up in the Silver Bullet and headed to town.

"Why we stopping here?" Peg grumbled in the back as I pulled up to the curb at the funeral home.

I climbed out and told him before shutting the door, "Today I'm making the last payment on the car. I won't be but a second, so sit tight."

With cautious steps, I walked into the front entrance and was immediately welcomed by the scent of carnations and something else that was specific to this place, probably mildew but I chose to identify it as death.

"You're a sight for sore eyes, darlin'!" Morty spoke, startling me.

"Hey, Morty." I waved the check in the air like a victory lane flag. "I'm here to pay off the car."

"Well, ain't that just marvelous." His enthusiasm matched mine, but then panic rose as he latched his manicured fingers around my elbow and started pulling me too far away from the front door.

All I wanted to do was pay this last payment and be on my

way, but Morty led me deeper inside the funeral home and the next thing I knew I was in a viewing room where a cherry-wood casket was set up.

Morty introduced me to the living person standing by the dead person laid out. "Austin, honey, you know Beth? From the flower shop?"

I gave the woman a small nod and struggled to keep my eyes away from the dead man.

"Beth is setting up the flowers for Mr. Winkle's viewing. His family will be arriving in about a half hour. It's been so busy I don't know if I'm coming or going." Morty's hands were moving through the air as rapidly as he was speaking, but his mention of Mr. Winkle's name caught my attention. His eyes snapped to me when I sucked in a sharp breath. "Don't worry, honey. I did a thorough exam before I began embalming him. I made sure there was no waking up this time."

Like that would make me more comfortable.

The florist leaned close to inspect the man. "He looks so peaceful, don't you think?" Beth whispered as if she were try-ing not to wake him.

I wanted to reply that he just looked dead to me but figured that was too snide and speaking ill of the dead. His waxy com-plexion and frozen state left no doubt to that fact.

"Like he's just taking a nap," Beth added.

The overwhelming sweetness from the floral arrangements surrounding the casket reminded me of a woman who'd been too heavy-handed with the perfume bottle way past the point of pleasant. Holding my breath, I reversed out of the room and bumped into Morty in the hall.

"Oh! I didn't even realize you left me," I squeaked out.

"Honey, I told you I had to grab this from my office." He handed me the car title and a thick manila envelope. "Give this to Dave, please."

"What is it?"

"Your father's funeral arrangements." Morty flicked his wrist when I gave him a concerned look. "Lots of people make prearrangements to take the burden off their family."

The arrangements did nothing but burden me even more with worrying what Pa might try next to speed up the need for whatever was inside the folder.

The florist called out, needing Morty for something, so I took the opportunity to bolt out of the funeral home. Hopefully, it would be my last visit for a very long time. I tossed the folder and car title in the trunk to keep it away from prying eyes and hurried to the driver's door.

"What did you put in the trunk?" Peg asked before I even settled in my seat.

"Just the car title and some paperwork," I said quickly, committing to the lie of omission. It was starting to bother me how easily lies fell from my lips anymore. "Let's go get the haircuts over with and maybe if y'all behave right, I'll stop by the Piggly Wiggly and get everything to make ice cream sundaes."

That earned me lots of cheers and helped ease my guilt. "Hopefully, Walynn won't take long."

Peg leaned forward and said close to my ear, "I hope that lady ain't thinking Pa is gonna help scratch her itch."

"Peg!" I jerked around to glare at him.

He leaned back. "Just speaking the truth. That's what those ladies at the library were saying the other day."

"About Pa?" I met Peg's eyes in the rearview mirror and he shook his head.

"No. About Walynn always looking for a new man to help scratch her itch."

"Foxy says it ain't polite to scratch in public," Nash remarked.

"Foxy is right," I added quickly, wanting to move away from the scratching Peg was talking about.

In all honesty, I did not care for the likes of Walynn Posten. I could tolerate a lot of people, but the loud, hair spray–wielding woman who wore her pants so tight you could see her religion was not one of them.

Walynn had rode into town with one of the local boys who'd picked her up when he'd been stationed at Fort Knox the previous fall. Their little fling lasted long enough for a deputy to catch her attention, but the thing with Walynn's attention was that it didn't keep for very long, so the deputy made it until the day after Christmas. That's when the owner of Magnolia Garage became the focus of her love after he didn't charge her for changing the oil in her car. That whirlwind romance didn't make it to New Year's Eve. She moved through men faster than gossip at the beauty shop where she worked. And I'd just as soon stay away from her place, but Pa insisted we give her our business since most folks treated her salon chair like it had the plague. Only men took the chance of sitting in it, and boy, did that just add fuel to talk about her behind being on fire.

I led the long line of Fosters into the beauty shop, noticing

Walynn immediately. Her permed hair with the bangs teased toward the heavens was hard to miss. The sides were drawn up with a banana clip, showing off her dark roots. When she turned around, the neon-blue eye shadow and hot-pink lipstick had the younger twins wrapping their arms around my legs, confirming what I already knew. It was going to be a long afternoon. It wasn't that she was ugly, just loud. Something we plain ones were not exposed to much.

Walynn scanned the line of us before looking toward the door. "Austin, sweetie, where's your daddy?" Her optimism was louder than that blue eye shadow.

"He's at the farm," I told her and was satisfied to see some of that optimism dim.

She planted her shiny red-tipped nails on her hips and tsked. "That man is in dire need of a good haircut. I told him that Sunday and he seemed to agree."

I shrugged because it was true, but I wasn't about to use words to agree with her. Something had my hackles raised with this woman. "Well, we have a lot to get done. Can you get started?"

"Sure." Walynn motioned us to her chair and placed some type of riser on the seat. "Knox, sugar, you want to go first?"

Knox eyed the scissors while combing his fingers through his unruly brown locks, pausing to scratch near his ear. Out the corner of his mouth, he spoke to me. "Ox, why can't you just do it at home like you always do?"

I'd always cut the twins' hair, not often enough, since they'd started needing it done. Back porch trimmings is what we called it, but it was more like hack jobs. With them starting school, though, it was time for me to put my dull scissors and clippers away.

I bent down to meet his denim-blue eyes. "You and Nash are big boys now like your other brothers. You'll start getting your hair cut like them. Ain't that cool?" I lifted my eyebrows and smiled, a slight nod of my head hoping to coerce one from him.

"I don't wanna." The little guy's voice broke and that always made my chest pinch.

"How about I go first?"

Knox sniffed, wiped under his nose, and nodded.

I straightened and saw that Walynn was already removing the seat riser. I plopped in the chair and in a blink there was a cape being snapped around my neck. "Just a good trimming please."

"You got it, honey." Walynn took a comb to my hair but it struggled against the knots. She gave up on the comb and sprayed my hair with something that smelled like coconut. After that the comb glided through with little effort. "These natural highlights are gorgeous. I'd kill for them."

I glanced in the big mirror behind her station and eyed the chemically bleached-out blonde. Nothing natural about it. She caught me staring in the mirror and winked. Thankfully, the trimming only took a few minutes and soon Knox and I traded spots.

My fingers had a mind of their own and kept combing through my newly silky-smooth hair. If I didn't have such an aversion to the woman, I'd inquire what she used, but that was too conversational and my desire to keep her at a distance had my mouth firmly clamped shut.

The door jangled just as a man in a business suit entered the beauty shop and started in our direction. I swung around and caught Walynn grimacing at the side of Knox's head. Her comb froze in midair.

"Oh, shoot. I forgot I have an appointment with Mr. Kaden. Y'all gonna have to come back tomorrow or another day."

Before I could protest, Walynn had the cape whipped off and was helping Knox down out of her chair.

"But we're already here. Can't that man wait his turn?" Peg spoke up.

"No can do, sugar. He was scheduled. Y'all weren't." She gave us an apologetic smile that did nothing to provoke forgiveness.

"But Pa said we were scheduled," I protested, cheeks warming with anger.

"No, he said y'all would try to stop in today. No official appointment." Walynn sprayed some cleaner on her chair, her back turned dismissively.

"Well, Pa ain't gonna take kindly to how you treatin' us." Peg was nearly shouting, so I grabbed his arm and began pulling him toward the door with the others following. "Who you think you are?"

"Hush, Peg. You're making a scene," I whispered on a hiss. "Pa sure won't take kindly to that."

Charlotte waved to the line of hair stations. "Someone else can do our hair then. We don't need you to do it." She pointed to the empty chair next to Walynn's. "Can't Mrs. Jill do it?"

Walynn gave the other stylists a meaningful look, ticking me off more. "No! Everyone has a full schedule today. And Mrs. Jill is on break. Sorry."

"Y'all a mighty sorry hair shop," Peg spat out.

"Hush," I told my mouthy brother again. After shoving him outside and ordering him to get everyone loaded up, I all but tossed the money for my haircut at her. The effect was lost when the ten-dollar bill just floated to the floor by her chair where the man was already settling in.

"Austin, sweetie, I'm sorry."

I whirled around and stormed away without acknowledging her feeble apology. I knew I didn't like that woman. Pa always said not to be too quick to form an opinion about someone, but he was wrong in this case.

I backed out of the parking lot and regarded all the frowns in the rearview mirror. "None of y'all wanted a haircut anyway. You should be smiling." Their expressions didn't change and I got it. We'd just been treated like outcasts, and embarrassment always had a way of outweighing positives. "I'd rather have ice cream sundaes. How 'bout y'all?" That seemed to lift the mood a little, but it was like the humidity outside. Too heavy to escape completely.

We made a pit stop at the grocery store and then set out to the farm in relative silence. Turning in to our drive, I noticed a candy-apple-red Volkswagen Beetle with its blinker light on behind us. There was only one of those in Magnolia, the very same one that had recently been parking at the chapel each Sunday.

"What does that woman want?" I grumbled under my breath as she followed our dust trail up to the farmhouse. I yanked the car into park and hurried to the trunk to grab the grocery bags, only offering the envelope from the funeral home one brief glance before leaving it behind to deal with later. "Boss, bring the ice cream and stuff inside, please. And be sure to put the ice cream in the freezer." I handed him the bags and turned to wait on our unwanted visitor. "What do you want?" I snapped at Walynn as soon as she exited the car.

Walynn had the decency to look ashamed. "Austin, I'm sorry how I brushed y'all off . . ." She retrieved a bag from her car. "But I didn't want to embarrass you at the salon. Little Knox . . . well . . . he has head lice. And it's against salon policy to cut someone's hair who has lice."

Mortified, I swung around and eyed the twins standing behind me. "Y'all got itchy heads?"

Knox nodded and Nash reached to give his scalp a good scratch to be sure. Undoubtedly he found it itchy because he kept on scratching while nodding.

"It's best to check everyone's head and figure out who needs treatments. I stopped by the drugstore on the way here." Walynn lifted the bag slightly.

Once Boss returned, we lined up like farm animals waiting for inspection at the 4-H tent with hopes of taking home the blue ribbon from the county fair. Luckily, after thorough examinations, only the younger twins turned out to be victims of the menacing mess. They'd been attending a summer day camp, and that had to be where they'd picked up the problem. I made a mental note that they'd be spending the rest of the summer at Camp Tobacco Barn.

"Dave's head needs to be checked too," Walynn pointed out.

I shook my head. Pa never got within arm's reach of the

twins, and it was doubtful he'd picked up lice from across the room. "He's not feeling so good. I'll see to him later. For now let's figure out what to do to get those boys' heads clear." I towered over the petite woman, but she didn't seem to let that or my curt attitude intimidate her.

Walynn pointed a long red nail somewhere behind me. "Does that hand pump by the shed work?"

I glanced over my shoulder at the black apparatus with an aluminum bucket hanging off the lip of it. We'd washed up there and quenched many a thirst over the years. Not sure why, but the water out of that pump tasted better than any I'd ever had. "Yeah."

"Perfect. If you'll get me a chair off the porch, I'll work on the boys' heads out here and you can work on washing all their bedding and any dirty clothes. That should take care of disinfecting inside."

The groan rose up my throat, knowing that equaled at least four loads of laundry. I hated doing laundry. But there was no time to groan. If Walynn was going to help me straighten out this mess, I'd have to suck it up.

Charlotte came rushing from the kitchen with plastic wrap coiled around her head. It reminded me of Foxy's head wraps, except this one was transparent.

"What are you doing?" I started moving around her to grab the cleaning supplies, but she blocked my path with the roll of plastic wrap.

"Let me wrap your hair first. Then we can start cleaning." She started unraveling a strip.

"Why?"

Rolling her eyes and sucking her teeth. "So those bugs don't jump in our hair. Duh."

"Fine. Just hurry." I stooped down and my sister had my head wrapped so tight that my eyes were pulling upwards. I had no clue if lice could jump, fly, or magically teleport from one head to another, but it seemed wise to err on the side of caution.

We made quick work of moving all the linens and clothing to the laundry room. By the time I rotated the laundry and had wiped all the hard surfaces down in the bathroom and their room, Walynn not only had the boys deloused but she'd also cut their hair.

After she completed the others' haircuts, I handed Walynn the money Pa gave me earlier for the haircuts and added a fifty of my own money to cover the treatment kits and her time.

"I think the best way to wash this day off is to go for a swim."

Everyone agreed but Walynn. She grabbed her bag and turned to leave.

"Miss Walynn, ain't you gonna swim with us?" Knox asked, trailing behind her.

"I can't, sugar. I have to get back to work." She offered him a kind smile. "Perhaps another time?"

Knox nodded his head vigorously. "Okay!"

"Y'all go get your suits on and leave your dirty clothes by the washing machine." I waited until everyone was inside before speaking. "Miss Walynn—"

"Just Walynn. We're probably closer in age than not," she said, but I figured she had to be more than ten years older than me, not close at all.

"I just wanted to apologize for calling you nasty names."

"You didn't call me any names." She fished a tissue from her bag and dabbed her forehead and cheeks with it. The humidity had melted a good bit of the caked-on makeup off and had taken the tease out of her bangs. She should have taken us up on the swim.

"I said them in my thoughts, and Pa says that's just as bad as speaking them out loud." I shrugged and shoved my hands in my back pockets.

She giggled even though my admission didn't hold any humor. "I'm used to being called ugly names."

And that just made me feel even more lousy. "Being called names isn't something you should have to be used to, nor should you put up with it. Again, I'm sorry."

"I've earned most of those ugly names. It's on me." Her smile wobbled but she quickly righted it. "But I'm working on it. See ya Sunday!" She waved with exaggerated friendliness and quickly left, as if she couldn't get away from her confession fast enough.

I stood at the end of our walkway and stared long after the dust of her departure settled, thinking about Walynn and her kindness and how I'd not extended none to her since she'd started attending church.

"Hey, Ox. Ain't you gonna change?" Raleigh asked from behind me.

I turned and saw that everyone was ready. "Y'all a good-looking group with your new dos."

My compliment was brushed off, the only thing on their minds being swimming, so I left my thoughts about Walynn for later and hurried to my room and made quick work of changing. A peek inside Pa's room found him where I knew he'd be. Curled in a ball on Mama's side of the bed, where he gravitated to when he was at his lowest. The only thing I knew to do for him was pray, so I offered that in silence and crept outside to join my siblings.

It had been a long day, and a few hours of swimming on top of that had worked up mean appetites for all of us. We set up underneath the overhang of the packhouse, where three picnic tables sat, and had ourselves a proper ice cream social. The conversation kept circling back to Walynn and it was no secret that she'd won over the entire lot of us.

"I like Miss Walynn." Nash grinned, using his hand to clean the chocolate sauce from his chin, only to smear it worse. "I hope she goes swimming with us sometime. She's nice."

Knox and Nash had never experienced the sweet gift of having a mother. I wondered if it was possible to miss something you'd never had. With the way they clung to Walynn and her attention today, the answer was pretty clear.

Later that night, the guilt of them missing out on the sweetness of Mama had me reading a second book at bedtime and then having the boys say their own prayers as I patiently knelt beside them. This routine had become rushed and taken for granted, but it was time to put a stop to that for my brothers' sake.

Standing in the darkened hallway, I inventoried those behind each closed door, my failures for each one stacking up high, more stifling than the damp heat outside. It was time to stop pretending to be some naive teenage girl and refocus on the responsibilities that were mine, no matter how difficult the burden could be at times.

Chapter 10

A SEASON OF CLARITY

September 1985

"We gonna have ourselves a Harvest Day celebration next Sunday. We'll meet at the pond." Pa stood tall and proud in front of the congregation. He'd gotten top dollar for the crop at market the prior week, and he said he wanted to celebrate this blessing from God. I'd heard of other churches having Harvest Day celebrations, but our little congregation had never had one before.

From what I gathered, a typical Harvest Day included a short sermon and special singing, followed by a covered-dish dinner. Of course, that wasn't how Dave Foster rolled.

"What do we need to bring?" Walynn asked from the front pew she'd claimed as hers.

"Just your swimsuits. Everything else will be taken care of." Pa grinned proudly as the rest of the crowd side-eyed each other with a measure of skepticism.

Morty cleared his throat. "So . . . we're swimming on Harvest Day?"

"That'll be a part of it, yes. But only if you want to. We're gonna have a picnic and just some good, old-fashioned fun."

There are seasons in a life that one may choose to remember best. A time where the good outweighs the bad enough that the bad is pushed into the foggy crevices of the mind, while the good is crystal clear. Sure, the good may be shined up with a bit of embellishment, but that's sometimes necessary in order to survive the more desolate seasons. The whole year of 1985 is one of those seasons for me. I hold on to that year like a talisman, allowing my memory to shine it up in such glowing appeal that I can hardly recall any shadows it might have held.

Tobacco season was the smoothest, most prosperous.

Vance's kisses and attention the sweetest.

Peg the most agreeable.

Both sets of twins laughed more than ever.

Boss continued to be boss.

And what shines the brightest is the fact that a familiar version of Pa finally arose from the shell of a man he'd become.

1985 could also be called the season of indulgence for the Foster family. Pa had come home with things every so often that floored us kids, like an electric ice cream churner that blew our minds. We literally had ice cream at every meal for two solid weeks before giving that poor machine a rest. Pa got wind of the elementary school redoing the playground, and the next thing we knew, he was hauling in their discarded metal slide, which he mounted on the end of the dock by our pond. A merry-go-round and seesaw showed up next and were set up in the side yard.

That was all great fun, but the most memorable thing he brought home had to be the giant portable radio and a box of cassette tapes to go with it. Up until that point, all we had was the record player in the living room and a small AM/FM radio that stayed at the eastside tobacco barn because it was the only one with electricity.

"It's a Panasonic Platinum boom box," Pa declared the day he brought it home. He presented it the same way he'd presented us with the funeral home limousine, so I was skeptical at first, but the shiny, silver behemoth of a radio turned out to be a blessing just as the limo did.

Anyone who declares music not to be therapeutic is not to be trusted for their opinions. I witnessed its effect on the entire farm, from the humans to the animals to the crops.

There hadn't been one trip to the fields where we didn't lug that bulky thing along and have it blaring at full volume. Suckering tobacco and then cropping it never went by so fast as it did while listening to a steady stream of music. It seemed as long as the music carried on, so did our lifted spirits. Anything from Van Halen to Whitney Houston, from Cyndi Lauper to Journey. The genre didn't matter to us. Prejudice was something we didn't care for in any form, and that included music.

The mistake of not carrying a supply of extra D batteries only happened once. That first time the boom box ran out of juice, we pretty much did too. I also think all of us kids thought the music was the cause of Pa's resurrection to the land of the living, so we were careful to keep it playing most all the time for fear he'd leave us again.

Midnight swims had started up again. Pa would wake us, and no matter how tired we were from a hard day of working, we'd find a second wind and play like those characters from *Where the Wild Things Are*. Pa was our king of the shenanigans and we were his wild creatures, ready and willing to go wherever he led. And wherever that was really didn't matter, because we had our father back, and we knew we were up against a time clock before we'd lose him again. I think we were all on the same page of sacrificing sleep to make those good memories with Pa.

The shiniest memory of them all that year has to be Harvest Day. After his unexpected announcement, Pa kept grinning and everyone continued staring at each other. No one ever addressed Pa's spastic ways, but looks can tell more than words.

It was for that reason that the small group showed up the following Sunday, carrying towels and a good bit of doubt. But boy, did Pa prove us all wrong.

He had stayed up the entire night before, cooking and setting up tables in the shade around the pond. Even stringing up tarps to offer more shaded area. *Picnic* doesn't really describe what we had that day. It was more along the lines of a feast. A roasted pig, a giant cast-iron pot of chicken bog, baked beans, corn on the cob, slaw, potato salad, watermelon. The only thing I had to do was make enough sweet tea and Tang to keep a small army hydrated.

"I'm mighty glad y'all have come to celebrate Harvest Day," Pa began after everyone settled at the tables he'd arranged in a U shape. He stood at the mouth of the U in his swim trunks and a ratty T-shirt. "Harvest Day celebrations began way back in the 1800s. It's a time set aside for the church to celebrate the provisions God has made for us and to share that with others. So I say let's start out by sharing what provisions God has made for us this year. Who'd like to start?"

After a few beats of silence, with each of us looking around to see who would volunteer, Tripp stood. "I got a lot to thank God for, mainly for you folks accepting me. I also got word at my last doctor's appointment that I'm gonna get a new eye." Tripp pointed to his glass eye. "This one ain't ever fit just right. I go in next month and Miss Wise said she's gonna take me." Tripp turned to Miss Wise, who was in the chair beside him, and leaned over to place a kiss on her cheek. She'd become a mother figure to him over the last little bit of time. It was sweet to witness two such withdrawn people come out of their shells to reveal a softer side behind their prickly exteriors.

"I'd like to come along with y'all. Miss Wise?" Pa asked.

She nodded her head. "Of course."

As Tripp took his seat, the group clapped and Miss Wise stood. She fiddled with the cuff of her shirt, one she would wear over her swimsuit the entire day to conceal the numbers on her arm. That was something she'd not gotten comfortable with sharing yet.

Clearing her throat, she spoke softly, emotion making her accent thicker. "Two young ladies have taken upon themselves to make a donation to something very close to my heart. Their act of kindness is a harvest that I'd like to thank God for today." She gave me and Charlotte a knowing look, and I was glad she kept the details of that donation just between the three of us. I was a firm believer that good deeds were best left private.

More applause rippled through the group as she sat down. Then Peg, of all people, stood up next, his chin held high with pride. "I've gone four whole months without cussing."

A wave of laughter rang out among us, echoing off the water and the rock face behind it.

"We all mighty proud of you, Peg. How about making four years your next goal?" Pa spoke on a chuckle. It was baffling that my brother even spoke in such a way, considering neither Pa nor Jinx ever did. I guess the summer farm help had rubbed off on him.

"I'll do my best," Peg declared, taking his seat.

Boss jumped up, happy to get in on the fun. "I grewed all them watermelons with Mrs. Foxy!" He pointed to the table lined with the fat melons. "God provided us a good dessert today, Pa."

Pa tipped his head, grinning ear to ear. "He sure did, Boss."

Boss sat and Jinx rose to his feet. "My lady and I want to thank our good Lord for the news we got from Louisiana. Our niece just had us a great-niece."

Everyone oohed and aahed at his news as Foxy smiled with pride. I'd let my nosiness get away from me once and had asked her why they didn't have children of their own. She said it wasn't in the cards for them and left it at that, but the sadness that small confession produced said there was so much more to it.

Once we settled down from congratulating them, Walynn took her turn. She wore a floral sundress over her bikini and looked ready for a day of frolicking in the water, except her hair was perfectly teased to the heavens and she had on a full face of makeup. "The women at the beauty shop invited me to their girls' night." Her cheeks blushed underneath the artificial pink. "I think they're finally accepting me."

"Well, why wouldn't they?" Pa asked. Then, quick to make sure she knew her place with him, he added, "You're a great friend."

But her smile didn't dim. "Thank you, Dave. It's good to feel like you belong somewhere. Y'all made me feel like that from the start, and now the women at the shop are too, and . . . it's just really nice."

As Walynn sat, Raleigh stood, which surprised me. He normally kept to the background, as I preferred to do. He looked at me and his lip wobbled. "I'm real thankful God saw fit to heal Austin's leg last year." His voice grew hoarse.

Charlotte popped to her feet, coming to her twin brother's rescue as she always did. "And we're thankful it didn't fall off! It was looking iffy for a while there." She wrinkled her nose, causing the group to laugh. Thankfully, we'd gotten to a point where we could joke about it, even though I still had a scar.

I stood to help move on from that for Raleigh's sake. My poor brother still carried a heavy burden of guilt over my snakebite, no matter how much I reassured him he shouldn't.

"God has provided us all with health this year. I want to celebrate that today."

I motioned for the twins to have a seat. As we did, Vance stood. He gave my shoulder a soft squeeze before speaking to the group. "So I've been calling Austin my girlfriend for over a year now, but she *finally* agreed to it last week."

The group laughed again. It was one of the long running jokes around the farm. All summer Vance would make some dig about it and I'd act like I didn't hear him. Last weekend, he'd joined us for a late-night swim and ice cream. Peg was hounding him about something and so I finally spoke up and told him to leave *my boyfriend* alone. It was a done deal after that.

As the laughter died down, Pa walked over to Vance and guided him to have a seat. "Yeah, and as long as you keep being good to her and be respectful, I'll allow it." Pa might have said it with a smile, but it was a warning all the same.

Morty had been noticeably quiet during the testifying and so it wasn't until he stood that most of us realized he'd been crying. A hush settled around us. The hissing of the grill and the rustling of the trees were the only sounds besides Morty's sniffles. "I'm ashamed to say I don't feel very thankful today. I've been struggling . . ." He sniffed and wiped his eyes with the collar of his wildly patterned shirt. "My parents won't have anything to do with me. It's like I don't exist ever since my brother passed away. . . . I don't get it."

Pa stepped around the tables and allowed the weeping man to lean on him as he gave him a bear hug. "Morty, sometimes folks don't make a lick of sense. They grieve in ways that they don't even understand."

Pa raised his head slightly and met my eyes. "I know it hurts, but you can't take it personally. Just know you are God's kid no matter what, and we are here for you." He hushed and let the poor guy cry it out for a spell. When Morty's tears dried up, Pa slapped him on the back and said, "Besides, this rad group here sure does care about you and likes having you around."

Morty shook his head. "Dave, you cannot pull off saying *rad*. Just doesn't fit you." The group laughed. "Thank you for caring so much about me. I'm sorry I put a damper on our Harvest Day."

"Nonsense. I'm cool enough to say *rad* and *tubular* and whatever else kids are saying these days." Pa's thick eyebrows arched distinctively. "And you got nothing to be sorry for. If you can't open up to us when something's buggin' you, then who can ya?"

Morty settled in his chair, finally smiling.

"Now Nolia Farms may have had a bountiful tobacco season, and I'm grateful for that, but I'm with Austin. I'm thankful for each one of you and your health." Pa started to return to the front of the tables, about to wrap things up, but Walynn motioned for him to stop by her chair.

She was subtle when she whispered the petition to Pa. "Dave, the little guys . . ."

Pa's eyes widened with awareness as he whirled around and focused on the twins. "Oh yeah. You boys got anything you want to thank the good Lord for?"

Those two cuties bent their heads together and communicated much like the older twins often did. Nash nodded and Knox nodded back before he looked at Pa and said, "Miss

Walynn." My heart ached at his admission, and from the whispered aahs and Walynn's sniffles, everyone else was clearly affected by it too.

Recounting what each person had shared as their harvest, I realized material possessions were not mentioned. Perhaps our group was known for their wrongs, but I'd just witnessed them getting something absolutely right—the true meaning of Harvest Day. I know God smiled down on us right then and there. The tightening in my chest and the goose bumps skirting along my arms testified to that truth. I often reflect on this as one of the most significant church services I've ever had the privilege of attending.

Once we settled down, Pa spoke again. "There's a lot we can learn from King David. He had difficult seasons of life and knew it was okay to cry out to God during them. That cat also knew how to celebrate God in the better seasons after being restored. He wasn't ashamed to shout out praises, to sing, to dance . . ." Pa turned in a circle, eyeing each person. "How about for today, we choose to leave our heavy baggage back at the entrance of Nolia Farms and just enjoy ourselves."

Gazing at the diverse crowd, I thought that maybe we were more like King David than not. He didn't fit the bill as a perfect leader, but he was a child of God. The First Riffraff of Magnolia certainly did not fit the bill of a normal congregation whatsoever, but we were God's children just the same.

"King David danced to celebrate God's grace and mercy, so I say we do the same!" Pa walked over to the boom box and cranked that sucker wide-open.

I seriously doubted King David danced to anything like

Chaka Khan's "I Feel for You," but no one seemed to mind. Everyone was too much in a celebratory mood to fuss over such details.

The day passed with feasting, swimming, and dancing. Peg didn't swim in front of others because it required him to take off his prosthetic and that was something he wasn't comfortable doing, so he appointed himself as DJ. Foxy didn't know how to swim, so she played his assistant. Those two kept the music pumping nonstop.

Surprisingly, Miss Wise could swim like a fish and spent the day racing Morty from one side of the lengthy pond to the other. Both sets of twins kept to the shallows, giggling and frolicking as children should do at their ages. Pa, Vance, and Tripp entertained us with their daredevil flips and dives off the rock ledge lining the backside of the pond. It made me nervous, but Pa hadn't worn a smile for that long at a time since before Mama passed away, so I wouldn't be doing anything to take that away from him. And that included sitting back while he risked breaking his neck.

I spent the day staying along the edges of the celebration, just soaking it all in. Each one laughing and playing and chatting freely, that was the harvest for me. It was as if the weight we had all been bearing lifted as easily as the smoke rising from the large grill, wafting up to heaven.

As night drew near, the swimming slowed down and the dancing picked up. The small beach became our dance floor. It was pretty comical watching Walynn get shot down by Pa. She would dance close, but he continuously evaded her advances.

Peg cackled as we watched on. "Watch him . . . There!" He

cackled again when Pa patted Walynn's shoulder and turned away from her. The exact same brush-off move he used with us kids when he'd had enough of us but didn't want to hurt our feelings.

Walynn was a beautiful woman, and the more time that passed, the less tight her clothes became. I still wouldn't refer to her as modest, but she had become more tasteful in her attire. And she doted on the younger twins in such a loving way that I wished Pa would pay her attention for the kids' sake if nothing else. Even though it seemed he'd woken up that year, he remained closed to that woman's affection.

"Poor Walynn," I said on a snicker.

Peg wrinkled his nose. "Poor Walynn? Shoot, she'd be better off dancing with me."

"You dumping me for her, Peg?" Foxy tsked.

That was all it took for Peg to put in the Tina Turner cassette tape and drag Foxy to the center of the dancing.

Walynn finally took the hint and danced with Tripp as Pa danced with Charlotte. Vance and Morty took turns dancing with Miss Wise. And just let me tell ya, that Jinx had some moves and before we knew it, he was teaching some of those moves to the kids. Watching Boss do the robot beside Jinx was close to being the highlight of the night until a familiar song came on.

"That's our song!" Vance yelled from the beach and rushed over to me. We began slow dancing to "Heaven" as the small gathering clapped and Tripp whistled. Looking over Vance's shoulder, I took in our surroundings. Everything was glowing under the numerous lanterns and portable lights. Each table housed a lamp and Pa had lined the dock with even more. The moon wasn't full, but the night sky was clear, so the stars helped to show off the festivities. As I swayed in Vance's arms with others joining in, I thought about prom of all things. About how Malorie had gone on and on that year about *The Blue Lagoon* theme. Smiling, I knew tissue-paper flowers and metallic streamers had nothing on this moment.

"Ole Dave knows how to throw a proper celebration," Vance commented as he lowered me into an unexpected dip. "Best Harvest Day I've ever attended."

I laughed. It was all I could do at the moment.

Vance righted me as he gazed at me with affection. "That laugh of yours has to be my most favorite sound in the entire world." He leaned close and placed a quick kiss onto my smiling lips.

"All right now!" Pa hollered in our direction. "I'm watching you, boy!"

Vance put some space between us as the group roared in laughter.

After our song concluded, I remained out on the small beach with Vance and the others, dancing the night away. I even tried doing the moonwalk at one point.

When Sister Sledge's "We Are Family" came on, Tripp yelled with as much enthusiasm as Vance had earlier, "That's our song!" More laughter and more dancing followed.

It was too good. Too shiny. Too normal. No matter how much I wished, prayed, begged, I knew this season wouldn't last. There was no way Pa would be able to keep up at the rate he was going. Like a race car leading the pack to victory, nearing the finish line, only to take the last curve way too fast. Losing control to the point of taking out those that were following too close in his wake.

Yes, I knew it wasn't going to last and a darker season would return. But I had no idea it would return so thick, like a glob of black ink, blotting out all the good underneath.

Chapter 11

HANGMAN

April 1986

The most annoying game to ever play with a bunch of young'uns who didn't put much effort into spelling was Hangman. It was torture with two five-year-olds and one mentally delayed twenty-year-old, but we soldiered through when it rained because there wasn't much else to do since Pa refused to put a TV in the house. We'd all but begged, but he said that was inviting Satan into the home. Well, I was fairly certain that sucker was already roaming the hallways, so there really was no reason to deprive us of a TV.

I certainly could have used the distraction of a TV show during that bleak spring and the humdrum life on the farm. There were always needs for me to meet and always the exhausting task of keeping up with Pa. He'd begun drifting off the farm for a day or two before drifting home like an indecisive ghost, never sure where he wanted to haunt. The fear of him drifting away permanently robbed me of rest at night, and so like most nights I had wandered up to the loft of the packhouse to ponder and worry about matters that were out of my hands.

As I studied the yellowing maps on the far wall of the loft, the incident at lunch last week came to mind. I closed my eyes and rubbed my temples, wishing to block it out but it was no good.

Pa had been all over the kitchen, plundering through the doorless cabinets. "Where the heck are the knives?"

I knew where the knives were and took them down when I needed them. Pa never ventured into the kitchen for much of anything, so it had been easy to keep them out of sight. Until now, I suppose.

"I . . . uh . . ." Before I could finish stumbling over an answer, his big paw met the side of the roasting pan on top of the fridge, the contents jangling from his force. "I put them inside the pan to keep them out of reach of the younger twins."

Nash and Knox sat at the table munching on a tin pan of Jiffy Pop I had just finished making for them. The space held the aroma of butter and a slight burnt smell from me almost taking too long to remove it from the burner, but it didn't stop their hands from dipping inside the foil dome for more.

Pa craned his neck around and actually looked at the boys—something he rarely did—while moving the coffee cups out of the way of the roasting pan. "You boys got enough sense not to mess with knives, right?"

"Yes, sir," they both muttered, eyeing Pa with a measured amount of fear.

Pa carried the roasting pan to the table and plopped it in the middle. His sudden movement and the loud clanging caused the boys' shoulders to jolt. After shoving the sleeves of his thermal shirt up to his elbows, he took the lid off and plucked a paring knife from the collection. "Y'all know what'll happen if you fool with sharp objects." In a blink, he flicked the blade against his forearm. A thin line of red bloomed instantly.

Everyone's eyes widened as we released staggered gasps.

"Ox, put the knives back where they belong." Pa tossed the paring knife in the sink and stalked out of the kitchen.

I opened my eyes to get away from the image of Nash's and Knox's frightened faces while they watched our father purposely hurt himself. Shaking my head, I returned to scanning the Texas map for a while. After hunching in the corner for longer than I should have, I got to my feet and stretched out my tired back before moving to the open window. It was time to head inside and go on to bed, but there was a restlessness rolling heavily in the pit of my stomach. From my view, a light coming from the front of the farm caught my attention. At first I thought it was headlights passing by, but the light remained several minutes later when I glanced that way again. Thinking someone must have left the light on in the chapel or produce stand, I climbed down and headed toward the light to take care of it.

A soft breeze rustled through the fields and reached me. It was a refreshing companion on my walk down the driveway, as well as my daydream of running off to live with Vance on the lake. I missed him to the point of pain when Pa got still in his despondency and, in effect, isolated me in it too.

A calamity rang out from inside the chapel, startling me out of those dismal thoughts.

We kept a tobacco stick propped by the door to whack the wasp nests down. I grabbed it up and barreled inside, preparing to whack a vandal. I lost my grip on the stick and it banged against the floor as I came to terms with the sight before me.

"Pa!" I ran to the altar, where he lay wrestling with a thick rope that looked like an anaconda wrapped around a victim. I fell to my knees and helped unravel the rope. Both our hands fumbled as if they were boneless, but we finally managed to free him of it.

"Pa, what's going on?" I asked, spotting the harsh streaks of red branded into the skin on the side of his neck. "Did . . . did you try hurting yourself?" I stopped short of adding *again* to the question. The answer was obvious anyhow and it had bile burning the back of my throat.

"Just wanted the hurt to stop," he whispered so low I wasn't sure he actually admitted it. He coughed. "It's so dark . . ."

I helped him to his feet and over to the front pew. When he said nothing else and my heart settled down to a manageable gallop, I focused on hiding what had just transpired—placing the overturned stool by the piano, coiling the heavy rope and tossing it out the door with the intention of burning it later, and sweeping up the splinters of wood scattered on the altar and floor.

Breathless from Pa's botched hanging and the rush to hide it, I plopped on the pew beside him. We both focused on the

damaged wood beam overhead for a long spell. A lot of time
went by with Pa regarding the beam in such a defeated manner, shoulders hunched, mouth in a harsh frown, that I began
to grow restless and worried if he was figuring out how to give
it another go.

"You can't, Pa. You can't do that again."

On a long sigh that ended with a raspy chuckle, Pa rubbed
the side of his neck and winced. He quickly dropped his hand,
giving away how bruised he really was. I felt quite bruised too.

"Yeah, you're right. Guess that answered my question."

Scared to look at him, I studied the scratches in the floor.
"What question?"

"The beam is weak."

Ya think? Of course it would be too weak to hold the two-hundred-
and-twenty-pound man trying to dangle from it. My sarcastic
remark remained trapped behind my clenched jaw.

Sighing, my gaze flicked to the buckled chunk of wood. It
now had fingers and was barely managing to grasp on to some
semblance of the solid structure it once was. Sneaking a glance
at the man sitting beside me from the corner of my eye, I didn't
miss the ironic similarities to him and the busted beam.

"Why were you wondering about the beam at one in the
morning?"

Pa's thick eyebrows puckered as he sought out the small
clock by the piano, apparently having no clue to the time. The
man just seemed to have no clue, period, as of late. "I . . ." He
scanned the sanctuary and stopped on the giant magnolia wreath
propped against the wall, pointing at it with a shaky finger. "I
wanted to surprise Charlotte by hanging that up." He offered the

excuse as if it made perfect sense. It was, after all, a skill we'd all perfected—hiding behind the pretending and excuses.

I gave up on getting a straight answer and turned my attention to his neck. He was holding it at an odd angle, clueing me in on it hurting him pretty badly. The rope burns were getting angrier and purple splotches were blooming all the way up to the scruff of his beard.

"Do I need to take you to the ER?"

Pa gingerly moved his neck side to side, front to back, and then swallowed several times. "Nothing a few aspirin won't take care of." He slowly stood and I joined him and we both made a quiet exit, not wanting to disturb the awfulness of what had just transpired.

We began the mile-long walk home, letting the darkness of night keep us company. Seemed that was the only companion Pa preferred anyway.

Once we neared the porch, I whispered, "There's some of Foxy's aloe ointment in the top bathroom drawer. It would do those scratches on your neck good."

"Yeah. I'll do that. You get on to bed now," he ordered in a hoarse whisper but I couldn't move.

"Pa . . ." The words rattling around my mind wanted me to ask why he tried killing himself again. They also wanted me to demand he go get some help, but in the end I chickened out. "I love you."

He returned the sentiment before disappearing inside the dark house. Shaken to the bone, I followed.

With less than three hours total of sleep, I managed to get everyone to school and dropped off Boss to Tripp.

Needing a break as well, I decided to swing by Miss Wise's house but her car was gone. Disappointed, I continued on toward the farm. With the images of Pa crumpled in a heap of rope and splinters fresh in my mind, the Silver Bullet shot right past our driveway. It happened with such ease that I decided to see how long that feeling would last.

It lasted all the way to Lake Murray, but after sitting on the brick steps of Vance's porch for the better part of an hour, that ease began to morph into a ragging anxiety in the pit of my stomach. I'd peeped into the garage. The truck was parked inside, but his new sports car wasn't in its spot. The car was what he preferred to drive to campus, claiming it was easier to park, so I figured he must have gotten held up at school for some reason.

Another half hour passed before the black Mustang pulled past the gates. My relief at watching it circle around to the garage was short-lived as three more shiny expensive cars pulled in behind him. A parade of fresh-faced preppy types exited the cars and moved toward me, each one with a grocery sack. Guys in an assortment of pastel polo shirts, collars flipped up in that annoying style, pressed Bermuda shorts, and tan boat shoes. The three girls were a feminine reflection of the guys, but with bright-white Keds. Each one offering a fake smile.

A brown-headed guy popped his Wayfarers on top of his head and gave me an exaggerated once-over. "Well, hello, beautiful." His chest puffed out as he swaggered closer. This fool's behavior reminded me of what Pa called peacocking. I expected the guy to start strutting and clucking at any moment.

I stood and smoothed my palms over the sides of my ratty

jeans, looking around and finally spotting Vance making his way out of the garage with his own grocery sack and a bag of ice. Wearing a preppy outfit himself, he caught sight of me and offered a quizzical smile.

"Hi," I mumbled to the guy without taking my eyes off Vance as he neared us.

"You have your own driver, sweetheart?" Flirty Guy asked with an air of arrogance.

I leveled him with a look. "Yeah. Me."

He balked. "You're a limo driver? Wow. Got a card so I can book your services?" He gave me a devilish grin, looking rather pleased with himself.

The shiny group chuckled and giggled behind him.

"I thought you had people for that, RJ," a redheaded guy spoke dryly.

RJ combed through his hair, blatantly eyeing parts of me he had no business eyeing. "Yeah, but I wouldn't mind having this one all to myself." He winked a dark eye, looking slimy instead of enticing.

I didn't admit it out loud, but I knew RJ was Robert Joseph Warner III. The son of our current governor. I was sure that if I paid more attention to such, the identities of the others would have been obvious, but there was only so much intimidation I could endure. Of course Vance had found his people at school.

It made me wonder what in the heck was I thinking going to him, regretting my rebellion of driving past the farm earlier. Surely I had no business amongst this elite group.

"Austin," Vance said, his voice surprised yet guarded, clearly missing or ignoring RJ's flirty comments.

I stepped away from RJ's advances and mumbled a rough "Hey" to Vance.

He made it to the bottom of the steps and looked up at me. "Everything okay?"

"Uh, yeah . . ." I scanned the curious onlookers behind him, all looking like Ken and Barbie dolls, before resettling on Vance's brilliant-green eyes. "Just wanted to stop by and say hey." I hitched a thumb toward the Silver Bullet. "But I'll come back another time."

"No." Vance took the steps two at the time and I braced myself for one of his full-force hugs. My throat even tightened with anticipation and need for his comfort. He zoomed right on past me to unlock the door, reaching inside to turn off the alarm. A few beeps later he returned to the porch. "You guys head on inside." He beckoned his friends and handed off the bag of ice and sack to a dark-blonde permed prep, who seemed to think the gesture was quite special.

RJ paused by the door. "Audrey, you should join us on the boat." He disappeared inside before I could correct him.

Vance closed the door and turned around. His cheeks were a warmer shade of bronze. I wasn't sure if he was embarrassed or shocked. He glanced at the limo, making it clear it was an embarrassment, which in effect embarrassed me. Coming to the lake had been a mistake.

"What's up?"

"Nothing." I shrugged a shoulder and shoved my hands in my front pockets to keep from pinching him for making this so awkward. My body trembled with the effort of keeping it together, so close to crumpling. Couldn't he see that?

"It can't be nothing for you to drive out here in the middle of the week."

I'd witnessed my father trying to take his own life, so it was far from nothing, but no way could I confide in this snooty version of Vance Cumberland. That made me want to punch him in the gut, the same spot where mine ached. "You said I was welcome anytime. Even gave me the code to the gate. Remember?" I whispered instead of yelling like I wanted to.

The door opened. We both twisted to see RJ popping his head out. "Cumberland, the chicks are whining that it's too chilly on the dock. You have any sweatshirts they can wear?" He asked Vance but his eyes were on me.

"Yeah, man," Vance answered in his public persona tone. He turned to me with a pleading expression on his handsome face. "I'll just be a sec. Okay?"

Even though I completely opposed his audacity of putting other girls and that prep squad before me who was supposed to be his girlfriend, I gave him a reassuring nod. He was in fake politician's son mode, so I knew to keep my mouth shut and remember my place.

RJ lingered after Vance went inside.

"Seriously, join us on the boat . . ." His dark eyes coasted over me. "I bet Vance will let you chauffeur us." He bit his bottom lip and I bit my tongue.

Someone yelled from inside, so he finally shut the door and I took my cue to haul tail out of there.

A mile or two down the road, several stinging realizations hit me square in the chest.

Vance hadn't touched me.

Vance hadn't introduced me.

Vance hadn't invited me in.

Vance had left me on the porch like an insignificant pet.

I pulled into a gas station when my vision blurred past the point of seeing the road clearly. After putting the car in park, I flipped the visor down and stared at my reflection, finding nothing appealing. Red-rimmed eyes with black circles underneath. Lips chapped and swollen from chewing them with worry. Cheeks hollowed due to the lack of appetite lately. Hair limp and unkempt. Whatever sickness Pa had seemed to have infected me too. So gradual that I'd not noticed, and Vance certainly hadn't just now. No, he was too busy focusing on his fancy friends' needs to have noticed anything about me.

Slapping the visor shut, I rested my head on the back of the seat and let all the bitterness of hurt and disappointment wash over me. The venom much more potent than the snakebite I'd endured two years ago. Bone-deep, this was a painful admission of defeat.

I was tired from searching for hope. For the first time, while parked in a strange parking lot, I experienced a new symptom of Pa's illness. It was the symptom of wanting to end it all. I cracked one eye open and then the other to get a better look at the bridge up ahead, but I could only see the car plunging off the side of it. It was a thought with a brief flash of comfort, finally making me understand why Pa kept chasing that fleeting moment of peace before his attempts. The idea of having a way to make it all stop, the pain, the grief, the frustration, the hopelessness . . .

A loud tap on the driver's window pulled me from the dark

idea. "Ma'am, you got car trouble?" a burly guy in a cowboy hat asked loudly through the closed window.

I reached a trembling hand over and sent the window down halfway. "No, sir. Just needed a minute . . ."

He bent slightly to get a better look at me. "You need some help?"

I needed a lot of help, but nothing the cowboy could offer. "I'm fine. Thank you for checking though." I sent the window up, making it clear we were done. He seemed to not buy that. How was my dismay so clear to a stranger yet Vance overlooked it? He stood by the window for another beat before tipping his hat and walking off.

I closed my eyes to regain the comfort I found in the image of the car plunging into the water. Instead, the faces of Boss, Peg, Raleigh, Charlotte, Nash, and Knox formed. Even Pa's face. Just as quickly as the symptom of suicide formed, it dissolved. There was no way I could do that to my family. They needed me. Yet there I was, on the side of the road, because I'd selfishly gone seeking comfort from my boyfriend. Talk about a reality check.

Expecting tears to show up to give some form of relief, I braced myself, but the only impact was that of anger and resignation. All aimed at Vance Cumberland.

Pa and my siblings were my world, and apparently boat rides with a bunch of preps were his. We simply did not fit together, and I was tired of wasting energy on it. His worry was keeping debutantes warm on the lake while my worry was whether Pa had found the hidden rope and a strong enough beam to get the job done.

Chiding myself for the momentary lapse in judgment for leaving Pa alone, I slung the car into drive and made the thirty-minute drive in twenty. Those minutes were spent begging God to let Pa be alive still, and I breathed a sigh of relief when I found him holed up in his bedroom with an ice pack on his neck. If Pa had enough wits to tend to his wounds, then surely there had to be a speck of hope in there somewhere.

In years to come, I would often wonder if I'd been a little more mature, a little more brave, whether it would have made a difference that night. Perhaps if I'd asked Pa what my mind screamed for me to, that botched hanging could have been a turning point instead of another cover-up. Could I have prevented some of the nightmares and episodes? The what-ifs plagued me.

———————

Perhaps I wasn't ready to come to terms with what needed to be done with Pa, but by Friday I was ready to get the job done when it came to Vance Cumberland. Most Fridays the pickup truck would ease up to the house and deliver the farm boy version. The one in torn jeans, work boots, dirty ball cap, and a dimpled smile. It was my very favorite version and I never hesitated to meet him at the driver's door to deliver my kiss of welcome. We would hold each other as if it had been months instead of days. I would trace the faint freckles on the bridge of his nose. He would comb his fingers through my long hair. Then the kids would burst outside and interrupt our intimate bubble, knowing Vance had treats for each of them.

This Friday my siblings weren't there to interrupt. I'd made sure of it, dispersing them between the people I'd grown to trust—Miss Wise, Foxy, and Walynn. They'd had a front-row seat for the entirety of my relationship with Vance, but this part needed no witnesses.

The truck rolled up as expected, but I remained sitting on the porch steps. When it became apparent I wasn't going over to meet him, Vance climbed out, a familiar brown bag in his hand. Even though he'd driven the farm boy vehicle, he'd shown up in his businessman facade.

"Ain't you all fancy today," I quipped.

"My father had me sit in on another board meeting." He unraveled the tie from around his collar and tossed it inside the truck before closing the door. "I was bored out of my mind."

"Tough life." I quickly averted my gaze toward the sprouting tobacco fields as he walked toward me.

"No hello kiss? And where's the welcome wagon?" Vance asked. The bag crinkled in his grasp as he waved it, playing off what he must have known would be a serious encounter after what had happened on Wednesday. He hovered nearby before finally taking a seat beside me.

We sat in silence until Vance exhaled, frustration and wariness both quite audible. That made two of us.

"Talk to me, Austin."

I settled my gaze just past my bare feet, following the brick walk's herringbone pattern. "Why talk now, considering you weren't in the mood Wednesday?"

He grumbled, "You showed up unexpectedly, and I had plans and . . . I was shocked. And before I had a chance, you left. Everybody was there and I couldn't just leave . . ."

Out the corner of my eye, I watched him rub his forehead. I wish my issues with Wednesday were so insignificant as his. I almost told him that, but then it would mean confessing what had transpired the night before that spurred my unexpected visit. Doing so would only make what I had to do next even harder. Just as I had to cut school off my list in order to manage my responsibilities, it was time to do another trimming.

Needing to get it over with, I angled toward Vance. "Look, I didn't mean to embarrass you in front of your friends. Had I known you were having a party I'd have never gone in the first place."

"You didn't embarrass me." Vance combed his fingers through his newly trimmed hair. It was way too short, too neat. I hated it just as much as our current predicament. He dropped his hand, noticing I was scowling at the new hairstyle. "I was just caught off guard, is all."

No, that weren't all, and I could point out how he hadn't welcomed me or introduced me to his friends, but it really didn't matter anymore. No. What mattered was that I had a broken father upstairs who seemed too paralyzed by some unseen sickness that he couldn't even free himself from his own bed.

"It's cool." I shrugged with indifference and scooted over when he reached to wrap his arm around my shoulders.

"No. It's not cool." He unbuttoned the collar of his dress shirt and yanked on it for good measure. "I called, but you wouldn't talk to me. I even got in an argument with Peg about it." His tone lightened, wanting to play it off. On another day . . .

maybe another easier life, I would have laughed it off with him and teased about Peg letting him have it about calling all the dang time.

"I have had my hands too full to be on the phone," I told the half-truth.

"I've tried talking you into coming out to the lake house for the last two years. You cannot hold it against me for being shocked at finding you there for the first time."

"I don't."

"Good." He moved closer again, and the late-afternoon light glanced off the green of his eyes. "How about coming back this Wednesday? We're taking the boat out again. That way I can properly introduce you." Hope joined the light in his gaze, sparkling even, but it needed to be extinguished.

"Nah. Not my scene." My tone remained detached even though I was livid. How could he play off his reaction to me in front of his posh friends? How could he not have chased after me? How had he not picked up on the fact that I was distraught? But then I wanted to kick myself, for two reasons. One, we weren't some stupid romantic tale where the hero saves the heroine. Two, I'm ashamed to admit that I'd become somewhat better at lying and camouflaging my feelings. That second point was about to come into play.

"They're nice once you get to know them. You'll see."

"I'm sure they are, but I'm not interested."

"Not interested? Not interested in making an effort for me?" Vance snorted a haughty laugh and jabbed a finger toward his shiny truck and then the newly planted field. "Yet all this time I've found interest in every aspect of *your* world!"

"You playing Farmer Joe for kicks and giggles at your convenience is not showing interest. More on the lines of you finding this poor girl and farming entertaining and a break from your posh lifestyle. I think you get a thrill out of getting dirty every now and then, but news flash, Mr. Mayor's Son, I'm *always* dirty. This is my world and it ain't changing."

"I'm not asking you to change. You won't completely let me in your world. That's on you!" Now his finger jabbed in my direction.

"And there you just hit the nail on the head. Our worlds are too different and it's too much work trying to fit into each other's. It's exhausting, and I'm over it, quite frankly."

Vance's brow furrowed. "Austin—"

"This has been our problem from the start."

"Problems can be solved. We just gotta work harder at figuring it out."

"It's too much of a commitment . . . Honestly, I'm too young to make this kind of commitment. I need some freedom."

His bronze complexion warmed a few shades more. "No." Standing suddenly, he yanked me to my feet and anchored me in his arms. *"No."* His crisp cologne, a mix of leather and citrus, blanketed me.

Holding my breath, I shoved out of his hold and moved down the small brick walk.

Heavy on my heels, Vance grabbed my wrist and whirled me around. "Austin. Please. I'm this close to finishing school." He held up a hand and touched his thumb and index finger together.

"Good for you. That'll come in handy when Miss Right

comes along. Sorry, but it ain't me." My words were supposed
to be a repellent. Instead, he stepped closer and took my face
in his hands.

"Don't do this, Austin," Vance demanded in a gravelly whisper that hurt me to the core. "Don't you dare."

I answered with silence, shoring up the wall between us.
Too many words shared would reveal too much, and he'd be
less likely to walk away. The barn cat strolled out into the sunshine and stopped at my feet. I plucked her up and into my
arms, knowing Vance's aversion to cats would encourage him
to keep his distance.

"Maybe you're right about being too young, since you're
acting like a child with this silent treatment." His lips pressed
into a severe line as a disgusted look washed over his face.

"You should probably head on out." I tipped my head toward
his truck and took another step back, putting more distance
between us. Tears burned trails down the back of my throat
and I couldn't help but wonder if a well-worn path had formed
over the past few months. Hidden deep inside, it was the only
choice I gave the tears and anger.

Hands tossed in the air, he began stomping toward his
truck. His door slammed, the engine roared to life, and the
truck did something I'd never witnessed before. It kicked up a
dust storm as it sped down the dirt road.

Even though I knew my motive was to do him a favor,
to free him of the sickness infecting the farm, my insides
crumpled.

Placing the cat on the ground, I managed to stumble into
the house, to the comforts of darkened rooms and heavy

silence. Pa was still up in his room, so paralyzed by his deso-
lation that he'd not been able to make it out of bed. And wasn't
that just fitting—misery certainly did love company.

I planned on keeping my misery to myself by means of
staying downstairs and self-medicating with the carton of
butter pecan ice cream I had hidden in the bottom of the
deep freeze. The tin of chocolate-dipped caramels Miss Wise
gave me when I dropped Charlotte off caught my eye as I dug
a giant scoop of ice cream out and into a mixing bowl. The
cereal bowls were too small to hold the proper dose. I popped
the lid, plucked a chocolate out and into my mouth before
pouring the rest on top of the ice cream.

With the bowl in hand, I shuffled into the living room
and plopped onto the couch. The silence was too loud, so I
thumbed through the records to find something to help hush it
and drown out my miserable thoughts about Vance and already
regretting letting him go. But to keep him would have just been
selfish. At least I tried talking myself into that truth.

Settling on the Allman Brothers album, I turned the volume
low and started shoveling ice cream in my mouth, chewing
thoughtfully on the sticky caramels. I kept at it until "Dreams"
started playing. It drew everything to the surface like a salve
drawing out poison. I set the spoon down and let it do its worst,
thinking perhaps the tears would show up to at least wash
some of the pain away. The song ended without tears.

I'd erected such an invincible wall between me and the outside world that an inner wall had gone up between me and my
emotions. I'd tried countless times to tear it down, but nothing
had been found to penetrate it. I knew the simple act could

be so freeing in so many ways after witnessing it expressed in various themes amongst our small congregation.

Surprisingly, Morty Lawson had shown the purest forms of crying. Smiling cheeks damp and hands raised in the air as he shouted *amen*, his were tears of praise and worship.

A river of heaviness marked by trails of mascara, Walynn Posten was the epitome of brokenness and regret. Cries so violent her narrow shoulders shook.

The most profound tears I'd witnessed had been subtle ones accompanied by an appreciative smile from Miss Wise when Charlotte and I had surprised her with a packet of significant paperwork last year. We'd pooled our earnings Pa paid us from the tobacco season and made a donation to a museum whose sole purpose was to preserve the history of Holocaust victims. Our donation was enough to have two brick pavers added to the museum's garden engraved with Helena Wisniewska on one in her honor and Irene Wisniewska on the other in memory of Miss Wise's sister. Those were tears of healing.

Staring at the melting ice cream drowning the beautiful chocolates, I longed for a combination of those tearful expressions or just one, but none showed up.

Not showing up seemed to be the current theme of my life, so it was no surprise when Pa decided not to show up Sunday morning to lead the service. I had banged on his locked door, pleading with him to come out, but the only response was the squeaking of the mattress springs when he apparently rolled over. At least I knew he was still alive, so I had no other choice but to leave him and go face the congregation. It wasn't the first time, but it was becoming harder and harder to lie to them.

I stood in front of the small group, shifting from foot to foot, staring at the back wall while trying to muster up an excuse as to why Pa was absent once again. Comments were being made about the beautiful magnolia wreath hanging just above my head. Considering the state Pa had been in since his botched hanging, I had no idea how or when he managed to fix the beam and hang the wreath.

"Umm . . . Good morning," I mumbled. A few returned the sentiment but with less hesitation. "Hope y'all had a good week . . ." I was stalling, coming up short on what to say next.

The side door creaked open to my right. All eyes turned to it and watched Pa enter. Temperatures were at least in the mideighties outside, much too hot for a turtleneck, yet there he was, wearing one. He would have fit right in on that Beatles album cover where they were all wearing black turtlenecks.

There was no denying the fact that my father was a handsome man, in a walking dead sort of way. Even though he'd recently lost some weight, Dave Foster still had a profound presence. If anyone found it odd that he was dressed in such a way—and hello, they undoubtedly did—no one said a word about it.

Pa gave my shoulder a pat, dismissing me to get out of the way, and I did with no hesitation. From the back pew I watched him place his worn Bible on the small podium as he cleared his throat.

"I ain't feeling too well today, so I'll be brief." He paused to clear his throat again. His raspy voice sounded like razor blades had shredded it, although I knew it was a rope that got the job done. He seemed to be flipping through the Bible aimlessly in such a lethargic manner that I wished he'd just stayed home. Finally he lifted his eyes and fastened them to me. "I heard the song 'Dreams' by the Allman Brothers the other night. . . . The lyrics spoke to me."

"Why don't you sing it for us, Dave," Tripp encouraged.

Pa's glassy eyes slid briefly to Tripp. "I would, but I have a sore throat." He sure wasn't lying about that. It would take longer than a few days to get over the damage he'd inflicted on himself this time. He refocused on my eyes, which worried me. "Those lyrics . . . they talked about having a hunger for dreams you'll never see and how the world seems to fall down on you. Y'all ever feel like your world is fallin' down on ya?"

Responding yeses rippled through the group, but Pa didn't acknowledge them as he remained honed in on me. Everyone else faded and it was just my father and me, both broken and weary, teetering on the edge of throwing in the towel.

"We all dream of what we want our lives to be, but some will just never . . ." His voice gave out, so he paused to clear his throat again. "I might not know how to fix things for you, for me . . . Just know that you can take it to God."

"Amen," Foxy said softly.

Pa dropped his gaze to the Bible on the podium and flipped more pages, the ruffling of the thin paper the only sound penetrating the heavy silence. "Almost half of the Psalms are lamentations." Looking up again, he began reciting several verses. "'Have mercy upon me, O Lord; for I am weak: O Lord, heal me; for my bones are vexed. . . . I am weary with my groaning;

all the night make I my bed to swim; I water my couch with my tears.' 'Why standest thou afar off, O Lord? Why hidest thyself in times of trouble?' 'How long shall I take counsel in my soul, having sorrow in my heart daily?'" His lips quivered as he wiped his eyes.

"Help him, Lord." Foxy was whispering, but it was so quiet in the chapel we all heard her anyway.

"In Psalm 3, verse 4, David said, 'I cried unto the Lord with my voice, and he heard me out of his holy hill. Selah.'" Pa closed the Bible and looked at me once again. "Just as we can dance like King David in the good times, we can cry out to God like King David in the difficult times. If I could take the pain away, I would, but I can't. It's a part of this life, plain and simple. We all fall, make mistakes we aren't proud of . . ."

He rubbed the side of his covered neck gingerly. "It's up to us to make the choice to carry on. When it seems you have no one to turn to, remember to turn to God. Bring your pleas, your burdens, your anger, whatever it is—just bring it to him. Don't put your faith in me. Put it in God."

This message could have been directed to any soul in the congregation, but I knew it was for me and me only. Pa begging me to beg God to heal us. Behind Pa's blank expression he wasn't just crying out to God but screaming for help. I knew it and he knew it.

Chapter 12

FALLING

November 1986

Autumn had sashayed into Magnolia's town square, spreading its decor everywhere—pumpkins, gourds, maple tree leaves. The aroma of apple cider, popcorn, and smoked meats on the cast-iron grills added to the festivities of the town and today's fall festival. For a chilly fall day, Magnolia was lively and in a celebratory mood. A Southern rock band crooned from the steps of the courthouse at the northern end of the square while a chorus of giggles and squeals from children rang out from every direction.

Situated near the middle of the square with other vendors, I spent the day working the Nolia Farms booth with Foxy. It gave me a clear view of the game booths on the other side of the grassy square, making it easy to keep an eye on both sets of twins as they played and explored. Sadly, it had also given me another view I had no desire seeing. A view that had started during the midmorning parade, where the mayor's family joined the Fitzgeralds on the Magnolia City Council float to lead the procession around town. Malorie Fitzgerald had planted herself beside Vance on the front of the float and had remained planted by his side for most of the day's festivities. With Malorie dressed in a fur-trimmed jacket and brown leather heeled boots and Vance in dark-washed jeans and a plaid jacket, they were a vision of youthful class. The perfect match, really, and it turned my stomach so sour that I couldn't even enjoy the caramel-and-chocolate–dipped apple Miss Wise had Raleigh bring to me earlier.

The normally reclusive lady was actually participating in the festival, manning the bobbing for apples game. Once a kid snagged an apple, Miss Wise would dry it off and dip it in the kid's choice of deliciousness. Vats of buttery caramel, melted chocolate, and cherry-flavored coating that reminded me of those red suckers the bank teller gave out to the young'uns when I stopped in the bank to make a deposit. Not surprisingly, Miss Wise was the most popular woman of the day.

"We're out of blackberry jam," I informed Foxy after placing the last jar in a brown bag for the customer.

"Did you check the back of the truck? There are a few more crates last I saw." Foxy looked around our booth as if some would magically appear.

"Yes. The only thing left is a batch of pepper jelly and pickled okra." I plucked the blackberry sign from the table and stashed it underneath, where we were keeping elixirs and such. No signs were needed for those. Folks only had to make eye contact with Foxy and she all but read what they were wanting to purchase out of sight of others.

"Selling out is a good thing." Foxy rearranged our display, moving jars of strawberry preserves over to the empty spot.

"I'm going to grab up the pepper jelly. Be right back." I cupped my hands and blew some heat to my frozen fingers and then rewrapped my scarf around my neck. Tucking my hands in the pockets of my corduroy coat, I walked over to the library, where we'd parked earlier, and grabbed the crate of jelly.

On the way back, I caught sight of Malorie with her head bent close to Foxy's as they spoke intently about something. I slowed, not wanting to have to speak but also curious as to what potion from underneath the table Malorie was purchasing. They exchanged money and then Malorie slipped the small bag into her purse before rushing off. Of course Miss High-and-Mighty didn't want to be caught at the witch doctor's booth.

My mouth opened before I could stop it. "Malorie! Did you need a receipt for your purchase from Foxy?"

Malorie ducked her head and speed-walked away, though I knew good and well she heard me hollering.

"What was that all about?" I plopped the crate on the edge of the table and began unloading it.

"Ah, she was in need of some tea," Foxy answered vaguely, adjusting the burgundy gingham tablecloth to conceal the lined shelf set up underneath the table, but not before I noticed the empty spot where the last pouch of fertility tea had been earlier.

"What'd she want with fertility tea?"

Foxy's onyx eyes slid to mine as she patted the side of her golden head wrap. "What do you think she wanted with it?"

I swallowed with great difficulty and blinked away the hurt that provoked. It had been almost half a year since I broke things off with Vance, so I knew it was none of my business. Too bad my heart didn't get the message.

Evening started coming around after a while. Our merchandise had dwindled considerably and so I was ready to call it quits when a formidable man walked up to our booth. A much more petite woman holding the hands of two cuties trailed behind.

"Hey, Pa. Whatcha up to?"

He glanced over his shoulder, appearing rather annoyed by his shadows, and then gave me a pleading look. "The boys are getting tired. You about finished?"

"I have to help Foxy pack up. Maybe another hour." I angled my head and gave the younger twins a smile, even working one loose to give to Walynn. "Y'all having a good time?"

"Yes!" both boys all but shouted and then began talking over each other to tell me about spending the evening playing games and such with Walynn.

Knox wiggled something out of his pocket and waved it at me. "Look what Morty gave us!"

I took it and examined the refrigerator magnet shaped like a casket with *Lawson Funeral Home* written along it in script. "Umm . . . I have no words."

"Look what he gave me!" Nash held up a plastic tumbler with a tombstone on the side of it. The funeral home's address and phone number were the epitaph.

"That Morty has a way with advertising. He said he's going to stop by the salon next week to help me design a business card and maybe some flyers." Walynn's shiny red lips stretched with genuine excitement.

I barely contained a cringe. Morty ran the only funeral home in Magnolia. Surely he didn't need morbid swag to draw customers.

I returned the casket magnet to Knox. "I thought Charlotte and Raleigh were watching you boys."

"They were, but I thought they should have some time to explore with kids their own age. They're over at the corn maze. I told them to meet you here after that." Walynn ran her orange-painted nails through Nash's brown curls, absently and motherly at the same time.

I slid my attention to Pa. He looked off, absent and not at all fatherly.

"Have you seen Peg or Boss?"

Pa rubbed the back of his neck. "Yeah. Boss is helping Tripp put away the street cones. Tripp said he'd give him a lift home once they're done. Peg was over by the courthouse, listening to the band last I saw him."

"So are you taking the boys home now?" I swiped a handful of popcorn from the bag Pa was holding and crammed it in my mouth. The gnawing in my stomach from not eating all day was starting to get the best of me. I could still smell the hot dogs and bratwursts roasting away on a nearby grill. Maybe that would be my first stop after we finished packing up the booth.

The giant man fidgeted. "I was thinking . . . maybe you could and I'll stay and help Foxy."

Walynn brought those manicured nails to Pa's arm and squeezed. "Dave, you were just telling me how tired you were. I don't mind giving you and the boys a ride home. That way Austin can stay a little while after working all day and have some fun herself." Walynn winked at me. "I think she's earned it."

Again, I looked to Pa and again, he was fidgeting. It was rather amusing. "That's mighty kind of you, Walynn ... but ...," I began and Pa's stiff shoulders relaxed, making me want to chuckle. "Well ... you know what? I think I would like to hang out for a while. Thank you."

Pa grunted in surprise and Foxy coughed to try covering her snort, but the boys were loudest, cheering their excitement about getting to ride in the "red bug," as they called Walynn's Volkswagen Beetle.

"You liable to get a talking-to when you get home for that," Foxy commented, still laughing after Pa had stomped off.

"That's what he gets. Walynn is just being kind and the little boys have really taken a shine to her. Pa should be grateful."

"The man acts like he's scared to death of her." Foxy handed me a basket full of our little signs, shaking her head.

"Well, Walynn is a bit much, but I'm just glad she's provoked any kind of emotion out of him." I shook my head too and concentrated on neatly folding the tablecloth and then tucking it into one of the empty crates. Pa had become even more withdrawn in the last few months, almost as though the dormant fields around the farm had dictated his emotions. Seeing him responding to a situation, even if it was a reaction of awkward nervousness, gave me some sense of relief.

Three crates were all that remained to carry to the truck, so I offered to handle it and encouraged Foxy to go find her man amongst the crowd. She didn't have to be told twice. Laughing off how fast she disappeared, I didn't realize I was being followed until he spoke and near about caused me to drop the crates in the dark parking lot.

"I'm sorry, Austin. I didn't mean to scare you." Vance reached for the top crate, steadying it and then taking all three crates out of my arms.

"I had it," I grumbled, defenses up and attitude pronounced. I snatched the top one and slid it into the bed of the truck, the scraping sound hushing whatever he was about to say. I twisted around and yanked the next crate, repeating the task two more times. I wanted to leave, but my siblings were wandering around the festival, making a hasty escape impossible.

"Of course you had it. Don't you always?" Vance clamped his hands on my shoulders, stopping me from turning to leave. "Will you be still for a minute?"

I yanked out of his hold. "Where's Malorie?"

He drew a step closer and angled his head to the side to meet my eyes. "I don't know. Why should I?"

Being this close to him physically hurt, so I backed up until bumping into the side of the truck bed. "Don't act naive, Vance. The two of you have paraded around together all day."

"It's not what it looked like." He combed his fingers through his neatly trimmed curls. "She's a family friend. Period. Nothing more."

"You don't have to explain yourself to me." I buttoned my

jacket and pulled a knit cap out of my pocket, cramming it over my head just to have something to do. "It doesn't even matter anymore."

Vance straightened my cap and tucked a lock of hair behind my shoulder, caring and affectionate as always. And all too familiar. "It still matters to me."

"Why?" I asked, whiny and exasperated. My huffed breath clouded between us.

"Because one day we're both going to finally grow up and figure out our future."

I sidestepped him, putting some much-needed room between us, and then opened my mouth to use some snark to help widen the gap. "Your future looks golden from where I stand. Magnolia will be all about a town royalty wedding. You and Malorie . . ."

The muscle in Vance's jaw flexed harshly as his eyes grew glassy and the tip of his nose reddened. His painful expression cut off my biting remarks. The last thing I wanted to accomplish was hurting him, yet I'd pulled it off with very little effort as always.

Vance cleared his throat and set his gaze past my shoulder. After a few slow blinks, he looked at me. "I miss you, Austin, but I sure don't miss this." He motioned between us.

I deflated. "Look, I'm sorry for being nasty. Seriously, Malorie is a nice person. You're a great person. You deserve to have a nice life with someone like her."

"Malorie is a nice person and a great friend, but she's not you. . . . I want *you*. I want a life with you."

"Let's not do this."

"I've had my fill of having to explain my friendship with Malorie to you. If you must know, she's dating a friend of mine from college. It's pretty serious and he's even bought a ring."

"Awesome. Good for her. Take care now." I turned to walk away, but Peg's hollering stopped me short.

"Austin, we lost Raleigh in the corn maze!"

I ran across the parking lot so Peg didn't have to run-hop any farther. "What do you mean you lost him?"

He slung his hands in the air, white clouds puffing out of him like a choo choo train. "I walked the whole dang thing, calling out his name, but I think he's freaked out. Charlotte's still in there looking."

"Okay." I picked up my pace and left Peg behind, intent on getting to the maze and finding my little brother. I had a feeling he was hiding in there somewhere waiting for me.

After a few twists and turns in the maze, I realized Vance was heavy on my heels. "Stop following me," I growled out.

"You're going the direction I want to go," Vance growled back as several boys darted past us. One knocked into my shoulder and had Vance yelling out at him, "Watch it, kid!"

I motioned for Vance to go around me. Once he did and took a right, I took a left in hopes of losing him. My focus needed to be on finding Raleigh and that couldn't be done when that man and his familiar cologne were following me.

The maze was tricky, and I'd have to commend Pa for helping design it if I ever found my brother and our way out of the blame thing. It definitely reflected the arduous puzzle that had become our life with Dave Foster. Twist after twist. Turn after turn. Dead end after dead end. All the while, I called out

Raleigh's name. Not quite in a holler, knowing he wouldn't answer, but wanting him to know I was near.

Panicked and freezing, my searching grew desperate, going as far as tearing down a section of cornstalks when I thought I heard my brother. It turned out to be two teenage lovebirds sneaking a kiss. Spinning away from them, I darted down another path.

Finally I heard Vance call my name somewhere off to my left. I cut through another wall and found Vance crouched down beside Raleigh, where he was cowering in a corner, rocking back and forth, cheeks wet with tears.

"I've worked up a sweat, trying to find my way out of this crazy maze," Vance was saying. "Your daddy sure knows how to design one of these things. You mind wearing my coat so I don't have to carry it?" he asked as he shucked off his coat. It made little sense to me until he managed to get Raleigh to stand and pull on the flannel coat. The tail of it was long enough to cover the dark stain on the front of my brother's jeans.

My heart sank even as it swelled, witnessing Vance offering my brother compassion by helping to conceal his humiliation.

I decided to give no words to any of what had happened and instead focused on getting everyone rounded up. After telling Peg to drive them home in the Silver Bullet, I walked to the truck with a bone-tiredness settling in. Luckily, in the last year or so, Peg had finally gotten used to working the pedals with his left foot. It was nice to have someone else to help me out with the driving duties.

"Austin."

I shook my head and pulled the keys out of my pocket.

"Please, Vance, not tonight. I need to get home to Raleigh."
Before climbing inside the cab of the truck, I paused.
"Raleigh . . . he's sensitive." Each life storm seemed to leave
Raleigh's bladder in a more weakened state than before, but I
kept that part to myself.

Vance held a palm up. "You don't have to explain. Accidents
happen to the best of us."

I took a deep breath and let it out slowly. When I continued to speak, it was only in a whisper. "Raleigh came in right
behind me the night I found my mother . . . the night I found
her dead." I focused on the lights strung over the tops of the
trees around the town square. "I froze. Couldn't do anything
but stand by the door and scream. He was only seven years old,
but Raleigh didn't even hesitate to push me out the way so he
could scoop up the blue baby. The one not breathing. I don't
know what possessed him, but he jiggled the baby in his arms.
A frenzied jiggle." I blinked as the lights became blurry and met
Vance's glassy eyes. "He jiggled the baby and the next thing
I remember was the baby squalling and turning red. Raleigh
saved Nash's life that night."

Vance stepped closer, but I put the wall up and hurried into
the driver's seat. "So when I say Raleigh is sensitive, you best
believe he has every dang right to be." I didn't thank Vance
for helping me find my brother. I didn't thank him for helping
Raleigh keep some measure of dignity. I should have, but pride
is a terrible greedy thing and wouldn't let me.

Vance caught the top of the door and refused to let me close
it. "Three years, Austin . . ." He slowly shook his head. "Three
years together. Yet this is the first time you've ever opened up

to me . . . Wow." He rubbed his chest with his free hand, show-ing me just how deep the hurt of that went.

"We're not together anymore," I blurted, continuing to inflict more pain like the vile person I was.

"Exactly!" He released a derisive snort. "I'd have done any-thing to right whatever wrongs were going on out on the farm for you, if you'd just let me in . . . You never did." He gently closed the door, eyes pinned to mine through the window before he turned away.

Through a haze of regret, I watched him walk off into the dark. Ever the gentleman, Vance bowed out of the way of my pride and let me go.

A dreadful longing for Vance Cumberland had become my only constant company in the last few months. It was no sur-prise that it was now taking up most of the space in the cab of the truck. I missed everything about him. His flashy green eyes, the lopsided smile that showed off his dimples, those shy freckles barely visible on the bridge of his nose. He'd been a part of the tapestry of my life for several solid years, weaving himself into it with such ease that I'd taken it for granted.

Now that I'd pushed him away, I felt it in every part of me, and with the secure thread of Vance removed, I began unrav-eling quicker than a frayed afghan.

Chapter 13

A SEASON OF RUIN

May 1987

Tobacco season was more like a carefully paced marathon than a sprint. From start to finish, it consumed most our entire year. At least after setting the plants, we could have a break. I laid my head on my pillow tonight, finally taking a breath. We'd set the last field just hours earlier, and even though my hands were tinged yellowy green and ached a little, there was a deep satisfaction in knowing this step was complete.

Sleep found me fast. So fast, in fact, that not even a dream could interrupt it. Oh, but a nightmare surely could.

"Ox, get up!" Pa shook my shoulder hard, scaring me awake.

I jackknifed in the bed, slinging the cover off and stumbling to stand. "What's wrong?"

"Get dressed. We got a mess!" Pa was out of my room in a flash and hollering at Peg to get up from the room next to mine.

I looked toward the window and found no light and no answer to what was going on. A glance at the alarm clock on my small nightstand answered my question on the time: 11:43. Thinking someone must be sick and in need of a trip to the ER, I hurried into a pair of jeans and a T-shirt before bolting downstairs.

Peg and Boss stood at the foot of the stairs, similarly dressed haphazardly in wrinkled shirts and jeans. Boss's eyes were closed and Peg was rubbing his.

"What's going on?" I asked.

"Pa has lost his ever-lovin' mind is what's going on!" Peg whisper-yelled.

"Peg!" I shushed him just as heavy boots stomped across the front porch.

The front door slung open, snapping our attention to Pa waving for us to hurry up. "Let's go. Lots of work ahead of us."

I ushered Boss and Peg out, hoping to not wake the entire house. Pa was already off the porch and climbing on the idling tractor with a trailer behind it. "Climb in!" he yelled over the puttering.

The tractor was on the move before my brothers and I could decide to do the same. With no other choice, we hopped in the trailer and waited to find out whatever fate lay ahead.

Peg elbowed me and pointed to a pile of broken tobacco plants. "Where'd those come from?"

I shrugged, still thinking this was just a nightmare. When

the tractor pulled to a stop in the front tobacco field and I noticed a few rows had been plucked clean of the plants we'd set earlier, the nightmare grew in intensity.

"Seriously, Pa, what's wrong?" I asked as soon as we'd all unloaded and were following him to a row that still held their plants.

He leaned over and began pulling them in a rapid speed. "The plants are diseased. Gotta get it out of my fields."

I grabbed a plant that had slipped out of his grasp and saw no sign of disease, just a tender plant bruised and ruined. "There's nothing on these plants, Pa. They look perfectly healthy."

"I don't see nothing either," Peg agreed, examining a plant he'd pulled from a hill.

Pa whipped around, his fists full of broken plants. "You kids think you know better than me? Ya disrespecting my authority?"

Our heads shook immediately. "No, sir. It's just...," I started, not knowing how to maneuver us out of this mess in a way not to set Pa off even more. His dark-blue eyes held that frenzied gleam that scared me every time it showed up.

"Just nothing!" Pa gestured toward the rows lit by the full moon. "They all gotta go. Get to it."

Boss was silently pulling plants, going at two rows at once. Right reach, pluck. Left reach, pluck. And I was close to tears, witnessing all of our hard work being ruined.

Peg let out a resigned sigh. "Can't we just plow 'em up?"

Halfway down a row, Pa shook his head. "No! Every plant has to be tossed in the trailer. Can't have disease. It's like yeast.

If any is left behind, it'll spread and infect all the healthy new plants."

Peg grumbled and groaned. "We'll have to replant! This is messed up!"

The first hour out there in the middle of that dark field passed with Peg and I taking turns trying to talk Pa out of pulling all the set plants, but he was in some sort of trance and wouldn't budge. Our protests eventually tapered off as we went into our own trance, maybe our way of protecting our fragile state, and worked robotically through the night. The only sounds besides the rustling trees on the far side of the field and the frogs croaking amongst them were our grunts that grew right along with our weariness. At least the breeze kept the sweat and mosquitoes at a more tolerable level.

Jinx showed up around the same time dawn arrived. Barely able to stand straight, I tossed a handful of plants into the trailer and waited for Jinx's reaction to the mess.

He scrutinized the trampled field and then Pa, who was still going at it like a frenzied machine on full throttle. Shaking his head, Jinx started back to his truck. "I'll be right back."

Thinking he probably hightailed it away from the crazy, I shuffled over to the next perfectly planted row and began ruining it like the others. Days, hours, or maybe just minutes passed before Jinx's truck returned to the spot by the tractor.

"Dave, you want us to bring this load up to the packhouse and get a clean trailer?" Jinx asked, calm as ever, not even questioning what in tarnation was the matter.

Pa stood straight and blinked a few times as if just realizing where he was at. He eyed the growing mound of damaged plants. "Yeah." He beat a path to the tractor and was pulling away as we stood frozen in slumped states.

"Y'all get in," Jinx ordered, inclining his head toward his truck.

The boys climbed in the back and I joined Jinx in the cab and filled him in on what had transpired. His lips remained pressed in a tight line behind his mustache as he nodded at a few of my comments.

In her nightclothes and a headscarf, Foxy stood beside Pa and the parked tractor by the packhouse. He was shaking his head at the offered thermos in her hand. We climbed out of the truck and joined them.

"But I made it extra strong, just the way you like it."

"I don't have time for a coffee break." He turned and began unhitching the trailer from the tractor.

"The caffeine boost will help you be more productive." Foxy kept on until Pa finally took the thermos and all but chugged it.

"Leave me some, Pa. I could use a caffeine boost too," Peg grumbled, limping toward him with a hand reaching for the thermos.

Foxy tightened the robe around her thin waist and blocked Peg's path. "I made you some too. Just give me a minute to get it."

"Where's it at?" I asked her, barely able to speak past the dust clinging to my tongue and throat. Between the thirst and the sharp pain in my lower back, I'd need more like a miracle than caffeine to get through the day.

Pa groaned, drawing our attention away from the pursuit of coffee. He staggered, bumping into the side of the pack-house. The thermos dropped to the ground as he braced his hands against the wood siding. His lips smacked loudly a few times before his body started sliding down to the ground.

Jinx caught him. "Here, Dave. Why don't you have a sit inside for a minute?"

Pa slurred a protest.

Jinx grunted under Pa's weight, all but dragging him inside. "Just long enough to catch your breath."

Pa groaned again and went down like a felled tree, knocking over a stack of hay bales. The momentum of his fall kept on until he was laid out flat on his back.

Jinx moved a bale off Pa that had landed on his legs before leaving him be.

Eyes bugged out, Peg waved a hand at Pa. "What'd you put in that coffee, Foxy?"

Foxy shooed off his concern, flicking her wrist. "Just something to help Dave relax for a spell."

"Relax? The man looks dead!" Peg hobbled over to Pa and placed two fingers on his neck. Checking for a pulse was unnecessary, considering the giant man began snoring a steady rhythm.

"How long you reckon that *coffee* will have him knocked out?" I narrowed my eyes when Foxy shrugged my question off.

"Long enough." She motioned for us to leave the packhouse. "Y'all get washed up and go to bed."

I used the collar of my shirt to wipe the grit from the corners of my scratchy eyes and looked around the yard, catching sight of the three dogs and Pixy on the back porch scratching at their empty food bowls. At the moment we had a pair of basset hounds, one mutt that had a good bit of golden retriever in him, and a potbelly pig who remained confused about her species. "There's too much to get done for that." I sighed while stretching my back. "Plus there's the issue of needing to get plants and needing to get them in the ground fast."

Foxy linked her arm with mine, pulling me along with her up the porch. She paused long enough to dump food into the dog bowls and then led the way inside. "Let my Jinx handle the plants. I'll round up Charlotte and Raleigh to take care of the chores. Then we'll bring the younger twins up to my house."

I didn't hug Foxy much, but I did right then in the kitchen, going as far as choking out, "I . . . I don't know what to do about Pa. . . . It's getting worse."

Foxy patted and rubbed my back but gave me no empty promises or reassurances about us going to be okay. It hurt, but I respected her honesty in being silent. Really, what could she do?

After Foxy left with both sets of twins, I sent Boss to run through the shower first. Peg and I moved no farther than the dining table, slumping on our elbows. Too tired to even blink.

"I hate him," Peg rasped as soon as the water pipes squeaked above.

My head swam with such heavy exhaustion that I wasn't sure if I heard him right or not. I looked over and met Peg's glassy red eyes. Swallowing down the grit and despondency, I whispered with very little conviction, "You don't mean that."

"Yes, I really do." His voice held a heavy amount of dejection but no malice could be detected. I understood how he felt.

"We hate whatever is wrong with him, but we don't hate Pa."

I stared at the dingy dog-eared copy of the *Farmers' Almanac* and Pa's open Bible beside it. The Bible was so well-worn that the spine no longer held the pages in tightly. A few verses in John were circled in blue ink, so heavily that the page had been torn from it.

Let not your heart be troubled: ye believe in God, believe also in me. In my Father's house are many mansions: if it were not so, I would have told you. I go to prepare a place for you. And if I go and prepare a place for you, I will come again, and receive you unto myself; that where I am, there ye may be also. And whither I go ye know, and the way ye know.

I reached over and closed the Bible, trying not to think about all of Pa's attempts of going on to the Father's house. I grabbed a toothpick from the small tin canister we kept on the table and worked on digging some of the caked dirt from underneath my tender nails.

With my focus on my stained nails, I spoke quietly. "Mama once told me loving your family means you love them during their sunshine and even during their thunderstorms."

Peg grunted. "I'd agree with that if Pa's thunderstorms weren't more like tornadoes."

I sighed, wiping the sprinkling of dirt onto my palm and then tossing it and the toothpick in the trash. My body was too sore to return to sitting, so I braced my elbows on the back of the chair. "Yeah, but that's when he needs us the most."

"Sure, Ox, but what about us?" Fear and hurt inflamed his

eyes. "What happens when his tornado levels us? Ain't gonna be no coming back from that."

"What other choice do we have?" My mind screamed in frustration as loudly as my body screamed in pain.

"I'm so sick of it!" Peg flung his hands in the air, much like I wanted to do, but that was never an option for me.

"You think you're the only one sick of it?" The water shut off overhead just as I was about to go on a tear. Taking a few deep breaths to tamp it down, I lowered my voice. "No matter how sick of it I get or you get, we need to remember there are six others in this house who are counting on us, and that includes Pa. We can hate what's going on, but we cannot hate our father." Someone had to find reason in the midst of our chaotic lives, though I was beginning to run out of it right along with patience.

Unsaid words flickered through Peg's eyes. They were filled with anger and confusion. Moments passed, as well as a few tears, before his expression dimmed with resignation. He stood, wincing more like an eighty-year-old man than an eighteen-year-old boy.

I touched his shoulder as he limped past me. "We don't hate him, Peg. We can't."

He barely tipped his head in agreement before heading upstairs to shower.

We'd managed to replant the fields and by the mercy of God, the crops flourished, but the tobacco season ended abruptly midsummer, cut short by a Pa tornado. It didn't level us, but it came pretty dang close.

One minute I was staring at the most bountiful tobacco crops we'd had in years. Leaves so healthy and fat that the plants hung heavily toward the ground. Then the next minute, Pa's comatose demeanor flipped to madman rage. I can still see him rushing around, yelling that the storm was going to wipe out our entire crop. Ordering us to strip each plant of all its leaves instead of taking the bottom leaves for the first cropping of the season. We'd packed barns past full, but over half of the harvested leaves remained in trailers or on the ground. Two days of rain was what a storm system from off the coast delivered to us. Rain that would have nourished the plants and would have made the next cropping just as prosperous as the first.

After the rain subsided, the stifling heat steamed the exposed tobacco until it soured. One of our hired hands for the summer ran his mouth and somehow the paper managed to sneak photos of the mishap. The images of withered, moldy leaves piled up in ruins weren't easily forgotten. The entire town had proof of Pa's madness and our embarrassment displayed right on the front page of the newspaper.

Pa told me once that fighting hate with hate will only produce more hate. Ever since that morning I told Peg we couldn't hate Pa, I'd poured as much love out as possible, but it did nothing to suppress the hate that seemed to be increasing in my brother. A resentment was beginning to reflect from each of us in various ways and times.

"Whew-ee, is the Lord good!"

I pushed the hopeless case aside as best as I could and focused on Pa's grinning face at the front of the church. Even that was impossible with the familiar blond head a few pews ahead of me.

Months had gone by with no sign of Vance Archer Cumberland, as if the years before had only been a figment of my imagination, but today he'd suddenly appeared. He was the same yet much different. Familiar yet a stranger.

Before I could look away, he glanced over his shoulder and caught me staring. Instead of offering me the typical dimpled, lopsided grin, Vance frowned. The ever-present sparkle in his grass-green eyes was absent.

I shook my head and glared a warning. *Not today.* He shook his head too but with resignation. He was too handsome to look so sad and I wanted to live in a world where I was allowed to make him happy, but it didn't matter anymore. There was no point in wasting his or my time on what could never be.

I broke our gaze first and focused on anything else but him and the dang ache searing against my breastbone—Charlotte's hot-pink jelly shoes, Pixy oinking and bumping into my leg, feeding Knox and Nash a snack, hushing Peg's grumblings . . .

Pa concluded the service much like he began it. At the untuned piano, he played that thing like he was Jerry Lee Lewis. Shoulders shaking, long legs bouncing to the beat, singing a lively version of "Just Over in the Glory Land."

Afterwards, I instructed Charlotte to take the younger twins to the house. "I'll be there shortly. Just fix some eggs and toast for lunch."

Charlotte fiddled with the end of her long, dark braid while glancing at Vance, who remained sitting in his pew. "You sure?"

"Yes." I handed her the empty cracker wrapper and my

Bible. Dusting my palms against my pants, I took a few steps forward and joined Vance on his pew. Staring forward as the door closed and blocked out the socializing in the small yard, we said nothing. I'd come to the conclusion there was nothing else to say, but his sudden appearance today said otherwise.

"I see you're still wearing those corduroy pants and hippie sandals," he commented.

The collar of my white V-neck T-shirt slipped off my shoulder when I shrugged. I pulled it back into place. "You popped up out of nowhere today just to poke fun at my outfit?"

"I've always loved your seventies style, Austin." Vance angled in my direction and draped an arm behind me along the top of the pew. His boyish face now held more sharp angles and a shadow of facial hair. The once-wild, unruly blond curls had been tamed with a close haircut and styling product. In his blue suit, Vance looked like the CEO of Cumberland Finance that he would eventually become.

Looking at him weakened places inside my chest with each blink, so I moved my gaze to the giant magnolia wreath. Stupid choice because that hurt too. "I know you're not here to talk fashion, so why are you?"

"To make sure you're doing okay. You look so tired." Vance sighed, his breath tickling the side of my neck as he fiddled with a strand of my hair like it was his right to touch me even though we both knew it wasn't.

"Gee, thanks." I dropped my head and let the long curtain of my hair help conceal the dark circles under my eyes. "It's been close to a year, Vance. Why now?"

"I heard about y'all losing half your crop."

Everyone had heard about it. It still felt like a really bad nightmare. The pain in my chest transformed into a burning deep inside my stomach. That pain wasn't new, either, and no amount of Pepto or chewing on mint leaves as Foxy suggested alleviated it. I'd even lost my taste for Miss Wise's handmade chocolates. "Yeah. So?"

"So are you okay?" He scooted closer, and the familiar notes of his crisp cologne reached me, but I refused to look at him.

"Yes."

"Financially?"

My head snapped up to meet his green eyes. "That's none of your business, but just know that we ain't completely stupid. We have savings . . . no mortgage . . ." I let out a humorless laugh and tapped the thinning material of my corduroy pants. "And I'm quite frugal."

"Don't put words in my mouth." Vance's arm moved until he had me cradled against his side. "I just wanted to check on you."

I shouldn't have allowed it, but his warmth and tender touch overrode my better judgment. "Seriously, Vance, you don't have to pop in here every time something goes amiss."

"Yes, I do." His other hand moved until resting on top of mine that was grasping my knee to hide the tremble.

"Why?"

"Because you're going to have to eventually accept the fact that I'm showing up for you no matter what . . ." He released my hand and combed his fingers through his perfect curls. "God only knows why exactly, Austin, but I can't figure out how to stop loving you."

I swallowed past the tightness in my throat. "I can't figure out how to stop loving you, either."

Vance dropped his hand and eyed me with furrowed brows. "If you love me, then why push me away?"

I pointed in the general direction of the farmhouse. "Because I love you enough to push you on to better things. You deserve happiness, and you dang sure ain't going to find that out here on Nolia Farms." I leaned over as naturally as breathing and placed a soft kiss to his frowning lips before standing.

Vance's fingers locked with mine as I began to step into the narrow aisle. "He's getting worse, isn't he?"

I knew he was talking about Pa, and he knew without me having to confirm it, because everyone else knew no tobacco farmer in his right mind would ruin a bountiful harvest the way Pa had.

"Thanks for checking on me." I gave Vance's hand a squeeze, tugging him to his feet and walking him out.

"Just because you won't talk to me about Dave doesn't change the fact that he's not well." Vance gestured toward the small podium before I closed the door. "Even today it was pretty clear."

Sighing, I tucked my hair behind my ear and gazed past his shiny black truck. "I need to go check on everyone."

"May I come with you?" There he went, trying to wiggle his way back in.

I jabbed a finger against his chest once in warning and started walking backward. "How many times do I gotta tell you that it's for your own good that you get from here and not come back?"

Vance grabbed my wrist and hauled me against his chest as he moved us to the shaded side of the chapel. "What about me, Austin, and what I want?" Vance asked in a steely voice. "Ask me if *I'm* okay?" When I remained quiet, he answered for me. "I'm not!"

There were no answers I could offer for comfort or for whatever he needed, so I slammed my lips against his and kissed him like my life depended on it. It was frantic. Desperate. A strangled groan rose from deep within him as Vance pushed closer, his hands tangled in my hair, anchoring us to the side of the building. The kiss was bruising to both my lips and heart. The entire push and pull of being with this man always left me bruised.

Even though I swore to myself that it was for the best to leave him alone and to be an adult about it, I gave in to my selfishness for a spell as we hid in the shade of the magnolia tree in the side yard. No, the kissing and clinging to each other didn't magically make us okay, but at least the bleakness ebbed briefly.

"I don't want to walk away from you, Austin. You're impor- tant to me, and you always will be. I'm willing to do whatever it takes to work things out between us," Vance declared sternly even as his fingertips gliding along my cheeks delivered a deli- cate caress.

"I can't do this right now . . ." My bottom lip wobbled, so I turned my head and pressed a kiss to his palm to conceal it.

Vance dropped his hand and whispered an oath.

Hurting Vance made me hate myself. "You deserve better than this," I insisted. I didn't give him a chance to reply, just took off down the drive like a shot, making it to the farmhouse in record time. Thankfully, the rumble of his truck drifted in the opposite direction. He'd let me win this round. I sure didn't feel like a winner, though.

The crowd was gathered on the porch, hunched over Raleigh as he clutched something close in front of him. Could it be the ice cream maker? My mouth watered, already longing for the sweet fruity taste of peach ice cream. It was possible, considering peaches were still in season. The glance of nostalgia had me wishing I'd invited Vance up instead of running him off.

A smile began tipping my lips as I took several rushed strides to the porch to join them, but then I got a better look at my siblings' faces. Anger streaked wet paths down their cheeks, lips thin and holding grimaces.

"What's wrong?" I pushed past Boss to see what Raleigh was doing. "Oh, Raleigh." The smell of urine was strong but it didn't deter me from settling on my knees and wrapping my arms around him tightly.

"Pa did this." Raleigh sniffled while holding the shredded baby blanket together. It was just as futile an attempt as me wanting to hold this family together. "He even took Mama's bottle of lotion." A sob cut his words off. "Said . . . I needed to grow up . . ." His body shook.

"What in the world happened? It's only been like fifteen minutes since services got out."

Peg roared with indignation, stabbing a finger in the direction of the packhouse, where I heard loud beating and banging. "That lunatic flipped out is what happened! Raleigh's fingers got slammed in the front door. It hurt him, doggone it! He had a right to cry!" He crossed his arms while a few expletives tumbled through his lips.

I reared far enough away to seek Raleigh's wounded hand. It wasn't hard to spot the swollen red-and-purple fingers he carefully held against his chest. "Charlotte, grab us a dishcloth full of ice, please. And some aspirin." Ice and pain reliever were the only things I could offer to fix the swelling.

A loud clanging rang out from the barn. I looked that way but only saw shadows moving around inside. "What on earth is he doing in there?"

"Probably finishing ruining the dang boom box." Peg motioned to the small side table on the porch. "He knocked it off the table and then kicked it while showing his behind. I'm tellin' you, Austin. I've had enough!" Peg stomped inside and commenced to adding his own beating and banging to the mix.

Everything was getting out of hand, and I felt helpless as to how to get it back under control. As a glass crashed in the kitchen, I scanned the porch floorboards, noticing fragments of silver plastic. Broken and scattered, much like life on Nolia Farms. Rooted on the porch under the weight of a debilitating fear of what was to come, I held Raleigh tighter and begged God to hold us together.

The tobacco season, Pa, each of us Fosters . . . everything was rapidly unraveling. We'd not only reached our limit, but we'd all picked up some of Pa's symptoms and made them our own.

Boss seldom talked.

Raleigh often cried.

Peg continued to grow moodier and would lash out in a blink.

Charlotte had withdrawn from us, basically moving in with Miss Wise.

Knox and Nash had taken to wandering off.

I battled a constant burn in my stomach and stinging in my chest.

As for Pa, his clarity became more muddled. His silence grew louder. His shadows, more vibrant.

Chapter 14

NO CALM
BEFORE THE STORM

July 1988

Drought was one cruel companion during the summer of 1988, leaching the life out of anything it could dig its craggy fingers into. It was ravenous, gulping every last drop from the swimming hole and sucking the nutrients from Nolia Farms' vulnerable crops to the point of decay and despair. We couldn't get rid of the destruction any more than we could the dust, which had become a permanent accessory to the hems of our jeans and the brims of our hats, while dark lines of grit wriggled into the sweaty creases of our skin. The barren season seemed to have no exit in mind.

It was because of this unwanted guest that had worn out its welcome that I didn't realize a storm was brewing. Or maybe

I chose to ignore it, considering we'd just barely managed to make it through another year since Pa ruined our crop and made the newspaper. But things had started unraveling faster than I could knit them back together.

Folks like to say there's always a calm before the storm, but that never seemed the case out on Nolia Farms. What started out as a normal suppertime that night ended in an explosive outburst. Nothing calm about that.

Just as we were about to dig in, Pa heaved a clipped sigh. "Raleigh, stop leaning on the table. You're making it rock."

All eyes wandered to Raleigh, who looked downright confused, seeing as how he was sitting back in his chair with both his elbows away from the table.

"Sorry, Pa," Raleigh apologized, even though he'd done nothing wrong.

Forks resumed clanging against plates, but I kept side-eyeing Pa when he didn't return to eating. He had an edginess about him, hands shaking and eyes wildly roaming around the room.

"Boss, now you're doing it," Pa snapped.

"No, sir." Boss looked to me for answers as to what was going on, but I had no clue.

"The dang table must have a loose leg." Pa jerked to his feet. "Everyone get up." He shooed us away as he crawled underneath the table.

I pulled the younger twins further away when Pa kicked a chair in our direction to make more room for his large form. The table shook as he inspected each leg, muttering nonsense to himself the entire time.

"Pa, I don't think the table is loose." Peg placed a hand on top and bore down, showing that no wobble could be found.

"You callin' me a liar?" Pa asked sternly, shoving his way out.

"No, sir," Peg answered slowly as the tension grew thick.

I didn't know what was about to happen, so I took a step in front of Peg when Pa moved closer to him.

Pa reached a big hand out and grasped the lip of the tabletop, picking it up and dropping it in rapid succession to emphasize each of his words. "The. Table. Is. Off. Balance!" Tea glasses overturned and a few forks pinged against the floor.

"Yes, sir," I said with most of my siblings echoing in agreement.

"Now you mocking me?" Pa's crazed eyes twitched as he glared at me. Before I could answer, he upturned the entire table, breaking off a leg and most certainly making it off-balance. Dishes shattered and supper ruined, he stormed out the door, leaving all of us shaking like leaves while staring at the chaos he'd just created.

"This has to stop!" Peg yelled, shoving a chair out of his way.

"Not now, Peg," I said through gritted teeth as Nash and Knox began to cry. "Charlotte, take the boys to the living room while I go make us some sandwiches."

"Come on, boys," she whispered as she led them out of the room.

"Peg—"

"I know! Clean up Pa's mess." He leaned down and started collecting all the brokenness, with Boss and Raleigh joining in. "All we do is clean up his crap . . . and hide it . . ." Peg grumbled this and some other choice words under his breath, but I had no energy to reprimand him about it.

No, tonight we had much bigger issues than swear words.

By the time we had the mess cleaned up, I decided to leave Pa be for a spell to cool off while I tried settling everyone down. I had no other comfort to give them but Twinkies and hugs. After giving out both to each of my siblings and making sure they were in their rooms for the night, I ventured outside, thinking I'd find Pa on the porch in his rocking chair, but he wasn't there. Dragging my feet from not wanting to deal with him, I checked the chapel next. It was empty, and so was the produce stand across the driveway from it. No sign in the packhouse or the tractor supply barn.

I was all but ready to call it quits when I peeped inside the shed and found a pool of blood by an open tackle box. The fish filleting knife was gone. Leaving the shed with my heart pounding and ears ringing, I could just barely make out the rusty melody of a Creedence song coming from the tobacco field. It was difficult to pinpoint his exact location. Each time I started down one row, the rasp of his singing shifted in the breeze and came from another direction. I wanted to holler for him to get still so I could find him, but the grip of fear told me his plan was to not be found this time.

"'I want to know . . . you ever . . . the rain . . . coming down . . .'" His voice was weak either from his giving up or his impending death, I wasn't sure.

I knew drawing attention to myself wouldn't help, so I pinched my lips tightly shut and wove through the rows. Shrouded in heavy clouds, the night held no light from the moon or stars. It reminded me of being lost in the corn maze and unable to find Raleigh. My brother was eventually found, so I held on to a speck of confidence that I would be able to find my father too.

With only Pa's weak voice as my beacon, I kept searching through the sea of plant decay. The tobacco stalks should have been loaded down with healthy fat leaves, clinging to me as I passed by. Instead the shriveled plants were more like the prongs of a yard rake, scraping my legs and arms, leaving sharp stings. This crop was opposite of the crop we'd produced last year, even if we lost half of it, but the dark madness was exactly the same.

I rubbed my forearm and held my breath. A groan echoed from a few rows over. I about-faced and shot a line straight through the brittle hills of tobacco, pummeling them in my wake.

Five hills over, my legs collided with something solid and sent me tumbling to the ground, knocking the breath out of me on impact. My right palm landed in a puddle of dampness in the midst of the desert. Blinking the dust out of my eyes, I brought my hand close to my face. It was shiny and dark, the only details I could make out. Dropping my hand, I looked over to see what I ran into and met a hollow set of eyes barely detectable in the darkness. The sticky dampness on my palm and the metallic scent in the air both showing me the direness even though I was unable to actually see it clearly.

"Pa . . . ," I breathed more so than spoke.

Lying on his side in the rut between rows, his eyes locked on mine but he made no acknowledgment of my presence.

"'Have you ever seen the rain . . .'"

"Pa." I spoke firmer this time, cutting off his singing.

His eyes drifted shut as he rolled away from me to his other side.

I wrapped my hand around his wrist to stop him, finding it slippery. I wiped and wiped but a flow of liquid continued bubbling from his arm. "Pa! What'd you do?" A sliver of moonlight pushed through a cloud and gave just enough illumination for me to see the long, angry slashes on his arm, wrist to elbow. "Why? Why would you do this?"

"I needed to get it out . . ." His murmurings made no sense.

"Get what out?"

"The darkness." His thick arm pulled out of my grasp as he flopped on his back. "Get on to the house now."

"I ain't leaving you out here. . . . We need to get some help." I looked around us, trying to figure how in the world to reach him. The glint of a knife in the dirt caught my eye. Snatching it off the ground and pressing the blade to my own arm was what it took to conjure a response from him.

Pa blinked and then blinked again before drawing his eyebrows together. "Give me that," he said in a tired voice void of any emotion.

"No." I scooted on my butt until I was out of his reach. "I live your darkness. Just like you, Pa. I need to get it out too." The blade pinched the skin at the crook of my elbow as I pressed harder.

Pa sat up and lunged for the knife. I dodged away from him, his big form sluggish from his comatose state or the blood loss, I wasn't sure, but it gave me enough time to keep away from him.

"Austin," Pa groaned as he slumped against a tobacco plant, breaking it in two. His lethargic reaction was worrisome.

"You can give up and die right here in this field, but you best bet it's going to be your fault that I die right here beside you. Or we can go get you some help. Either way, it's going to end tonight."

Pa made another swipe for the knife, causing me to slice through the skin of my forearm. The sting drew my attention long enough for him to snatch the knife out of my hand. I lunged for him as Pa added another wound to his arm, knocking us both sideways. It was like wrestling a drunk bear. We rolled to sitting, our hands locked around the hilt of the knife. I knew Pa was stronger than me and that he could very well kill us both, but I was willing to accept that if it meant finally being able to put an end to the downward spiral our lives had taken on.

The vortex of destruction that began way before I was old enough to recognize it whipped through the field on a mighty roar. The wind picked up and a rumbling vibrated the ground.

"Let go," I cried out in frustration as beads of sweat dripped into my eyes, causing more discomfort.

Pa's lips snarled in response and he yanked so hard my shoulder popped, but I still refused to let go of that dang knife. We somehow managed to climb to our feet only to stumble. My hip smacked hard against the unforgiving ground. A flume of dust enveloped us. A tiny part of my mind wondered if this was how Jacob felt when he wrestled with God.

Choking on dirt and panic, I realized I'd lost my grip on the knife. I watched Pa crouch to pick it up. I sprang to my feet and charged like a crazed bull, shoving Pa with all my might. It caught him off guard and so I took him down with surprising ease. The momentum of his fall brought me with him, but the knife was all mine. He made no move to get up. I gripped the knife tighter as I scrambled to my feet and took off in a dead run, cutting through the decaying field and then the small patch of woods that led to Foxy's.

I banged on the door and screamed, "Help! I need help!"

A dizziness slammed into me as soon as the door opened. In a skipping reel, I barely recalled Foxy picking up the phone. Another skip and I was following Jinx through the woods. Blinking, my bloody fingers were pointing at the dark, unmoving body between two rows of tobacco. Was I too late?

Another blink.

The air shifted around me, a subtle warning, just before fat drops fell from the sky and pinged against the tin roof of the barn and then reached my overheated skin. The cool rain almost hurt, but that gave me some sense of relief that I was still able to feel anything.

Flickers of lightning joined the pattern of blue-and-red flashing lights whirling around the tobacco field as I swayed in place, taking in the chaos that was building right along with the storm. A rumble of thunder formed in the distance, sounding like a boulder on a runaway path. It was so fierce I could have sworn it formed within the very marrow of my being. Another sharp bolt of lightning. This time making my teeth sting. I swiped my tongue over them to get rid of the tingling sensation and swallowed, but the metallic taste clung to my palate like the dust to my skin.

Rebelling against humidity, the fine hairs along my neck stood on end. The air crackled with energy as if it were tiptoeing across a live wire. All warning signs that this was far beyond a gentle rain cloud. The panicked yelling of orders for the EMTs to get the lead out, the staticky screech of CB radios spewing indecipherable codes, the ringing in my ears . . . also warning signs.

This night not only marked the end to the drought, but also the end to the long-held secret we'd kept hidden just past the magnolias of Nolia Farms.

As it began to rain in earnest and the red lights faded into the night, the sheriff broke away from a small circle of police officers and came to a stop beside me. My eyes were fixed to the ambulance as it rushed down the dirt road, kicking up dust the rain hadn't had the chance to tamp down yet.

"Austin," Sheriff Inman spoke, using a tone better suited when dealing with a two-year-old girl instead of a twenty-one-year-old woman. He exhaled harshly. "Who—?"

"Pa . . . Pa did it to himself . . ." A staggered sob rushed up my throat, nearly choking me. "It's not the first time." The putrid-green fields swirled around me as the ringing in my ears grew to a nauseating pitch. The field angled sideways, but a hand grasped my shoulder to keep me upright.

"Whoa there, young lady. You okay?"

I sipped a mouthful of balmy air and nodded while demanding the dizziness and bile to recede.

"I need you to come with me." He spoke louder as the rain picked up its own volume.

"Why?" I blinked away raindrops clinging to my eyelashes.

"Just to answer a few questions. Won't take long."

"But the young'uns . . ." I lifted my hands so that the rain could wash away some of the blood and guilt. Fingertip to elbow, I was thickly covered in both. Just like the dust, I had my doubts of ever ridding myself of it.

The sheriff's eyes were trained on the ribbons of crimson rolling off my arms as he pointed in the general direction of the farmhouse. "Foxy and Jinx are with 'em."

"Head count?" I rubbed my hands together, wishing for a bar of Lava soap. It could handle tobacco gum with ease. I wondered how it would stand up against sticky blood.

"Six. They all accounted for." He steered me toward the cruiser and opened the back door. "Everyone's fine."

"Boss?" I asked, worried the most about my older brother. Boston's mind was the youngest and most fragile by far.

"He didn't see anythin'. He's okay. Everyone is," Inman reiterated and motioned for me to get in.

I glanced at the disturbed rows of brittle tobacco where the secret had just spilled out. Maybe the rain would last long enough to wash away the crimson stains. A quick scan confirmed my shorts and T-shirt in no better shape, equal parts dirt and blood. "You got a towel or something I can sit on?"

"Don't worry 'bout that. Just get on in fore this storm picks up."

As soon as I climbed in the back, the door slammed at the same time another clap of thunder shook the earth, jolting my entire body and pumping a new dose of adrenaline through my veins. A sting drew my attention to the laceration on my forearm, where it began to trickle again. It was insignificant compared to the whole scheme of things, so I pressed my palm over the wound to stanch the flow. It would heal soon enough, even if nothing else did.

The sheriff settled in the driver's seat, turned down the CB radio, and put the cruiser into gear. "Everyone's okay," he said for the third time, making me wonder if he was trying to convince me or himself. "You hear me, Austin?"

I ignored him, along with the bloody smudges I was leaving on the gray vinyl surface of the back seat and the mud puddling on the floorboard around my bare feet.

The car bumped down the mile-long drive that led out of the farm and away from tonight's nightmare, passing a few barns and then the farmhouse, where every window was lit. I was too ashamed to look for the shadowed figures who were sure to be peeping out. It was my duty to protect those shadows and tonight made it clear how severely I'd failed each one of them.

As the brakes let out a squeal at the end of the drive, a flash of lightning illuminated the small clapboard chapel where it stood by the entrance. It was as much a part of farm life as the farm equipment in the barn, which meant it was also a witness to our downward spiral. A heavy sheet of rain moved between me and the building, obscuring my view, so I closed my eyes to it and welcomed the end that had been a long time coming.

Even though we finally made it to the end, we certainly didn't make it out unscathed. My grip tightened around the proof of that, but a flesh wound came nowhere close to the scars that were about to be completely exposed.

The reel skipped again and now I stared at the enamel

table before me. The blanket around my shoulders did nothing to ward off the tremors attacking my body. "I need to see Pa."

A can of Coke was placed in my sight. "I just got off the phone with the hospital. They're done sewin' up his arms and are keepin' him for observation for a couple of days."

I looked up at the sheriff. "Why?"

He sat in the folding chair in front of me. "Austin, your father tried to kill himself."

The time for lies, excuses, and omissions had come to an end, so I nodded my head in agreement.

"You said earlier that this wasn't the first time he's tried something like this?"

"Pa . . . he's struggled since Mama died. Over time, it's gotten worse."

"Has he ever hurt one of you young'uns?"

"No, sir. Never. Just himself." I popped the tab on the can and took a long sip to wash down some of the grit and anguish. "Sheriff Inman, you know Pa is a good man. He's just haunted by something I don't know how to help him overcome." My words barely came out as my throat closed around them.

Inman patted my arm just below the bandage someone had put on my cut after we'd arrived at the police station. It was already stained red. "How about we let the doctors work on helping him, okay?"

"Okay."

"Now how about I take you on over to the hospital to let someone see about your arm. And then you can go see Dave."

"Yes, sir."

Hours slipped by but the darkness outside the hospital window told me the longest night of my life wasn't over yet. I sat by Pa's bed, eyes zeroed in on his thickly bandaged arms. Whatever they gave him knocked him out so hard, his mouth was too slack to hold in the drool. Seeing him sleep so heavily exhausted me but my scratchy eyes refused to close.

Movement by the door shook me out of my stare, but I didn't look away from Pa's still form, considering the nurses rotated in and out what felt like every few minutes. The doctor informed me Pa was on a seventy-two-hour hold for assessment and evaluations, which meant they were keeping a very close eye on him. As quickly and quietly as the door opened, it closed again. A shadowed figure dropped in front of me where I sat by Pa's bed and engulfed me in an ironclad embrace, arms wrapping around my waist as a curly head settled in my lap. I marveled how his strength held such tenderness, how his gentleness always cradled me within the barriers of safety.

I greedily breathed in the fresh scent of his cologne. It was the scent of comfort and reassurance. The one fragrance in the world that always showed up in the midst of the overwhelming stench of my life.

We remained quiet, only the echoes of medical machines and voices drifting just outside the door in the hallway interrupted the stillness. Questions rolled through my thoughts about how Vance knew Pa was in the hospital, that I was here too, but there was no energy within me to verbalize anything.

I was just profoundly grateful that he did know and that he was here holding me.

Vance's hands glided over my back, brushed my hair behind my ears, traced down my arms, and then froze on the bandage wrapped around my forearm that now had stitches. "He hurt you?"

"Not intentionally. I, uh . . . I got in the way of the knife."

"Let me take you home."

"I can't leave him alone. What if he wakes up while I'm gone?"

"I don't believe he will. They have him heavily sedated." Vance sensed my hesitation, holding me closer and whispering in my ear, "If you let me take you home, I promise to come right back and not leave him. It'll do you good to take a hot shower and change clothes."

I knew he was right. Even though my shirt and shorts were mostly dry, they were stained with blood and in spots smeared with mud. I wiggled my toes inside Pa's work boots that I had swiped as soon as Sheriff Inman brought me to the hospital room, feeling the grit and grime between them. There were tater patches on my neck and dirt caked underneath my nails, so there was no other choice but to agree with Vance.

Slowly rising from the chair, my muscles protested and made it known what they'd endured in that tobacco field. I eased closer and looked Pa over. It was the most peaceful I'd ever seen him. Too bad drugs knocking him out was what it took to achieve it. I brushed his long, wild hair off his forehead and then smoothed the side of his bushy beard, praying to God that this would be a turning point. Considering we'd already passed the breaking point, I guess there was nowhere else to go but to make some sort of turn.

Vance drove me home and walked me to the door. Cupping my cheeks in his palms, he said resolutely, "We'll get through this together." He pressed his lips to my forehead.

I was tired of getting through everything by myself, so I really liked the sound of that. Clearly I was failing anyway. "'Kay." I leaned forward and kissed him. It was just a brief peck, and then I let myself in the house.

I autopiloted through a thorough shower, rebandaged my arm, and dressed in a clean shirt and pair of shorts so I'd be prepared for whatever showed up next. I fell face-first into the bed. As my body began to float in a doze, the bed dipped on both sides. I rolled over and stretched my arms out in invitation. Two small bodies snuggled close. Clinging to the twins, I let go for a while and gave in to sleep.

Chapter 15

AFTERMATH

An entire day was lost after Pa's catastrophic tornado, as if the turbulence from Friday night had managed to wipe away Saturday. The hospital called to let me know they were not allowing visitors, so it was best to stay home and work on recovering myself. Once the nurse reassured me Pa was resting and would remain sedated, I took them up on it and hunkered down with my sister and brothers the entire day.

We barely left the shelter of my room. At one point Charlotte pilfered the kitchen and came up with two loaves of white bread and a jar of peanut butter that sufficed as breakfast, lunch, and dinner. No one wanted to leave the room or talk, so we mainly rested. Vance was somewhere in the house, but not invading our personal moment of mourning and coming to terms with all that had transpired. No one gave him permission to stay, nor did he ask for it, but it was a comfort to know he was there if we needed him.

Sunday morning, a persistent tapping on my shoulder arrived a lot earlier than I was ready to deal with, so I swatted it away and drifted in the haze of sleep, but the dang tapping started again. Mindful of the little person burrowed against my back, I turned my head and pried an eye open and found Peg standing by the bed beckoning with a hand for me to get up.

"Pa?" I whispered.

Peg shook his head.

I scanned the bedroom and counted off the sleeping bodies piled along the floor. Raleigh and Boss were near the door. Charlotte was curled up on the rug to the left of the bed, and the younger twins were snuggled underneath the covers on either side of me. All were accounted for, so I started to roll over and resume catching up on some sleep.

"No, Ox." Peg yanked on my shoulder. "We got another problem."

He'd have the entire room woke up if he kept on, so I climbed over Knox and made my way into the hallway. I closed the door once Peg joined me and asked him, "What is it?"

"Everybody showed up for church."

I lifted my hand to comb the hair out of my eyes and winced. Parts of me hurt that I didn't even realize had been involved in Friday night's battle. "Why didn't you tell them to go home?"

Peg sighed heavily and rubbed his puffy eyes with the heels of his hands. "I did, but they said they needed to see you."

"For what?"

"I dunno." He stood staring at me just like all the others always did. It was a look of expectancy. A look that said to please handle it.

I was so sick of handling it, yet I shouldered past him to go handle it. Whatever *it* was. As I reached the bottom of the stairs, I noticed Vance sleeping on the couch, so I lightened my steps to the door. I glanced over my shoulder, wishing I could climb underneath that afghan with him and hide for a little while longer. But hiding had never worked for me, so I eased the door open as quietly as I could. The steady drumming of heavy rain on the roof made me pause long enough to shove on a pair of rubber boots and snatch an umbrella off the hook by the door. I traipsed down the muddy driveway, amazed at how quickly the barren summer had turned into a sloshy wet mess.

As I neared the chapel, a car drove by on the highway. The thought of flagging them down and begging whoever was inside to help me escape had my fingers twitching, but I managed to keep them balled by my side. Running away had never been an option for me either.

Refocusing, I walked to the side door with the plan of peeping my head in and announcing the services were canceled. It wasn't a new idea but an old one that I'd repeated sporadically over the last several years. I caught sight of Foxy and Jinx through the hazy window and wondered why in the world they hadn't canceled it for me.

Taking a fortifying breath, I cracked the side door open just enough to peer inside. My eyes fastened on the abandoned podium as I offered an excuse. "I'm sorry, but there won't be any services today. Pa ain't feeling well." With butchered arms and a tortured mind, *not feeling well* wasn't even close to the truth.

"Wait a minute, honey," Morty called out before I got the door shut. "We need to have a talk."

I didn't like the sound of that, but I closed the umbrella and took a tentative step inside. I looked no further than the worn floorboards where my rubber boots were forming puddles. A dark hand caught mine and sent my gaze to rise.

"Foxy?" I questioned, frowning at her head. It was the first time I'd ever seen the woman without a scarf of some sort covering it. From her right ear to the crown of her head, the dark bald skin was beveled in scars. The black hair on the other side was shorn close to her scalp.

"Today we gonna witness," Foxy said softly as she rose from her pew and walked to the podium, gesturing for me to stand beside her.

"You okay?" I whispered.

Foxy met my eyes, winking at me before turning to the congregation, but I couldn't look away from her. "Austin knows firsthand that I steer clear of confrontation. She's even called me a coward a time or two." Her hand locked with mine and squeezed to stanch my reaction. "My girl is right to an extent. I've been hiding what happened to me back home in Louisiana." She smoothed her palm over the bald part of her head. "I was twelve years old. Some men thought lighting my hair on fire would make for fine entertainment. I let that hate crime rob me for the better part of thirty years, until Dave Foster took me and my Jinx in and treated us as his equal and showed us our lives mattered to him and his family. A family I consider my own."

Jinx said, "Amen."

Foxy gave him a warm smile. "I walked a long time alone, and once Jinx became a part of my life, I thought I was fine." She turned to me. "But you, child, wouldn't accept that. Since the day we arrived, you've walked by my side out here on the farm, in town, it didn't matter where. Thank you." She drew me in for a long embrace before turning to the congregation. "Who's witnessing next?"

Rattled by what was going on, I did a double take when Miss Wise stood from her pew and took Foxy's place beside me. She wore a short-sleeved blouse. As far as I knew, it was the first time she'd done that in public.

Chin lifted and shoulders back, Miss Wise told of her horrific imprisonment in Auschwitz. Her accent thickened when she shared about losing all of her family at the hands of Hitler. I'd heard her harrowing testimony before, but shivers stung my skin and nausea hit my stomach as if it were the first time. As she talked about losing her sister, Irene, I reached for her hand, and she willingly let me hold it even though it meant making the faded numbers on her arm more visible.

"I still remember the day I moved to Magnolia. Dave and Edith Foster showed up at my door to welcome me. The woman was round with child, but she and her husband helped unpack boxes all day until it was time for school to let out." Miss Wise cleared her throat and shook her head. "I'd not seen love lived out in a very long time, but that man . . . he loved his wife. He wore it as good as he does a denim shirt, as Edith would have said. Witnessing their love made me want to stop hating."

The mood was somber, sniffles filtered around the room,

and I was surprised again when I realized some of the sniffles were my own. My eyes had grown damp and my nose was turned on like a leaky faucet.

Miss Wise produced a tissue from the pocket of her dress slacks and handed it to me before continuing. "Dave Foster is a stubborn man. He refused to take my no as an answer when he invited me to church. I finally gave in just so he'd stop showing up at my door. I guess he taught this one beside me to be just as stubborn. Neither one would leave me be until I agreed to forgive my past and to start living." She gave me a sidelong glance, her thin lips curling into a slight smile. "Austin was fourteen or fifteen when she told me she believed forgiveness and getting over being mad was a gift for ourselves, not for the ones who wronged us. She also said she would be praying for me. I think it's time for us to return the prayers for her and her family's sake."

My eyes were so flooded that I could barely see her walk away and Morty take her place. One blink and two fat tears plopped down my cheeks. It was then that I noticed Morty was dressed down in a plain blue T-shirt and a pair of jeans. His hair lay flat instead of fluffy and feathered. His face even held a shadow from not shaving.

"Dave Foster was the first person in Magnolia to speak to me on a personal level after my brother died. To Dave, I was more than the son of the funeral home owners who lost their other child. I didn't have to try to stand out to get his attention. He has a knack for noticing people, and never did he just speak in passing but would stop to actually listen." Morty's lip wobbled, so he stopped a moment. He shot a look at me and snickered. "And this one . . . this young lady is cut from the same cloth as her father. Shoot, she was there that day Mr. Hal came back to life, yet she still talked to me after that incident. I've been made to feel like a nobody most my life, but the Foster family invited me to be a somebody to them. They accepted me as is and have shown me that God does too."

A muffled sob tumbled free from me as Morty gave me a hug and called for the next witness. All this time I'd looked at myself as an afghan unraveling. Even though I was falling apart in front of these people, the fraying parts were being replaced by a stronger binding.

Tripp joined me, which was surprising because we weren't as close as I was with the others. What was more surprising than that was the fact that the man actually cleaned up nicely. His long hair was even pulled into a neat ponytail and his face was clean-shaven. In a crisp white button-down, he shoved his hands into the pockets of his navy dress slacks and took a deep breath.

"I ain't much on public speaking, but it'd be wrong not to for Dave. I only had one person to visit me the entire three years, seven months, and two days I was incarcerated. I didn't know Dave Foster before all that, yet he showed up and made himself my brother. It was a bad time. You see, other inmates don't take kindly to anyone accused of hurting a child, so I was the punching bag. And after that crazy guy took a pen to my eye, Dave was there when I woke up from surgery."

Miss Wise marched to the front and handed Tripp a tissue when he couldn't continue. That ornery lady patted him on the shoulder and returned to her seat.

"Thank you," Tripp muttered to her as he wiped his eyes. "Not many know, but it was Dave who fought for the state to review my case even before they discovered the remains . . . And then once I was exonerated and decided I was going to rebel and show out . . . I don't know how that man knew when I went to the juke joint, but he showed up each time to drive me home. He spoke a lot about Jesus during those rides home, and somehow it stuck. Do you want to know why? Because Dave never gave up on me." He turned to me and I made sure to focus on his good eye. "And we ain't giving up on him either."

A woman I hardly recognized took Tripp's place. A natural beauty, with her hair tied in a low bun and her face free of makeup. She wore a loose tunic over a pair of stirrup leggings that looked better than anything I'd ever seen her in.

"Walynn?" I was beginning to wonder who these strangers were.

"Hey, sugar." She wrapped an arm around my waist and secured me to her side while facing the group. "I've been called a lot of names in my life. Most I've earned. I let my mistakes and what people said about me dictate who I was, but it was this young lady who made me realize I'm better than my mistakes and didn't have to put up with people calling me names." She tapped my hip. "Most men I've encountered who showed me attention expected something in return. I thought that was the way it worked, but Dave Foster taught me kindness could be shown without it costing me my dignity. He invited me to church. He sent his children to my chair at the salon for haircuts when others refused to give me business. Dave never wanted anything but my betterment in return, but I think it's time for Dave and Austin and the Foster family to allow us to return the acceptance and support they've given us." She gave me a hug and then moved to the front pew.

The room grew quiet as I stood up front by myself, processing what had just transpired.

Foxy hid behind mystery and headscarves.

Miss Wise hid behind a scowl and long sleeves.

Morty hid behind a wink and silk shirts.

Tripp hid behind bar brawls and a rough exterior.

Walynn hid behind big smiles and blue eye shadow.

Although they all had valid reasons for hiding the way they did, they were finally calling themselves out for doing it. And now here they all were, gathered together to call me out for hiding behind tobacco fields and family loyalty.

The windowpanes rattled as thunder tumbled past the church. With the heavy rain pinging against the roof, the flood of emotions released from me. Body trembling, tears pouring, I lay right there on that altar, crying out to God that I couldn't take it anymore. And then I was surrounded by voices praying over me. Each one crying out on my behalf, forming a harmony with the other voices, and it was the most beautiful symphony I'd ever heard. All I could do was lie there, letting loose until I was wrung completely dry. I'm not sure how long we remained on the floor in the chapel, but the reassurance of them being there for the long haul couldn't have been more clear.

As the prayers tapered off, Foxy began softly singing, "'All to Jesus, I surrender.'" Others joined in until we were all singing. Pa would have loved to be in the midst of the beautiful moment. It was the very thing that he always strived to share with everyone. Well, he did until whatever was attacking him took over. It was the first time that I had a hope of finally getting him some help.

As the song concluded, Jinx stood from the group, grabbed his Bible, and returned to sitting beside me. He flipped through the pages until coming to Ecclesiastes. "Chapter 4, verses 9 through 12 are verses your daddy has brought to life." Jinx gave me a meaningful look and then read the Scripture to us. "'Two are better than one; because they have a good reward for their labour. For if they fall, the one will lift up his fellow: but woe to him that is alone when he falleth; for he hath not another to help him up. Again, if two lie together, then they have heat: but how can one be warm alone? And if one prevail against him, two shall withstand him; and a threefold cord is not quickly broken.' Austin, I know y'all feel broken, but you're not. We'll help you get Dave some help if you will allow us."

"I don't even know what he needs."

Walynn reached over and placed her hand on mine. "Sweetie, we'll figure it out together. The point of today is to help you realize you're not alone in this."

Her words released another surge of tears.

Miss Wise spoke up. "And we'll do what you always do. We'll research and educate ourselves on what Dave will need." She scooted closer. "I'm going to go up to the house and help Charlotte pack. I'd like to invite her to stay with me for a while or for as long as she wants, if you're okay with that."

"I . . . That would be Pa's decision." As I said that, I knew he wasn't in the right state to be making any type of decision.

"We just want to help," Walynn reassured me. "If you agree,

I'd love to bring Nash and Knox home with me this week. That way you can focus on caring for Dave."

"And since Boss works with me and I have an extra bedroom, he's welcome to stay with me for a while," Tripp offered.

"Raleigh and Peg will stay with us," Foxy said.

I looked around at the concerned faces surrounding me, wondering when they'd come up with this plan. Truly, I did have a lot to figure out with Pa, and giving my siblings a break from the farm seemed like a solid idea.

Chapter 16

CHANGES

Monday, the doctors insisted on moving Pa to a facility. Tuesday, I insisted he be moved from the facility. They diagnosed him with something called manic depression, but he wasn't a lunatic. And that first place housed folks I considered to fit that description. Patients in wheelchairs randomly dotted the hallways. In comatose states, they just slumped in the chairs, as if they either gave up on their destinations or were left for dead by someone. Wails and high-pitched screams came from some unknown location as I had maneuvered around the wheelchair statues. The smell of urine and body odor did me in, and even though I added my own high-pitched fit, it took over a week to finally get Pa out of there. An ambulance picked him up and moved him to a nursing home with a small ward for high-functioning mental health patients. Whatever that meant. The place didn't stink and the patients seemed to be cared for, so I felt okay with Pa staying there until I could find better accommodations.

In the meantime, I had a lot of research ahead, but that meant going to the Truett Memorial Library and coming to terms with acknowledging what the town had long suspected about Pa.

Swallowing my pride, I straightened my shoulders and walked up to the front desk at the library with purpose. Miss Jones looked at me with pity, but I ignored it.

Recalling how brave Miss Wise was to share about her past, I held my chin up and rounded up some gumption. "Miss Jones, would you please help me find books on manic depression?"

"Of course." She didn't hesitate with her response. "Whew. I was worried for a moment there you were going to ask me to pull books on UFO sightings."

Brow furrowed, I stared at her, but when she winked, the tension dissipated as I realized she was cracking a much-needed joke. "What's wrong with UFO sightings?"

She scoffed and readjusted her glasses before typing something into her new computer. "What's wrong with them is they ain't real."

"I wouldn't be so quick to dismiss it." I fiddled with the stack of bookmarks. "After you round up my books, would you mind seeing about a directory or some kind of information about mental health facilities near us?"

"We can do that. Sure. Let me pull these books and we'll

get right on it." Miss Jones stood from her chair and walked around the long desk, giving my hand a squeeze in passing.

An hour or so later, I had four books on mental health disorders, and a directory of mental health institutions would be delivered in a few days for me to check out. I stepped outside, retrieved my melted slushy I'd left under the edge of the magnolia tree. After taking a syrupy sip, I tossed the cup in the trash and started across the side parking lot.

I looked up and had a moment of déjà vu. There, leaning on the side of the silver mile-long car with a brown bag in his hand, Vance raised his other hand in a small wave. Dressed today in a sharp charcoal-gray suit with a teal striped tie, the man would never stop being a sight for sore eyes. I knew he should have been at work instead of hanging out in the library parking lot, but I wouldn't tell him that.

No, I was tired of running him off and so I quickened my steps just to make sure he didn't decide to do that on his own. As soon as I was within reach, he hooked an arm around my waist and pulled me close.

Worry and empathy crinkled the corners of his green eyes as a sad smile tugged on his lips but didn't produce much of a curve. I got it. Grief and anger had mine constantly pulling in a deep frown as of late.

Freeing me from the books and papers, Vance opened the car door, placed them inside along with the brown bag, and closed it. He didn't look around one time to see who might or might not see us as he threaded his fingers through my hair near the base of my neck. With a gentle tug, he angled my head and leaned down to press a familiar kiss to the corner of my mouth. It was his tender kiss of concern, the one filled with giving and wishing. Tears pricked my eyes as I captured his lips with mine to deepen the kiss and discovered the fruity taste of Razzles candy.

After just one more kiss, we held each other for a while. I'd not been a good person to this man and I wanted to share a million truths to make up for all of the half-truths and omissions I'd told over the years, but his embrace felt like he already knew and didn't care.

A throat cleared from behind us. I looked over Vance's shoulder and found Jinx standing there. "What's wrong, Jinx?" I asked because there was always something wrong.

"Nothing's wrong. We just got some business to handle." Jinx and Vance exchanged a nod that did nothing to make me think it was *nothing*, but I had no choice but to follow them through town.

Vance and Jinx whisked me off to Cumberland Finance without much of an explanation. By the time we were situated in the fancy conference room, I was shaking like a leaf.

Vance clamped his hand firmly over my wrist. "Calm down, Austin. It's nothing bad. Just some changes." He let go and straightened his tie as his father and another suit walked in. Thankfully, Jinx was dressed down in Dickies work pants and a plain navy T-shirt, which made me a little more comfortable in my ratty bell-bottom jeans and one of Mama's frumpy blouses. Dressing in her clothing gave me some comfort at least.

"Yeah, well, I've already had my fill of changes lately. I'm not sure I want any more," I whispered, but Vance seemed to not hear me.

"Gentlemen, thank you for joining us," Vance said formally as he stood to shake their hands.

It kept striking me out of nowhere that he was an actual grown, successful man and not that teenage boy who used to goof around the farm and steal kisses from me. I had no idea where the years had gone, no more than I knew where they were going. By the looks of these men at the conference table, they were able to tell me. Or try to at least.

Ed Cumberland directed his focus on me. "Jinx and your father met with my financial team a few months back, along with Mr. Fitzgerald." Vance's father tipped his head toward the man I knew was Malorie's father and the town's favored lawyer.

My stomach began to churn.

Mr. Fitzgerald took that as his cue. He handed me a thick folder. "Dave made the necessary provisions in case . . . in case something was to happen to him, to provide for you and your siblings."

The envelope Morty had given me three years ago with Pa's funeral arrangements came to mind. Pa had never intended to make it through any of his suicide attempts, yet he did. "He's okay," I whispered.

"Of course." Mr. Fitzgerald gave me a sad smile.

Jinx spoke up from beside me. "Austin, your daddy will be okay, but we need a plan to take care of the farm and you young'uns till he gets there."

I leaned close to Jinx and whispered, although I'm sure they could hear, "Was Pa in his right mind when he made these decisions?"

Jinx reached over and clasped my fisted hand. "You know I wouldn't let him do this if he wasn't. He'd talked to me about it a lot in the last few years."

I nodded, trusting Jinx. "Okay." In his early fifties, he wasn't old enough to be my grandfather, but I had come to view him as one anyway. He was a wise man. I returned my attention to Mr. Fitzgerald.

"As per Dave's request, Jinx will take over all the farm duties. Cumberland Finance is overseeing the contract negotiations for mining the coquina from the back acres of the farm. I'm not sure you realize, but y'all have been sitting on a gold mine out there. You and your family will be financially stable if the earnings are handled properly. There will also be plenty of money to take care of your father's medical costs." Mr. Fitzgerald handed me another envelope, adding to the overwhelming information.

Long after the conference room cleared out, Vance patiently went through all of the paperwork and explained everything to me once again. I already knew about the coquina, but it was surprising that Pa had actually made the decision to have it mined when he'd never wanted to do that before. Maybe he was more aware of how dire things were getting than I realized.

"How'd Pa even know to go to your father?"

"It was my father who went to him about all this."

I glared at him. "This was none of your father's business! You know I don't take too kindly to that."

"Be mad at me about it, not him. I asked him to do it. My father knows how much you and your family mean to me. We wanted to help. You can't deny how much y'all need it right now." Vance ran his hands through his hair and heaved a long exhale. "Hopefully, with things getting squared away, you and I can have a real chance too."

"We're at different stages." I motioned toward him. "College is behind you—you're living on your own, helping your uncle run a daggum million-dollar company, for heaven's sake!" I rubbed my forehead. "You're a grown man and . . ."

He grabbed my wrist. Using his free hand, he gestured between us. "My feelings aren't going to change, so this will keep. Now is your chance to maybe go to college and do the stuff I've already done. Heck, do none of it. Regardless, do every single thing you've ever wanted to but put to the side for your family. Either way, I'll be right here where you leave me."

"But that's not fair to you, Vance," I said on a hoarse cry. "And what about Charlotte and my brothers?"

"What about them?"

"Boss is slow on the uptake. And Peg—"

Vance snorted a laugh. "His handicap doesn't give him any trouble."

I mimicked his snorting laugh. "No, but his mouth does. He'd be in jail or the hospital if I weren't paying enough attention to keep him in line."

"There's plenty willing to help out with Boss, and as for Phoenix, he's near about grown, Austin. It's time he realizes, just like your father, that you're not always going to be there." He dipped his head and searched my eyes. "You know it's past time."

"Probably." I glanced at the fancy clock on the wall. "School will be letting out soon. I better go." I eased out of his hold and began gathering the mountain of paperwork.

Vance rose, pulled another packet out of his briefcase, and led me out to the limo, holding my hand the entire way. After helping me settle into the driver's seat like the gentleman he was, Vance leaned into the car and gave me a somber kiss.

He pulled back slightly and offered me the glossy packet. "I know we hit you with a lot today, so give this a look when you're ready."

I placed it on top of the other paperwork that joined the books on the passenger seat. "What is it?"

"You'll see." Vance's warm lips pressed against my forehead and then he straightened. "I still haven't figured out how to stop loving you, Austin Foster."

Our gazes connected and I slowly tipped my head in agreement. "I can't figure it out either."

"One day, Austin, we're going to give in to this love and let it have its way with us. I'm looking forward to that day." He took a moment to cup my cheek before backing away and closing the door.

I watched him stroll down the sidewalk, greeting people as he went. I could have sat there and watched him all day, but it was time to move forward.

I made my rounds, visiting Knox and Nash first at the salon, where they'd been going after school. I found them in the break room putting together LEGO kits Walynn had purchased for them. In the week that she'd had them, she'd been spoiling them rotten. Not surprisingly, they didn't want to go back to the farm. I asked each day to be sure, just as I did with the others. No one wanted to go back, so I took turns staying at different houses most every night.

As I pulled away from Miss Wise's house after supper, the stack of books caught my attention from the passenger seat, so I knew tonight I needed to stay at the farm. Five minutes later, I pulled up to what appeared to be a haunted house now that it sat empty and quiet. Funny how I'd always complained that the place was too filled with life and noise.

Once everything was organized on the dining table, I took my seat, and suddenly the enormity of the task slammed into me. Slumping away from the table, I took several deep breaths and began to pray, because there was absolutely no way I could do it on my own. When the anxiety abated to a more manageable level, I scooted my chair in and pored over the books, scribbling notes when something struck a chord. Words and their meanings stared back at me.

> Patients experience extreme mood swings. Emotional highs: euphoric, high energy, insomnia, quick to become agitated, chatty, delusional in extreme cases. Emotional lows: loss of appetite, moody, body aches, lethargic, suicidal.

Certain sections of the books described Dave Foster to a T. Those sections also outlined treatment options, and some of the options—like shock therapy—made me cringe. But what made me cringe more was the fact that there had been help out there all these years. I was ashamed that we let pride keep us from reaching out. Tears rolled down my face as I mourned for my dad and what he'd quietly endured. He'd been traveling further and further into his darkness. He'd been too far gone to be reached. I just hoped it wasn't too late to bring my father back to us.

I chose not to look through the fancy-looking packet that night. There was just too much to process already without adding more. It remained on the dining table beside Pa's almanac and Bible as I channeled my energy into finding the right facility for him.

That task had become a bigger endeavor than I would have ever imagined.

The slowest month of my life passed as days were spent in medical offices. Having medical power of attorney for my father, all the decisions fell on my shoulders. I'd been doing just that for years. But that was out on a farm surrounded by fields and farm animals. This was a new setting, one that intimidated me and often left me feeling ignorant.

"We think you'll do well here, Mr. Foster. We've added a new state-of-the-art gym and an art studio to the campus recently. We take field trips to Folly Beach." The institute director sounded like a used-car salesman, but he made Pa chuckle as soon as we began the meeting, and that was a first in many months. His name, Donald Butkus, suited him. It was probably a magnet for laughter.

Pa chuckled again. "Art and field trips . . . wow. You make this place sound like a school instead of an asylum."

How Pa could joke was beyond my understanding. I found

nothing humorous about the situation or anything else, for that matter, and hadn't in a very long time. I gave him a weak smile when he looked my way. It was the best I could do, considering we were sitting in the office of a mental hospital with Pa's sliced-up arms on display. His skin had taken on a sallow tone and the circles underneath his eyes were the darkest I'd ever seen them. If I didn't know any better, I'd think someone had punched him in both eyes.

The gray-headed man leaned his elbows onto his messy desk. "Educating ourselves and then applying what we learn is much like a school. Shoot, sometimes we even have to send class members to the principal's office." Both men chuckled at that.

"Are you ready to attend, Mr. Foster?" Mr. Butkus spread his arms and gestured around his office as if it held all the answers to Pa's problems. I sure wished it were that simple, yet nothing so far had been.

"I need to discuss it with Austin and then have a good long prayer about it, but to be honest, this is the first time a place has felt right."

The director rose to his feet, a big smile on his face. "Well, I'm honored you feel that way, and I'd be even more honored if we are able to work together on your health."

On the way out, I asked, "You want to grab something to eat before heading back to . . . ?" I hated saying *the nursing home* or *facility*, so I left it hanging there.

Of course Pa picked it up and joked, "The loony bin?"

"Pa!" I wasn't a fan of that term, nor of my father using it in association with himself.

He stared out the window. "I could go for a loaded hot dog and onion rings from Duffy Dogs."

"Sounds like a winner to me." I just hoped he'd actually eat it. His appetite had been nonexistent since he'd entered treatment.

I was grateful the doctor had been able to lower his meds. Hopefully, his appetite was returning too. At first he'd been transformed into one of those zombies—staring off at a distance with drool dripping from the corner of his mouth. He'd been there in body only. I hated it too, much like a lot of everything else that came along with my father's mental disorder, but I loved him with a fierceness that kept driving me forward to find solutions to help him. Sure, there'd been setbacks and the doctors had warned us. Each time I crept close to the point of giving up, I'd recall the witnessing in the chapel that stormy Sunday and remind myself how Pa had never given up on a single soul. Those reminders—and a whole lot of praying— fortified me to keep on keeping on.

We arrived back in town by late evening. After we ate, me devouring a burger and Pa picking at his food, I returned Pa to the nursing home and understood we still had a very long row to hoe ahead of us.

Upon arriving home, I found Jinx and Peg on the porch in rocking chairs.

"You know our boy wants to fly?" Jinx asked.

"Huh?" I looked at Peg for confirmation, but he kept his eyes pinned to the porch floorboards, face high in color. I hated that because it meant he felt ashamed about dreaming. Why had that become a thing amongst us Fosters? And why had I started hating everything? Both needed to change.

"He said something to Vance a while back, and come to find out Vance done took it upon himself and sent an application to an aviation school up in Colorado." Jinx plucked the letter he had jutting out the top of his shirt pocket and handed it to me. "Phoenix has been accepted."

I scanned the letter, and sure enough, a door had been opened for my brother. "That's . . . Wow."

Peg huffed and crossed his arms. "I can't go."

"Why the heck not?" I kept reading and found that he'd been awarded a disability scholarship that covered the entire tuition. "All we have to do is get you on a flight by the end of September. I think we can handle that."

"With everything going on with Pa, I can't leave y'all." His face reddened as tears streamed down his cheeks. "We gotta get Pa better."

"Pa and the doctors have to get Pa better. Not you and not me," I pointed out.

Peg slapped the tears off his cheeks. "You spend all your time meeting with doctors and doing research at the library, so don't try feedin' me that bull."

"We've found Pa a place near the coast. That's where I've been all day. It's a good facility that is faith-based. He'll probably be moved there the beginning of next week, so chew on that."

Pixy hobbled up the steps, oinking in what sounded like agreement. She went right over to Peg and rutted until plopping down between his feet.

"I don't know if I can do this," Peg confessed quietly.

"Can you fly with only one leg?" I asked.

His head popped up, his long locks flopping in his eyes. "There's hand control, Ox."

"Then you ain't got any reason to be saying you can't. This is the opportunity of a lifetime, and I won't allow your aggravating butt to pass on it."

"Austin's right," Jinx interjected. "And none of us is gonna let you pass on it."

And just like that, we were heading inside to pack Peg's bags so he could pursue a dream.

It amazed me right then and during the months to come how God answered my prayers in ways I'd not trusted him enough to handle. I had begged God for years to heal Pa, to protect my siblings, and to give us a life outside of the shadows we hid behind out on Nolia Farms. Growing weary, I'd concluded that I wasn't being heard. Or that I was just flat-out being ignored.

God proved me wrong. In his own timing, he answered me far greater than I could ever have imagined.

———————————

The fancy packet sat on the dining table for another month. Between nearly having to beat Peg to get on the blame airplane to head off to the aviation academy and then coming to terms with Pa having to stay at the facility he was in for at least three more months before he could come home, my mind had been too preoccupied to wonder what was inside.

No one wanted to come home to the farm until Pa could return, so that left me mostly living on my own at the house. Mid-September, I sat at the table one night staring at the packet. Giving in, I opened it and immediately picked up the phone to call Vance.

"Hello."

Needing a moment to simply take in his rich voice that always sent warmth through me, I didn't immediately respond. Clearing my throat, I whispered, "It's me. Austin."

"Hey, beautiful. Everything okay?"

I stretched the cord and leaned to grab the stack of papers. "What's with this filled-out application for Baptist College at Charleston?"

There was some shuffling on his end and then a muffled groan, sounding like he was settling into a chair and readying himself for a debate. "You deserve a chance to explore different career avenues besides farming."

Hackles raised, I stood straighter. "What's wrong with farming?"

"Nothing's wrong with farming. But it's wrong that you've never been given another choice besides that." Vance heaved a grumbly breath. "I knew you'd be difficult. Why's everything always have to be this way with you? With us?"

"I don't mean to be. It's just . . . this isn't something you should have done without talking to me."

"All I did was fill out the application. The rest is up to you. I will say that my father made some phone calls, and you're in for the spring semester if you want."

"There y'all go, getting in my business again."

"You didn't have a problem with me doing it for Peg."

Dang it, he had me there. I leaned on the wall beside the phone mount and tapped the back of my head a few times to find some reasoning. "What if things aren't in a good place for me to go then? Ain't that like two hours or more away from here?"

"It's only an hour and a half. And if the spring semester doesn't work, then we can talk to admissions and have it moved to the fall semester." His confidence made it sound so easily doable.

"It's going to be hard on Pa and the young'uns when he gets home." I twirled the cord around my fingers, nervous yet excited all at once. College had been something I'd never allowed myself to want, but now? Now I wanted it more than just about anything.

"You're right, but Dave will need to adjust to doing things without relying on you. Austin, you can't always be the buffer. It's time to step out of the way." Vance sighed. "Same for your siblings. The entire church is committed to helping you, aren't they?"

"Yes, but . . ." I couldn't figure out a *but*.

"Besides, you can come home every weekend to help out."

The man made it sound so easy, and I was terrified that it might just be. Now I knew why Peg was so torn about leaving, but I couldn't expect him to set a good example for the rest of our siblings when it came to pursuing their dreams and passions if I wasn't willing to do it myself.

"We'll just have to play it by ear," I finally conceded.

"Good enough," Vance agreed quickly. "Now how about coming to the lake to see me. I miss you."

"If I go see you, I can't promise I'll ever leave."

"That doesn't sound so bad to me."

"Vance . . ." I sniffed the tears and swallowed. "You have no idea how much I want to—"

"I know. The timing isn't right. But the timing *is* right for college and for going and acting like a teenage girl."

I snorted. "I'm almost twenty-two."

"Exactly. You missed all the selfish teenage angst. Go do all that and get an education."

"What if . . . what if that includes a guy asking me out?" I said it in tease, but afterwards it didn't feel that way. I'd seriously not done any normal teenage living, and a handful of "dates" with Vance was all I had to go on.

He didn't respond right away, perhaps thinking it through just as I had done. "Then say yes if he's a nice guy."

I have no idea how much that cost him to say, but I respected Vance for it and knew that answer gave away the extent of his love for me. It made me love him even more.

The year 1988 would always go down in my family history book as the year of accepting change. Of new beginnings.

The beginning of Pa's diagnosis and treatment.

The beginning of my siblings' lives being lived apart.

The beginning of college life for me.

Sure wasn't easy, but nothing in life worth having ever is.

HEA: HEALING EVER AFTER

I regard the regal woman sitting before me in the wingback chair, wringing her manicured hands. Wearing a tailored outfit with her makeup and dark-gray hair flawless, the woman's exterior is impeccably put together, yet her interior is falling apart. It never ceases to amaze me how easily we as a society have perfected the art of hiding our internal storms behind shiny facades.

"What will people think of me?" Sylvia looks away from me and busies her hands with checking each button on her blouse to make sure they are in line. She repeats this three times, always ending on an odd number.

"If you choose to share, they will know you are brave. But, Sylvia, it really doesn't matter what others think. Your worth won't be found in someone else's opinion of you."

"Yes, but what about first impressions?"

"First impressions can be important, but they can also be misleading." I place the pen in my grasp on my desk. "Tell me, what impression do you have of me?"

Sylvia is a new patient who drives from two counties over just so she won't be seen entering a psychiatrist's office. A matriarch in her town and obsessed with keeping up appearances, Sylvia battles OCD behind closed doors, but recently her compulsions have reached the point where she's unable to control them on her own.

She gives me a once-over, much as she did during the first session she had with me last month.

"You are a wise, perceptive person. Well-put-together . . ."

"Go on." I tip my head and give her an encouraging smile.

Her thin shoulder hitches upward. "I wish my Jimmy would find a decent woman such as yourself. All he seems to want to bring home to meet me are rough ones, if you know what I mean." She scrunches her nose and then readjusts her glasses. Then moves to adjust her earrings that are as perfectly fine as her glasses were. When she completes her accessory circuit, she catches herself from starting over and picks up the stress ball I gave her to help redirect her focus away from the impulses.

I unbutton the left cuff of my blouse and roll the sleeve up to my elbow. It's a rule of mine to not share much of my personal life with my patients, but Sylvia needs to get over her hang-up about maintaining a proper appearance if we're ever going to make any progress. Shoot, she won't even take the silly ball home with her for fear someone will see her with it and think poorly of her.

I lay my arm on my desk to display the scar from long ago and the tattoo lining it. "Does this tattoo give you a different impression of me?"

Sylvia frowns. "Well, I wasn't expecting that on you . . ."

"May I tell you the meaning behind it?"

"I suppose."

"A dear friend of mine was a Holocaust survivor. She wasn't given a choice when they tattooed her identity number on her skin in about the same spot as mine." I traced the inked symbols, each no bigger than my thumbnail, with my fingertip. "This is in honor of her. Each symbol stands for something very personal to me."

I touch the dainty white flower, where the story begins. "The honeysuckle bloom is in memory of my mother, who died when I was only thirteen. I cannot smell the sweet aroma of honeysuckle without hearing her laughter." Being mindful of not getting carried away in the first part of my story, I move to the red outline of a heart, where the right side doesn't close completely. "The open heart is a reminder to keep my heart open to possibilities and to love others openly. To not ever hide my love." I trace the sky-blue cross next to the heart. "The cross symbol is where I find my hope in this life of chaos. It's the center symbol to remind me to keep God centered in my life. First and foremost."

I laugh softly at the next symbol. It's the one that I receive the most compliments about, even though it's considered inappropriate in most social circles nowadays. The pink flower is beautiful and impressively detailed. "This is a tobacco plant bloom. It's the symbol of my history, considering I was raised on a tobacco farm. It taught me a strong work ethic and loyalty." I tap the last symbol with the tip of my finger. "The semicolon is in honor of my father and my family surviving his suicide attempt. I'm beyond grateful that God wasn't finished with his story. And I placed it on the end as a reminder that my story continues also."

I roll the sleeve down and refasten the cuff. "Now that you know the history behind the tattoo, do you still feel the same as your first impression of it?"

"No . . . That's courageous."

"Do you see my point? If you only allow people the first glimpse and don't share more, you give them the power of assumption. Show them you're more than that. Show them you're also courageous."

We wrap up the session, and after Sylvia leaves, I lock up and do the same. I pull out onto the highway and head toward Lake Murray, but nostalgia has me taking a detour.

Pa is doing much better these days and still delivers a sermon in the small chapel every Sunday, but I like to pop in and check on him when I can. He's learned to live with his bipolar depression. Although he's able to live a more stable life, he will always have to cope with his mental illness. The constant ups and downs of medication adjustments, the revolving doors of new counselors, and relapses will make sure of it. Thankfully, we all figured out it did no one any good to keep his illness hidden. Nowadays, Pa tells us when he's having a bad day and we talk about how that affects us. It's amazing how freeing conversation can be. It's healthy and I highly recommend it.

Mental illness is much like cancer when choosing a victim. Neither discriminates. Pa has no control over his affliction, but he can and does choose daily to manage his symptoms. And each one of us who are a part of his support system must continue to lift him up when he starts declining. To not allow him to give in to the darkness that tries so hard to overwhelm him at times.

What began in desperation to educate myself about Pa's disease soon grew into a passion to help others going through similar mental illness. It was pretty easy to declare a major in psychology with my focus on becoming a counselor one day. During my senior year of college, I actually interned at a clinic near campus and was met by a great deal of criticism from my supervisor when she caught me praying with one of the patients.

"This is a clinic to treat mental illness. It's not Bible study or prayer service. Can you leave your God out of our counseling sessions?" she asked me after giving me a lengthy berating.

I told her, "That's impossible. God is in everything."

Luckily, I found other facilities to work at that reminded me of the mental institute where Pa had been treated. I love helping others in the same situation my siblings and I endured most of our childhood.

Within miles, the city gives way to a rural setting of planted fields and barns. It has evolved, like everything else, to an extent. Most of the outdated dirt roads are surrendering to their destinies, trading in their dusty worn jackets for shiny black dressings.

Before I get too lost in the landscape of my childhood, I hit the Bluetooth button on the steering wheel. A few moments later the most alluring voice fills the inside of my SUV.

"Hey, babe. What's up?"

Grinning, I reply, "Hey, handsome. I'm going to swing by the farm before heading home."

"Everything okay?" There's a touch of caution to his tone, but that has become a norm if the farm is ever mentioned.

"Yes. I just want to make a quick visit."

For the record, Vance Cumberland was a man of his word when he said he wasn't going anywhere all those years ago. The day I completed grad school, I drove out to Lake Murray and told him I was done waiting, and if he was in agreement with that, then we should go ahead and get married. I had a ring on my finger before I left that night. Apparently Vance had been prepared.

Vance pushes out a breath, sounding relieved. "I have one more meeting before wrapping things up for the day. I'll pick up something for supper."

"Make one of them young'uns of yours do it. Ain't it 'bout time we make them heathens earn their keep?"

Vance's rich chuckle echoes through the vehicle. "I love it when you talk country to me." He grunts, turning on his flirt. "You getting me all riled up right before going into this meeting. You're gonna owe me."

"Oh, behave," I tease. "Seriously, though. Have the twins order something for supper and I'll pick it up."

Three years into our marriage, Vance finally talked me into the idea of having a child. I emphasize *a* child. I should have known I'd end up having twins, boys at that! After getting those two kicking boys out of my body, I declared two children was my limit and Vance agreed. I did get a little even with them over the whole two-baby trickery, naming them after cities in Texas. Vance thought I'd lost my mind, and we had a pretty heated argument when the nurse came in with the birth certificates, but I've never been one to back down and won out in the end.

Brookshire Vance Cumberland was born three minutes before his brother Beckville Archer Cumberland. Brook and Beck may never completely forgive me for their names, but they will learn to appreciate the sentiment behind them, just as my siblings and I did. I love that my mother gave us odd names, and I love that it's unique to us.

"I'll call Beck here shortly. Brook is still on phone restriction, correct?"

"Yep. That punk has two more days until his sentence is complete." I laugh in spite of myself. Even though Brook and his twin are blond carbon copies of their daddy, Brook reminds me so much of their mouthy uncle Phoenix, always popping off at the mouth before thinking it through. For Peg, it appears that becoming an international pilot for a major airline has calmed my brother's temperament to a more agreeable level. "And you have a meeting, so I'll call Beck before I start home. I think I'm going to kidnap Boss from the farm."

Even though Pa leases the farmland to other farmers to work these days, Boss runs the produce stand. Foxy turned him into one fine gardener over the years. He likes to keep close to the farm and our father, but he's always game for coming out to the lake for a week or two at a time. The weather is perfectly warm and humid, so I think it's time for another kidnapping, as we've come to call it.

"Sounds like a plan, my wife. Tell Dave and Walynn I said hello if you see them."

The fact that Pa married Walynn took me quite a bit of getting used to. But it turned out that learning the truth of Pa's imperfection seemed to be the perfect reason for Walynn to finally be able to admit her feelings for him. She stepped into the mother role for not only Knox and Nash, but also for the rest of us Fosters, as if Mama had somehow reached down from heaven and passed her the maternal torch.

I flick the blinker light on and make a left. "I hope Nash and Knox are around too."

"Be there in a minute," I hear Vance tell someone, probably his secretary. "Are they back from Zambia?"

"Walynn said they got in a few days ago." Identical twin missionaries are a big hit in foreign countries, and so Knox and Nash are constantly being asked to join various mission organizations to help with their cause. I know Pa couldn't be prouder. I'm just glad that he finally worked out how to not associate them with the death of our mother and to discover a bond so late in the game with them. "Okay, I'm for sure hanging up this time. I still haven't figured out how to stop loving you."

"Me either, babe. I quit trying a very long time ago."

We conclude the conversation the same way we've been doing for as long as I can remember. Vance gets me like no one else ever could.

After taking another left, I park the SUV in the small yard

beside the weathered chapel. The structure is a testament to the Foster resilience. We may not have made it to this point unscathed, but by golly we made it.

Staring at the clapboard structure through the windshield, a bevy of memories play out before me. All the times I'd witnessed Miss Wise spitting on the steps were outnumbered by the times I'd sat on those steps with my siblings, talking about nonsense while trying to make some sense out of life.

I exit the vehicle and recall standing in the yard and tossing birdseed in the air as Charlotte rushed out the door, clinging to her groom, whom she'd met after moving to Charleston to open an interior designing company. The celebratory day helped some of the harder memories fade a little more into the background of our history. Seems we Fosters have become diligent with doing just that.

I open the back hatch and take out the yellow ribbon stashed in the storage compartment. I walk over to the magnolia tree in the side yard and admire what appears to be hundreds of yellow ribbons tied amongst the branches. Raleigh joined the military right as soon as he turned eighteen, saying he wanted to find his bravery. He'd found it way before turning eighteen, but I've come to understand that some things people have to figure out on their own. I can only hope he has discovered that his bravery presented itself with compassion and tenderness as a young boy. And I pray each day for his safe return home from overseas.

After securing the ribbon amongst the collection and whispering a prayer for him, I kneel at the hem of the magnolia tree's skirt, wishing I had brought a rake. And wishing even more that I could send it underneath to retrieve a gift wrapped in a beautiful ending for my story.

I look into the shadows under this magnolia tree, recalling how dark some moments of our story have been. Lots of prayer and determination were the driving forces to get us to the point of no longer hiding. Such a freeing place. One we discovered was right there all along.

I'm not one to believe in the hype of happily ever after. I most certainly know better. But I do believe in healing ever after. It won't happen fully in this lifetime, but I've had tastes of healing's nectar along this journey.

The day Pa walked out of the mental health facility with a newfound grasp on reality and a peaceful smile on his face.

Finally saying "I do" to the man I know without a doubt God sent to me.

The miracle of my body birthing two perfect babies.

Witnessing my siblings reach those moments of career, marriage, and children for themselves.

Those milestones celebrate the fact that the Fosters overcame the hardships life tossed our way. Truly, we have survived, and we live to tell the tale.

A lot may have been hidden out at Nolia Farms, and that which was hidden may have come mighty close to leveling the Foster family, but the freedom from unearthing it helped us find our way to a healing ever after.

ACKNOWLEDGMENTS

To Team Lowe. Life is a team sport. One cannot manage a successful season of life alone. We are supporting players, rooting Lydia on at a softball game, helping Nathan prep for another year of college, critiquing Bernie's love of golf, or cheering me on as I near the finish line of another novel. No matter what, we are in this together. Bernie, Nate, and Lu, I'm honored to be on your team. Love you to the moon and back.

I'm indebted to my reading confidantes, who are always my first choice in reading new manuscripts: Trina Cooke, Lynn Edge, Teresa Moise, and Jennifer Strickland. Your honesty and consistent support keep me on track and make me a better storyteller. Love each one of you!

Christina Coryell, my critique partner and author sister, I recall your text after you finished reading the manuscript for *Under the Magnolias* before I sent it to my agent. You said if my agent didn't like it, she was nuts! (LOL. Thankfully, she's not.) You mean so much to me. Can't thank you enough.

I want to thank my brilliant agent, who is not nuts whatsoever, Danielle Egan-Miller. I still pinch myself every so often to make sure it's true that you are my agent. Such an extravagant gift for me as an author to have you in my corner. Your passion for this novel tells me all I need to know. I think we did good here! I couldn't have done it without you. Again, thank you.

I am honored to be a part of the Tyndale House family. It's always an exciting journey to work with you on bringing a story to readers, this one in particular. My city gal, Jan Stob, and my country gal, Karen Watson: you ladies rock! I treasure you both. Can't wait to see what God has in store for this book. Thank you for believing in it.

This book would not be as strong had it not been for the guidance of my editor, Kathryn Olson. You sent me an email recently saying that it's always fun to work with me. I feel the exact same way about you. I told Danielle from the get-go that I trusted only you with *Under the Magnolias*, knowing your vision would be in tune with mine. Even when you throw those curveballs, I trust and respect your instincts.

My lovely publicist, Amanda Woods, I so enjoy our email exchanges and love talking book boyfriends with you. Your enthusiasm is contagious and I truly enjoy working with you on promoting my stories.

I cannot write a book about tobacco farming without acknowledging the Prince family. In my youth, I learned many a lesson in your tobacco fields about life and the importance of hard work. I've carried those lessons with me, and I know they were fundamental in shaping me into the woman I've become. Thank you.

My readers, what can I say? I view you as my friends and cannot thank you enough for supporting my little dream to write by reading and sharing my stories. I seriously could not be T. I. Lowe without you!

My heavenly Father, we sure did have some long conversations about this book. I have no doubt that you gave me this story with an important purpose. My prayer through this journey has been that I wouldn't get in your way. Still praying I don't.

DISCUSSION QUESTIONS

1. A secluded farm in rural South Carolina in the 1980s provides the backdrop for much of Austin's story. How does the setting shape the novel?

2. The folks of Magnolia choose to live by the idea of "Out of sight, out of mind." What are the pros and cons of this mindset?

3. At age thirteen, Austin loses her mother and gains responsibility of her six siblings as well as her mentally ill father. How does she handle this unexpected life change?

4. Vance Cumberland decides early on that Austin is the woman he wants to spend his life with. Did you like that element of the story? Was Austin right to keep him at arm's length for so long?

5. Hard work and loyalty are just as important as bountiful crops on Nolia Farms. How do these characteristics help, or hinder, Austin and her family?

6. Austin and her siblings all adopt different coping strategies. Was there one character or coping strategy that you particularly identified with?

7. Each person who comes into the Fosters' lives influences Austin's life story: Foxy Deveraux, Miss Wise, Morty Lawson, Tripp Murphy, Walynn Posten, Miss Jones. How do each of these people affect her? Which one speaks to you the most? Why?

8. How did Dave Foster's private struggle with mental illness affect you as a reader? Did you empathize with him? Want to snatch a knot in his backside? Both, at times? Why?

9. Austin tells Miss Wise, "I also believe forgiveness and getting over being mad is a gift for ourselves, not for the ones who wronged us." Can you think of any examples of this from your own life?

10. Dave Foster is about as different as they come, and not just because of his mental illness. He says in the novel, "There's nothing wrong with being different. What's wrong is when people refuse to accept it." How have you seen this play out in our world today?

11. At the end of the book, we read how some of the characters' lives have turned out in the years since the main action of the book. Did any of them surprise you? Which endings did you like the best?

12. Discuss the title of the book, *Under the Magnolias*. What are some of the literal and metaphorical examples of hidden things in the story?

UNDER THE MAGNOLIAS
PLAYLIST

"Have You Ever Seen the Rain" by Creedence
    Clearwater Revival
"Here Comes the Sun" by The Beatles
"Don't Let the Sun Go Down on Me" by Elton John
"Dancing in the Dark" by Bruce Springsteen
"Harmony Hall" by Vampire Weekend
"Heaven" by Bryan Adams
"Between the Raindrops" by Lifehouse
"Let's Hurt Tonight" by OneRepublic
"I Think It's Going to Rain Today" by Bette Midler
"Can't Help Me Now" by Rob Thomas
"Let It Rain" by Crowder & Mandisa
"I Can See Clearly Now" by Johnny Nash
"Landslide" by Stevie Nicks
"Walking on Water" by NEEDTOBREATHE
"Bring the Rain" by MercyMe
"Still Rolling Stones" by Lauren Daigle

ABOUT THE AUTHOR

T. I. Lowe is an ordinary country girl who loves to tell extraordinary stories and is the author of nearly twenty published novels, including her debut, *Lulu's Café*, a number one bestseller. She lives with her husband and family in coastal South Carolina. Find her at tilowe.com or on Facebook (T.I.Lowe), Instagram (tilowe), and Twitter (@TiLowe).

DISCOVER LOVE IN SUNSET COVE WITH THE CAROLINA COAST SERIES FROM T. I. LOWE

Beach Haven

Ex-Marine Lincoln Cole lands in Sunset Cove harboring deep hurts. Almost before he realizes it, free-spirited boutique owner Opal Gilbert's well-meaning meddling begins to heal his wounds . . . and capture his heart.

Driftwood Dreams

After a tragedy, Josie Slater's let her dreams drift by. Then a friend from her past returns, hoping Josie will give him—and her dreams—a fair chance.

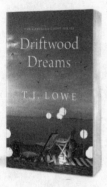

Sea Glass Castle

Both reeling from heartbreak, Sophia Prescott and Dr. Wes Sawyer aren't looking for love in Sunset Cove. But what they aren't looking for may find them anyway.

JOIN THE CONVERSATION AT

Settle in for a cup of coffee and some Southern hospitality in

OVER 100,000 SOLD

Lulu's Café
— a novel —
T. I. LOWE

Available in stores and online now

CONNECT WITH T. I. LOWE ONLINE AND SIGN UP FOR HER NEWSLETTER AT

tilowe.com

OR FOLLOW HER ON

f T.I.Lowe

instagram tilowe

twitter @TiLowe

g T_I_Lowe

CP1684